ENDORSEMENTS
THE FORGOTTEN AWAKENING

In *The Forgotten Awakening,* Douglas McMurry steals your heart away to a time in America's Pacific Northwest where human value and dignity were the centerpiece of its cultures. I grew up in Washington's Puget Sound and Montana's Rocky Mountains and took great identity in the beautiful landscape portrayed in Doug's book. However, I was unaware of its early history and my heart was instantly captivated by Doug's honesty and integrity in letting history shine its light on a truly redemptive American story that took place there. It is a story we can all appreciate, the story of *us,* filled with the grand adventure of both heroism and tragedy. But more importantly, it is a humbling reminder that the Master of Life was behind the scenes all along, carefully weaving all of its strands together. It is stories like this that need to be told to awaken our national consciousness to our moral responsibility — we must remember and not forget. It is for us, the living, who must wrestle with the issue of reconciliation, carry its legacy into the future and pass it on to the next generation. Thank you, Doug, for writing such a masterful work.

—Darrell Fields, Author: *The Seed of a Nation*

Our Creator calls men to walk in His love without compromise and to live by our convictions. Doug and Carla McMurry are such people—people of prayer who speak His love with not only words but actions that prove His love in and through them.

America is in desperate shape in part because of actions taken to Christianize or culturally convert the Native people of this land. The message Doug shares will bring revelation that will challenge you to become a catalyst for change.

The truth sets men free when they acknowledge and act on it.

We can no longer turn a blind eye to the deeds of the past and the effects they have had on America's First Peoples. Now is the time for us to recognize our responsibility to act and reap the harvest for truth and justice.

There are still thousands of natives who have yet to realize that people actually care about them and the conditions they are in as a result of past treatment.

Doug and Carla are non-native leaders who are standing up to say "We care and we are doing something about it." Doug has done the research and presents the truth in a way that will lead the descendants of both perpetrator and victim on the road to freedom.

—Jonathan Maracle, Founder and Director of "Broken Walls"

In this historical novel, Doug McMurry takes us back to a time when God breathed a vision of peace and friendship between Native Americans and the recent arrivals from England. In this extraordinary story from a long-lost, pristine era, you will have all your stereotypes of Native Americans and English explorers shattered, and above all, your vision of God and His vast workings with humanity will be expanded. Doug McMurry is a master story-teller who leads you into genuine friendship with the characters of this lost history. Through knowing their hearts you will be led deep into the ways of God. This novel is a prophetic invitation to restore God's vision for the people and the land that we know today as the United States and Canada.

—Brad Long, Executive Director, Presbyterian Reformed Ministried, International

THE FORGOTTEN
AWAKENING

Douglas McMurry

A HISTORICAL NARRATIVE

THE FORGOTTEN AWAKENING

HOW THE SECOND GREAT AWAKENING
SPREAD WEST OF THE ROCKIES

DOUGLAS McMURRY

Deep River
BOOKS

SISTERS, OREGON

THE FORGOTTEN AWAKENING
A Historical Narrative
How the Second Great Awakening Spread West of the Rockies
© 2011 by Douglas McMurry

Published by
Deep River Books
Sisters, Oregon
http://www.deepriverbooks.com

ISBN 13: 978-1-935265-63-4
ISBN 10: 1-935265-63-6

Library of Congress Control Number: 2011926409

Printed in the USA

Cover design: Robin Black, BLACKBIRD CREATIVE
Interior design: Juanita Dix • www.designjd.net

Contents

Maps

With highest respect for the tribes of the Columbia Plateau,
whose story has won my heart.

Preface

In 1987, during four all-day God-led trips to the Library of Congress, I discovered a national treasure. Plowing my way through old books that looked like they hadn't been checked out for decades, I stumbled across several eighteenth-century tribal prophecies about Jesus from the Native American tribes of the Columbia Plateau.

When I say these were prophecies of Jesus, I should clarify. Though God was clearly revealing Jesus to the tribes, the name "Jesus" was not yet being used.

Sometime prior to the advent of horses in the area (in other words, prior to 1730 or so), the Flatheads and the Kalispels received word of the cross and began to wear crosses into battle to ward off evil. The shape of the cross was known to be important to God—revealed by the Salish name Amotkan, He-who-dwells-on-high—and so it was considered to have great spiritual power. Of course, they did not receive the meaning of this cross, but only a glimpse of something significant about it from the Creator. They would wear crosses into battle, and they believed that this talisman protected them from harm.

About a generation later, the Coeur d'Alenes received revelation of the birth of a Savior long ago, and they began celebrating Christmas annually in the middle of the eighteenth century. This tradition came entirely through prophetic revelation to respected leaders—much like what the Persian Magi must have received at the time of Jesus's birth—prior to any contact with Europeans. Since it was revealed through the cultural forms of the Coeur d'Alene people, they likely did not celebrate this birth on December 25.

Moving in a westerly direction, about a generation later, the Spokanes received a prophecy about the Bible—"leaves bound together that the white-skinned ones will bring." At the time, none had met a white person or seen a Bible. But when white fur trappers came bearing Bibles, the Spokanes were not surprised. Had not their greatest leaders predicted these things a generation before?

These tribes did not know the name Jesus; they spoke instead of "The Master of Life," as I will show in the following pages. They believed, at first, that this being was somehow connected with the sun. They learned his ways as best they could and tried to find out more about him. Their efforts culminated in a historic delegation to Saint Louis in 1831 to request Christian teachers for the Nez Percé tribe and possibly for other tribes as well. All alike recognized that Jesus Christ was the person about whom their greatest prophets had spoken.

It is this connection between tribal prophecy and the very earliest preaching of the gospel on the Columbia Plateau that I portray in *The Forgotten Awakening*. At the time of the 1831 delegation, no one in the East suspected the motivation that produced it, nor the events that had already happened to produce such hunger for God. It is only by piecing together the events of those early years that we can discover what God was doing.

I describe the prophecies and the events that followed in their wake, leading to the preaching of a Native evangelist, Spokan Garry, and a Christian spiritual awakening on the Columbia Plateau at the headwaters of the Columbia River in the 1820s.

As I read of these amazing prophecies, I remembered the writings of Don Richardson. In his books *Eternity in Their Hearts* and *Peace Child*, he showed how God has a habit of revealing glimpses of Jesus to cultures just before those cultures are introduced to him by the Christian church. I suddenly realized—God did this right here in America. God was communicating his vision for America, a vision which included indigenous people along with everyone else.

I had read the story of Bruce Olson, a Minnesota Lutheran who was plucked from the frozen north to be an ambassador for Jesus among the Motilones of Venezuela. This tribe let him into their midst (without killing him!) because tribal prophecy had alerted them that a tall blond man would bring "the banana leaves out of which God would come." Bruce fit the description and fulfilled the prophecy.

Fascinated by what God did during those early years in American history, I devoted several years of my life to further research, concentrating on the writings of eyewitnesses, mostly fur men, missionaries, and the remembrances of indigenous people describing their own story. Then I visited the sites where these events happened so that I could accurately imagine and describe them.

The original primary documents, of course, do not record actual conversations between the players in this drama. But because previous generations were much better than we are at keeping journals, we are able to piece together events with some accuracy. For example, we do not have much written by Spokan Garry about his experiences at Red River, but we do have the complete unpublished diaries and letters of the Reverends William Cochran and David Jones, who were among his tutors. David Jones, in turn, passed on a verbatim copy of Garry's letter of 1828 to his father and tribe, and he happened to mention Garry's original Indian name, Slough-keetcha. Though my book does include fictional elements for the purpose of telling an effective story, they have been kept to a minimum.

We do not know the precise content of Garry's preaching—but all historians testify to the results of that preaching throughout the Plateau tribes, and I give these testimonies verbatim in my epilogue. We can only wish that the first Christian evangelist west of the mountains had written down more about his own life. But as with the great explorer, mapper, trapper, and ardent Christian Jedediah Smith, some of whose journals were apparently lost in a tragic fire, the unknown parts of these men's lives can be pieced together from the writings of others. (In Jedediah's case, the journals of his clerk, Harrison Rodgers, pieced together by Dale Morgan with the journals of William Ashley, James Clyman, Alexander McLeod, and others, form a more complete picture.)

My goal has been to imagine real events and make them come alive again out of the distant past. Perhaps we can discern, if we look carefully, the loving heart of God revealed long ago when two peoples first began to mingle on this continent.

Just imagine how it might have been . . .

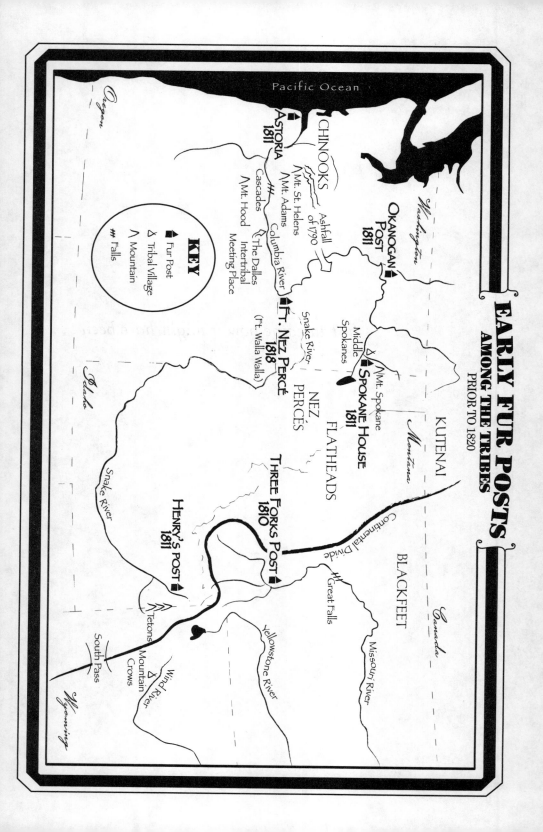

Part I:
The Promise
1782-1811

Cornelius, a Spokan chief, in 1841 a man of about sixty, gives an account of a singular prophecy that was made by one of their medecine-men, some fifty years ago, before they knew anything of white people, or had heard of them. Cornelius, when about ten years of age, was sleeping in a lodge with a great many people, and was suddenly awakened by his mother who called to him that the world was falling to pieces. He then heard a great noise of thunder overhead, and all the people crying out in terror. Something was falling very thick, which they at first took for snow, but on going out they found it to be dirt; it proved to be ashes, which fell to the depth of six inches, and increased their fears, by causing them to suppose that the end of the world was actually at hand. The medecine-man arose, told them to stop their fear and crying, for the world was not about to fall to pieces. "Soon," said he, "there will come from the rising sun a different kind of man from any you have yet seen, who will bring with them a book, and will teach you everything, and after that the world will fall to pieces."[1]

—Wilkes, *Narrative of the United States Exploring Expedition, 1841*

There was a lot of green grass at the bottom of the Bitterroot Range, and the people stayed there to feed their riding ponies and pack horses for two or three days. Then they continued on to Kingston, where they made their winter quarters for the year 1740.

It was here that the first Christmas was celebrated with appropriate ceremonies. Twenty years before this, Circling Raven had announced to his people that the Savior of the world was born at this time. All the young children and the babies grew up with this happy thought. He told his people that it had happened a long time ago, and that they and their enemies should avoid further bloodshed. They should stop and think about this event.[2]

—Chief Joseph Seltice, *Saga of the Coeur D'Alene Indians*

---

1. Taken from Christopher Miller, *Prophetic Worlds*, 45. A more complete account is located in Ruby and Brown's *The Spokane Indians*.
2. Joseph Seltice, *Saga of the Coeur d'Alenes*, 17.

In order to understand many of the features of Flathead past and present non-material culture, one should know something of the story of Shining Shirt. Both the Flathead and the Kalispel claim this hero . . . My oldest informant who claims to be over a hundred years old says that these events took place long before his grandfather's birth. All the elderly informants are sure that he died long before there were any horses in the country.

According to the legend Shining Shirt was both a chief and a shaman. After he was a grown man and was in charge of his people, a Power made a great revelation. The Power said that there was a Good and an Evil One of which the Indians knew but little so far. Yet the time would come when men with fair skins dressed in long black skirts would come who would teach them the truth. The Indians had never heard of a white man at that early date . . . The Power then gave Shining Shirt a talisman of terrific strength. This was a piece of metal inscribed with a cross.

Then he told them that there is a God. His true name was not revealed, but he was temporarily called Amotkan, He-who-lives-on-high. It is the people's duty to pray to him, especially the chief who must do this every morning and particularly at the Midsummer Festival.[3]

—Harry Holbert Turney-High, *The Flatheads of Montana*

3. Harry Holbert Turney-High, *The Flatheads of Montana*, 41-42

One

The village of the Sin-ho-man-naish[4] was in torment. An anguish with an invisible cause, beyond explanation and completely new, had descended on them. An enemy not human had attacked them, an enemy very different from the Okanogans, whose depredations were familiar and easily guarded against. This torment was caused by an enemy no one could see or understand, and they were helpless against it.

Enemy? No one, looking at this quiet village, would even suspect that it was under attack by an enemy. The village seemed to bask in a lazy ease that had hovered forever around these waters below the falls that stopped the salmon. Here, large pines, emitting a sound like labored breathing, hovered over reed-mat lodges of different shapes and sizes, each large enough to house several families. The lodges, weathered gray, exhaled smoke that filled the camp with a sluggish, oppressive air.

The smoke was kept in the camp by pine-covered hills, which hemmed in the river and caused it to loop, forming a kind of city limits on three sides, or a beautiful village moat. But if the moat had been meant for the protection of this village, it had utterly failed.

---

4. The Salmon-trout people, that is, the Middle Spokanes.

Alarming the friendly ravens that always hovered about, anguished cries now shattered the air, the cries of women weeping—the nasal keening of old women, mingled with the clear, quiet sobbing of young girls astonished at the first tragedy of their lives. As for the men, they had learned not to weep openly.

Death, proud and vicious, was stalking the camp in the form of a new sickness. It began with coldness and shivering and ended with a kind of suffering The People had never yet imagined.

Yuree-rachen, Circling Raven, was filled with grief and dismay. Medicine man of the Sin-ho-man-naish, he was a tall man who painted his face the black of the ravens. A single black coup feather hung down behind his long, raven-black hair. In his face was mingled the fading strength of youth with the emerging wisdom of years. He was in the prime of life, yet he felt as if he wanted to die.

They mean to destroy the whole village, the shaman observed, thinking of the spirits behind the sickness. He was afraid.

Soon after the dying began, he walked away from camp, seeking a quiet place, a sanctuary among the pines, where he could let out his emotions. He lay on the ground, the precious, immovable earth reassuring him of its constancy. When life itself is fleeting, the permanency of the earth is a comfort. He wept for sheer frustration and fear, his tears wetting the red-brown pine bark scattered on the ground. The pines, too, were some consolation, for they were solid and secure, like the earth itself. They spoke their peace into his heart. The wind was a spirit in the vocal chords of the trees, whispering to soothe his grief and fear. The breeze gently dried his tears.

But Yuree-rachen was not so easily comforted. He had only to walk back to camp to see the same wrenching sight of an hour before. It was a nightmare from which one could not awaken. Already, dozens of lodges had been touched by the sickness. The dead were everywhere. Their bodies, full of running sores, exuded an offensive odor. The smoke that hung in camp seemed to come from them. The stench was everywhere. There was no escape from it.

Days passed, the most evil of days.

"Is the world coming to an end?" asked Yuree-rachen's brother, Smilkus, Buck-without-antlers, who lived in his lodge.

But the black-face had no answer for him. Circling Raven was seeing how thin was his knowledge, how narrow his influence over these spirits.

He kept his thoughts private. My wisdom is a *sumesh* pouch full of dust. We are helpless! We have done nothing to deserve this. The Piegans deserve this maybe, but we have harmed no one. This affliction of evil tears the heart out of a man. Who can stand up to it? Who can understand it?

Circling Raven's people respected his wisdom. They had rewarded his years of spiritual leadership with buffalo robes, a sign of prominence. His lodge was made of them. His mother, brother, children, daughter-in-law, and sister all lived with him. He had prided himself for sheltering them in one of the better lodges.

Protection? Shelter? Phah! Buffalo hides are no improvement over tule mats. They are no protection from the sickness.

Only last week Yuree-rachen had said to his brother, "The summer buffalo hunt during the Moon of the Camas Root was profitable. Better than usual. We eluded the Piegans and had only one skirmish with the Dakota. We brought home more meat than usual, and hides, too. The thin hides will make someone a good lodge."

These words, spoken at a time of prosperity, now returned to mock him. What good are buffalo hides to dead people? It is horsehides that one uses as grave markers.

Circling Raven made his rounds, chanting, performing cures, sucking out invisible darts of sickness. He wore himself out. His knees ached with kneeling over the sick. His voice was weak from chanting. Never before had so many people sought him out—and then turned their faces from him, grievously disappointed. The ancient rituals had been ineffective.

Late one night, the shaman entered his lodge after an unusually tiring day. He saw the look in his wives' faces—the same look he had observed elsewhere among the women of stricken families. Fear. Reproach. Grief.

"Something has happened?" he dared to inquire. He followed their wordless gaze, looking down where they looked.

Two Bears? My son? Is it now come to you? He dared not speak the thought. Yes, Yuree-rachen's people respected him, but the evil spirits did not.

The disease strikes rich and poor alike, aged headman and helpless baby, man and woman, shaman and warrior. All alike are vulnerable. Evil respects nothing! Yuree-rachen looked down at his son, but eight years of age.

"Father, I am cold. My head! It hurts!" the little one cried pitifully. He shivered uncontrollably.

Aagh! Not Two Bears. My son! The shaman repeated the words to himself in disbelief. The spirits are cruel. They prey upon little children, who have done no harm. They love to afflict the innocent. He thought the words. He did not speak them. Why is life so difficult, so full of suffering? Is there no reward for goodness, for uprightness? Do the powers of the shaman amount to nothing? The questions harassed him. The sickness mocked his hopes, his beliefs.

He had sought Quilent-satmen, He Made Us, for cures, for answers. He had prayed for hours. He had danced, had chanted, had reviewed carefully the ancient lore. Yet no spirit had spoken to him in a dream, and none of the elders could give further answer. Where was Quilent-satmen now? Practitioners of the herbal lore had also done their best. Nothing brought relief.

True, by now a few people had managed to survive the sickness. The Ant People had done their work. But even those few survivors had ended up hideously scarred. Old Laughs Alone had gone blind. The People were losing confidence.

Two Bears grew steadily worse for three days. Hot, yet chilled and shivering, he lapsed into delirium. He cried out frequently. Circling Raven was much in prayer over him, chanting, dancing. His dance was a prayer.

On the fourth day, the fever broke. Two Bears returned to consciousness. This seeming improvement would have encouraged Circling Raven, but he had seen the same in at least a dozen others already—and yet they had all eventually died. He tried to hope, but he could not.

On the following day, the dreaded red spots appeared on Two Bears's neck and forearms, the worst of all omens. They spread out, deepened, and widened as the days passed, until the boy's entire body was covered with running sores. Two Bears cried constantly. Each sore was a firebrand on the skin. He could not lie down without pain. Neither could he stand.

At this point in the sickness came the most difficult part of the search for healing. The shaman dutifully called for Talks Much, the practitioner of herbal arts, whose job it was to scrape each of the pustules. The scraping increased the suffering, yet it had to be done, for in the scraping was the only hope of healing.

Carefully, the woman scraped each of the boy's running sores. His screams of pain could be heard throughout the village. They tore at the heart of Circling Raven and his two wives. The entire village, hearing the wailings, averted their eyes from each other in grim silence.

Then Talks Much carried the pus out to an anthill south of the village. She threw the pus on the anthill. Yuree-rachen followed at her heels and carefully observed how the ants treated the pus.

Good! The ants are eating the pus. The sores will disappear now.

The cure of the Ant People worked sometimes, and when it worked, the treated person would never suffer from boils again.

But it did not work for Two Bears. After several more days of intense suffering, Two Bears breathed his last. Circling Raven wept silently as he washed the body of his son, then painted the boy's face earth-red as though to prepare it for the red earth.

After the time of mourning, the shaman wrapped the body in a deer hide. He placed in the hide beside the boy a wooden carving of a raven in flight. Yuree-rachen had made the toy himself—a gift for his son. He took the corpse to a nearby hillside along the river. The pines mourned with him. So did the dogs running at his heels. The women followed, shrieking their grief to the treetops. The burial ground was strewn with horsehides hanging from tree limbs and poles—grave markers for dozens who had recently died. Who could have imagined that horses, introduced fifty years before, could be so useful.

Circling Raven buried his son in a shallow grave heaped with stones. Then the women of his lodge trudged the sun-drenched path back to the lodge, where they cut their hair short with flints. The lodge of Yuree-rachen added its mourning to that of all the others.

Circling Raven felt numb, empty of tears. He had grieved too much. His grief was turning to bitterness. It was as though his spirit had dived beneath the troubled waters at life's surface to confront the dull brown mud of despair at the bottom—and the mud-covered shapes of long-buried doubts and fears.

Let the women weep. It is their duty.

Circling Raven was dealing with perplexity so deep that emotion could not grapple with it. He struggled not only with the death of his son, but with the futility of life, the impotence of all human effort. His crisis, he sensed, would not pass away even should other sons replace the one he had lost.

During the Month of the Onion, the spirits devoured a quarter of the village. As the disease spent the last of its wrath on the Sin-ho-man-naish, Circling Raven's family sensed his despair. They sent a runner for White Horse, brother of Circling Raven. A close bond tied the shaman to White Horse, who was chief of another village to the north. Perhaps, they said to one another, White Horse will find words to ease the pain of Circling Raven.

White Horse arrived the following day. He slept in the lodge of Circling Raven and rose up with him the next morning. After the morning sweat bath, while they were walking back from a cold plunge in the river, White Horse spoke.

"Elder brother, you have been silent too long. Is it that the death of your son still eats at your heart?" Though directly related to Circling Raven, but used the term out of respect and familiarity.

Immediately came the reply. A tongue full of bitterness spat words beyond the thin veneer of composure that had existed a moment before.

"Why did Quilent-satmen take my son, who did no wrong? But he leaves bad people on the earth to kill and destroy. Is there no justice? Is there no reward for righteousness? Does the Creator punish the innocent, while rewarding the guilty? Faugh!"

White Horse was astonished at these frank words of doubt. But he remained calm. It was a time for listening, for pondering and sympathy.

After a few days, he met again with Circling Raven to continue their conversation of great thoughts and few words. The black-face spoke to his brother in the gall of bitterness:

"Our laws are a mockery. Let us abandon them. There is no God. Let us agree together on it!"

"All right," replied the other. He felt giddy, as though stepping over a cliff. Momentous decisions seemed imminent, yet neither man knew where they would lead.

White Horse measured his words. "Agreed. We will live like the animals. We will abandon our laws. We will proceed as if there were no Creator. But first, my brother, do this one thing. Go to The Mountain and fast four days and nights. Then come back just before noon on the fifth day. If you find no proof of the Creator, we will disband our laws and live like the animals."

Without delay, clad only in a breechcloth, Circling Raven ascended the pine-covered slopes of The Mountain.[5] Here he had gone thirty winters before, to make contact with his *sumesh*, his guardian spirit, when he had entered into manhood. Then, the spirit of the circling raven had spoken to him, had promised to be his guard and guide.

Now in the prime of life, he came to the very clearing where he had gained his new name and his guardian spirit. The place was full of little stone shelters where other youngsters had gone to pray for their guardian spirits.

Full of poignant memories, the shaman built a fire in the center of that clearing, rebuilding also the broken-down stone shelter that he had erected years before. Then he sat in the middle of it and lifted up a chant.

---

5. That is, Mount Spokane.

The Forgotten Awakening

As the days passed, he prayed, fasted, cried out to the Creator, sang the songs of the fathers, maintained vigilance, and hoped—yet despaired.

Aiya, haiya, aiya, haiya.

With each chant, there went up the question: Is there not, somewhere, some good worth living for, some evidence of God? Is there no righteousness in the world?

On the fourth day, before dawn, there came without warning a burst of light, a shattering of the veil that separates the visible from the invisible. It was a dazzling injection of a living future into the dead body of the present. That there should be no misunderstanding about it, Circling Raven heard the voice of Quilent-satmen, the Creator:

"Look down into the future of your people."

As he looked over the pines toward his village to the southwest, he saw no pine-treed landscape, but a procession of strange beings, a true vision manifesting before his very eyes. The beings were people unlike any he had ever seen. Their skin was as white as the clouds. They wore strange clothes, even on top of their heads. The vision of these beings was somehow merciful, though he couldn't say why. They bore in their hands leaves bound together. The leaves, which they held in their hands, was the source of the mercy. It was as though the leaves bound together were a new *sumesh* pouch, a bundle of treasures in which one could put great confidence. After a time, the strange beings evaporated. The vision was complete.

Descending the slopes at the end of his fast, the shaman was full of glory. Despite his weakness, he flew down the mountainside like one of the wild horses. The Creator had spoken! He had entrusted to him a vision!

Circling Raven found his way home, took White Horse his brother aside, and told him, "The Creator has spoken! We should not give up our laws, but live as men, seeking righteousness!"

Yet he did not confide to anyone the vision he had seen. It did not seem to be the right time. This he knew: Quilent-satmen had revealed to him a glimpse of some future mercy. What form this mercy would take, he didn't understand. But he had received vision enough to hang his trust upon it. He was content.

Two

In the eighth winter following The Year of Great Sickness, another event occurred that shook the Sin-ho-man-naish to their roots. A mysterious premonition of evil descended on the village.

Several of the older ones were awakened by it, but not wanting to alarm the children needlessly, few spoke of it. They stared at smoldering fires, plagued by a growing fear that some disaster was drawing near.

Deer-without-antlers, awakening in the night to relieve himself, noticed that the sun-of-the-night was no longer visible. He heard, too, a strange rumbling sound. The ground itself trembled lightly. Strange specks filled the air, like ashes from a large campfire. He returned to his bed, wondering.

Hours later, there grew a strange polluting of the air, a sort of fog that came into the lodges through every opening. By the early hours of the morning, the fog was so thick that Circling Raven, now advanced in years, could scarcely see to the opposite end of his lodge. People blinked their eyes from the desire to see more clearly or to rid themselves of the burning sensation.

The Forgotten Awakening

Something in the air was keeping The People from seeing clearly.

For the past several years The People had lost their vision, had been plagued by vagueness and uncertainty—foggery. The plagues had shaken them to the core. Though the dead had long been buried, and no sickness had recurred, yet a sense of doom had lingered in the village, a sense that the future held a tragedy of which they had known only the first part. Now this rumbling confirmed an impending tragedy, and the fog reminded them of their lack of vision.

By early morning, the plague of fear had grown to explosive intensity. The hour of daylight arrived, yet night refused to give way to it. There was no dawn.

At the first tardy signs of light, a few villagers ventured out of the lodges. As they peered out, their worst fears were confirmed. The coming of daylight had been delayed because the sky was falling! Yes, the sky was actually descending in ashes like snow—gray, dry snow that wasn't melting. Five inches of it had already fallen, burdening the roofs, blanketing the rocks, bending the branches of the pines.

"Aieee!" screamed a woman, Camas Root.

Others, pulled between curiosity and fear, looked cautiously out to see what was the matter. Soon all were huddled together in front of the lodge of the young chief, Illim-spokanee, Child of the Sun and Moon. All were now chattering at the top of their lungs, releasing pent-up emotions that had been accumulating all night long. Children were crying uncontrollably. Their mothers, frantic with fear, tried to shield them.

"What shall we do? It is the end of the world," they cried, their voices bleak with despair.

The words soon became established fact. Even the dogs whined and howled as though about to die. Panic was drowning an entire village.

Illim-spokanee observed that both sun and moon were blocked from view. In fact, almost everything was blocked from view. The air was thick with whiteness. The chief could not even see to the edge of the crowd pressing in around him. He tried to quiet them, but the panic still grew.

It was not he, but Circling Raven who succeeded in quieting them. The black-faced shaman was a rock of certainty in a sea of confusion.

Climbing an ash-coated boulder and raising his hand in the sign of silence, he shouted, "Be quiet! I have a message for you."

Astonished at his words, the crowd listened intently, for he spoke with authority. Circling Raven's stature in the village was unequaled. All suspected that he had been carrying around a secret, and curiosity about that secret had risen to a fever of interest during the intervening years. Maybe now, the man of faith would reveal the word that had come to him on the mountain. If anyone could clear away this foggery and give The People vision, it was he.

"This is not the end of the world," he said. "Much more must come to pass before that time arrives. The Creator spoke to me at the time of the great sickness. A strange people with skin of a different color, speaking a strange language and wearing peculiar clothes, will come to us before the world ends. They will bring with them teachers who will carry leaves bound together in a bundle. Much later, the world will fall to pieces. Until these people come, the world will continue. Let us get to work and clean up these ashes."

With the itch of curiosity scratched at last, the people wanted Circling Raven to scratch the itch some more. "Tell us more, Yuree-rachen."

The old shaman replied, "The newcomers will be *chipixa*, the white-skinned ones. They will be friends to The People. That is all. I am finished."[6]

The people trusted the old shaman. They believed him. He turned fear into rejoicing, despair into hope. He was, surely, the greatest *sgu-moiga* in the history of The People.

The Sin-ho-man-naish created a new dance to commemorate the occasion[7] and to help them keep in mind the words of the great Yuree-rachen, to teach them to their children and to their children's children until the time of their fulfillment.

---

6. The prophecy was almost certainly articulated by Circling Raven during the explosion of Mount Saint Helens in 1791.

7. The so-called "prophet dance" or "dream dance" dates from this and other prophecies throughout the Plateau. Other tribes also practiced it, indicating that there were many other prophecies. Perhaps we don't know half of them; some may have been lost to memory.

Three

Twenty winters after these events broke in among the Sin-ho-man-naish, an even more extraordinary thing happened. Finan McDonald broke in among them.

He was riding a horse and leading a packhorse along the trail from the east. As fishermen along the river looked up, they could not believe their eyes. Here was a man more massive than anyone had ever imagined possible—surely a descendant of the giants of old. He had hair not only on the top of his head, but on the bottom as well, and it covered his mouth! This incredibly ugly hair was not black, nor yet was it gray. It was more nearly the color of red earth, and it hung in profusion down to his waist! His skin was nearly as white as the clouds! He was *chipixa*—a white-skinned one. He wore clothes of unimaginable material, colored in strange crisscross patterns and flopping down over his face.

This apparition now rode up to the bank of the river across from the village. Frightened children ran away, shouting uncontrollably. The whole village came to know that something monstrous and wonderful was approaching from the east. A growing crowd of awed villagers gathered around, a picture of astonishment and curiosity.

Finan McDonald leaned back in his saddle and heaved an uproarious belly laugh that echoed off the hills. Then he spoke:

"*Latha math dhuit!* Good day to you!"

His belly laugh they understood. But his words were strange.

With this giant rode another man of more normal appearance, but wearing equally outlandish clothes and speaking gibberish. He was Jaco Finlay, mixed-blood clerk of the Northwest Company. These men dismounted in front of Illim-spokanee.

By now the Child of the Sun and Moon was an old man. His hair was prematurely white. He had married late and had fathered many children, but he appeared to be their grandfather, not their father. He was a guileless man with deep facial lines that spoke of wisdom, not treachery. He wore a bear-claw necklace and a single swan feather behind his neck.

Trembling, he boldly approached the monster and gestured palms up, palms down, palms outward in the traditional greeting, wondering all the while if this creature was even a human being and whether he could understand the universal language.

"Ha-ha!" cried the Celt, and he laid hold of the astonished headman in the friendliest of bear hugs.

The chief could only think, this man is descended from the giants for sure. This is a strange greeting.

The giant was not disposed to make war, but peace. He went to his horse, searched his packs, and held out gifts to the chiefs, who were standing in a circle wondering what was coming next. Then he spoke:

"*Chan 'eil eadar an t-amadan agus an duine glic ach tairgse mhaith a ghabail, 'nuair a gheibh ei.* There is no difference between the wise man and the fool, but to accept a good offer when he gets it."

During the following week, with a hundred villagers watching their every move, the strangers began to build a lodge on a patch of prairie near the east bank of the river, just across from the village.[8] Saws, axes,

---

8. The site of Spokane House is just west of Spokane, Washington.

guns, knives, awls, traps, wool blankets—all came out of packs as villagers watched. Finan remarked to Jaco that it was like building a house in a stadium full of spectators.

And this lodge! They made it of pine trees cut short and stacked, one atop the other, with clay packed in between. These were miraculous days, days of prophetic fulfillment. All The People's wondering was turning into wonder.

When the lodge was finished, the men brought out from their cavernous packs the final and most certain prophetic fulfillment of them all: leaves bound together. *Ledger book*, they called it. In this book they would make scratchings with brown water flowing from a feather.

Illim-spokanee marveled at the accuracy of the prophecy, yet he wondered at its meaning, its implications. What could The People learn from scratchings such as these?

The two white men knew nothing of the prophecies of Circling Raven. They were simply fur traders responding to a British appetite for beaver-felt hats and trying to make an honest living at setting trap. Soon they proceeded to build two other wooden lodges like the first.

As the weeks passed, the strangers taught the villagers how to trap beaver in the white man's way. In return for the skins, the *chipixa* were willing to trade the inventions they had brought with them. In time, every lodge was adorned with English conveniences—mirrors, beads, spoons, axes, knives, cups, plates, blankets, and articles of clothing.

• • •

One day, the two hat-wearers were joined by another man who rode in from the east. David Thompson was his name.

Clearly, he was a man of authority, both chief and shaman combined. On the one hand, he gave orders even to such a one as The Great Redhair. On the other, he spent much time gazing at the stars through an instrument of great medicine. Surely, this was the man foretold, who would teach The People the mysteries they had long awaited.

But what good was a name like "David Thompson"? It meant nothing. This man would be *Koo-koo-sint*, Star-gazer.

The whites were also busy renaming things. This unsettling trait might have disturbed Illim-spokanee, but they were naming things after him. The Sin-ho-man-naish were renamed "The Spokans." The big river they named "Spokan"; the little one, "Little Spokan." Even their trading post was called "Spokan House." Illim-spokanee was honored.

Koo-koo-sint brought gifts to the chief. The chief looked deep into Koo-koo-sint's eyes. Kindness was there. A face lined with goodness stared back at him from under shoulder-length black hair with bangs clipped straight across the eyebrows. How did Koo-koo-sint trim his hair so straight? It was a mystery. Burning coals did not do such a neat job, nor flints.

With his snub nose and short stature, Star-gazer did not look like a great chief, especially when standing next to Red-hair. But Illim-spokanee sensed another sort of greatness, a greatness even Red-hair respected. There was inner power, knowledge of the mysteries that had produced the wonders even now adorning his lodge.

Illim-spokanee received a London fusil, a cheap gun designed for trade, a gift from Koo-koo-sint. That night he called a counsel of all the chiefs to show them the trade gun and to call for war against the Okanogans to the west. The Kalispels and the Sahaptins had been working out an alliance for days.

"Now we have guns," he said. "We have the white man's arrowheads. We are strong. We can make the Okanogans fear our name. Let our young men ride forth in honor. Today the prophecy comes true that was given us long ago. White men are indeed a blessing to The People."

"Oy, oy!" they all chorused.

Yet no sooner had they agreed upon war than two messengers, Pock-face and Eyes-full-of-tears, entered the circle in the council lodge. Turning to the right and walking behind the seated guests, Eyes-full-of-tears placed vermilion and tobacco before the chief, then announced:

"My elder brothers, we bear with these gifts a message from the *chip-ixa*. Koo-koo-sint does not bring the smoke sticks so that The People can fight the Okanogans. He brings them so that the young men can bring in game, and the people of Illim-spokanee will not starve. This is what Star-gazer says. Remember: only one winter ago, The People were as defense-less as the Okanogans. They hid from their enemies and lived on roots and berries. If The People insist on fighting defenseless neighbors, Koo-koo-sint will have to bring guns and steel arrowheads to their neighbors so they can defend themselves against you. If you must fight, join your allies and fight the Piegans to the east. For the Piegans have made slaves of your young women and have murdered and scalped many of your young men. So speaks Star-gazer."

Illim-spokanee meditated on this teaching during his stint fishing the river.

New ideas are entering the village with the new gifts. Star-gazer is saying that the strong should not violate the weak, but protect them! Those who believe in peace must band together to protect themselves from murderers and pillagers. These are good ideas. This is reasonable counsel. Circling Raven would have given such counsel as this. Star-gazer has wisdom from the stars. But when will Koo-koo-sint share with The People all the treasures of his knowledge? And there is yet this mystery: the prophecy said that knowledge would come not through the stars, but by leaves bound together, which the white-skins will bring. There is much yet to be explained.

Added to this confusion was another surprise: Star-gazer did not remain long at Spokane House. David Thompson was a busy man with many a mile to travel. He was charged with surveying and mapping the entire region of the northern Rockies and establishing the Northwest Company there in fur-trade power. Star-gazer was soon gone, an enigma, unwittingly promising much, but withholding even more.

Four

At the same time that David Thompson had been making his way west toward the Salmon-trout people, an American ship was breaching the treacherous gravel bars at the mouth of the Columbia. The revelations of Lewis and Clark had induced a vision in the mind of John Jacob Astor. Herr Astor seldom prayed and never fasted. He got his visions in a sound, German, businesslike way: by reading the newspaper. He saw that the mouth of the Columbia could be utilized as the hub of a great fur empire, provided his ship could reach it before the British traders did. If David Thompson wanted to map the Rockies, Astor wanted to own the world. That was his vision.

So, when the *Tonquin* had unloaded her thirty-three men on the south shore, they named the spot for their visionary.

Astoria.

It was April 12, 1811.

• • •

The hammering of axes, like the staccato sounds of a pileated wood-pecker, announced the American invasion to the Oregon fog. Gulls and ravens screamed the tidings to nearby villages of Chinooks. During the passing of two months, an acre of ground was cleared of huge spruce and red cedars—some fifty feet in girth. Amidst these beginnings a young Scotsman named Alexander Ross prepared himself for wilderness hardship.

Ross, like the others of his party, was an unlikely lord of the wilderness. Acutely aware of his inexperience, he felt like a meek Scottish terrier barking into the dark woods to make it seem less threatening. Even now, he clung to Weasel, his Scottish terrier, for protection.

As he worked to build Fort Astoria, Alex was appalled that none of his superiors had any more wilderness ken than he had.

Ten weeks after the founding of Astoria, Alex heard the barking of seals playing up river. Looking toward the noise, he was surprised to spot a canoe making its way toward them around Tongue Point to the east. This canoe was not an Indian canoe, for it had a large British flag jutting up from its stern. Besides, the canoe itself was not of Indian design. As these men docked, Alex noticed that the vessel was ingeniously crafted with cedar clinkers sewn together and seamed with gum—a light craft perfectly designed for both river travel and portaging. Obviously, these men were experts in wilderness lore.

Duncan McDougall, the Astorian leader, immediately recognized the well-dressed man in the stern.

"David! David Thompson!" he shouted. "Are ye a sight fer sore eyes. What brings ye to these infairnal regions?"

"Can't you guess, Duncan? They've got me mapping these 'infernal regions'—and bringin' in furs as well."

Alex, standing nearby, sputtered acid thoughts. English! Curse them! Maybe they willna stay long.

But McDougall was cheery: "Can ye stay wi' us fer a season? Plenty o' room here, an' ye could help us deal with these infairnal Chinooks."

"I'll need to be on my way up river again in a fortnight," David replied.

"In a fortnight! Eh, we'd be ready by then to start us an exploring tour of our own. Don't suppose ye'd be open to us makin' the wee journey togither now?"

"Well, yes," replied his friend. "The delay'll give us time to caulk our canoes and repair our traps." Turning to his men, he shouted, "*Mes voyageurs! Desirez-vous manger, dor-mir et jouer deux semaines?*"

The men guffawed. No one had any objection to a two-week holiday. A spirit of camaraderie warmed and united the seven French-Canadians and one Owyhee[9] under David's leadership.

But Alex Ross disliked the English, and he was not in the habit of guffawing. He was a Presbyterian.

And so at Astoria a competition was begun that the Americans had no chance of winning. Alex's sense that Americans were inexperienced novices in a world of English experts proved only too accurate. The English were better at trapping, better at map-making, better at exploring, better at relations with Indians, better at canoe craft, better at trading, better at fighting, better at winning, better at organizational skills, better at everything. In the end, these Astorians would give up, handing over their fort to the British, who would call it Fort George.

After ascending the Columbia, winning a hard-won friendship with the Okanogans, and marrying an Okanogan woman, Alex would found Okanogan Post. Then he would trade sides, working for David Thompson's Northwest Company, preferring to align himself with winners, not losers.

As for the other Astorians: considering themselves loyal Americans, they would make a different kind of decision, and a different kind of history. Somehow, they would find their way east, desperately hoping to survive thousands of miles of bitter wilderness travel all the way to St. Louis, and then back home. And they would manage it, barely—just barely—finding, in the process, almost by accident, a pass that would become legendary, a pass to the south of the one Lewis and Clark had discovered.

People would call it: South Pass.

---

9. Hawaiian.

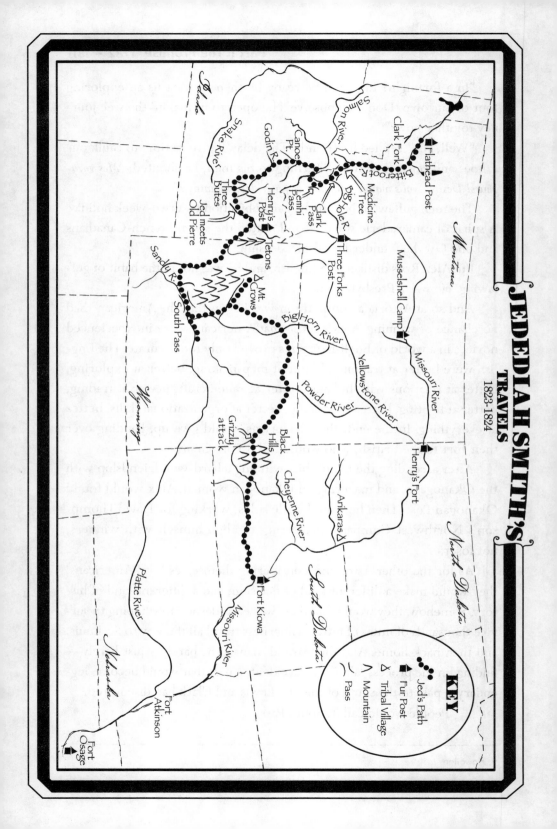

Part II:
The Great Shaking
1811-1824

The extent of the earthquake's effect westward across the plains and mountains remains uncertain and it could have been only a coincidence that late in 1812 a series of exceptionally violent shocks destroyed missions in California. That so monstrous and general a phenomenon should have gained so little notice in American history, and none at all in American folklore, is one of the stranger anomalies of our career as a people.[10]

—Dale Van Every, *The Final Challenge*

Jedediah Smith, perhaps the greatest of all the American mountain men, was as devout a Christian as a Scotch Covenanter.

—Robert G. Cleland, *This Reckless Breed of Men*

(T)he observant Jedediah had watched the spectacle of the winter trade with the Flatheads, Pend D'oreilles, Kutenais, Nez Perces and Spokanes, written in his journal, worked on his maps, and—if one highly esteemed source is correct—engaged in some missionary work that was to have considerable significance for the Hudson's Bay Company.[11]

—Alson Jesse Smith, *Men Against the Mountains*

---

10. Dale Van Every, *The Final Challenge*, 105.
11. Alson Jesse Smith, *Men Against the Mountains*, 227.

One

Back east, beyond the great rock barrier the tribes called The Backbone of the World, the quiescent body of the earth suddenly went violent. On December 16, 1811, without warning, the continent went into grand-mal epileptic convulsions. It was a great shaking in the crust of the earth, a splitting open of things such as this land had never before seen. The New Madrid earthquake exceeded the 1791 explosion of Mount St. Helens for sheer terror. It was as though the earth were making a statement on both sides of the Backbone, announcing trouble and change.

The location of the great shaking was significant. Saint Louis: the very gateway through which French, then American trappers had already entered the Missouri highway that would take them to the western tribes and beaver waters. Saint Louis: future home of William Clark, ambassador to nations who were already calling him Chief Red Hair. As the home of the first Superintendent of Indian Affairs, Saint Louis would be the meeting place for countless tribal delegations from as far away as the

Columbia Plateau. But the earth opened this chapter of history with an act of violence.

A quiet coldness had descended on the Mississippi Valley that night of December 16. Settlers of the valley between Saint Louis and New Madrid were sleeping peacefully. The days of late had been unseasonably warm. In Saint Louis, late-night revelers were wandering home from William Christy's public house, singing bawdy French songs at the top of their lungs.

"Fermez la bouche, imbécile!"—The shout of a wakened sleeper came from inside one of the vertical-beam cabins that lined the crisscrossing lanes of mud that passed for streets. The revelers made their way home. All was quiet again. Saint Louis slept.

But no. At 2 a.m., a huge, guttural rumble began calling to the city out of the west as though the earth had caught something in her throat. The noise was like thunder, but it was not thunder.

Everyone in the valley was instantly awakened, awed by the menacing roar. People braced themselves. Who could understand this voice, this message? The earth herself was crying out, her cries filling the air, now rattling windows, now banging shutters. Everyone sensed that something awful was about to happen. No one knew what. Few had experienced an earthquake before.

The noise, intensifying by the second, ripped into valley settlements like a thousand cannons exploding at once. An earsplitting roar shook every molecule of matter. Thumbs tried to save eardrums from intolerable vibrations. A violent shaking toppled chimneys, demolished roofs, sent French heirlooms crashing to the floor.

With loud curses, drunken boatmen and French patricians rushed out of their houses, trying to discover what awful fate had come upon them. What they saw utterly terrified them.

The ground was undulating like the sea! Waves of earth were traveling toward them at the speed of ocean surf! Then these amber waves of grain stalks would burst open, shooting a surf-spray of sand, coal, and water forty feet into the air.

Day dawned, but it was no comfort. The daylight merely showed more clearly the monstrosity of their hell.

Sacré bleu! Trees were pitching over. Shacks and trees disappeared in deep, twenty-foot-wide crevasses that were opening up to swallow whatever or whoever might fall in.

Some tremors were vertical, others horizontal. Vertical tremors produced the most earsplitting noises. But the others were the ones most devastating to the pitiful dwellings of the valley. Trees shook with such violence that they broke one another's branches. They were fighting battles! Oak fought willow, and willow fought cottonwood.

Birds were so frightened that they stopped flying about and sought shelter in the bosoms of fleeing men and women. But the men and women knew no better than the birds where to find shelter. From such a disaster as this, there was no shelter.

The earth was in travail. Tyrannical powers kept on torturing the ground at intervals. A pang advanced, then a few hours of breathing space, then another pang. But what was this travail bringing forth?

Blackening dust rose to a great height. A yellow, sulfurous vapor filled the air as if some malignant spirit were troubling the earth. The stench was overpowering. There was no escape from it. Clouds of sand and dust eclipsed the sun. The day became like night.

From the midst of this unholy blackness, mysterious flashes of light could be seen around the Saint Louis horizon, or so her citizens later testified. By evening the landscape seemed aglow, not with departing sunlight, but with the very flames of hell. To this day, no one has explained these infernal visions.

The lethargic waters of the Mississippi became violent. Impressive flood tides rolled up on land and back again, washing away thousands of trees. Pirogues and keelboats were swept away to accumulate on snags downstream. It was the only time in history that the Missouri River was ever known to flow upstream.

Both downstream and up, floods were preparing to drown anyone who had not the sense to flee to higher ground. Thousands lost their homes. One island, a nest for pirates, was entirely swept away.

The Forgotten Awakening

As the floods receded, they left a residue of white sand that covered whole counties, to remind future generations of those violent days.

The New Madrid earthquake was no brief or local disaster. During the following year, tremors would be felt as far away as Baltimore, New Orleans, and the Dakota villages of the West.

Two

The New Madrid Quake gave Saint Louis an evil reputation. It associated the place with judgment and doom. It placed a sense of foreboding around the fledgling town, located so promisingly on the junction of the two greatest rivers in America.

Yet, eleven years later in 1822, Jedediah Smith didn't balk at all when it came to paddling a canoe from his home in Ohio, down the Rock River in winter, all the way to the mouth of the Missouri, to join up with William Ashley's new fur brigade—at Saint Louis. He purposely designed to go through the gateway of evil reputation into the place of foreboding beyond.

His mentor, Dr. Titus Gordon Vespasian Simons, had given him for his sixteenth birthday a copy of *The Journals of Lewis and Clark*. The book had changed his life. It had opened up a vision of a vast continent full of the wonders of God waiting to be discovered. The picture beckoned to him like an enchantress.

The Forgotten Awakening

At the heart of the West roared the Great Falls of the Missouri, topped by a huge, sun-bleached cottonwood skeleton crowned with an ancient eagle's nest for hair. Vast grasslands to the east of this sentinel fed huge herds of beasts unfamiliar to easterners. To the west, foreboding, impenetrable mountains of eternal snow blocked passage to the great Columbia and her triumvirate of peaks, "St. Helians, Adams and Hood"—as Lewis and Clark had named them. And all this was full of people who had lived there forever, people Jedediah Smith wanted to meet and to know. They were part of the fascination.

What is it that impels some few of us to embark on foolhardy adventures, when others prefer the comfort and ease of a quiet fire and a good book? But for Jedediah, the book had the opposite effect. It pulled him away from the fire.

To Jedediah's youthful mind, the scene evoked in the *Journals* was like the allurement of an ancient walled garden, beckoning to him to find his way inside and see what was beyond the lichen-encrusted barrier that was supposed to keep him out. Faith, too, drew him. Somehow, Jedediah knew that behind this fascination was a fascinating God who was calling to him in the writings of Lewis and Clark. So he left his comfy fire and abandoned his girlfriend, Louisa Simons. He set out for the gateway that opened to the pathway that led to the walled garden that led to—what? Nobody knew. That was the fascination of it. Nobody had been there and lived to tell about it. Nobody, that is, but that ragtag group of Astorian fur traders who had abandoned Astoria and fought their way back to Saint Louis.

As Jedediah departed for the gateway, he took two books with him as his only treasures: *The Journals of Lewis and Clark* and his Bible.

Through countless arguments with his father, Jedediah Senior, and his brothers, Nelson, Ira, Peter, and Austin, he had tried to convince them of his reasons for going. Of course, there were the practical realities. The bank collapse of 1820 had put everyone in desperate poverty, and Jedediah was hoping to supply his family with income. It was said that beavers were good money, so he would learn how to trap them. That was the motive you could put into words, the reason that was reasonable.

But are there not deeper, higher destinies that latch on to our hearts and pull us forward, as though a voice from somewhere within were imposing itself on us, impelling us to travel down an invisible river? And all the shakings and fearsome threats in the world cannot convince us to pull our canoe out of the river and camp along the side of it when such a call grips us. Jedediah believed he had a destiny, and his destiny was for no other but him alone. So that first winter of his planned odyssey, he paddled to Saint Louis alone, or rather, with only God for a companion.

· · ·

While Jedediah Smith was enticed by the female wonder of untouched creation beckoning to him softly with whispers, the New Madrid earthquake, macho and warlike, was to be a more accurate picture of life once he arrived in Saint Louis.

William Clark, who now resided in Saint Louis, had written in his report to President Jefferson, "The Missourah and all its branches from the Cheyenne upwards abound more in beaver and common otter than any other streams on earth particularly that proportion of them lying within the Rocky Mountains." This was the enticement of the decade, attracting hundreds of fur men to ply those waters, which unfortunately moved in the opposite direction from their lucrative headwaters. And yet there was but one road west, and the Missouri was it, even though it was a treadmill moving the wrong way.

That was not the only problem with the Missouri River. This was no ancient, lethargic, meandering, spent river of bygone glory like the Mississippi. The Missouri was a young, rebellious, cantankerous teenager that ripped holes in keelboats, froze you out with her four-foot-thick ice, impoverished you with her vast stretches of treeless plains, and still hid herself in unexplored mystery. Here was a challenge that shook Jedediah Smith and all of Ashley's trappers out of their ease and comfort. In fact, before they had even arrived at Fort Osage, after a mere three weeks of river travel, the river got the better of them and sank their keelboat, stranding the whole party before they had even left the realm of civilization.

A shaking of confidence. A comeuppance for pride. The river argued belligerently, "You're not coming up here if I have anything to say about it."

• • •

When William Ashley himself showed up to rescue them in another keelboat, the next challenge presented itself to Jedediah. Growing up on an Ohio farm, isolated from neighbors, with church being the main social outlet, he had enjoyed quietness and peace among friends. But now, cramped on a twenty-by-fifty-foot keelboat, he was thrown in with some of the most notorious scoundrels of the age. Mike Fink, known as the most formidable rough-and-tumble fighter of the American wilderness, now past his prime, but seasoned in foulness, had decided to try trapping with Ashley's outfit. Brash and arrogant, the man was as dangerous to his friends as to his enemies.

Then there was Ed Rose, whose nose had been bitten off by "a big Chillicothean." He looked either monstrous or comical, and it was sometimes hard to decide which. But you just had to learn not to notice the nose of Rose. The man didn't like to be laughed at, nor to be ostracized for his appearance. You had to pretend to like him. He was needed for his skill as an interpreter, being the only one of the lot who had lived with Indians. Other than interpreting, he didn't believe in work, even when there was much work to be done.

These were rough customers of the sort Jedediah, at the age of twenty-two, had never before encountered. Yet he was in close company with them daily, and he had to get used to it. It had been easier floating down the Rock River by himself. These men shook Jedediah out of his peace. Often his thoughts returned to his parents, to Peter and Austin and Louisa back home, and the comfort of the small four-room farmhouse in Chenango County he had left behind. Yes, the house had been cramped, but at least he had enjoyed the people he was cooped up with.

After many weeks of backbreaking labor on the treadmill, Ashley's trappers joined Andrew Henry at the mouth of the Yellowstone. In October, Jedediah accompanied a party up to the mouth of the Musselshell. They built four shacks for winter survival and surrounded them with a palisade. In December the river froze over, and the magnificence of infinity settled in and rewarded them for finding their way to its bosom. Purity unimaginable to civilized people stared up from the ground everywhere, free to be enjoyed by all who had eyes for it. Lewis and Clark had been here. Otherwise, this was virgin wilderness—except for the people of the land who had lived here forever. But they were nowhere to be seen. The panorama had been unpeopled for weeks.

One day, a huge herd of buffalo appeared out of nowhere, crossed the ice and approached the camp. Fascinated by the men, they insisted on sticking around. Hovering near the stockade for much of the winter, the buffalo provided an endless supply of food. The beasts did not understand that they ought to be afraid. When one of the men killed a buffalo, the other beasts couldn't comprehend what had happened to it. This was profligate abundance in the midst of stark emptiness.

Unfortunately, Mike Fink and his two friends, Talbot and Carpenter, were there to spoil the scene. They were always arguing about something. But arguing with a man like Fink was not recommended. Finally, he proposed a contest to prove (for the one hundredth time) his great skill as a marksman. He required friend Billy Carpenter to put a cup of whiskey on his head for Mike to shoot at. Friend Billy did so. Mike said, "Hold your noddle steady, Carpenter, and don't spill the whiskey, as I shall want some presently." He plugged his friend an inch and a half above his eyes, dead center. Carpenter fell forward dead. And Fink replied, "Carpenter, you have spilled the whiskey."

This event, observed by Jedediah, was an earthquake in the middle of paradise. He had been watching the arguments grow for weeks. It dawned on him now that out here in the middle of nowhere, there was no law, no accountability, no restraint. The ground of Jedediah's soul was shaking again. He was getting an education in the extremes of human nature.

By contrast to such gross backwoods foolishness, Jedediah had been fascinated by the people of the land, the tribes Lewis and Clark had described. From his first reading of the *Journals*, he had seen them as the crown jewels in the fascinating diadem that was the American West. Part of what fascinated him was that they were different from himself. He wanted to know them as a man wants to know a woman whose differentness is her attraction. Upon glimpsing the Plains tribes for the first time, he had written of his fascination, toying with a longing to "live the lazy, carefree life of an Indian." This was not a moral judgment, but a sudden realization that there were other ways of life that might actually be preferable to the agricultural one he had grown up with. Seeing the pristine conical lodges of the Sioux, Jed saw that their way of life could be just as worthwhile and honorable as his own. At least, he thought it might, and he wanted to find out.

Ed Rose, the only man among them who had spent any appreciable time among the tribes—the Mountain Crows—spoke glowingly of the sexual opportunities out there among the people of the land. Jedediah couldn't imagine how any woman would be interested in this noseless man. But Rose presented himself as the expert with all Indians everywhere, especially women. He called himself by his Crow name, *Chee-ho-carte*, Five Scalps, and liked to wear tokens of Indianness, eagle feathers and other doodads.

Jedediah was interested in the tribes for other reasons hard to pin down. Whether it was the influence of the Bible or the *Journals*, he couldn't say. But in his mind was the ambassadorial leadership modeled by William Clark. He was determined to take that example and traverse the entire West, discovering the people no one had met.

Three

On May 31, Jedediah Smith's destiny came dead up against a wall. A team of thirty Missouri Fur Company trappers, led by the huge one-time army lieutenant Michael Immel and his clean-shaven sidekick Robert Jones, had gone further up the Missouri to trap. The Piegan war chief, *Mehkskehme-Sukahs*, Iron Shirt, had lured them with promises of trade. Then, with a war party of Piegans and Bloods, Iron Shirt ambushed them, killing seven out of the thirty, including the two leaders.

News of the "Immel-Jones massacre" spread downriver immediately and landed among Ashley's men. Joshua Pilcher's Missouri Fur Company was finished—completely demolished as if by a powerful earthquake. No business could sustain itself in the face of such loss of life. Few men had the heart for such risks—as Iron Shirt was well aware.

William Ashley reached back to a conversation he'd had with William Clark before he had left Saint Louis, explaining to his men that the real enemy was the English up north. They were selling London fusils to the tribes and encouraging them to kill any American trappers they might find. Around the campfires for nights on end, long-smoldering hostilities toward English traders were fanned for weeks.

But then it was Ashley's turn. William Ashley left Andrew Henry at the mouth of the Yellowstone to take his furs back to Saint Louis. Above the Great Bend, he stopped to visit with Gray Eyes in the twin Arikara villages on the west bank of the Missouri. When the trappers had been lured into trade by the wily old chief, the Arikaras opened fire without warning—and killed fourteen of Ashley's men. This was much harder to blame on the English. It seemed the whole fabric of White-Indian trade was experiencing an earthquake on the Upper Missouri.

The French, trading for decades, had never encountered any such thing. The Chouteaus, with quiet consistency, had gotten rich trading here. To them, it was a highly profitable business. All they needed was a little business skill to make it succeed. And they were still making it succeed. Why didn't the tribes attack the French? It was a mystery.

But now, for some reason, came a great shaking for Americans. Some wondered if the problem was that the Americans were no longer relying on the tribes to do their trapping for them. The Arikaras were perhaps afraid the Americans were coming in to take over the trapping and cut the Indians out of the deal altogether. Were the tribes feeling excluded?

In the midst of the crisis, Jedediah and a French trapper named Baptiste rode west, picked up Andrew Henry, and returned to wreak vengeance on Gray Eyes. Colonel Henry Leavenworth, hearing of Indian hostilities, came north with his bluecoats to "teach the Rickerees a lesson in American military superiority." But the Arikaras didn't seem to know about Leavenworth's superiority. They thumbed their noses at him, then packed up silently in the night and escaped, though the two villages were completely surrounded by soldiers and trappers with specific instructions not to let them escape.

The colonel ended up merely looking foolish. None of the trappers or soldiers, of course, admitted to having fallen asleep during the night watch. Everyone was pretty well disgusted with everyone else. The Rocky Mountain Fur Company, what was left of it, descended the river and reconnoitered at Brazeau's Fort, renamed Kiowa, a property of the prosperous French Fur Company.

. . .

The ugliest fort on the Missouri, Kiowa looked like a surgical mistake on the skin of the earth just below Great Bend. The place was especially dry and dusty on account of a drought that summer. The whole country had suddenly become very unpromising.

In the courtyard, Andrew Henry, William Ashley, and a dozen men who remained of the Rocky Mountain Fur Company met together to consider their options.

Andrew Henry, a tall, slender man with dark hair, blue eyes, and a commanding presence, looked tired and beat. The first to take a party of trappers to the headwaters of the Missouri, he had already experienced this sort of disaster in 1810 at the hands of the Blackfeet. Not to be deterred, he had crossed over to the west side of the Rockies and built Henry's Post beyond the Tetons. But the white silence of wilderness winter had frozen him out—much like his wife, who had divorced him after two years of marriage. The Arikara fiasco had now finished him. At least for the moment, he was ready to divorce the wilderness. A studious man who played the violin and loved to read, he was conspicuous in this meeting by his silence.

Another man conspicuous by his silence was Bill Sublette. Like many of the others, he was young, barely twenty-three. In the last two years, he had lost both his parents, and he had joined Ashley's trappers to get away from painful reminders. Now, after the deaths of many of his trapping friends, it seemed as though his whole life was consumed by death. He was going through deep grief that few others understood or knew how to help.

As if to sympathize with the obvious pain emanating from the most silent ones in the circle, Tom Fitzpatrick, who had immigrated from Ireland six years before, let go with a series of invectives against "the Rees."

This got the whole circle going for a while, including Tom Eddy, a recent immigrant from Edinburgh. But those who knew Fitz best had learned to just let him blow off Irish steam, and then he'd be back to normal after a while. Encouraging him with sympathy tended to make things worse, and then everyone ended up unhappy. Unfortunately, that's the direction the conversation was going.

Jedediah Smith stood behind William Ashley, lost in thought. The invectives against the tribes were just what you might expect after a massacre. And yet, he felt no desire to join in. Why? he asked himself. Why do I feel no bitterness?

As the others had their say, he began to realize that for twenty-three years, he had heard preachers preach about sin. "All have sinned." That word, from the book of Romans, had gotten into his blood and altered his way of looking at people. He had grown up with doctrines of sin. Been shaped by them. Now he felt he was joined by sin to all other members of the human race. Sin was a common principle, a basic, unquestioned understanding of the human condition. There were no good guys and no bad guys. He could not say "Indians are treacherous" in such a way as to imply that white people were not equally treacherous.

Mike Fink. Gray Eyes. All of us have sinned and have the potential just to haul off and shoot somebody. Somebody who trusted you, who just wanted to be a friend. But something gets inside you and makes you think you should kill 'em. A mystery, but it's just the way things are in a fallen world.

Lost in these thoughts, and deeply troubled by the tone of the conversation, Jedediah remained as silent as Bill Sublette and Andrew Henry.

As things got more heated, Jim Clyman, a long-haired aristocratic Virginian in his late twenties, came to the rescue. He had the slowest, steadiest nature of the group. An educated man, upon first being introduced to the Ashley men a year ago, he had written in his diary "Falstaff's Battalion was genteel by comparison." Fitz's salty anger grated on Clyman, and he intervened in a slow drawl that always had a tendency to slow everyone down.

"Hold on there, friend. Ah do b'lieve we're here to talk about the future, not the past. The Rees got away in a right clever move, an' my hat's off to 'em. There's nothing we can do 'bout it now, except be more cautious the next time."

Dave Jackson, the only older man in the group (in his forties), helped put the brakes on too. Jackson was in an entirely different situation from the others, being married with four children. He had signed on to be Ashley's clerk, and he talked like one: "Let's hear what our Mr. Ashley has to say."

William Ashley, who had borrowed $100,000 from Tracy and Wahrendorff for this enterprise, was now $100,000 in debt with very little to show for it. But he had not yet walked through years of desperation like Andrew Henry, and he was willing to give the mountain trade another go in spite of everything. In fact, he recognized that being $100,000 in debt was a bad place to end his story, and he was desperate to keep it going somehow. On this cool, sunny fall day, with a voice thick with his Virginia origins, he could afford to be optimistic.

"Men, Ah have nothin' to offer you now but the conviction that our fortunes and our destiny lie beyond the mountains. We've all learned the hazards of river travel. Lose one boat, and $10,000 disappears in a day. But if we could buy horses and outfit a party to explore the streams beyond the Divide, who knows what we might find? Mr. Rose knows the Mountain Crows and has been across Union Pass. He reports, from his journey with the Astor's men, that this pass is just waiting for us to cross it, and there are plenty of beaver beyond. Ah wish that Mr. Rose had made some maps as he was exploring west. But, well . . . he didn't. But at least we know the pass exists.

"Ah b'lieve Mr. Smith'll be the best one to lead the party; Mr. Henry ain't interested this time around. Mr. Rose will go as interpreter. As free trappers, y'all stand to make or lose a fortune. All Ah can promise is: Ah'll wear down ten teams o' pack mules to get there with next year's supplies, and Ah'll purchase your furs from you at the going rate. Pilcher and his Missourah Comp'ny's done, so he's willing to loan us a few mules as pack animals. Says he has no use for 'em. We'll aim for the end of September to depart. Will any o' you follow Mr. Smith through the Rockies?"

Then came their answers:

"Aye," said Tom Eddy.

"Yep," echoed Bill Sublette.

"Sure will," Dave Jackson put in.

"I'm in favor, aye," Tom Fitzpatrick said.

James Clyman merely nodded while cleaning his piece.

Ed Rose had already been volunteered, but he was off somewhere sleeping. Two other men, Stone and Branch, known to be city slickers, came on later.

Most of the men were young, born in 1799, the same year as Jedediah. And now, at age twenty-three, they were heading out to discover the walled garden of Jedediah's dreams and see if they could find their way through.

Somehow, the fact that he was on his way to penetrate that walled garden was no surprise to Jedediah. His life, it seemed to him, was right on track.

Four

As September phased into October, the party, led by a French guide borrowed from Fort Kiowa, made its way through endless empty hills of brown grass. The landscape was a study in pure loneliness. After weeks, they arrived at the Black Hills, then emerged on the other side among wild plum trees and prickly pear cacti. October weather was producing a cold rain.

One day, without warning, there came from the left an ominous pounding of the earth. Then the cry, "White bear! Look out!"

Jedediah ran out of a clump of underbrush directly into the path of a monstrous grizzly. The half-ton beast picked up Jedediah's one-hundred-and-sixty-pound frame by the head. The beast's wretched breath enveloped Jed's face. Its teeth felt like they were tearing his head all to pieces. Then, with a snarl, it threw him away like a piece of trash. Charging again, it aimed a blow at his ribs. The blow hit Jedediah's knife, bending several ribs beneath it.

Faced with challenges from Sublette and the others, the grizzly decided to lope away, but not without pawing a few more times at Jedediah's head. As it ran off, the fat on its back, covered with white-tipped hair, shook like jelly. Its lower lip bounced in an arrogant swagger. The thing knew it had won.

As they gathered around Jedediah's wracked body, the group—greenhorns every one—knew that this was the worst of all possible disasters. They were out in the middle of nowhere. No medical possibilities whatever. Ed Rose, who might have been of some help, had disappeared ahead.

"What's ta be done?" asked Tom Eddie.

"We gotta do something," said Sublette. "He'll bleed to death."

"Why don't you?" retorted Fitz with Irish pique. He often translated panic into anger.

Everyone debated the situation. After several minutes, Jim Clyman, the Virginian, got down close to Jedediah and asked with a kind of reverence, "Sir, what should we do?" They were asking their leader to please lead them—from his position flat on his back.

Jedediah didn't seem to know he was supposed to be in shock. It was almost as though the body on the ground was not his own. His voice weak but calm, he replied, "One or two of you, go for water. Clyman, see if you can find that needle and thread of yours. How bad is the damage?"

"Old Ephraim warn't kind," Clyman drawled. "Scalp's gonna need some repair work here'n there."

Clyman fetched his needle and began stitching Jedediah's face back together. But the ear was dangling by a thread of skin, and Clyman said frankly, "There's no hope for this."

But Jedediah disagreed. "Oh, you must sew it on somehow or other," he moaned irritably.

Jim did the job, but it was all rough work. Jedediah was not a pretty picture by the time he was done.

With Clyman apologizing for not doing a better job, they rode to a nearby stream, one of the tributaries of the Cheyenne, and set up camp. Privately, none of them thought their leader would survive.

• • •

For a week, Jedediah went in and out of delirium as he lay on his back next to the babbling stream. The picture of the inside of the bear's mouth was a hard one to get rid of. So were the animal sounds, the enveloping ferocity, the experience of being lifted off his feet by violence, his face personally assaulted. Yet, deep in his heart, a quiet peace continued to steady him. This unexpected peace had been there the whole time. There was grace for this ferocity.

Often as he lay there, his thoughts went back to Ohio, back to Louisa with her quiet confidence in him, her insistence that he would become someone important one day. Why had he chosen to leave her? Everyone had expected the two of them to get married. It was inevitable, they thought. His decision to leave home for the western wilderness had caught them all off guard. No one could have predicted this. Dr. Simon, Louisa's father, had wondered if he had made a mistake, giving Jedediah that book.

Marriage? Well, one day—yes—perhaps. He had hoped, assumed, dreamed. But for now, Louisa's face was only a distant comfort, held pleasantly in a dozen cherished memories. She was gentle and innocent and wonderfully female.

Jed's parents had imparted their faith to him, and that faith was now tested as never before. His family had never been interested in religious externals or Christian foofaraw. Either Jesus Christ would change your life, or he wasn't worth your time. The Puritanism of Jedediah's ancestors had played itself out, becoming legalistic and external. But then had come the recent outpourings of God in the wilderness, with all the stories that had circulated in wilderness communities.

Leaders during the Great Awakening—eighty years ago now—had made a big deal about how God would always conduct himself with decorum, abiding by the rules of dignity and decency. They defended the outpouring by insisting that it was "entirely without outcry." But in these latter days, the present move of God was full to overflowing with "outcry." Wilderness people in places like Kentucky did not need a great deal of decorum, and God seemed to know that. The outcries God had created were controversial in the extreme. But controversy is a good publicist, and the stories of God's great deeds had been breathed around among all the wilderness communities for years, beginning with the year of Jedediah's birth, 1799, the year the Kentucky revival began.

He remembered the stories now, stories not of religion and church, but of God and his great power. How James McGready had stirred up prayer for "the worst place in America," Logan County, Kentucky. Most people knew the place as Rogues Harbor. Then McGready had gone there and prayed on-site for the conversion of some of the most desperately wicked people in the country. One day, without warning, all the scum from Rogues Harbor had shown up at James McGready's little prayer chapel during a communion service. It was as though they had been invited to a birthday party—yet no one had invited them. And whose birthday was it, anyway?

McGready, seeing that his prayers were being answered, set up a pulpit under the trees and preached of Jesus. And God was suddenly there, more real than anyone wanted him to be. The rogues of Rogues Harbor were stricken down and thrown into a violent trembling. God was shaking them bodily—and they were crying out for mercy. The shaking didn't quit until they let God write his laws on their lawless hearts. There was absolutely no decorum there at all. James McGready, the ugliest preacher east of the Mississippi, had given up on decorum years before.

To others, God had revealed himself differently—as the circuit-riding preacher Peter Cartright had described it: "Divine light flashed all round me, unspeakable joy sprung up in my soul. I rose to my feet, opened my eyes, and it really seemed as if I was in heaven; the trees, the leaves on them, and everything seemed, and I really thought were, praising God."

The Methodists, more than anyone, had followed God's power out into the wilderness places to nurture and train those who were touched by it. And so Jedediah's family had become Methodists. They were interested in a real God, a God who is there. Not like the God of William Ashley, who, upon arriving in Saint Louis from Powhatan County, Virginia, had helped start the first Episcopalian church there. Jedediah couldn't help but feel that Ashley was just starting a social club for wealthy entrepreneurs, though he hesitated to pronounce such a harsh judgment on his employer. Not his employer anymore, come to think of it. His supplier. Jedediah was his own boss now.

Civilization holds more danger than the wilderness, Jedediah thought, as he lay on his back looking at the sky and the quivering aspen leaves overhead. Didn't Jesus go out into the wilderness to find refuge from the greater danger of the city? For Jedediah, the Cheyenne River became a place of baptism into an outdoor faith. "God is here," he said to himself repeatedly. It was a deep inner knowing as to the care of God, tested and confirmed by suffering. Jesus had hinted that suffering could be a baptism into something new, and now, here was that baptism. Some said that God stayed east of the Mississippi. Those people knew nothing of God. God goes to hell and meets people there, and there is no hell so deep, no violence so terrifying that God cannot meet you there. Jedediah now knew this about God, and no one could convince him otherwise.

Now that the encounter was over, Jedediah looked to God for his healing. Another story from his childhood came back to greet him: how Charles Wesley had become deathly ill, but in the middle of the night, a neighbor, Mrs. Musgrove, had appeared in a dream and said, "In the name of Jesus Christ, be healed." And when Charles woke up, he was healed.

That was the God Jedediah believed in. And that God could heal him out in the middle of nowhere, on an unnamed tributary of the Cheyenne River, with no other help available to him.

As the days passed, he turned to his Bible. Pages fell open to the book of Job:

Man is chastened with pain upon his bed,
and the multitude of his bones with strong pain:
So that his life abhorreth bread
and his soul, dainty meat.

His flesh is consumed away, that it cannot be seen;
And his bones that were not seen stick out . . .
Then is God gracious unto him, and saith,
Deliver him from going down to the pit; I have found a ransom.
His flesh shall be fresher than a child's;
He shall return to the days of his youth:
He shall pray unto God, and he will be favorable unto him:
And he shall see his face with joy:
For he will render unto man his righteousness.

It was astonishing to Jedediah how words from the Bible so frequently leaped out at him and took hold of his life. It was beyond explaining, but it seemed true what the Bible said, that Jesus Christ had ransomed him from death for a calling: "For we are his workmanship, created in Christ Jesus unto good works, which God hath before ordained."

Jedediah had peered into the jaws of death, had smelled its stench. Yet the encounter had awakened him to life. The preaching of a thousand sermons congealed themselves into a Savior's presence. The ransom of God was so real that he could sense the scales tipping him into his wilderness destiny. Baptism with suffering opened his eyes to the mystery, beauty, and joy of life. That he lived seemed a miracle. It was a miracle beyond explanation that anything at all lived. The jaws of the beast had been a womb. Through them he had entered into deep discovery.

What inventiveness is all around—look at the bunch grass! Those buffalo berries! See the majestic cottonwood tree, with its praying branches. The aspen leaf! Look—how it is hinged twice, like wrist and elbow. So this is the secret to the shimmering aspen! God has supplied it with jointed stems so all the leaves will quiver, with no more purpose than to please us, who alone have the eyes to see it. Quaking aspen.

From the day of this inner awakening, Jed began to collect leaves, seeds, and minerals that fascinated him. The reflected genius of the created world, though grown wild and violent, held for him a magnificent wonder.

We live in a fallen world, but that's a different thing from a godless world, he mused. God uses monstrous beasts to shape and prepare us for his callings. Somehow, Jedediah knew that his life had never seriously been in danger. The deep shaking of the grizzly didn't destroy his wilderness calling, but strengthened it.

He had discovered a new nugget of truth: "Though our outward man perish, yet the inward man is renewed day by day." Jedediah was filled with gratitude at the very moment when others might have said he had nothing to be thankful for.

After ten days, Clyman removed the stitches. The next day, Jedediah rose with the dawn and got out his razor to shave. His ribs hurt terribly, and it was difficult to breathe. He pulled his mirror out of his pack. William Clark had convinced Ashley to take along a whole box of mirrors to be used as protocol gifts, because it was important to honor the chiefs of the tribes. William Clark was recommending that all parties take gifts when going into tribal areas. But when the first keelboat had capsized, the box of mirrors had been swept away. When Jedediah rescued it, Ashley had rewarded him by giving him a mirror.

When he looked at himself in that mirror, he was shocked at what he saw reflected back to him. Mauled by a monster, he now looked like a monster. An angry red scar connected his eye to his hairline. He was missing an eyebrow. His right ear, resting at an angle, was growing back to his head askew. His hairline was grossly jagged, as though someone had tried to scalp him. This scarring would be for life.

He sat down, shaken. "Ephraim warn't kind," he repeated Clyman's words softly, dazedly. Maybe Louisa wouldn't want him after all. He was as ugly as Ed Rose. As ugly as James McGready.

Five

A pristine vision greeted Jedediah Smith as, weeks later, he led his party into the village of the Mountain Crows nestled on the banks of the Wind River. The village was the antithesis of the drab mud villages of the Arikaras. Frost-white tipis poked up through cottony snow, providing counterpoint to the mountain peaks of the Wind River range. The tipis, all facing east, were elaborately painted with red and yellow antelopes, bison, coyotes, and deer. The cones were taller and narrower than most Plains tipis, creating a sleek, crisp effect. From their summits blew long strips of rawhide used as ties when tipis were packed up for travel. The ties blew like streamers in the brisk wind.

Ed Rose, impatient with Jedediah's recuperation, had gone ahead with a loaded pack mule. He now emerged from the southernmost lodge, his mouth grinning from under his truncated nose. Next to him stood Long Hair, the head chief, a man of sixty with a profusion of silvery hair pouring from his head like a cascade. For the moment, it was rolled up in two bundles and tucked into a girdle at his waist. Rose claimed that this hair was over eleven feet long. Though he spoke the truth, no one believed him.

Wanting to establish himself as the true leader of the brigade, Jedediah gave presents all around in return for lodging for his men.

The arrival of the white men scarcely made a dent in Crow comings and goings. They were preparing for an important buffalo hunt. For two days, an old shaman had chanted over a buffalo skull which pointed east down the valley to bring roaming buffalo from high ground. Now the animals had appeared close to camp, descending from the mountains as they were accustomed to do for the winter.

The village was in a hubbub. Only the village guards stood still, posted at the outskirts of the village to keep any self-seeking brave from attacking the herd on his own and driving it away. Others kept watch on the plain for Blackfoot or Shoshone raiders who might intentionally scare the herd away.

Delicately tattooed women, with braidless hair flowing over long skin-and-elk-tooth dresses, prepared to cut and dry meat and to dress hides. Their husbands located their treasured buffalo horses and strung their bows. Many stopped off at a painted, grass-decorated buffalo skull, where they offered a prayer to the buffalo spirit: "Do not let your spirit touch my spirit to do me harm." Others rode to a well-known buffalo-shaped rock, where they offered prayers and gifts to the buffalo spirit. They approached it with religious fear and trembling. This hunt might easily make the difference between full stomachs and starvation this winter. That night, further ceremonies were ordered by the medicine men to ensure a successful hunt.

By the following day, all was ready for the hunt. At the crack of dawn, Jedediah and his men were invited to join in. Chief Long Hair rode at the head of his warriors, proudly displaying his hair as it blew magnificently in the wind.

"When he was jist a little sprout, the chief dreamed that his strength'd be in his hair. He thinks that if his hair should ever git cut, why, all his power 'n' wisdom'd vanish jist like that," Rose explained with a snap of his fingers. Jedediah could not help but think of the Nazirites of the Old Testament, who had held exactly the same belief.

A line of footmen, armed with fusils, took their stations downwind, unobserved by the buffalo. Jedediah, Jim Clyman, and Ed Rose took their stations at the north side of the herd.

At no particular signal, the brutes started moving. A dozen riders hastened to close the circle, driving the herd toward the line of hidden footmen. The chase was on, as mounted warriors, naked to the waist, rode through freezing winds, firing arrow after arrow into the mob of beasts. Jedediah was astonished by Crow endurance of the cold. He was also deeply impressed by the footmen, who stood their ground in front of the stampeding herd.

The trappers on horseback soon discovered Crow wisdom in using the bow and arrow. Crow warriors were so skilled that often a second arrow was in the bow before the first had struck. Muzzle-loading, by contrast, took perhaps fifty seconds—six arrows could be fired in that time. The white man's ways were pronounced clumsy and artless.

The frightened herd rushed toward the footmen, heard the report of the fusils, and turned back, confused. Few escaped the slaughter as each Crow hunter picked out his winter supply of food. They hunted quietly, methodically, as though the hunt were a solemn religious occasion. From their view, the buffalo spirit was giving up its own that the village might be fed, sheltered, and clothed.

Before the slaughter was finished, already the women were bringing knives and tomahawks to buffalo hide—chopping, ripping, and slicing. Here and there, the young men surrounded the last few old bulls on foot. Shouting *hai, hai, ha*i, they jabbed them with spears, shot arrows into flanks, waved pieces of red cloth before their eyes, lassoed their horns, jeered and joked. They seized a bull's tail and tried to jerk him about. Mad with pain and enraged by the jeering, the bull charged them, snorted and hooted—but to no avail. Finally, he grew weary and dropped dead from loss of blood.

Hunters sang victory songs. The people gorged themselves on livers, kidneys, brains, and fat. They drank blood and warm milk, and fed their dogs and their children.

Squabbles broke out among the women about ownership of meat and hides. Grizzled old-timers remembered: "It was better in the old days when we drove the buffalo over a cliff. All the meat belonged to everyone; no one claimed anything for himself. Everyone worked for the common good. But now? Hah! The women fight each other for choice bits. And the young bucks? What vanity!"

These quarrels produced ugly interruptions in an otherwise joyful and prosperous scene. As a rule, the brave whose arrow made the kill took the hide, and anyone else was permitted to take what meat he could, up to two-thirds of the carcass.

By night, wolves were gathering around the scene. Sentries were posted throughout the slaughtered herd to fend off the prowlers until, on the following day, the cutting could be completed and the boneless meat carried back to camp.

Jedediah's men insisted on hacking out "good roasting pieces, cut with the bone after Christian fashion." But when they had to carry the heavy boned pieces back to camp, they soon learned the wisdom of the Indian way. These men had much to learn, and the Crows had much to teach.

After the hunt, women hung strips of meat from tripod racks over fires for drying. These quarter-inch strips were destined to become jerky. For Bill Sublette, it would be his first taste of a food he would crave the rest of his life, even in days of retirement as a wealthy fur baron in Saint Louis. Even then, with the finest gourmet food at his fingertips, he would send off to the Crow camp for genuine Crow jerky.

Every lodge feasted for a week. Guests roamed freely. No invitations were needed. The men sampled tongue, *depouille, boudins*, blood-clot soup, and other delicacies that were not so delicate.[12]

---

12. *Depouille* was buffalo fat; *boudins*, the intestines.

Eventually, dry wood ran out, and the village moved upriver. A few old-timers, the fire-keepers, put glowing embers in fungus punk, sealed them in stoppered buffalo horns, and carefully guarded the latent fire to the next campsite.

The way led past gorgeous red, purple, and amber sculptures of stone, jutting knifelike toward the skies. Women gathered heaps of juniper firewood, while the men searched the valleys for another buffalo herd. They found one at the foot of a bright yellow cliff and continued the harvest. No starving times this winter.

At the new camp, the women set to work on the hides. The summer hunt had produced thin, almost hairless hides for tipi covers. Now these thick, dark, winter hides would be used for robes. Stretching out each hide on the ground with stakes, women cleared flesh off the inside with bone fleshing tools. Then they spread brains over each hide to soften it before scraping it with a pointed graining tool for further softening.

The Crow camp was a school for wilderness tailoring. By February, the trappers had made for themselves moccasins to replace worn-out boots; leggings to replace ragged cloth trousers; tassled, full, pocketless deer-hide shirts to replace purchased flannel ones; and buffalo-hide saddle blankets they called *epishamores*. They learned to carry their odds and ends tucked inside their shirts.

Back in the days of Herr Astor's experiment at the mouth of the Columbia, the German fur king had sent a land party to find the Columbia overland from the east. This ill-fated expedition was a hedge on Astor's bets—just in case the *Tonquin* never made it. The party had discovered a wenching, hard-drinking guide named Ed Rose, who showed them a way through the Rockies at Union Pass, just south of the Crow camp.

Now Jedediah Smith, driven by that mysterious passion for discovery, wanted to ascend the pass. It was a duel of passions—Jed's forcing Ed Rose out of his well-used bed, and Ed's driving himself back into it. Rose fumed, swore, and argued against the stupidity of crossing a pass in the middle of winter. But such was the respect of the men for their captain (and for dreams of "fur gold") that Rose was forced to go along with the plan.

On a sunny, windless day, they wound their way out of camp and up the side of the mountain to the south. For most of the men, it was their first experience of truly rugged mountain travel.[13] The horses' hooves perforated the surface of the snow, plunging the animals to their bellies in drifts. Jedediah was becoming acquainted with the wilderness virgin Andrew Henry had known: a beautiful lady, but hard as beaten nails. At the summit, her queenly beauty was displayed to the north, where the Wind River range lifted her white and blue-green monoliths, gargantuan and threateningly cold, like a woman whose eyes would rather stare you down than entice you. The midwinter snow was too deep for further travel; Ed Rose cried I-told-you-so.

"Now are you satisfied?" he whined. "You c'n see as well as me it'd take a whole herd o' buffler to clear the way through that! An' we killed all the buffler back thar, didn' we? Heh! Only a crazy man'd poke 'is way through ten foot o' snow."

"You're right," Jed admitted. "We'll have to find another pass. Rose, I'm relying on you to find an alternative. The Crows must know something. You talk to 'em."

Rose, half-toothless, grinned at the thought of going back to his bed. "All in good time. For now, let's hightail it back to camp afore dark."

• • •

The next day, Wandering Buffalo, the town crier, awoke the camp early as usual. It was his duty to remind the village of the events planned for the day and of the virtues of water in beginning the day correctly. "Drink your fill; make your blood thin. Touch your body to the waters. Water is your body! Keep your blood thin! You will not get sick!"

One by one, the Crows came out of their lodges, walked to the river, broke through the thin layer of ice that had formed overnight, and waded in. Some filled their mouths with water, squirting parts of their bodies

---

13. They were moving to the southwest of present Dubois, Wyoming.

like a shower. The Crow penchant for cleanliness—both inside and outside the body—stood in sharp contrast to the conviction held back east that "all Indians are dirty."

By contrast, most of the trappers hadn't had a bath in months. They adopted many customs of the Crows, but never the one about bathing. Trapping involved taking many baths involuntarily, and they were not about to take a bath if they didn't have to.

Crows ate at any time, day or night. Many kept a stew pot to which they added and subtracted morsels more or less perpetually, whenever they had a mind to. The whites, on the other hand, still believed in three square meals a day.

After breakfast, Jedediah and Jim called Ed Rose and a few chiefs to their lodge for a lesson in geography. Jedediah addressed Long Hair:

"Do the Absaroka know of other passes through the great Backbone of the World?"

Rose interpreted, using his hands more than his voice. "The Long-knives seek *mirapa*, the beaver, from the streams west of the mountains. Can you tell us a way to find these streams?"

As Rose spoke, Jim Clyman reached for his epishamore, spread it on the ground, and began covering it with piles of sand. With gestures, he explained that these piles represented the mountains to the west.

The Crows replied, "The Long-knives will like the streams beyond the Backbone of the World. They abound with beaver. Beaver are so abundant that you do not have to set your traps for them. Only walk along the banks and club them with a stick."

Rose continued, "The captain wants to know: how do you get there from here? The pass yonder is closed."

Long Hair picked up more sand, adding a few mountains to the south and drawing in two more rivers on the buffalo skin to show that a pass existed south of the Wind River Range.

"It is an easy way beyond the mountains," Long Hair continued. "A whole tribe could ride through it abreast. It is at the head of Popo Agie." Here he indicated a branch of the Wind River, where it bent to the right. "But be careful of the *Poo-der-ee*, the wind in the pass."

The map helped Jedediah crystallize his plans, and he quickly sketched the sand-drawn map in his journal.

• • •

The next day, the bad weather returned, but it did not prevent Jedediah from packing up and moving his men east along the Wind River, then south, on the Popo Agie. It did, however, prevent Ed Rose from going—he had planned all along to stay with the Crows as long as they would have him. Jedediah was glad to be rid of him. God would be his only guide from here on out, once Long Hair's directions petered out, "and God never rides out too far ahead, either," he mused out loud.

As they ascended the south fork of the river, a strong smell of tar filled the air, a black smell on a white landscape. After five more miles of riding, they came upon the cause: a spring of oil—they called it "coal tar"—oozing out from the base of a bluff. Great piles of the ooze had accumulated below, accounting for the stench. The country looked as barren and uninviting as it smelled. They had seen no game for days, and they were carrying precious little of the buffalo they had killed among the Crows.

Each rider had but one horse, and the horses were already weakening from starvation. Sublette and Clyman went hunting, riding out in foot-deep snow in search of buffalo.

The next afternoon, they showed up half-dead, with a few strips of frozen blue buffalo meat strapped to their epishamores. The men were so hungry they devoured the chewy stuff raw.

They continued on to the source of the Popo Agie, crossed a low ridge to a nameless river, and camped. The wind was a raging torrent—as though all the molecules of space were rushing over the plain at this one point. Jedediah spent the entire first night trying to keep his blankets from blowing away. He remembered Long Hair's warning about the *Poo-der-ee*, but now that he was in the midst of it, he was at a loss what to do about it.

At first light, he and Clyman rigged up a few blankets on some stumpy juniper boughs for a windbreak, but the back current blew ashes into their faces. When they removed the screen, the wind blew the fire away, logs and all!

Jed and his men moved the camp east to a clump of willows, cleared the crusted snow away, and camped again. Oh for a good, thick, spruce tree to lay our beds under, they kept thinking. On the following day, they walked east down the river, reached a narrow defile, and camped, trying to get relief from the wind. But the place was a wind tunnel.

Just before nightfall, Branch, a city boy, the greenest of greenhorns, looked up, saw a mountain sheep overhead, aimed carelessly with chattering teeth and shaking limbs, and fired. Miraculously, the beast fell at his feet, the first meat for three days. Everyone congratulated the novice with great cheer. The men emerged from their beds just long enough to eat their meat raw, then took to their blankets again to hide from the stampeding wind.

The wilderness was trying to blow them east, to prevent them from entering her sacred garden. Yet the trappers refused to be cowed. They thought of William Ashley, who trusted them to rescue him from financial ruin. And they dreamed of beaver and glory and wealth too—of bank beaver so plentiful they could walk along a stream and club them by the dozens, as Long Hair had described. Surely there, just yonder, gold equal to the wealth of Peru awaited them, in rich streams to the west, just west, always farther west. Who could say whether, if they stopped now, they wouldn't stop two miles short of gold and glory?

And so they refused to let the wind beat them. The men closed their eyes and cursed the wind, while Jedediah prayed.

• • •

In the middle of the night, Jim Clyman awoke. Something's different! What is it? Hey! The wind is gone! Silence is so noisy, it woke me up!

He rose up, kindled a fire, and began heating some stones while the others slept. Jim loved times like this, alone with his thoughts, when a sage fire crackled, the rocks glowed orange in the flickering firelight, and the stars twinkled in the heights. All was at peace again. Nature had turned amiable.

Jim was learning Indian ways. He tied a buffalo paunch to a tripod of sticks and filled it with water. He put hot rocks into the water, Crow-fashion. Within a minute, the water was boiling. He cut off strips of sheep and plopped them into the water. Soon the smell of boiled meat awoke the others, and they feasted. Never had a meal tasted so delicious. The men talked until daylight, swapping stories of hardship and endurance. It was good to be alive.

Jim went scouting, returned, and told Jed of a favorable campsite downriver. They filed through the ravine to where it opened onto a broad sagebrush plain. A wet snow began to tumble from the heavy sky in great, globulous flakes. The air was warming! The men camped in the middle of a herd of mountain sheep and waited for spring.

At last, spring showed up and chased the sheep away. Jedediah took the hint and turned his face west to search out the elusive and legendary South Pass.

Before they left the site, the men dug a cache. It was arduous, mucking, thoroughly unenjoyable work. A fire was required to thaw the ground first; then they dug the pit five feet deep, broadening it at the bottom, designing it after Andrew Henry's caches at Fort Henry. Before throwing in the pelts they had traded from the Crows, they lined the pit with aspen boughs against leached moisture. Camouflage was difficult in the snowscape, so they built their last campfire over the cache to divert suspicion and mark it for the future. Just as they were heading out, Jed pointed to the budding aspens that surrounded the cache and said, "Remember this aspen grove. If we get split up or anyone gets lost, try to make your way back here at the end of the spring hunt, about June 10th."

They headed west up the nameless river.[14] They trekked on for days, looking for some sign of a mountain pass. But the country was a blank, sagebrush plain. They could see the Wind River range to the north, but

---

14. Today, we know this river as the Sweetwater.

there were no mountains where they were walking, only gentle slopes full of gray brush poking up through drifted snow. Monotony ruled the days; cold, the nights.

After six days, Clyman and Sublette killed another buffalo bull. The men were learning to eat meat raw. Making a fire in the snow was too much trouble. No fresh water had been available for days. They held their raw meat in one hand and a handful of snow in the other, alternately devouring meat and lapping snow with their tongues.

After fifteen days of travel over rolling, barren hills, they struck another river. The wind had scoured the slopes of snow, leaving large brown patches that relieved the threat of snow blindness. At one patch, Bill Sublette began to stare at the new riverbed meandering in a snow-and-ice-filled ravine. Hoping for some real water, he began to hack away at the ice, several feet thick. After half an hour of hacking, he shouted, "Froze clear to bottom!"

But Jim Clyman approached the hole from the circle of spectators, saying decisively in his Virginia drawl, "We'll jus' see 'bout that!" Drawing his pistol, he fired into the hole. It spouted a thin stream of water!

Jedediah studied the hole curiously, then reached down and hacked at the ice some more to see which way the water flowed. Soon he saw: the water was flowing west! They had crossed the Great Divide without knowing it. Below were beaver streams and the river the Crows had called *Siskadee Agie*, the Prairie Chicken River.

Immediately, he saw the potential of the situation. Here, no doubt, was the thoroughfare Robert Stuart had discovered on his way back from Astoria. Ha! He could almost see those Astorians, haggard and ragged, stumbling east across this desert, wondering if they would live to see Saint Louis again. If this was the same pass, then the Platte River couldn't be far away—for the Platte had guided the Astorians back to Missouri.

New thoughts rushed in, all bunched together—Why, a wagon could roll through here, no trouble at all! Here's the answer to William Clark's quandary—how to get western furs to eastern markets. It was Jedediah

Smith's first major discovery: South Pass, the fabled southerly passage through the Great Divide.

But Jedediah discerned that he stood only at the near wall of the great garden he had always dreamed of exploring. He was standing at a break in the wall on a massive heap of stones weathered into gravel through count-less ages. The western garden beckoned to him—this Rocky Mountain expanse of which Lewis and Clark alone had published news (for David Thompson's Rocky Mountain manuscript lay discarded and forgotten in some Northwest Company desk drawer). Now the wilderness was once again vulnerable, this cold, disinterested virgin that Andrew Henry and a few Astorians had come to know before him. And despite her reputation with them, Jedediah was disposed to be gentle with her.

Six

During the next year and a half, Jedediah trapped the newly discovered streams, sent the furs with Clyman and Fitz down the Platte, and then explored north. With his small group of men, he ascended north to a mountain range Andrew Henry had told them about, the Tetons, to explore the beaver waters on the west side.

Jedediah trapped the streams of the Snake Basin, thoroughly aware that this was contested country—England was here already. But Jedediah believed that this land was to be part of the United States, so he mapped as he trapped. With the grandeur of the Tetons reflecting the late afternoon sun, he and his six men would set their traps at eventide, retrieving and skinning their catch early in the mornings.

During the following weeks, they worked their way slowly north to Henry's Post, the first log structure on the west flank of the Rockies, built by Andrew Henry himself. It was nothing but a ramshackle collection of rough-cut log cabins covered with chartreuse moss and dappled gray lichens. The place was full of evil memories, spoken into Jedediah's memory by Andrew Henry himself—memories of bitter cold, starvation, and disappointed hopes.

The men, too, were aware of the history. But following Jedediah was proving to be different from following Andrew Henry or William Ashley. Dave Jackson, Tom Eddy, and Bill Sublette had never understood how he could so consistently find his direction in this uncharted wilderness. But Jedediah Smith, like John Dickson before him—the very first trapper to bring a haul of furs from the western mountains—had gained confidence in the secret guidance of God and had learned to follow it unreservedly. His friends didn't understand how it worked, and Jedediah didn't either—but they had all learned *that* it worked, and so they spoke of him as having a sextant in his soul.

The plains west of Fort Kiowa had tested this sextant and found it reliable. Jedediah recalled those first few weeks as leader of a fur brigade. They had enjoyed no trees for landmarks. No nothing but a miserable white river that made everyone constipated when they drank of it. Then the Frenchman who had been assigned as guide simply rode off and disappeared. On top of that, the greenhorn Branch had fainted dead away, unable to go further. Jedediah had insisted on being the last in line, just to make sure Branch didn't get left behind, and now Branch was lying on the ground, stricken with heat prostration. Jedediah received an inner word to bury Branch in the sand, up to his neck. He obeyed the word, and treated Branch's friend, Stone, with the same treatment. Then he rode off to fetch a couple of mules and water from the main group five miles ahead, promising to return.

The men learned from this, and countless other lessons, that Jedediah could find his way anywhere. And that Jedediah would care for the weakest and most vulnerable men in his brigade, even at risk and great discomfort to himself. So this was how it was: Jedediah trusted God, and they trusted Jedediah. Not once had they been disappointed in him, though at first they had tested his patience sorely with their complaints, their doubts, and their fears. In more recent days, their complaints had trailed off into silence as they marveled at Jedediah's uncanny way of leading them into good fortune. Their respect for his authority preserved this group from the kind of bickering that had plagued the *Tonquin* team fielded by Astor at the mouth of the Columbia.

Jedediah had the look of a leader now, no longer a callow boy. The vacancies on his head he tried to cover with a black silk scarf, his favorite headgear. But the scarf only made him look like a pirate, and it did not really cover up his deformities, except the bald scar at his hairline. By contrast to the other six men, he made a vain attempt at civility by shaving every day after his morning quiet time with Jesus. But this habit only revealed more scars on his bare chin, where the wilderness had marked him for life.

As Jedediah traipsed up the streams emptying into the Snake, he recalled his trapping mentor's instructions when he had first learned to trap. His mentor had been a youngster named Chapman, nearly as green as himself, but with some trapping experience. Back at their first arrival at the mouth of the Yellowstone, Chapman had shared the lore with him: "Keep yer eyes skinned fer beaver sign—trees gnawed to a point, mound-shaped lodges, dammed-up creeks, beaver slides, drag paths, an' tunnels mined out o' the banks. See there? Don't never move downstream to set yer traps. Move upstream an' let the water carry yer scent away." At one point, when the terrain was too swampy to take the canoe, the tutor disembarked and took a trap out of his burlap trap sack. It took powerful arms to open the trap jaws. Master and apprentice did it together over Chapman's leg, hooking the trigger, or "dog," under the pan. The pan would release the trap when stepped on by an animal—or pressed accidentally by a careless thumb.

A stoppered vial was slung over Chapman's shoulder, and he carried a large pole of dry wood and a small barkless twig.

"Got to make beaver come to medicine, see." Chapman had taken the stoppered vial and showed it to Jed. "This here is castoreum. Medicine. Mr. Beaver uses it to stake out his territory."

The stuff smelled as if cinnamon had turned rancid. Chapman had dipped the twig into the yellow-brown preparation and pressed it into the creek bank. Then he carefully placed the trap in four inches of water near the bank.

"Don't need much medicine to bring Mr. Beaver, see, so don't waste it. Mr. Beaver smell medicine, an' he come close. Gonna see about strange beaver in his stream. He step up here to find out more—an' whap! Here. I set it so as to git his right rear leg. Don't set it in the middle o' the path. Beaver don't have no leg in the middle, see. Hee hee."

Chapman had stretched the five-foot trap chain out toward deeper water and driven the trap pole through a ring at the end of the chain and into the creek bottom. "You try the next one," he said as he finished.

The young men were wet and cold, but Jedediah would learn to get used to the chill. Since beaver pelts were best in spring and fall, trapping was a cold-weather career. Summer pelts were worthless.

The next day, Chapman had taught Jedediah how to skin the beavers they had caught. Each animal had bright orange teeth and a flat, scaly tail. Chapman slit the skin on the four paws, then broke off the feet. Cutting around the tail, he slit the skin to the throat. Working around each side, he separated the skin from the meat, popping each leg out until the skin was removed. He also removed the castor gland at the base of the tail, an eight-inch piece of flesh. The hides were turned over to the camp keepers for graining, curing, and pressing into bales.

Usually, the work was done by 9 a.m.

Every time Jedediah would go out setting trap in the evening or retrieving animals in the morning, he would remember Chapman. Then he would go out under the closest tree and remember God.

• • •

Here on the Snake, Jedediah addressed God with a practical question: "Where are we going to winter over?" His catch was in. The traps were lying to the side under a cottonwood. The river was bubbling brightly. The sun shone on the Tetons to the east. The approach of winter reminded Jedediah of how faithful God had been the previous winter. One challenge of faith, successfully met, continually strengthened him for the next.

The Blackfoot River slithered through a dreary and barren wilderness, which got more barren the farther west they traveled. He remembered the grim tales Andrew Henry had told about the peril of snow blindness here, the specter of brute starvation, and the silent isolation that descends on these parts five months out of the year.

Should we go west, or turn back and hole up at Henry's Post? Guide me, Jesus.

No answer came at that moment, but Jedediah knew that silence from God was not an indication that God had vanished.

Later that day, the men were setting up camp on a stream southeast of the Three Buttes, which rose up stark and majestic above the horizon of the plain. Jedediah was staring at the buttes, mesmerized by their lonely beauty. Suddenly, startlingly, within twenty feet of camp, a voice began speaking out of a clump of scrub willows as though the trees had learned a curious blend of French and English.

"*Mes amis, écoutez!* You there, my fran's! Please! Be good chap and help us."

"What the . . . ?" blurted seven surprised Americans.

Out from the trees where they had been hiding, probably for hours, came a dozen men, apparently Hudson's Bay trappers, looking sheepish, helpless, and lost. At their head, wearing a red cloth belt, tattered wool trousers, and very little else, was their leader.

"*Je suis Pierre. Vieux Pierre! Parlez-vous Français?* You *Américains.* Please! I beg you, my fran's. Do not harm us. Bannocks came down an' rob us good. Make sport of us. The Horse, he took all our pipes and traps. Eugh! Him a very bad man! Now we have nothing but a few miserable peltries, which we offer you if you protect us. Please have pity! Without you we dead men!"

Jed was full of questions. "You say you are called 'Old Pierre?' Where do you come from? How did you get here?" [15]

---

15. Trappers used the word "old" as a sign of familiarity, but, in his fifties, Old Pierre was very old for a mountain man. "Pierre's Hole," a valley surrounded by mountains, was named after this man.

"M'sieu Ross, him *bourgeois*. Him promise to meet us over there, you see, where *Rivière Goddin* meet up with that big mountain, *là-bas*." Old Pierre pointed to one of the three buttes, then continued, "But them Bannocks cam' down here an' took all but these peltries. One hundred and five, count them." He led the men around a willow trunk to where they had hidden the furs.

"Where is your Mister Ross now? When were you to meet him?"

"Just now, *Monsieur le capitain. Parbleu!* We late already! If you but lead us to him, we are happy to make you know him. Him very nice chap, *oui!* A very patient *bourgeois, oui!* You will like him. He will like you. *Oui, oui!*"

Jed smiled and turned to Bill Sublette. "I believe we'll just follow these men to their rendezvous with this Mr. Ross. Then we'll tail them to their winter quarters and make maps the whole way. And for the privilege of doing it, they will pay us a fare of one hundred and five beaver!"

The sandy-haired Sublette joked, "Ha! We'll be their chauffeurs and take 'em back home. A hundred five beaver ain't too much fer such kind, personal service."

"Nope. And besides, we chauffers'll be able to keep an eye on these English and report the extent of their hold on Oregon. I bet Senator Floyd'd be interested in what we find."

Quickly, Jedediah and his party prepared to travel north. Striking their makeshift tents, caching their furs in the ground, and unhobbling their horses, they traveled to Goddin's River, where they met up with a party of Hudson's Bay men waiting for Old Pierre and his crew. The combined party moved northwest around the buttes and through a waste of "pumice stone," as Jedediah called the huge expanse of lava. For a week, they traversed mountain passes and undulating valleys. Finally, they attained Canoe Point on the Salmon River.

Here, the long-suffering *bourgeois* Alex Ross had been waiting for the return of his freemen, for this was now the second search party he had sent after them. *Freemen* were mostly self-employed Natives to whom the Company sold supplies and looked to supply them with pelts. They were not Hudson's Bay employees, yet the HBC relied on them for much of its harvest each year. Ross had been spending his idle time getting furs stamped and pressed into bales for transport back to Flathead Post. He looked up from his press to find that his freemen and their rescuers were leading not pack animals loaded with furs, but seven Americans—and no furs. The men wore sheepish expressions and would not look directly at him.

"Mister Tevanitagon!" barked Ross. "May I have a word wi' ye in my tent?" The two ducked into Ross's quarters, a tent that looked utterly official and British, as though it were standard-issue army—so different from the makeshift tents handcrafted by the seven Americans as they adapted Crow arts to the tastes of white men. And no two alike. Sublette, Eddy, and the others were already erecting their tiny shelters downstream from the British camp.

Ross was clearly fuming. "Pierre! Those're Yankees or I'll eat my hat!"

Pierre spoke with his hands, animatedly. "Need not eat hat, m'sieur. Them Bostons, yes. Them good men. Save us from Bannocks, they did." The unpleasant interview reviewed the events of the last several days and ended as quickly as possible. Then it was Jedediah's turn.

As Jedediah entered the tent, he was barely greeted by the man he had been invited to see. Alex Ross was not a man known for warmth, despite Old Pierre's recommendation. A narrow, blustery Scot with brown hair combed straight back, he exuded ordinariness and smallness—so different from the usually large and violent fur men who had tamed the wilderness thus far.

Ross met Jedediah's gaze. He was impressed with the sincere demeanor of the man. Yet he couldn't help but notice those horrendous scars, that missing eyebrow and misshapen ear. Was this man really as innocent as he seemed? Alex Ross thought not. Nobody who wore black silk scarves could be an honest Christian. Ross had become chronically suspicious in his middle years, and his mistrust immediately enveloped Jedediah. After all, had not this Mr. Smith been introduced to him by the plot-hatching hen, Old Pierre? Alex suspected collusion between the freemen and the freedom-loving Americans.

"Old Pierre tells me you just happened along when they were desperate?" the older man asked. He had failed to shave that morning. His face was lined with stubble and worry.

"Yes, that's right, sir." As Jedediah told of the encounter, his smile disarmed Ross. His story matched Pierre's except that, according to Jedediah, Pierre had given him one hundred and five furs (and not just forty dollars). This catastrophic news did nothing for Ross's already sagging opinion of Pierre.

"I ken your Mr. Henry has intentions to cross the Divide an' trap the west side o' the mountains," Ross continued. "You have made your way from his fort on the Big Horn, have you?"

"No, sir," Jedediah replied, his candor evident. "I've been leading a separate party. We wintered with the Crows an' crossed the Divide in February. We've been trapping the Seedskeeder since March."

"I can well imagine you have done well for yoursel'?"

"Yes, sir, nine hundred skins, cached on the Snake in two caches. That includes the plews Pierre gave us."

Ross pursed his lips. "Wouldn't you prefer to sell the furs here than to carry them back to Mr. Ashley? We'll give you $2 a peltry."

As the stream burbled outside and ravens shattered the air with their gargling caws, Jedediah struggled silently to understand how anyone could imagine he would give away his pelts for so little. Was it just Ross, trying to play up to the reputation of a Scotsman, or did all British fur men try to commit highway robbery like this?

Here began a series of offers and counteroffers, to which Jed finally replied, "We'll take our plews back with us, Mr. Ross. To be sure, they're trouble. If you could give us $3 for 'em, you could have 'em. But if not, we'll try our luck in Saint Louis."

Ross replied to Jed by simply turning his back and blurting, "good day."

When Ross found out that Jedediah was a Christian, the news didn't much help their budding relationship. As a rule, Presbyterians cherished a low opinion of flaming Methodists.

Seven

Now that the freemen were back safe and sound, Alex Ross chafed to get back to Flathead Post for the annual trade fair. On Saturday, October 16, the party ascended the mauve hills east toward Lemhi Pass. Alex let the Americans ride with them. It was his strategy, when dealing with dangerous people, to keep them close so they could not form plots against him. Also riding with them was a small party of forsaken, bedraggled Nez Percés, who showed up just as the party was setting out. They had been out to steal some horses from the Piegans, had been ambushed by their intended victims, and wanted to travel under the protection of Ross's brigade. They were frightened and grieved out of their wits over the death of their friends.

Two days later, in the lush country of the Big Hole Plain, these Nez Percés came upon the remains of their six ambushed friends. The shimmering aspens still held their yellow leaves, and their silvery trunks rose up like columns of a cathedral. But in the midst of this holy stillness and awesome beauty, parts of bodies were scattered everywhere, decomposing and smelling of rottenness. The Nez Percés went into a frenzy of wailing, tearing their clothes and hair and cutting themselves with knives. Several removed their left little fingers at the knuckle, the traditional way of expressing bereavement.

Jedediah and Alex Ross shared the same thought: For how many generations has this heart-wrenching grief been wailed out to these hills? Are these people destined to remain forever torn apart, limb from limb and tribe from tribe? Jedediah remembered William Clark's attempts to bring intertribal peace by means of treaties. Alex Ross did too, and grimaced scornfully at Clark's naïveté. Alex had become completely cynical about that word *peace*.

"It's a dismal scene," observed Jedediah from the saddle.

"Aye, but one all too frequent among them," replied Ross, dismounting to examine the remains of a decaying body still adorned with the ornaments of war. The Scot had long since stopped feeling pity for these warring nations. Besides, compassion was foreign to his nature.

Jedediah was not so cold. In fact, he spoke with passion. "One day, perhaps they will come to know Christ. Do you speak of him to them?"

Ross looked up sharply, momentarily at a loss for words. Just typical of a Methodist to ask such a thing! To Ross, faith was a private matter, to be kept separate from the workaday world by thick walls of mental brick. He quickly changed the subject.

"'Twas back there at the pass that Finan McDonald had his run-in wi' the Piegans just a year ago. McDonald chased 'em into a thicket, set the woods afire, an' shot all those who tried to escape. Sixty-eight killed, an' only six of our men. 'Twas a lesson they'll never forget, you can be sure o' that. Their bones be a-gleamin' in the sun, same as these."

The Nez Percés were still wailing, and Jedediah looked toward them as he replied, "We had some trouble with the Piegans, too, just about the same time. Didn't end the same as yours, though. Iron Shirt massacred the best of the Missouri fur men. His Piegans cut 'em off cold and lost not a single man. Then the Rees killed a bunch of our men on the Missouri, and got away in the night to brag about it. The summer of '23 was poor doin's."

Ross spat disdainfully into a melting snow drift. "Mark my words, Mr. Smith, the Indians'll be a scourge until they be taught a lesson. Ye canna let 'em get the upper hand like that. Sixty-eight Piegans killed by McDonald! Now there's a lesson in respect they'll no' soon ferget. An' we'll be thankin' McDonald for years to come. 'Tis the way it has to be out here. Sharin' the gospel is all verra well, but these people don't live by our rules."

Jedediah averted his eyes, recoiling from ideas he could not agree with. After an embarrassed silence, he replied, "Is it true, then, that our only hope for peace is in killin' them? Is there no more hope in Christ than that?"

Now it was Ross's turn for embarrassed silence. Ross finally shrugged his shoulders. "O' course, not all tribes live the same," he admitted with reluctance. Perhaps he sensed that his attitudes were tainted with unbelief. Or that he had overstated his case. Alex's Okanogan wife had a softening effect on him. When he was away from her, that effect disappeared entirely—not, he realized, always for the better. "Ye'll meet the Spokanes an' the Flatheads at the post. They be different, considerably different from the likes o' these."

As the party moved on, Jedediah grimaced over the conversation. Ross's God was as small as a buffalo berry. Alex Ross seemed to have no hope that God could ever change anything. Pure resignation lined his face and exuded from his gray pores. He might gain some inner resiliency from his own faith, but he had no idea of the power of God for anyone else. Jed wondered if all Presbyterians were like this.

Jedediah was not ready to believe that Jesus couldn't end the curse of enmity that ruled these people. Which was more powerful: the curse of tribalism staring at them from the blood-soaked ground, or the blood-soaked ground at the foot of the cross? Ross's pessimistic, narrow-minded ranting against Indian tribal warfare only made Jedediah more determined to prove him wrong.

The party made their way from Lemhi Pass to Clark's Pass during the first week of November, then dropped down to Ross's Hole, scene of a massive blizzard Alex Ross had encountered on the way into Snake country. Only an inch of snow covered the ground now.

That night, they camped near a well-known landmark, the Ram's Head Tree. It was a ponderosa pine with a ram's skull protruding from the side, adorned with all manner of trinkets hung there to honor of the spirit of the tree.[16] In the cold dusk, amidst the honking of geese, Jedediah examined the curiosity and wondered at its meaning. It spoke intuitions like a Sibyl giving omens. To him it seemed to say:

Beyond this point, you enter the domain of the all-powerful Hudson's Bay Company. They are the rulers here. They have been planted in the north country and have been growing strong there for generations, since the time your Puritan fathers crossed the ocean. You are but a young sheep, inexperienced and hoping foolish hopes among those more knowledgeable than you. They are lords of the forest. And you? Try out your horns. Soon you will discover that a tree cannot be knocked down by a sheep like you.

---

16. The "Medicine Tree" is presently marked by a National Forest Service sign at the east side of Highway 93 north of Sula, Montana. The ram's skull has long since disappeared.

Eight

Flathead Post, the Hudson's Bay terminal east of Spokane House, was a crude hotel: six narrow shacks of squared timber linked together in a straight line by a single long, sloping roof. The shacks faced Clark Fork River, peering out over two hundred feet of flat grassland toward the riverbank.[17] Upriver, the Northwest Company's Saleesh House had fallen to ruin, a symbol of that company's obsolete and violent ways.

"The Honourable Company," as the Hudson's Bay Company was coming to be known because of policy changes at the top, was enjoying a gentle impact on the Salish people. The whites, through sheer whim, had begun calling these people *Flatheads*, though their heads were just as round as anyone else's. "Flat" and "round" are all in the eye of the beholder, as Alex Ross was fond of saying.

No stockade surrounded Flathead Post, for whites had nothing to fear from Natives here, nor Natives from whites. Violence, seducings,

---

17. The post was located at Eddy Flat, Montana, between Thompson Falls and Plains.

and debauchery were discouraged by the Honourable Company and by tribal chiefs too. Trade could proceed happily because both sides were gaining from each other something they wanted, without violating each other in the process. In other corners of the continent, this sensible way of working things had eluded most people.

Shortly before Jedediah and the others arrived, the quiet valley of Clark Fork was coming alive with Natives making ready for the annual trade fair. Beginning on November 26, they came from all directions, bringing wives, pelts, dogs, children, horses, and lodges. They were soon setting up camp, renewing old friendships, racing their horses, swapping stories, telling jokes, smoking their pipes, and gambling furiously. All were getting ready for the once-a-year buying opportunity, hoping great hopes for what they could purchase. Behind the post, they pitched their tents, leaving the six shacks and the trading plain vacant. These areas were for the men whose coming had been promised.

From the west, at noon, came the pack train from Spokane House, bearing trade goods from England via Fort George. In the lead was the intrepid Peter Skene Ogden, who had spent the summer in charge of Spokane House. His party filled in the spaces around the post at the edges of the trading plain.

Chief Trader Ogden was one of those larger men the Company had hired to keep order on the Columbia. He wore a captain's cap, turned sideways so that it shaded his massive right sideburn, proclaiming at once his authority and his playfulness. He wore a striped blanket capote over his navy blue, brass-buttoned vest and gray wool trousers. He was barrel-chested, but not heavy-handed, nor very tall. The impression of large size came partly from his big heart and his enormous sense of humor. His deep-tanned face had the look of a dry humorist. He had the habit of cracking a joke without cracking a smile, though everyone else might be writhing on the floor hooting with laughter. His way of laughing was to curl his lip in a charming half-grin. He wore his black hair plastered to his forehead. He possessed no neck at all. He was an iron chunk of a man.

Ogden had married a Salish woman, and the Flathead tribe was gaining its first impressions about biblical ideas from him. Tribal prophecy throughout the area had alerted many tribes to the approaching white people and their knowledge of Creator. The Flatheads were no exception. Therefore, these tribes all competed with each other not only for the *chipixa*'s material possessions, but even more for Biblical understanding. Every tribe wanted its own Christian. Ogden was the Flathead's Christian.

Peter Skene Ogden did not have long to wait before the third group showed up from the opposite direction. It was Alex Ross's Snake Brigade. Ross and Ogden were good friends, despite their contrasting personalities. Alex led his party up, dismounted, and greeted Peter Skene.

It did not take Peter long to spot the seven Americans who rode with Ross. Americans wore skin clothing, seldom wool. Their habit of adopting Indian lifeways set them apart from the English. The Ashley men looked like white people trying to be Indians, a look that the English never attempted. The British believed that Christianity and civilization were inextricably bound together, and it was futile to try to separate them. American trappers like Jedediah Smith did not believe any such thing.

Looking at the uncouth Americans who had invaded their camp, Peter Skene raised an eyebrow at Ross and said, "This is a new twist. You've come back with more men than you left with. Don't tell me. You single-handedly saved the Americans from bein' tortured and burned alive by the Snakes!"

Ross never knew how to respond to Ogden's humor. "Nay," he replied. "Old Pierre got himself in trouble wi' the Bannocks. Mr. Smith, the youngster over there, came along an' saved 'em—fer a fee. Then Old Pierre led 'em to us."

"And you led 'em here?" Ogden asked, suddenly sobered. "Don't you remember Governor Simpson's orders to keep the Americans out o' here? No good'll come o' this, Alex."

Ross stiffened defensively. "What could I do? They would ha' followed us no matter what I said. At least this way I could keep an eye on 'em."

"Guv'nor won't like this. Ah well, it'll be fun to see the color o' his lily-white cheeks when he finds out." The "governor" was George Simpson, a newcomer to the north country who was quickly making his mark on the fur trade. But some still accused him of being a greenhorn.

At that point, Ross spotted his Okanogan wife, Sarah, and his children, Alexander and Margaret, who had come with the group from Spokane House. Running to them, he slowed down and greeted them with Scottish cordiality, shaking their hands awkwardly. Alex was not an affectionate man in public. His private and public sectors were cemented off from each other by a wall as solid as that separating his religion from his business life.

All hands set to building lean-to shelters against cottonwoods near the river or setting up makeshift little tipis on the edge of the trading ground. Ogden walked to the river's edge to hand Alex Ross a letter. Speaking in his peculiarly high, almost falsetto voice, he explained, "Guv'nor Simpson came to Spokane House on his way from York Factory to Fort George. He's determined to reorganize the whole district. Hah! He wants us to plant wheat, barley, lettuces, and Indian corn so we don't spend so much money importing foodstuffs. That'll go over great with the men. He left this letter for you at Spokane House. Probably full of gardening instructions."

With a friendly "Aye," Ross took the letter and retired with Sarah to a quiet spot near the river to read it. Sarah, who never interfered in her Scottish husband's business affairs, merely listened. As he read, Ross interpreted the letter into Okanogan for her.

"God be praised. It's the answer to my prayers! Governor Simpson is transferring us to the Red River Colony. I am to become headmaster in the school there. Says here, too, Governor Simpson 'could wish that two Indian boys of about eight years of age of the Spokane and Nez Percé tribe were got from their relations for the purpose o' being educated at the school and taken out with our family.'[18] Hunh." Alex scratched his

---

18. Quoted from Clifford M. Drury, "Oregon Indians in the Red River School," p. 52-53.

head. It had never occurred to him that a trading company like HBC would be concerned about the Christian education of Natives. The whole idea seemed odd.

"Where is this Red River?" queried Sarah, with a tremor in her voice.

"It is far away, far away," beamed Ross. To him, *far* and *away* were the most valued words in the language. Far away from the Snake expedition. He would prefer any job to this one. Any at all.

For Sarah, the words were not as welcome, yet they were not unexpected. Years before, she had prepared herself to leave her family and kin to follow Alex over the Backbone of the World. Now the news that two boys from the area would accompany them helped to ease her mind about being uprooted from all that was familiar, from her tribe and family.

Alex continued. "In the meantime, I am to take charge of Flathead Post. Peter Skene will conduct the next Snake Brigade."

This, too, was pleasant news. All the nagging questions about their future had been resolved for him. George Simpson was not called governor for nothing. He played the role to the hilt. Fortunately, Alex Ross's desires coincided perfectly with the governor's.

Nine

On Tuesday, November 30, Ogden sent for the Flatheads, who were camped at Horse Prairie several miles away. They arrived by midmorning in formal, diplomatic array. Ogden was accompanied by his Flathead wife.

The sun was taking the chill off the morning, and excitement filled the air. Their horses decorated to the ears, a solid line of mounted warriors pranced toward the post buildings, trade rifles in hand, chanting together the Song of Peace. They rode abreast through the prairie flats, stopped, fired a salute, rode further, stopped, and fired again. Protocol and honor were an important part of the peace that prevailed here.

Ogden nodded cheerfully to an employee who touched off the brass four-pounder brought expressly for the occasion. All these boomings and poppings reverberated off the hills, putting a stop to idle conversation and announcing as clearly as any words, "Let the trade begin!"

The Forgotten Awakening

The Flathead chief, La Brèche, just arrived from Flathead Lake, rode forward with the younger Insula at his side. He welcomed the traders: "It is the season of the trade fair. We come again to the house of the timbers to celebrate the enduring friendship between the Flatheads and the Long-hairs."

"Aye," Ogden quipped to his men, "a flat head and long hair make a right smart combination."

Using his hands, Insula spoke next. He was short and stocky, but he looked princely on his horse. With regal dignity mingled with voluntary humility, he honored the English traders in sign lingo: "We are very poor in trapping the beaver. We do not excel in this as the white people do. We would like to bring thousands of skins. As it is, we have brought only hundreds."

The chiefs dismounted and drew near the post buildings to smoke. Arranged according to rank, the warriors approached the houses, bringing their catches with them. Ledger books were opened. Each of the men made a short speech and brought forth his three or four pelts as though they were the greatest treasures in the world. Each was given wooden counters in return.

When it came time for the purchasing, the women rode up and joined their husbands. They all spent the afternoon in delightful haggling, examining four-point blankets with their bright yellow, red, and green stripes, fixing the price of dried buffalo tongues, arguing the relative value of fox, mink, fisher, and muskrat, and stocking their parflêches with pemmican and jerky. The round beaver pelts, blood red on one side, brown on the other, were tallied, stamped, pressed, and readied for canoe transport to Spokane House.

Jedediah observed all this and noted the low prices for which these people were willing to sell their furs. "Appears to me this monopoly does not work in favor of the Indians," he remarked to Bill Sublette.

Bill replied, "Was noticing the same. I 'spect we could use a little American free enterprise 'round here. So far, the Injuns don't know no different."

On the following days, other tribes were invited from Horse Prairie to join in the trade fair. Toward the end of the week, Illim-spokanee appeared with four lodges of Spokanes.

The news had spread around camp at Horse Prairie: "Bostons are here!" Now the Spokanes could satisfy their curiosity about the Americans for themselves. As he and his people approached the Bostons at the trading ground, Illim-spokanee noticed an astonishing thing: the captain of the Bostons carried with him a leather-bound book identical to the one Star-gazer had carried, and which he had often seen at Spokane House. The Boston man was younger, taller, and leaner than Star-gazer. Yet Illim-spokanee sensed that the scarred Yankee was of similar character.

The white-haired chief approached Jedediah one morning during a lull in the trading. He knew that, by acquiring a Flathead wife, the trader Ogden had become an avenue of information about the leaves bound together. He did not want to be left out of the spiritual power that might be gained from the leaves.

Jedediah had just come into camp from a jaunt to let his horse feed on a good stand of dead grass, and he was hobbling his horse with a rope loop attached to her front legs. Sensing someone approaching, he turned to greet the chief of the Spokane nation. They gave each other the universal greeting: palms up, palms down, palms toward each other. The Spokane started the conversation, speaking in a mix of sign language, Salish, and recently learned English. "I have heard that the Bostons come to us across the Backbone of the World?"

Jedediah replied, "Yes, we are Bostons, come from the east."

"Talk is, Bostons buy furs. Old Pierre say: Bostons pay more."

"Pierre is right. Bostons do pay more. We Bostons come from over yonder. Maybe soon, we trade with Spokanes? Pay more money!"

"It is good! We welcome Bostons! Come next year. You have guns? Knives? Axes?"

"Yes. Our chief brings these things even now, for trade."

"Spokanes like trade. Spokanes trade with Bostons."

"It is good," Jed signed.

The aging chief was developing for the American a fondness that went beyond the economic benefits he promised. Jed had a winsome smile. So did Illim-spokanee. The clean-shaven white man had also the marks of the grizzly on his face. Clearly, he was a man of fiber, a wilderness-tested man. He had crossed the Backbone of the World, too, a feat to be respected.

At last, the conversation led to a subject of even greater interest to the chief than trade, for the Spokanes were always inquiring about the one they called "the Master of Life." The Coeur d'Alenes, eastern neighbors to the Spokanes, were celebrating his birth each year, revealed to them, it was said, by the animals. But none of the tribes had any knowledge of his name. Confusingly, he was thought to be somehow connected to the sun. Perhaps he was the sun. Information had been traded at tribal trade fairs before any white people had joined in. But the name of the great being was still unknown.

The Spokane prophecy given by Circling Raven had concentrated on the book of the *chipixa*. So the chief pointed to the book the Boston carried with him. Jedediah tended to carry it inside his shirt, but just now, it happened to be in his hand.

"The chiefs of the white men always carry leaves bound together. Does it teach of the Master of Life? What is this medicine?"

"What? The Bible?" Jedediah's heart beat a little harder. He had dreamed of sharing the gospel with the Indians—he had not necessarily expected them to ask! He picked up his Bible and showed it to the chief. "The Bible teaches of God. It says, God sent to earth his Son, to show his love for us. The God who made us sent his only Son, an express message to every nation."

"Ah! He-made-us has a Son? Quilent-satmen has a Son?"

"Quilent-satmen?" Jed repeated, forming the unfamiliar name carefully. "Yes. Quilent-satmen has a Son."

"Ah!" Illim-spokanee leaned back in wonder.

This was a new idea to the aging headman. Totally new. Yet was it not Quilent-satmen who had told them in advance to listen to the words of the white men? Here, then, was the kernel of the mystery foretold: Quilent-satmen had a Son! This was what they had been trying to discover since the days of Circling Raven. Light was dawning. The morning mists were receding as the sun shone in.

Jedediah's eyes sparkled as he went on. "He has a name, too, the Son of He-made-us. His name is Jesus."

"Ah! Jee-sus!" Illim-spokanee's voice betrayed his wonder. The Name, revealed at last.

"Yes! You got it!" A smile of exhilaration crossed Jedediah's face and was reflected in the chief's wrinkled countenance like a mirror.

"What does the name mean? 'Jesus'?"

"It means, He-saves-us."

"He-made-us sent his Son, He-saves-us. Why such a name as this?"

Jedediah struggled with his limited vocabulary as he answered, "He saves us by bringing peace with God and with each other. He also rescues us from death. He wants us to live forever with God—with Quilent-satmen." He knew it was more complicated than that, but his vocabulary could only go so far, and he still had the tragedy of Piegan-Nez Percé warfare in mind. The wailing and disfigurement of the warriors haunted him with the smell of rot in the air. It was truly peace these people needed.

As for Illim-spokanee, he remembered the peacemaking counsel of Star-gazer about warfare with the Okanogans. He now recognized its source: the Bible the *chipixa* held in his hand. This book spoke of peace. Quilent-satmen wishes us to live at peace with him, and with each other.

Within Illim-spokanee, there arose a certainty that Quilent-satmen had spoken. It was the same certainty that had invaded his life the day the mountain had exploded with information about *chipixa* bearing leaves bound together. Now, here was one such person standing directly before him, telling him the answer to their prophecy. The wheels of the Creator turned slowly, but turn they did, and they always brought fresh insight into the will of Quilent-satmen. Nothing stays the same.

As Jedediah watched the light dawning in Illim-spokanee's eyes, he felt as though he had been standing under a warm waterfall of peace and joy. This had been a conversation of spirit with spirit, a current of divine love in the meeting of the eyes. Through the eyes, you can see into the heart. These two men had given each other the gift of trust—or it had been granted to both from the Creator. It was as though neither man had ever been hurt by an unkind word. Each had been given the secret gift granted to the pure in heart: they recognized one another as though they belonged to a secret society. They spoke a language deeper than words, known only to each other. It was as though God himself were the language.

Jedediah longed for the shower of peace to continue, for the meeting of spirits to endure forever. Illim-spokanee, a more experienced man, recognized that these gifts were not permanent, but could be cherished in memory. He clasped Jedediah's hand in a gesture of farewell, an unspoken hope that the Creator might grant such a meeting of spirits again. Jedediah, he sensed, had the power to fill the vacancy left by David Thompson's departure years before.

But fur men were not known for settling down anywhere, and the Americans were no better than the English at settling down. Illim-spokanee would never see Jedediah Smith again.

• • •

During the week that followed, one of the six shacks was converted into a business office. Another became a fur warehouse. Another, the equipment shop for the next Snake Brigade. Another, the store for trade, and another, an impromptu chapel. At the end of the week, the Spokanes left to accompany the furs west. Ogden ensconced himself in the business office to settle accounts with the freemen.

Alex Ross held forth on Sundays, leading worship and preaching in Scottish Presbyterian fashion. It was the first recognizable church service the Americans had attended in two years. But there was little in Ross's Presbyterian style that would cause them to beg for more. He was all formality, so unexpected in this backwoods place, and Jedediah could only breathe a sigh of relief as he finally stepped out into the good air that God had himself provided in the great outdoors. Besides, cooped up in that small room, the men stank. Remembering the Crows, Jedediah decided to take a Sunday bath in the river.

On December 20, the next Snake Brigade headed out under the aegis of Peter Skene Ogden. The Americans stayed behind with Alex Ross. Natives were still appearing out of nowhere, hoping to trade. Much smoking, gambling, trading, and joking was still going on. Jed hung around, looking for opportunities to share the news that He-made-us had a Son, He-saves-us. Among those who stayed to listen to him was the young Flathead chief, Insula.

Finally, after Christmas, Jedediah decided it was time to follow Ogden's slow-moving brigade back to Snake country. The Americans bade farewell to Flathead Post and rode east, following the cold trail of twenty-two families that had plodded through the snow before them.

As he moved toward reunion with his supplier William Ashley, Jedediah was full of gratitude. Not only had God provided a place for them to spend some of the winter, but love had flowed through him toward the tribes, and he knew beyond a shadow of a doubt that God had used him. "There is nothing like being in the center of God's will," he said to himself over and over. Perhaps this was the real, underlying reason he had found his way over the wall and into this secret garden.

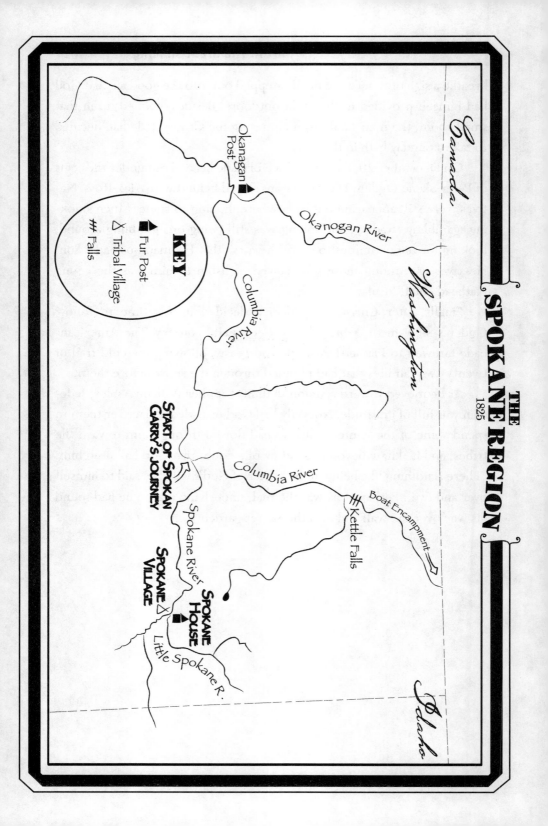

Part III:
The Search
1824–1825

The principal personage is His One Eyed Majesty Concomely a well disposed Indian; he lost two fine young men lately one of whom was to have been his successor altho the youngest; the only remaining Son Cassicus is a cruel Tyrannical blood thirsty Villain who has formed several plans to cut off the Fort; he and the old man are anxious that I should take his Son a Boy of about 9 years of age for the purpose of being Educated, but the lad looks delicate and if any accident happened to him it might be attended with unpleasant reflections & perhaps consequences I am therefore as yet undetermined on the subject.[19]

—George Simpson's Journal, 1825

Had a long interview with Eight Chiefs belonging to the Flat Head Coutonais Spokan and other tribes who assembled here for the purpose of seeing me; they appeared much pleased with all that was told them and promise well. Made them a present of a little ammunition and Tobacco. The Spokan & Flat Head Chiefs put a Son each under my care to be Educated at the Missionary Society School Red River and all the Chiefs joined in a most earnest request that a Missionary or religious instructor should be placed among them; I promised to communicate their request to the Great Chiefs on the other side of the Water with a recommendation from myself that it should be complied with.[20]

—George Simpson's Journal April 8, 1825

Two Nez Percés Chiefs arrived to see me from a distance of between 2 & 300 Miles; my fame has spread far and Wide and my speeches are handed from Camp to Camp throughout the Country; some of them have it that I am one of the "Master of Life's Sons" sent to see "if their hearts are good" and others that I am his "War Chief" with bad Medicine if their hearts are bad. On the whole I think my presence and lectures will do some good.[21]

—George Simpson's Journal, April 9, 1825

19. Merk, *Fur Trade and Empire*, 104.
20. Merk, *Fur Trade and Empire*, 135.
21. Merk, *Fur Trade and Empire*, 136.

One

In the suburb of Clapham in London, England, the righteousness of God was confronting an entire neighborhood. God had never been known to prefer the wealthy, and yet this was one of the wealthiest neighborhoods of England, full of the most powerful and influential men and women of the age. And God was there.

It was all the fault of Henry Venn, man of prayer.

Caught up in the English Great Awakening with George Whitefield, John Wesley, and John Newton, it was Venn who became convinced of the necessity of constant, intimate, listening, faithful, in-season, out-of-season prayer. Scratch the surface of the great transforming movements of the past, and you will almost always find such people as Henry Venn. Characterized by unimpeachable goodness, they spend much time with God, letting him transform them before they ask him to transform anyone else. Their lives of prayer are a fiery furnace that warms the whole house, yet the furnace remains hidden in the basement of history.

That is why so few today remember Henry Venn, or any of the others who stoked the prayer furnaces that led to countless other great social movements. After the Henry Venns of this world die, posterity forgets the love radiating from their faces, the power of their words, the goodness of their friendships, the wholesomeness of their presence, and their influence with God. History remembers hard facts recorded on paper, doctrines set forth in black and white writing, and new organizations founded with visible, quantifiable consequences. The subtle but profound influence of a life of prayer is hard to quantify, and it makes historians uncomfortable. Historians study history. Henry Venn makes it.

Henry Venn had invested several years of his life ministering at Clapham, only to move away to spend his best years among the poor of wretched neighborhoods that no one else wanted to shepherd. But then, at the end of his life he returned to Clapham, and that is where he died six months later, in 1797.

And then all heaven broke out. At Clapham.

The young aristocrat, William Wilberforce, member of Parliament, began to make serious headway against the slave industry. Barely five feet tall, by 1802 he was rapidly gaining the stature of a giant of social reform. Having gathered around him a group of men and women who wanted simply to do the will of God no matter what the cost, he set an example from which other citizens of Clapham soon gained courage.

On April 12, 1799, Wilberforce was the central figure in a group of sixteen who met at the Castle and Falcon in Aldersgate Street to consider the calling of Christ to make disciples of all nations. As if it were not enough to take on the slave industry worldwide, these Christians now sensed that they should pledge their lives and their fortunes to see to it that the nations of the world were acquainted with the love of Jesus.

Two centuries before, during the reign of King James, there had been talk of "converting the heathen." But throughout the centuries, people who talk like that have had a bad track record. And in that case, such talk had been little more than window-dressing to legitimize their money-making schemes in Virginia.

The Clapham Sect was different. As a result of intense prayer (such as that of Henry Venn), God was doing something different, something genuine. God can grip hearts with such passionate love that people will risk life and limb to obey his destiny for them. Passion!—like that of the German Moravians seventy years before, who had sent out the very first two Protestant missionaries to the Isle of St. Thomas to love African slaves with the love of Jesus. Filled with Christlike passion, they had been willing to become slaves, if God had called them to do it.

So too, God's passion gripped the Clapham Sect to form the Church Missionary Society, armed with a completely new vision that few Christians had given the least thought to for centuries. Wilberforce and his team were creating a new England and a new church, and they were heaven-bent on transforming the entire world.

By 1823, Benjamin Harrison, friend and neighbor to William Wilberforce in Clapham, took his place at the round table of the directors of the Hudson's Bay Company. His quiet influence in the Company, and that of Nicholas Garry, another Clapham Sect evangelical, enjoyed the same success that Wilberforce was having as a member of Parliament. By now, slavery had been eradicated in England, and Wilberforce was attacking the slave industry in the rest of the world. Under Harrison's influence, righteousness, justice, the abolition of slavery, and the proclamation of God's love worldwide became the business of the Company, which had extended its influence around the world.

• • •

It was this inconvenient gift from God at Clapham that taught the arrogant Governor Simpson, across the Atlantic Ocean in Rupert's Land,[22] a lesson in humility.

George Simpson was the self-confident and enormously gifted young clerk who had just been put in charge of half of North America. He had a cherubic pink mouth shaped in a permanent smirk, jade green eyes as

---

22. That is, Canada.

hard as ice, a ferret's nose, a pimply complexion, and dark red hair creeping up from his neck—hair which, even now at age thirty, was forgetting to entirely cover his head.

Simpson was a stickler for fine clothing. From the moment he arrived in the New World, he had dressed like an English nobleman: black suit fitted with *sous pieds*, white shirt with collar to the ears, velvet stock to button down his neck, and a black top hat of beaver felt, worth forty shillings—the closest thing to a crown that could suitably be worn in the wild. Over his black frock coat he sported a long coat of Royal Stuart tartan lined with scarlet, the robe of a king. All this comprised the grand presence of the Governor of the Northern Department, arguably the most powerful man on the American continent.

The Northwest Company that had mapped and explored the Northern Rockies under David Thompson had vanished, amalgamated into the HBC in 1821. The Hudson's Bay Company now monopolized the wilderness forests and prairies north of the fledgling United States and provided for them something like government.

Cursing the cold weather of the frozen north country where fate had placed him, Simpson was walking from Fort Garry, the Hudson's Bay post, to the home of Robert Pelly at Fort Douglas, just a stone's throw to the east along the Assiniboine River. "These missionaries are a bleeding nuisance," fumed the little king as he sloshed through the mud that claimed the name of "road" at the center of the Red River Colony.[23]

"And, of course, Pelly will want to cave in to their every whim," he continued, talking to the air. "No backbone whatever. What you'd call 'a fine Christian gentleman.' Phah!"

Suddenly catching himself, he looked around to see if anyone was within hearing distance. It wouldn't do to express aloud such unkind remarks toward the governor of Assiniboia, ineffective though he was. Assiniboia was the official name of the territory, and Robert Pelly was the official governor. But Pelly was a weakling, or so Simpson told himself as he prepared

---

23. Today's Winnipeg, Manitoba.

for his interview with him. The issue on the agenda was Christian missionaries and their proposed school for Native lads. Because of Pelly's general ineffectiveness, the official government of the territory was slowly giving way to the influence of the Hudson's Bay Company. And Simpson was himself, more or less, taking over the governance of the land.

Coddle him. Play with him. Sooner or later Pelly must shrivel up into nothing. Then you won't have to deal with him anymore, he assured himself.

But it wasn't Pelly the governor was really concerned about. It was Simpson's mentor, Andrew Colvile, one of the Company directors back in London.

Back in '21, Simpson had been a simple London clerk with no connections whatever—except Andrew Colvile. He had no future and no experience in the fur trade. Then, quite out of the blue, Colvile had nominated him to be Governor of the Northern Department. He owed all his present good fortune to the man. His benefactor was therefore the one person in all the world he could not ignore, pat on the head, threaten, or humiliate into compliance.

"Dear old Colvile," Simpson reminisced—for the old gentleman had been a true father to him, risking his own reputation on behalf of a complete nonentity. "He believed in me!" The thought still astonished him, and his face twisted into a grimace as his emotions collided.

"Damn, I'll not let him down. But it's still a bleeding nuisance! William Wilberforce is a nuisance, and so is Ben Harrison. The lot of 'em are as bad as West—I'm glad to be seeing the last of him!"

As Simpson fingered the letter from Colvile which had brought him to his present dilemma, he reflected on his unpleasant relationship with the obnoxious John West, the first of the Anglican parsons to be stationed as a missionary here. The specter of John West's face floated into Simpson's mind: that jutting jaw (which was always flapping at somebody); that clear, steady gaze and narrow face (like a horse with blinders on); that flawless, milk-white skin (fit for a lily-white psalm-spouter, which was just what he was.)

In 1822, soon after the board of directors had formed their alliance with the Church Missionary Society, they had sent the Reverend John West to pastor retired Company employees at the Red River Colony, a town which had been founded by Lord Selkirk, a friend of William Wilberforce and a full-fledged member of the Clapham Sect. Appropriately named, West was the first missionary in the American West. Once established in the colony, West had proposed a school for Indian boys. The school would teach Indian lads their ABCs: Agriculture, Britishness, and Christianity.

George Simpson was against all but B. He had argued scrappily that agriculture and Christianity would destroy the Natives' usefulness to the fur trade.

But John West was no meek little lamb. No! If George Simpson was blunt, lacking in social graces, and sure of his opinion, John West was his equal in all categories. He was the sort of sincere Christian who could start a new church against insurmountable obstacles, but could not make it prosper. He had a golden tongue, sharp as a dirk, with which he criticized Hudson's Bay officers for their lifestyles of Sabbath-breaking, drunkenness, and serial marriage with Native women. He had laid for his mission congregation the solid foundation of righteous morals, but he could not add the floor of love to make the place livable. George Simpson found him intolerable. In some ways, John West was too much like himself.

Simpson fumed silently as he trudged along. They'll not accuse me of being against philanthropy or the church. But trying to Christianize Indians? Faugh!

To Simpson, the word *Christian* meant the same thing as the word *civilized*. Now that the English had become civilized, he didn't see any need for the church, which, he earnestly believed, should quietly disappear now that it had outlived its usefulness.

For two years, West and Simpson had flailed away at each other. West had railed against the governor's habit of keeping a concubine at York Factory and of having children by her.

On May 20, 1822, Simpson fought back with a letter to Colvile:

Mr. West has some idea that through the interest and exertions of Mr. Harrison a fund may be raised or got from some of the Charities to open schools for the instruction and maintenance of Native Indian children; he takes a very sanguine view of this scheme which is to diffuse Christian Knowledge among the natives from the shores of the Pacific to those of the Bay and will no doubt on paper draw a very fine representation of the advantages to be derived therefrom, which may attract the attention of Philanthropists, but in my humble opinion will be attended with little other good than filling the pockets and bellies of some hungry missionaries and schoolmasters and rearing the Indians in habits of indolence; they are already too much enlightened by the late opposition and more of it would in my opinion do harm instead of good to the Fur Trade.[24]

Well, that was George Simpson's "humble opinion."

A year later, Colvile's reply had come—and it was this letter that the governor now removed from his breast pocket. He opened it and reread it for the sixth time:

It is incumbent on the Company, even if there were no Settlement, to have a chaplain in their country & at least to allow missions to be established at proper places for the conversion of the Indians, indeed, it would be extremely impolitic in the present temper & disposition of the public in this Country to show any unwillingness to assist in such an object. By uniting with the Missionary Society & the Settlement these objects are obtained safely, conveniently & cheaply.[25]

---

24. Frederick Merk, *Fur Trade and Empire: George Simpson's Journal, 1824-5*, 181.
25. Andrew Colvile to Governor Simpson, March 11, 1824. From Orin Oliphant, "George Simpson and Oregon Missions," 232.

These were patient, measured words, so different from those the Northwesters might have used five years before. The new breed of Hudson's Bay men had kindlier hearts than their predecessors. Yet their quiet words bore more clout than others' threats of violence.

As George Simpson reread the letter, he could almost hear his benefactor's patient voice. Andrew Colvile possessed an integrity that drew a person to want to please him. He didn't grasp at authority. He invited you to give it to him.

Chastened, the ferret-king took another look at the whole prospect of Christian evangelism. He allowed himself to have a change of mind, though few would have called it a change of heart. He was still George Simpson—tough, opinionated, a man whose heart was made of crocodile skin. A man who did not know how to weep.

Wiping the mud from his black leather shoes, Simpson arrived at Fort Douglas, knocked at the door of the main residence, and was greeted by Robert Pelly, who had been waiting for him.

. . .

From the opposite direction came a birch-bark canoe—from downriver, the direction of the church that John West had built. But it was not John West who paddled this canoe toward Fort Douglas. The Church Missionary Society had replaced him with a more patient, accepting man, the Reverend David Jones.

Jones, a Welshman, disembarked from the fragile, yellow-white birch bark. The art of canoeing was still foreign to him, and he was glad to set his foot on solid ground. He made his way through the cattails at the water's edge and past the lone maple tree on the path to the fort. He knocked on the door of the governor's home, a comfortable but simple residence of squared wooden logs laid *pièce-sur-pièce* between notched vertical corner posts.

The two who opened the door to him were dressed in the black-and-white finery of English gentlemen. They wore their clothing as a statement of faith that, yes, even Assiniboia could be, must be, and was being civilized. Here were that combative ferret, George Simpson, and the mild-mannered governor of Assiniboia, Robert Pelly. While Pelly had already become a cherished friend to David, the parson felt meekly reluctant as he entered the presence of Simpson.

By contrast to these distinguished men, the new parson had little about him to raise him above the commonplace. He was a young man of ordinary height and appearance, ordinary conversation and education. He wore moccasins in place of shoes, because his cobbler had made a mess of the shoes he had ordered for his journey to the New Country. Such acquiescence to Indian ways was not a distinguishing mark in the eyes of either Simpson or Pelly. David Jones was suddenly embarrassed by his own inadequate appearance.

"Let us get down to business, shall we?" said Simpson in an unnaturally pleasant voice.

"Agreed," said Pelly. "I know there've been some misunderstandings, but now I trust we are in agreement as to the benefits of educating Indian boys here at Red River?"

Jones looked nervous. Simpson's reputation as a man who devoured missionaries had preceded him. Still, the Welsh parson spoke first. "Guv'nor," he said, addressing himself to Simpson, "we see it as the first step in providing schools within the tribal villages themselves. Surely you can see that having English-trained interpreters among the Indians could be a blessing to the Company as well as to the Church Missionary Society. Are you with us, Guv'nor?"

"Certainly, sir! Heart and soul!" Simpson was effusive in words, even if his manner still seemed strained. Jones was astonished. He was supportive! Against all expectation!

Pelly added, "Governor Simpson and I have prepared a list of possibilities. At least it's a place to start, you know. Three here. Five there. If all goes well, the spark of Christian teaching will have landed in every district from the Atlantic to the Pacific, and from the Coppermine River to the Missouri."

Simpson pulled a scrap of paper from his vest pocket, referring to it as he spoke. "We've worked it all out. We will present to the school ten Swampy Crees, five Thick-woods Assiniboins, five Crees from the Isle à la Crosse and Athabasca, five Chippeways from Great Slave Lake, three Indians from New Caledonia, and two from the Columbia River District."

Simpson looked up at Jones and continued. "As to these last, I plan to cross the Rockies myself after the meeting at York Factory, and I will personally bring the two from the Columbia." He cleared his throat. He could not believe his own words, but he kept hearing Colvile's voice emanating from the letter hidden in his breast pocket.

David Jones regarded this statement as nothing short of a miracle of God. Looking vastly relieved, he still voiced one doubt. "I am grateful, Guv'nor Simpson. Of course, the sticking point is going to be getting men of influence among the tribes to lend us their sons."

"Ha! It is easily done, sir!" Simpson almost laughed. "We'll allow a stipend of three pounds sterling as an inducement to the chiefs of these tribes to give us their children. We'll be doing them a favor! Most of them would be only too happy for us to take their children off their hands. One less mouth to feed, if you see my point."

Pelly and Jones looked at each other, tight-lipped. Neither spoke. This was the old familiar Simpson. Brash. Arrogant. Presumptuous. The kindly and sensitive Simpson was just a façade after all, put on for the sake of good manners.

David Jones was unexpectedly firm in his reply. "Guv'nor Simpson, 'tis not money but prayer that will accomplish our objectives. God has his own ways of accomplishing his will. We need not contrive our own."

Simpson was about to respond when Robert Pelly jumped in. "Still, you don't just take thirty boys from the wilds and bring them into our care without incurring some expenses. I think we'll need that three pounds sterling to purchase clothing, seeds, and implements for the boys—will we not, Mr. Jones?"

"Surely. But the Society provides some money for these things. I will provide for the boys on behalf of the Society, if the Company will help to bring them to Red River. To be honest, I believe the Company bears the harder part of the bargain. I will pray for your success."

Simpson, not caring much about this prayer business, ended the meeting. Prayer never accomplished anything. It was a pastime for weaklings, fanatics, and dreamers. Simpson was a man of action, not prayer.

Two

The most grueling, dangerous, obnoxious wilderness trail of all was the one that led from York Factory on Hudson's Bay up the Beaver River, through the Lesser Slave Lake District, across the Great Divide at Jasper House, and then down the Columbia River to its mouth. It was this trail that Governor Simpson prepared to travel after his interview with Jones and Pelly.

Long forgotten were the days when he had first traversed the rough carriage road to Montreal. Then he had complained miserably that the roads were "one continued morass" and "the weather so bad that I had no opportunity of devoting much of my attention to the surrounding Scenery: my Vehicle was nothing more than an open Cart drawn by 4 animals unworthy of the Name of Horse and after about 50 Spills in which I had numberless bruises & contusions was compelled to have recourse to the Marrow bone stage the greater part of the Journey."[26]

---

26. Arthur S. Morton, *Sir George Simpson*, 14. The quote is from a letter dated April 28, 1820, Montreal.

It did not take George Simpson long to realize that such complaints were the sentiments, not of the conqueror, but of the conquered. In the three years since, the governor had learned to be a conqueror. He considered it his destiny to overcome offenses to the bone marrow. No rough carriage road was going to get the better of him again—and in the last three years, none had. Now it was time for the acid test, to see who was the boss here: a man, or a simple pathway leading through the woods to the ocean.

As George Simpson set out from York Fort on this path, he imagined himself treading on the neck of the enemy. He was determined, too, to squelch every gossipy suspicion that he was but a *blanc bec*—a "white-nose"—who belonged back in London behind a desk. Simpson fancied himself on an imaginary race against all who had ever trekked this trail throughout history, and he was going to beat them all. Let the race begin!

The trip began badly. On the first day, the whole party was forced by high winds to abandon ship in high surf on the river. All had to jump into violent, neck-deep water and unload the pitching, bobbing canoe. "Never mind. It is easily done," the governor assured everyone.

A week later, they were caught by heavy winds on Lake Primeau. The boat shipped a foot of water despite vigorous bailing by two red-capped voyageurs. The water-filled canoe was moving nowhere. Only by the most frantic efforts did they remain afloat. "The lake is just testing our mettle," Simpson observed casually from his pillow in the lead canoe.

The Beaver River was dry. Well, not dry, exactly. It was a long, narrow mud hole. They had to carry everything for miles through the mosquito-infested slime. One man sank down to his neck in muck. George Simpson pulled him out with a hearty word, as of father to child: "Pluck up, my man; there you are!" Such is the role of a lord, he mused.

Further west, the winds came up again, actually blowing down trees around their camp. Governor Simpson laughed in the teeth of the wind and examined the faces of his voyageurs for traces of fear. It was his lot to conquer even the winds—though it could not be said that they obeyed him.

Day after day, this *Georgius Rex* ordered his men up before dawn and had them paddling and portaging until late at night. As for himself, he always allowed one of the French Canadians to carry him piggyback through the shallow water and deposit him gently on his pillow in the center of the lead canoe. There he spent the day giving orders while others paddled and carried.

Crossing the Height of Land on horseback, the pack containing Simpson's wardrobe slipped off its mount, dropped into the river, and was swept away. By diligent effort, some of his clothes were retrieved. "Such things will happen. They are but clothes," he muttered.

Climbing the path toward the Committee's Punchbowl (as Simpson named the tarn at the head of the pass), they were overtaken by a storm. Eight inches of snow fell in one night. George Simpson, budding world traveler, took the hardship in stride. Who would have guessed that he possessed such a fund of endurance?

On the journey down the Columbia, as they passed by the Spokane, the Okanogan, and the Walla Walla rivers, firewood became so scarce that they had to burn horse manure for cooking fires. Simpson easily adjusted to the indignity. Strong winds blew sand into their faces, and, further down, they were invaded by vermin crawling into their clothes, hair, and packs.

But George Simpson was glorying in it all. Let the wilderness throw at him what it would, he would prove himself the master, molding the whole Northern Department into a productive fur empire. He would earn his title by sheer force of will. The wilderness must know its true governor. Move over, you spirits of tree and bear. Your new master draweth near!

As for the rough-hewn men who traveled with him (or under him, as was often the case), they were part and parcel with the wilderness. They too must be taught the lesson of respect for their betters. By journey's end, all would learn that nothing could conquer George Simpson— nothing! He was indefatigable, undeflatable, irrepressible. None doubted it now: Andrew Colvile had possessed rare discernment to have chosen such a one for such a job.

Mercifully, Simpson was learning to obey the HBC directors too. He was, after all, a man under authority in a chain of command.

The night before the men were to arrive at Fort George (Astoria, when the place had belonged to the Americans), the governor had them unpack their dress clothes: fresh red or white blouses with billowing sleeves, red wool caps and matching *L'Assompçion* sash belts, silky serge trousers bunched at the knee, knee stockings, and beaded moccasins. Away into packs went unsightly, ragged trail clothes. The men were made to shave, wash with soap, and comb their hair. Simpson would have them arrive in style!

On the following day, as they neared Fort George, they found the chief factor of the fort sporting with a sailboat on the river. This child's play made no favorable impression on George Simpson. Too bad for the chief factor. The governor never forgot first impressions.

Proceeding under overcast skies, they made their appearance at Fort George. The setting sun cast its rays through a break in the clouds, intensifying the reds of painted paddles and vermilion clothing. Simpson was dressed in his kingly robe, crowned with his top hat. The voyageurs proudly stroked to a cadence of chanted songs, some in French, some in English. A triangular pennant at the bow of Simpson's canoe pictured a beaver with the motto *Pro Pelle Cutem*, "Skin for Skin," from the book of Job.

A sentry, spotting the canoes, fired a signal gun from the fort. From the lead canoe, a kneeling piper dressed in full highland dress answered with the tune, "*Si Coma Leum Cradh Na Shee*": "Peace, If You Will It, Otherwise War." The fort responded with a seven-gun salute, followed by a trumpet voluntary announced into the wilderness air.

As the canoes drew near, the chanters broke into the standard Canadian tune, "Faintly As Tolls the Evening Chime." The bagpipe accompanied them until they were landed beneath the loading boom at the dock. The King of Rupert's Land had arrived at his remotest outpost to the accompaniment of antiphonal music not unlike a coronation service in Westminster Abbey.

The Forgotten Awakening

That night, everyone got roaring drunk—everyone, that is, except George Simpson and Dr. John McLoughlin, the new chief factor. The men were celebrating the winning of the race, for they had set a new record for this trek—eighty-four days—beating the old record by twenty days!

Three

The arrival of Governor Simpson at the mouth of *Tacousah-tesseh*, the Columbia River, was the event of the year at Fort George. As it was happening, Concomly, chief of the Chinooks, was standing at the edge of his village, Kaht-samts, on the north bank of the Columbia's mouth. He was superintending four of his three hundred slaves as they were trying to catch a sturgeon. They had angled for it all day, with their hardwood hook rubbed with wild celery root. Attached to the cedar dugout by a long fiber of cedar thread, the monster had led them on a wild chase across the mouth of the river, towing the four boatmen hither and yon, taxing their boating skills to the utmost.

Shouting his orders, Concomly instructed them on how to bring the fish in. The air rang with his orders, heavy with x, k, and w sounds unintelligible to anyone but Chinooks and their slaves. The twelve-foot monster was brought up to the surface, thrashing alongside the canoe. The slave at the bow pulled its ugly head over the gunwale. At a command from shore, with a twisting motion the slave skillfully and single-handedly rolled the whole body over the side into the canoe.

Meanwhile, another canoe was just arriving from across the river, bringing news of Simpson's arrival at Fort George. Immediately, Concomly began shouting more orders. He commanded the four slaves to string the sturgeon to a carrying pole. Then he ordered the other villagers to get ready for an ambassadorial visit.

After an hour of preparations, Concomly ascended the bank to his house, absorbed in thought. Will this governor be like that skunk McDougal? Or will he be a true king, worthy of an alliance? We choose to think the best, until proven otherwise. By trade have I, Concomly, led my people to prosperity. By trade have we amassed an unprecedented number of slaves and hyaque shells. By trade have we utilized the white man to our advantage. By trade have I cemented my place as chief. What has that dog, Sachla, done by comparison? Sachla is a mere salmon. I am the great sturgeon here. Sachla understands nothing. Hah! The way of nobility is to cement trade relations by marriage. I understood this from the first. Calpo and I knew how to build power!—by marriage. It is the way of kings!

Concomly smiled. His diamond-shaped face, broad at the cheekbones, was filled with the parentheses of skin folds.

He stopped smiling when he reached his house, for there was the daughter he had given to that Boston dog, McDougal. The disturbing remembrance of McDougal's cowardly betrayal still stung him. The great British canoe had come from across the ocean twelve years before, had come to take the fort away from the Boston men. Concomly had offered to help McDougal keep Astoria for the Boston men. After all, McDougal had become his son-in-law.

"The big canoe can never cross the bar," he had said. "They will send their little boats to the shore. I will post my men in the woods. We will fire on them when they land. We will take them by surprise. It is a foolproof plan."

But McDougal had refused to fight. Totally outclassed by the English. He had sold out to them and had abandoned his wife. And now the King

George men are here, the chief concluded in his review of unpleasant memories.

Ah! But the King George men are different! Maybe the coming of the King George men is a good thing after all.

Concomly pushed aside the round disc that hung by a thong at the front of his house. Behind it was a circular opening under the legs of a giant figure painted on the front of the house, a structure big enough to provide lodging for many families. Entering, he ordered his wives and daughters to prepare salmon as gifts.

The chief continued to meditate. King George men understand Chinook ways better than Bostons. They make better traders, better husbands. They know how to respect a king. Their dining rooms show this. English and Chinook are twin peoples.

Concomly sat by the fire as the women of his house cut down salmon hanging from the rafters. The whole house reeked of fish. The fire burned heartily from a square pit at the center, cut into the earth through a hole in the cedar-plank floor. Other fires smoldered from other parts of the huge house. Smoke drifted lazily through holes in the roof, but some remained trapped to smoke the salmon hanging above their heads.

The chief tried to visualize the new governor. New relations must be cemented with him. He must be kept from forming relations with that verminous Casseno on the Multnomah, with Schannaway and his no-account Cowlitz to the northeast, or with the scheming Clatsops south of the river. Marriage was the solution, a permanent answer for all perplexity, a perfect way of assuring successful business transactions for years to come.

Concomly got up and went to his friend Calpo, who lived nearby. "It is time to put our plan into action," he said.

George Simpson was about to become the target of a matrimonial conspiracy, and the last thing he had prepared himself to conquer in this wilderness was the charm of a woman.

• • •

The Forgotten Awakening

On the next day, a messenger arrived at Fort George from Kaht-samts to announce that the great Concomly was arriving to greet the governor of the King George men. Visible from the fort were four canoes, each forty feet long, plying the gray, choppy waters of the Columbia and heading directly toward them. The gates of the stockade were opened. A highlander piped "Rule Britannia." A grizzled old Canadian set off one of the two eighteen-pounders facing the bay.

As the Chinooks beached their canoes, British dignitaries lined up in front of the stockade. The last few leaves of vine maple, still clinging to wispy branches, added a splash of vermilion to the otherwise somber scene. A long line of slaves, all with unflattened foreheads in contrast to their masters, bore gifts of fish, pungent in the salt air. The last was the sturgeon caught the day before, which was placed at the feet of George Simpson and Dr. John McLoughlin, a towering, white-haired medical man who was destined to be chief factor of the Columbia District for many years to come.

As each slave laid his gift before the British, he said, "*Clar-how-ah-yah.*" By the twentieth greeting, Simpson turned to McLoughlin and said, "Do these slaves think I'm William Clark?"

Archibald MacDonald, veteran of the fort, answered. "It's Chinook jargon, sir; the trade language used all up an' down the coast. They're sayin', 'How do ye do?' You'll get the hang of it, sir. We use the jargon wi' all the tribes 'round here."

After the slaves had passed by, Chinooks came to offer similar greetings. Each had a flat forehead and a pointed cranium. The head-flattening, achieved by placing boards over the skull soon after birth, pulled up the eyebrows and caused the eyes to bulge. Foreheads sloped back in line with the nose. Black hair fell to the shoulders as from a fountain hidden on the point of the head. Simpson was having a hard time getting adjusted to people whose sense of beauty differed so appallingly from his own. These who bowed before him might have been descendants from some lost Atlantis.

At last there came Concomly himself. He was a short man with fat, unshapely legs, a squat body, and an oriental face. To cover his less than regal figure, he wore an otter-fur robe, sewn ingeniously from long strips of fur twisted so that the fur showed on both sides of the robe. On his head he wore, not the cone-shaped basketry hat of the other Chinooks, but an out-of-date tricorn, reminiscent of Revolutionary War days and the voyage of Lewis and Clark. At his side, under his robe, he wore a sword dangling from a cloth belt.

The most striking aspect of Concomly's appearance was his face. He had but one eye. His left eye socket was empty except for an ooze of yellow matter that partly filled it. This non-eye seemed to cause him no pain. The chief's face sloped outward toward a strong, beardless chin. His straight, coarse gray hair flowed out behind numerous earrings of hyaque shells. His earlobes were enormous. Under his nose he wore a large shell, suspended by a thread through the septum. Hyaques were used as Chinook currency. It was as though Concomly wore silver dollars or shillings in his ears and nose to proclaim his wealth. It was the same sort of thing that white people did back east, when they purchased beaver-felt hats for six-months' wages and wore them on their heads. And the taller the better.

As George Simpson and Concomly sized each other up, each sensed that the other depended a good deal on regal clothing to enhance his unroyal appearance. Neither man was large, powerful, or attractive. Yet each discerned in the other the authority to command.

Next to Concomly were his wives, Khayak and Keasno, his three sons, and three of his daughters. Each of the women was dressed in a shredded cedar-bark skirt and an upper garment of bobcat fur.

Next came Calpo and his wife. Behind them, presented as the culmination of the parade, was Chowie, the daughter of Calpo. The girl was an eighteen-year-old innocent, and beautiful in a Chinook sort of way. Lady Calpo explained in English, "She is true princess lady. She make some King George man one good wife!" As she spoke these words in English, she smiled garishly.

The princess Chowie stared alluringly at George Simpson, her face framed by her basketry hat, hyaque earrings, and a necklace of blue beads purchased from Lewis and Clark. The girl offered her *"Clar-how-ah-yah"* on cue. Simpson noticed, when the softly smiling girl approached, that she smelled dreadfully of fish oil. He also noticed that her mountain-beaver chemise revealed a good deal of her anatomy.

Other dignitaries, including the ambitious Sachla, came forward to greet the governor. Finally, it was announced that there was to be a feast.

Everyone promenaded through the stockade's double gate into the courtyard. Straight ahead of them stood the two-story factor's house behind the two eighteen-pounders. The dining hall stood to the left, sandwiched between the clerks' apartments and the blacksmith's compound.

A place was made near the governor for Calpo, Concomly, and their families. Since this was a diplomatic occasion, Englishmen and Chinooks sat at the same table. But everyone was still carefully divided by rank.

Lady Calpo, by her fondness for words, had taken the trouble to learn more English ones than any other Chinook. Now in her fifties, she possessed a rapidly fading beauty and badly stained teeth. Her many words had worn down her teeth almost to the gums—or so it seemed. A cascade of dark gray hair framed a brown face full of lines, mostly garish smile lines. She warmed up to George Simpson immediately, as she had done to a twenty-year procession of white men.

She turned to Simpson and said, "I have young slave girls. You like? Verra pretty. I have one slave just for you. Her name Quinault. You like her. Your men like her. I make her come to you tonight. I sell her one night for you verra cheap. She verra pretty. We make deal, yah?" She beamed.

Such crass forwardness took Simpson entirely by surprise. "I suppose you sell your slave girls to our men often? Do our men do this? Do they buy your slave girls for a night?" His face expressed his shock.

Lady Calpo's face broke out in laugh lines as she leaned back and hooted. "Yes, yesss. They are but slaves. Treat them as you like. There is Quinault," she pointed. "You see her for yourself. She has the head of a slave. Anyone can see she is a slave. She belong to me, Lady Calpo. I sell her cheap for a night. Make an offer and she is yours."

"It is not our way," replied Simpson.

Lady Calpo stopped laughing. Incredulity clamped down over her face, as though Simpson had asked her to believe a bald-faced lie. The look contained a thousand words, and Simpson retreated from his statement. "I—I mean, I do not do such things myself."

"What? You are married?" Lady Calpo looked yet more horrified.

"I mean, I do not buy women for pleasure. As for my men, they make their own decisions." Apparently they have been making a good many of their own decisions, and paying good beaver pelts for their pleasures, he thought. No wonder this place never makes a profit. Then he said, "You see, I hope to go back to England. There is a woman waiting for me there."

In fact, Simpson had already fathered several children by a Native woman at York Factory. The governor's mistress, Margaret Taylor, was the sister of his personal servant, Tom. But there was a clear difference, in Simpson's mind, between his relationship with Margaret and these men's liaisons with prostitute slaves. On the one hand, he didn't consider himself married to Margaret. On the other, he didn't want anyone else to have her either. He had considered installing a chastity belt on her during his long absence to the Columbia, just to ensure that she would be faithful to him. It was more civilized to commit oneself to one woman at a time than to spread one's seed around indiscriminately with prostitutes. Besides, he didn't intend to continue with Margaret forever. In his letters, he openly confessed that Margaret Taylor was nothing but "an unnecessary and expensive appendage" and unworthy of "a commissioned gentleman." He planned to get properly married to a white woman in the near future.

Lady Calpo did not receive Simpson's news well. But it only took her a moment to convert an obstacle into a challenge. It was not truly the slave Quinault that occupied her mind, but the hope of attaching her daughter to Governor Simpson on a more permanent basis. The slave merely opened friendly trade relations with Simpson. Quinault (whose Chinook-given name was merely the name of her tribe) was a mere appetizer, after which the Princess Chowie would be the coup de grâce.

"I am afraid I do not approve of your bringing your women and selling them to the men," Simpson said firmly. He turned to Calpo. "I must ask you, Chief Calpo, to order your wife to stop this practice. My men are being distracted from their real duties: taking furs."

But Calpo either didn't understand or pretended not to hear. He was the very picture of stoic and dignified silence, and his wife was not interested in interpreting the governor's words to him. Perhaps, thought Simpson, the man does not know English. He turned to Concomly, seated on the other side of him.

"The Lady Calpo tells me that slave women are brought to the fort and that they give their bodies to the men. This practice must stop. It distracts the men from their work."

Concomly took in these words like a breath of fresh air—not at all because their moral innocence was refreshing, but because the governor dared to contradict Lady Calpo, which even her husband rarely did. Here, truly, was a man after his own heart, a man of authority!

"It shall be as you say," the chief replied gravely, yet with a faint smile.

But in the days to follow, it was not done as Simpson said, nor as Concomly said. The slave girls still came. Concomly possessed much authority, but not that much. Concomly cherished the belief that he possessed the authority to stop the flow of women to the fort, as a favor to a fellow king. But in this he was deceived.

• • •

The days that followed that diplomatic soiree were busy ones for Simpson. The Columbia Department had not been turning a profit. Chief Factor Alexander Kennedy had been more interested in pleasure-boating and in providing English luxuries for himself and his men than in harvesting furs. Simpson, like Concomly, was a fanatic when it came to promoting trade. He ordered the removal of Mr. Kennedy, who was not.

In fact, after much scouting, Simpson and McLoughlin decided to remove the entire post to Jolie Prairie, a fine, grassy slope upriver on the north bank. There, crops could be more easily grown. The men would not be so dependent on expensive English imports. Above all, the north bank was safer from eventual American takeover. Simpson considered himself to be claiming the north bank for England.

The threat of American competition was becoming a nuisance. Simpson (like the Piegans under their war chief, Iron Shirt) had been directed to trap the region bare of beaver so that Americans would have no reason to enter the area. If they did, the loss of monopoly would bring with it the loss of control. Loss of control was but a descending staircase to fur-trade corruption: using liquor competitively as an inducement to Indians to trap, reintroducing drunkenness and violence among the Natives. The Americans—despite federal law—were notorious for their kegs.

George Simpson reviewed what the directors had dictated: If Americans reintroduced whiskey to the Indians, the Honourable Company would have to do the same. A scorched-earth policy was not normally favored by the directors, but in this case, it was the lesser of two evils. Trap the Snake bare to keep the Americans out. This order had already gone out to Peter Skene Ogden.

Simpson determined that the flow of whiskey must be entirely stopped. It wasn't that he considered whiskey immoral, but that using it was a very shortsighted trade policy. Indians, he wrote to the board, would use up their money for drink and then "we would not have the Means of continuing the Barter and we should be the sufferers in the long run."[27]

For the next three months, Simpson, the bumblebee, and McLoughlin, the white-headed eagle, flew about, trying to put the policies of the directors into operation. Concomly visited the fort from time to time and was eager to have Simpson for a friend. During this time, Lady Calpo was a frequent visitor to the fort. Always in her wake followed the Princess Chowie. The girl was a diplomatic weapon who had been kept hidden in a bunker, protected all her life from the normal attention of boys. She was shy, especially around her overpowering mother, from whom she could not escape except during menstrual isolation.

But her quiet spirit and beauty were proving attractive to George Simpson. He liked Chowie, and he took pride in being courted by a leading Chinook family. By January, too, he had taken up with the Chinook standard of beauty. Flat foreheads had become almost exotic to him.

---

27. Merk, *Fur Trade and Empire*, 110.

Four

By January, word had gotten to Kaht-samts—now moved to an inland location for the winter—that Simpson had removed Chief Factor Kennedy from being factor at the fort. Concomly smacked his lips and smiled. The decision demonstrated once again that Simpson was no jelly-kneed squid. Kennedy had been selected by the boastful Sachla for a marital alliance with Sachla's daughter. Now Sachla's futile and belated attempt at greatness would fall to the ground! Hah!

But as close as Concomly felt himself to Simpson, to George Simpson, there was still an ocean of distance between Chinook and British ways. That ocean widened one day when, exploring the north bank of the Columbia, the governor happened upon a dead body. It was lying in a marshy mud hole near the north bank. Birds of prey were feeding on it. It was the body of a Chinook slave, a boy. He had been shockingly mutilated—his fingers, nose, and ears cut off. Then he had been left in the mud to die. On his face was a terrified expression of lostness and despair, as of one who had already lived in hell many years. It was a nightmarish scene, and it deeply affected the governor.

Simpson's men chased off the birds of prey and buried the body. But the sight of such blatant cruelty and disdain for human life was like a knife through the crocodile skin of Simpson's heart. Few tragedies affected him—but this one shocked him. He almost shed a tear. He felt a little nauseated, in fact.

What sickened him most was the reluctantly dawning thought that Chinook society mirrored his own, that the passions that fired the breast of Concomly were the same ones that fired his own—brutality in the service of trade. Englishmen had gone to Africa and committed the same shocking horrors, against which good William Wilberforce now stirred Parliament, seeking to rid the entire British Commonwealth of the curse of the slave trade. The conviction that the Chinook and the English were twin peoples forced itself upon George Simpson, its very power causing him all the more resolutely to insist that they were not.

Crossing back to Fort George, the governor thought about what Archibald MacDonald had said about the early days of the post, how the white men with Chinook wives had insisted that their children grow up with unflattened foreheads. The wives, appalled at the thought, had tried to kill their own babies rather than let them grow up looking like slaves. Slaves were cattle. Non-humans. Unworthy of sympathy, dignity, or love. A slave was a commodity to be bartered, a chip put forward in a gambling game, merchandise that might easily change owners three times in a year. A slave only appeared to be a human being. But it wasn't really. Not at all. That was why all Chinook women flattened the heads of their babies, for an unflattened head was a boarding pass to a monstrous life, an existence of no value. It was the shape of your head that proved you were born to be slave or free.

Here was where the convenience of marital alliances broke down. The slave issue had driven a wedge between men and women—and discouraged also the wedding of Chinook and English peoples.

Chowie was Chinook. It was a whole forest of trees blown down across the path toward marriage for the sake of alliance—at least in the mind of George Simpson. Other traders and factors before him had adapted their thinking and attitudes, but Simpson could not. No, it was out of the question. Too many trees across this path. He just couldn't go there.

Yet no sooner had they returned to the fort than Lady Calpo showed up, offering the Princess Chowie once again. Chowie herself was not present, being in menstrual isolation, and that made for some frank bartering on Lady Calpo's part.

"You like her, yes? She love you, Governor George Simpson. I talk to her today. She want you. She make good wife. No man ever have her yet. She have no disease. She work like good wife. She carry big loads. You pay dowry. One hundred fifty skins. She not go for less."

The woman was staring at him earnestly. She was determined to have her way. For perhaps the first time in his life, Simpson felt his will giving way to a will that was actually stronger than his own. He could not endure her earnest gaze. He broke the visual connection, looking away. It felt like a victory for the other side.

A moment of silence followed, with the sound of the Union Jack beating nearby in the stiff breeze. They were surrounded by the log-built structures of the fort. The governor appeared to examine the flag, with its rope beating loud on the flagpole. In reality, he was just gathering strength for his next counterassault.

Presently, returning his gaze and looking Lady Calpo straight in the eye, he replied stolidly, "Princess Chowie is very beautiful. She will make a very fine wife for someone. But I will find a wife among my own people."

Lady Calpo kept talking—would she never quit? Simpson shifted his weight uncomfortably. The board of directors just needed to let him get married, that was all. Her voice was droning on, but he kept thinking private thoughts: If only they had let him get married when he had first requested it, then all this embarrassing, unseemly, and compromising chatter could have been avoided. Simpson had been willing to postpone marriage for the sake of trade, just to get this coveted job. But *marry* for the sake of trade? He was not willing to go that far. Never!

• • •

The ocean of distance between Simpson and the Chinooks widened yet again when John McLoughlin came to him before dinner in the dining hall. "Will you sit down, sir?" he said. "I have news from Kaht-samts."

Against the clatter of crockery coming from the kitchen, McLoughlin continued: "Two o' Concomly's sons died last week," the big man said in his throaty Scottish brogue. "Some sort o' plague swept through the villages. Only one son remains alive: that scoundrel Cassacas. And for each dead son, it is said, Concomly killed a slave to walk with 'em into the next wairld. Cassacas also killed the medicine man that failed to heal the twa bairns."

"Damn! These people and their slaves. It's an outrage!" Just then someone in the kitchen dropped an earthenware bowl, which shattered on the floor as if to punctuate Simpson's own punctuation.

McLoughlin continued. He was a contrast to Simpson in every way imaginable: slow, large, unflappable, seemingly under a cloud most of the time. And married to a Native, too. "I ha' already spoken to Concomly about it, sir. I told him that if he wanted to continue good trade relations with us, he must tell his people to stop killin' slaves."

"Well done!" Simpson exploded. "And what did he say in reply?"

"He said that the slaves were dangerously ill, by the same disease that took off his sons. They were almost dead anyway, and he did no' consider it a crime t' anticipate death by a few days or weeks."

"That weasel! He knew the right words to help him wiggle out of that one."

"I dinna ken that he did wiggle out o' it. I made it clear that we still consider it mairder, plain and simple. They are human beings, these slaves, and they should be treated accordingly."

"Well spoken! Couldn't have said it better myself! Colvile and Harrison will be eager to hear of these things. Rest assured, they know of the slavery these tribes practice. Damn, if Colvile isn't right about it. We can do some good here, and not just take furs. Doctor, I saw the most shocking sight yesterday: a slave boy, brutally maimed—fingers, nose, and ears cut off, then left to die in the mud. These things have got to stop."

"You have my word on it, sir."

Simpson nodded, satisfied, and the air between them grew quiet for a moment. "You know," he said, "there's something positively engrossing about this place. I feel as if I could spend the rest of my life on the Columbia. One could really do some good here, set his stamp, if you know what I mean."

"I've had the same feeling, sir," replied McLoughlin. "It's as though all my prior experience were a preparation for the present. Perhaps it's Providence, sir."

Five

By the early months of 1825, the Hudson's Bay men were ready to build the new fort on Jolie Prairie, seventy miles upriver. Timbers were cut for the factor's house, two storehouses, an Indian hall, and sheds for the men. As buildings were completed and covered with bark shingles, furniture and merchandise were transferred to the new location. The old post at the mouth of the Columbia was becoming an empty shell.

All this activity and desolation were observed by an anxious Concomly and received as the least welcome of news. The chief did not talk frequently with Simpson now. But he got much news from Lady Calpo, who was a newsmonger of the first order, both for the British and for the Chinooks. She plied the waters between Kaht-samts and Fort George with the regularity of a sentry marching back and forth at the gate of a city—for such was the mouth of the Columbia: a city, with the river a very broad Main Street.

Concomly sat at the fireside of his home next to his wife, Keasno. Steady rain beat upon the cedar roof. Through the circular door came their only remaining son, Cassacas. He was about thirty, a man with a dark look, the sort of man who is never satisfied unless he is inflicting cruelty. Concomly had placed his hopes on Selechel to succeed him, but now Selechel was dead.

"It is certain, then," Cassacas said, invading Concomly's troubled thoughts. "They are building a new fort just across from the village of Casseno. They are abandoning us, Father. It is as I have been telling you all along. The King George dogs are no better than the Bostons."

"There you are wrong, my son," replied Concomly. "They are not abandoning us. They are merely moving to a new place upriver."

"Hah! A new place right in the heart of Casseno's people! You are like the eagle who loses his prey to the vulture. And you do not even try to stop him. I say, let us surround the fort and cut off these traitors, or they will trade their guns, tobacco, and blankets to Casseno, and we will be cut out of the bargain."

Keasno spat into the fire that flared up from the hole in the floor. There was a sizzling noise.

"Father, why do you sit and do nothing? We must make them pay for their faithlessness. I say teach them a lesson. Surround the fort when half are away building the new fort. Then the other half can be easily taken. Cut them off and destroy them before they make Casseno great on the river. They must know who is the greatest chief. They must be taught to fear Concomly and to know that it is with Concomly they have to deal. Concomly arranges all bargains. Concomly governs all trade. Teach them this, my father." The young man was raising his voice.

Concomly, resigned to the hurts that come hidden in all friendships, rebuked Cassacas. "My son, it is not time for shedding blood. A plan such as yours would destroy friendship with the King George men, and with it, all trade! You like the quick way. You must have more patience." He let his one eye fix itself on the fire as his thoughts took form.

"Yes, it would seem easy to surround the fort, to place it under siege, to cut it off. You have tried it before. What did it get you? Lady Calpo herself warned the King George men of your treachery, and it all came to nothing. These flimsy plans of yours! They didn't work then, and they won't work now. Let your prowess be shown in more gainful ways. You, Cassacas, are to keep the Cowlitz, the Tillamooks, and the Humptulips from reaching the white man's fort with their furs. That is all the siege that is needed. We show the Cowlitz, Quinault, and Clatsop who is lord of trade here. They must know that only Concomly trades with the King George men, and all others must trade with us. That alone is worth killing for. But kill the King George men? It would be like taking all the fish from the river, so they will bite no more, or like taking all the beaver from the pond, so the pond will produce nothing. We must allure the King George men, not destroy them!"

There was a moment of silence.

Concomly continued, rising from the side of his wife. "The man Simpson wants to take a Chinook boy to be taught by their teachers. If we offer him your son, he will be obliged to continue in trade with us. Your son will be offered. He will help secure trade better than your violence will."

Cassacas took in this new idea in stunned silence. He stared at his father in disbelief. Sounds tried to come out of his throat. Finally, after what sounded like stammering, he managed to form the quiet, measured, white-hot words: "Give up *my son* to their teachers? Has it now come to this? What assurance do we have that he will not die among them? What assurance that the King George men will not all disappear up the river, like the Boston squaw McDougal?"

"Cassacas!" the one-eyed trader blurted. "You are now my only son. To you falls the right to be chief of The People. You must learn to take risks. You must learn that being chief requires much sacrifice. Have you learned nothing from the potlatch? He who would rise to the place of honor must give more than everyone, even from his own loins. He must sacrifice even his sons and daughters for the good of The People. It is the lot of a chief. Away with foolish plans. Cassacas must learn to master his hate. When he controls the flow of hate, he will then control trade on the river. The big sturgeon swims upriver, does he? We must put our hook in his jaw, so he takes us with him! Your son, like Calpo's daughter, is a hook for the jaw of the governor. This is a better way than killing the King George men."

Cassacas had no reply for his father. He left the lodge of Concomly in turmoil. He saw, for the first time, the degree of sacrifice necessary to remain the greatest trader on the river. He would have to offer his son as a sacrifice. Worse yet, he would have to pretend to enjoy giving his son away to be taught by the white men. Faugh!

· · ·

Lady Calpo had not given up on the original plan. She forced on George Simpson the company of the buxom Chowie, who used her grass skirt and fur capote to great advantage. She was voluptuous, round, young, and alive, possessing just the right combination of innocence and intrigue, exotic charm and womanly familiarity. Yet there was always the smell of fish oil about her, so very distressing to the discerning English gentleman.

Lady Calpo suggested one hundred beaver skins as an appropriate dowry. "Below that, no family of royal blood can go. It lower all high-born Chinook families to permit even such a dowry as this. One hundred beaver, and let us finally reach an agreement!" she beamed.

But Governor Simpson was a determined man, her equal in the complex art of trade.

The next day, Concomly and Cassacas appeared at the factor's house for a visit with George Simpson. They were wearing ponchos woven of rushes—a square mat with a hole cut in the middle and draped over the shoulders, the Chinook rainwear. Both also wore conical hats which extended wide over their shoulders. Only their arms were wet from having canoed across the river in the rain. With them was a frail nine-year-old boy who looked at the ground, always at the ground.

The governor invited them into his barren sitting room. Cassacas had made it a point of honor to learn none of the English language. He was forced to speak Chinook jargon, a language that consisted of some three hundred words borrowed from half a dozen languages, each word with a dozen shades of meaning.

"*Clar-how-ah-yah*," he began, while his father offered a British-sounding "Good day." Concomly had insisted, despite his greater familiarity with English, that his son do the talking. The governor must believe that Cassacas truly wanted his son to go with him across the mountains.

Simpson, who had learned Chinook jargon in the last three months, replied, "*Clar-how-ah-yah. Mika kumtux King George wawa?*"

Cassacas indicated that he did not speak English. Then he added, "*Papa wawa King George man by-by mamook teach Chinook tenas man delate wawa.*"

George Simpson picked up the gist of this: Concomly had told his son that Englishmen might teach a Chinook small man straight truth.

Cassacas added in Chinook jargon, "My son wants to go stay with the King George man who teaches. The King George man who teaches will teach my son."

Simpson looked at the boy for some trace or hint that he wished to go to the school at Red River Colony. The boy continued to stare at a spot on the floor two feet in front of Simpson's shoes. No expression. No desire.

"*Kloshe kopa nika*," replied Simpson to convey his pleasure at the offer. He was in a spot. He had a bad feeling about the whole proposal and was beginning to regret that he had mentioned the idea to Concomly. The boy looked frail, even sickly. He could not imagine such a boy traveling over the morass of evils that was the path to Red River Colony.

Cassacas continued, trying to smile, "Nika tenas he-he tumtum. Nika tenas delate hyas kloshe. King George man ticky nika tenas. My son has a jolly, good nature. My son is a perfectly good boy. Englishman like my son."

Simpson looked again at the boy. No expression. No desire. What does he see there, in front of my shoes? I must extricate my feet from his cold stare somehow.

Clearing his throat, Simpson concluded, "I must pray about it; I must make up my mind. I will come to Kaht-samts soon to tell my decision."

After sharing tea, the Chinooks left, leaving the governor to find a way to depart upriver without taking the little boy with him.

• • •

On the following week of February, George Simpson and John McLoughlin launched a canoe headed for Kaht-samts at its inland location. Keasno saw them coming and brought Concomly out to meet them. The chief invited them to sit by his fire, where Cassacas was already seated.

Simpson began, using the jargon. "I come to bring reply; I come to speak my heart."

"Good," replied Concomly. Cassacas looked nervous.

Simpson continued. "I would be happy to take your son to the Englishman who teaches religion. Do the two chiefs wish to send their son far, far away? I go very far away."

Concomly fished for words, trying to convince the governor how deeply they wished their boy to go far, far away. But McLoughlin interrupted. "Nesika mamook pepah copa King George man mamook teach. Nesika wawa: chahko yukwa copa Chinooks."

It was as though he had spoken magic words. Everyone immediately breathed more easily. John McLoughlin was proving to be a genius of diplomacy. Simpson thought, It is astonishing how he comes up with just the right words at the right time.

Cassacas smiled. Concomly smiled. All laughed together. They smoked, they joked. Finally, all departed.

Everyone was vastly relieved, for John McLoughlin had offered to bring the man who teaches religion to the mouth of the Columbia. By that diplomatic solution, Cassacas would not need to send his son away. Concomly would have the assurance of trade strategies yet to come. And Simpson would not have to explain the death of the frail boy en route to

Red River. McLoughlin was building a reputation as a diplomat superior even to William Clark.

As for Simpson's promise to David Jones, to bring him two Native boys from across the Height of Land, he had a persistent intuition that he should look for them from the tribes at the Columbia headwaters—and that his letter to Alex Ross would produce them.

Six

If Concomly had met Illim-spokanee, he would have thought of him not as a Child of the Sun and Moon, but as a mere child. He had no slaves, no hyaques, and no impressive cedar-plank house. The one-eyed chief would have thought, Illim-spokanee has profited little from trade with the whites. The Spokanes have much to learn—we who are wiser must lead them by the hand.

But the Spokanes had the remembrance of Circling Raven to lead them by the hand. They remembered the words of the prophet, and they longed to see where those words might lead them. It was righteousness, not trade, that had made Circling Raven great in their eyes.

At the same time that George Simpson was approaching Cassacas and Concomly, Alex Ross appeared at the village below the falls that stopped the salmon to open conversation with Illim-spokanee. The little Scot had brought with him from Flathead Post several Flathead and Kutenai chiefs. They sat on the ground around a pine-and-horse-dung fire in Illim-spokanee's lodge.

After the communal smoke, Ross began. "The white chief Simpson has written a letter." He waved it in the air as his interpreter talked. Then he continued. "In it he says he wishes to take two boys of the chiefs of your tribes to a school in the east, where they may be taught by the white men."

The translation of these words produced looks of indignation and much murmuring. After a time, the Kutenai chief, Le Grand Queue, gave reply. He was younger than Illim-spokanee. His face was painted entirely red. His words were translated by interpreters into both English and Salish:

"For many years, we have been told of the coming of the white people. But do the white people look upon us as dogs, that they think we should give up our children to go we know not where? Do the Long-hairs think we have no love for our sons, that we would give them up for such a journey?" The Lower Kutenais never crossed to the Great Plains on buffalo hunts as the Upper Kutenais did. They were content to hunt the deer and the salmon that the Old Man, the Creator, had provided for them on their own lands.

The others cried, "Oy, oy."

Alex Ross kept going. "But the teacher we have in mind is a minister of religion. He would teach your sons the secrets of our religion, that they may return and teach these things to you all. Besides, I go with my wife and children. I will take care o' your sons like my own. Surely, if the trail be not too hard for my little ones, it be not too hard for your sons."

After a thoughtful pause, Illim-spokanee spoke. "The Sin-ho-man-naish want the white man's teaching, as do our Salish brothers of the east and the San-ka of the north. Since the days of our fathers who sleep, it has been prophesied that white teachers would come from the rising sun. I have longed for this day, have dreamed of it, when my son will learn from leaves bound together. These things have been hidden from our eyes, but now we will have our eyes opened. You can lead us by the hand, share with us the white man's powers. How will we learn these things unless we take the risk? Does Quilent-satmen not watch over us? Did he not speak of these things long ago, which come to pass now?"

Turning to Ross and staring him in the eye, he added, "As for me, I give you my son, Slough-keetcha. He is the joy of my life. He is my youngest. He is in your care. Take him and let him go with you. I have spoken."

This speech produced a flurry of murmuring and debate. Finally, Le Grand Queue said to Alex Ross, "If the Long-hairs are ready to share their teaching about the Master of Life with our people, they might have any number of our sons. It is plain that the Long-hairs possess many valuable secrets, which we all want to hear of and learn. I, too, join Child of the Sun and Moon in giving my son, my youngest, to you."

Within a moment, a fearful prospect had been transformed into the opportunity of a lifetime. Other chiefs, not to miss out on a great honor, offered their sons. But Ross cut off the conversation there. "I have been authorized to take but two. Let me meet the laddies, and I'll be the judge whether they be fit for the journey or no. If you wish to give your son into my care, bring him to this place just one month from today, an' I'll choose the two lads most fit."

So ended the discussion.

Seven

Back at the mouth of the Columbia, on Wednesday, March 16, four canoes were readied for the final departure of Hudson's Bay men from Fort George. Only ten were to remain behind to occupy the fort, while John McLoughlin, Chief Factor of the Columbia Department, would reside in his new house at Jolie Prairie. In a few weeks, even those ten would be removed, abandoning the post to the mice and the woodpeckers.

A large number of Chinooks appeared for the send-off, despite the rain that fell throughout the day. Cassacas had threatened war, and rumors flew everywhere that he would attack the departing King George men. The Chinooks who had come to the fort were gloomy. Concomly was the gloomiest of all. All his dreams for the future of trade were disintegrating. Though he still had hope enough to keep his trade strategies alive, the departure of the British from Fort George still felt like abandonment. Showing as little emotion as possible, he shook the hands of the departing King George men. By his side, Chowie wore the appearance of failure.

At noon sharp, under leaden skies, the four canoes embarked. Simpson looked back at the crowds of Chinooks standing on the bank. Behind them loomed the buildings and the stockade, with a backdrop of fir, spruce, and cedar. The Chinooks stood disconsolately under their ponchos and conical hats. The governor waved good-bye, breathing a sigh of relief. Rapids, falls, rain, and wind would present the kind of relaxing challenge he was ready for, much easier than the complexities of tribal diplomacy. The wilderness of the earth was a safer, less complicated challenge than the wilderness of the human heart. As for the river, its treachery was well-known, and they had prepared for it.

At eleven o'clock Friday morning, the four canoes paddled into Jolie Prairie. The land here, by some miracle, had never been taken over by any Native village. Some said that there had been a plague here, and the place, once occupied, had been abandoned. The scene at *Skit-so-to-ho*, the Place of the Turtle, was one of untouched beauty and fertility, long sloping grasslands punctuated by clumps of fir, spruce, and big-leaf maple not yet budding. This land had already been decreed for the plow. The men walked the beaten path to the stockade at the top of the ridge a mile away.[28]

As they walked the path, the men cursed Simpson for his devilish decision to place the fort so far from the water. Simpson, who had sat idle in the canoe these last three days, scarcely noticed the extra steps.

The governor and the factor spent the night under bark roofs, receiving tribal delegations from up and down the Columbia and making last-minute plans for the new fort and the next year's brigades. But Simpson was in no mood to linger. The next day, he assembled all the people around the flagpole. As a bagpipe played "Rule, Britannia" over and over, Simpson directed the hoisting of the Union Jack. Then he swung a bottle of rum against the flagpole, loudly proclaiming, "In behalf of the Hon-

---

28. The original fort was located northeast of the present Fort Vancouver National Historic Site.

ourable Hudson's Bay Company, I hereby name this establishment 'Fort Vancouver.' God save King George the Fourth!"

The crowd cheered three hurrahs—and that was all. At 9 a.m., the governor was off, ready to drive his men back to Red River Colony as though he were a high-perched cab driver, and they, the horses.

• • •

The trip from Fort Vancouver to Okanogan Post took only eighteen days. As the party moved east of the Cascades, sterility and starvation hovered over the banks of the Columbia. The men dined solely on their provisions of salt pork and beef. No other food was to be had east of the Dalles.

Simpson and his men were continually approached by Natives begging for food. This was a barren land, and winter had taken a heavy toll on its people. Simpson called it "the most sterile tract country perhaps in North America." The only good thing about it was that it didn't rain so much here.

On the eighteenth day, the governor had his men waist-deep in the river, dragging the canoes through the rapids after dark. They finally arrived at Okanogan Post at 9 p.m. There, a Kutenai chief sought counsel with Simpson. His people had heard that the governor might arrange for a messenger from the Master of Life to come and teach them. Word to this effect had spread from tribe to tribe at Hudson's Bay posts during trade fairs. The Kutenais wanted a teacher on their lands, to teach them the mysteries of the white man's power and the divine being that had come from God. "Master of Life" was now the accepted term for him among the tribes.

Simpson promised to represent their wishes to the great white chiefs on the other side of the mountains.

A three-day horseback ride brought the governor to the Forks of the Spokane, where he had arranged to meet Alex Ross and the gigantic Finan McDonald from Spokane House. The boats continued slowly toward the same destination by river. By the time the boats arrived, Simpson had already established camp at the Forks, interviewed Ross and McDonald, and written letters hither and yon describing his plan to abandon Spokane House in favor of a new post at Kettle Falls.

In the afternoon, the governor arranged for the long-awaited interview with Alex Ross and the chiefs who wished to send their sons to Red River Colony. Eight chiefs had come with Ross down the road from Spokane House, bringing their families with them. These were camped in tents on the pine-covered grassland all around the English camp. The eight—the most important men of the Spokanes, Kutenais, and Flatheads—brought their sons with them to the meeting area in front of Simpson's tent, where Ross and Simpson were waiting. The chiefs were dressed in elaborately decorated buffalo robes; their sons in three-point blankets.

Spring birds were singing. The river laughed. The wind breathed peace through the pines all around. But the chiefs were unconscious of these things. Each was walking on the knife-edge of decision. Each struggled with a future thoroughly pregnant and about to give birth. But to what? They were bringing their sons to Governor Simpson. Two would be selected for a long journey into the unknown. Were they giving over their children to life or to death? To blessing or to curse?

The chiefs had always been gamblers. But in this gambling game, it would be impossible to know winner from loser. Yet the prophecies that had raged like a grass fire throughout the Columbia Plateau had pointed inexorably toward this day. These chiefs dared not let the moment pass without taking decisive action.

Simpson and Ross indicated that everyone should be seated on buffalo hides. They began by smoking a pipe around the circle. Both prudently waited for the chiefs to begin the conversation. The Kutenai Band Chief, Le Grand Queue, began. "My elder brothers: it is said that the Long-hairs wish to take our sons to their teachers, to teach them of the Master of Life. We have brought our sons. The traders have agreed to choose which shall be favored to go with them across the Backbone of the World. Choose now. We have long awaited this day. Our sons have agreed to go with you. We can see plainly: the white man knows many things which we long to hear. There is great medicine in the book of the Long-hairs. We wish to know its mysteries. Choose now from our sons, that they may return to us full of the white man's instructions, to teach us better ways. I am done."

Governor Simpson rose to speak. "We will choose two boys from among you. They will go with us to the teacher at Red River, who will teach them what the Master of Life has told the white men. They will return to you after several years."

"It is good!" grunted Illim-spokanee, and the others agreed with simple genuineness.

Simpson conferred with Ross, then spoke again. "We have chosen the sons of Le Grand Queue and Illim-spokanee." The two chiefs stared back stolidly, refusing the least sign of emotion. They looked into the eyes of Ross and Simpson without smiling, then clasped hands in a gesture of trust. Was it Ross and Simpson they trusted—or the Creator himself?

There was little else to be said. Words were cheap when spoken lightly, and none were wasted on assurances impossible to guarantee. The decision had been made. Now each of the eight adjusted his thinking to new realities. Six chiefs would have their favorite sons still with them. Two would not.

Eight

At last, the day of departure arrived: Tuesday, April 12, 1825. All was confusion at the mouth of the Spokane. Dogs and horses were everywhere. Voyageurs in red stocking caps ran to and fro, making canoes ready for the journey north and saddling horses for Spokane House. To add to the confusion, storms were blowing in from the northwest, bringing heavy hail, but nothing was permitted to hinder the departure of George Simpson. The work of organizing the district was complete, and the governor was still master of the wilderness. He never allowed weather to alter his travel plans.

About noon, as preparations were completed, two families approached the canoes during a break in the showers. Le Grand Queue and Illim-spokanee were ready to send off their sons. Dozens of people—mothers, brothers, sisters, aunts, and uncles, as well as favorite dogs and horses—were there to give their good-byes.

Slough-keetcha, son of Illim-spokanee, hugged his family one by one, then led the way to the water's edge. He was short and stocky for a fourteen-year-old. His smiling eyes and grim mouth reflected anxiety and grief painted over with courage. The last to bid good-bye was his favorite uncle, Chongulloosoon.

As the crowd neared George Simpson at the canoes, Le Grand Queue addressed the governor. He spoke loudly and firmly: "You see, we have given you our children, not our servants, but our own sons. We have given you our hearts—our children are our hearts—but bring them back again before they become white men. We wish to see them once more San-ka, and after that you can make them white men if you like. But let them not get sick or die. If they get sick, we get sick. If they die, we die. Take them. They are yours."

At that moment, there broke forth the most anguished shrieks of mourning that the governor had ever heard. They came from the women who surrounded the two boys. The noise frightened the horses, set the dogs to howling, and thoroughly unnerved the governor. Was it true, then, that these people considered their boys as dead?

Le Grand Queue uttered a command, and with the sign of silence, ordered the women to be quiet. Instantly, all was quiet except the belated howling of dogs, who soon sensed that they too were out of order.

This intrusion of emotion into the businesslike departure gave the governor an idea. He felt the need to provide reassurance to the families of the boys—and to himself. He quickly reached for a Book of Common Prayer from a pack destined for Spokane House. Snatching it up, he read the baptismal service, then reached down into the water and baptized the two boys.

Choosing the names of two prominent Hudson's Bay leaders, he renamed the boys as he baptized them. To Slough-keetcha, son of Illim-spokanee, he gave a new name, combining the tribal name with the name of Nicholas Garry, a Company dignitary who had helped establish the school. "I christen thee Spokan Garry," he said, and then he sprinkled water over the boy's head. As he baptized the son of Le Grand Queue, he said, "I christen you Kootenai Pelly," after Robert Pelly. Turning to the families, he concluded, "These two boys are now under the protection of God, whose ways they are going to learn."

For Simpson, who knew nothing of the Anglican Church and whose grasp of Christianity was tenuous at best, baptism was simply an excuse for giving people "Christian"—that is, English—names. He believed that the Natives would be dazzled by ritual, the way Anglicans dazzled people in the great cathedrals of England. "If they can do it, I can do it," he said to himself. His use of the ritual would have been vigorously resisted if John West had been there, but Simpson's thoughts continued: "Thank God, that pest West is not here, and I can do as I wish."

As to the parents of Slough-keetcha, the giving of names had always been a two-way street between whites and Natives. New names were freely given and freely received. But the baptismal ceremony healed no grief and calmed no fears. The families of the boys simply walked away without comment, not wishing to prolong a painful separation.

Slough-keetcha himself looked to his father to judge whether he should accept the new name. A look of acceptance communicated that he should treat the *chipixa* as agents of Quilent-satmen who bore his father's approval. Slough-keetcha nodded. He would trust his father.

This slender, elastic thread of trust between the boy and his father would stretch out across a thousand miles without snapping. It was a resilient thread, and by hanging on to it, Slough-keetcha not only accepted his new name, but accepted too the commands, teachings, warnings, corrections, and encouragements of these white men. He considered them his new family, by decree of Quilent-satmen, for good or for ill.

As for Ross and Simpson, they had only a dim awareness of their heavy responsibility for the children. They were caught up in their own dreams and ambitions. They casually led the boys to the canoe, entered it, and embarked on the most obnoxious and dangerous forest "road" known to the Hudson's Bay Company.

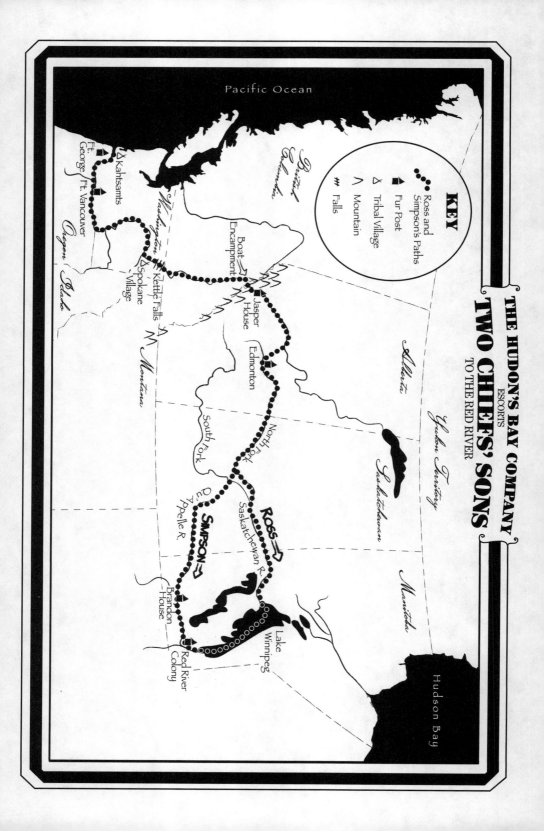

Part IV:
The Great Inundation
1825–1826

Had a long interview with the principal Chief of Thompson's River who came hither purposely to see me; he is the most respectable manly looking Indian I ever saw, appeared much pleased with what I said to him and promised faithfully to back and support us with all his power; I made him a present of a Medal bearing the C^oy arms which he seemed to prize greatly and gave him a few other triffles. We parted excellent Friends and this interview I think will go far towards the safety of the Establishment and future good conduct of the Indians; he enquired particularly if they might soon expect a "Messenger from the Master of Life" on their Lands (Meaning a Missionary because they had heard in the course of the Winter that I considered such probable) but I could merely tell him that I should represent to the "Great Chiefs on the other side of the Water" that such was their wish.

—George Simpson's Journal, Monday, April 4

This morning I went to the Company's Fort and had much interesting conversation with Mr. Ross, a Gentleman just come to the settlement from the Columbia, on the North West Coast, after a residence there of upwards of Fourteen years . . . He said that . . . their enquiries after knowledge of the "Master of life" are astonishingly earnest.

—Journal of David Jones, July 3, 1825

The glass windows were driven out by the current, the seats were shattered and mostly carried away, the pulpit swept from the foundation, the doors battered down, and all the plastering washed off, in short, the desolation was complete. But I could not help thinking this might be intended as a useful lesson to me, to teach me not to suffer my mind to wander from the main object of my ministry by any external circumstances.

—Journal of David Jones, Thursday, May 25, 1826

---

29. Merk, *Fur Trade and Empire*, 132.

One

At 3:30 a.m. on Wednesday, April 13, 1825, the cry went up in George Simpson's camp: "*Levez, levez, levez!*" Twenty-one hairy fur men opened bloodshot eyes to the predawn air.

Alex Ross jumped up at the call and awakened his family, Spokan Garry, and Kootenai Pelly. The party had managed to paddle only a few miles up from the Forks of the Spokane the night before. Alex felt a lingering responsibility to help the two Native boys adjust to the routine of travel, and he included them with his group.

By four o'clock, they were ready to embark. Governor Simpson was perched upon his pillow in the lead canoe. Ross and the boys followed in the consort canoe.

It being dark, the voyageurs sang to keep their spirits up. The foremen of the two canoes kept up a lively competition of skill and speed, all of which warmed the governor's heart. To see his men striving together to please him, all the while enjoying the spirit of *bon vivant*—it was half the joy of travel.

The Forgotten Awakening

The boys, Garry and Pelly, who were learning to recognize their new names, were eager to know what their fortunes would be at a place called Red River. They sat together, but not knowing each other's language, were unable to talk to each other except in sign language. The canoe was carrying them off into the wild unknown, as it was also carrying the Okanogan woman Sarah Ross—carrying them all into conceptions of life they could not imagine: carrying them into challenges and hardships that could end their lives prematurely, or propelling them to fame and fortune in the white man's world. Sarah, Garry, and Pelly felt as though everything solid had been jerked out from under them, and all that lay beneath them was running water. They could not give assurance to each other, for none spoke the language of any of the others. And so they sat in silence, neither smiling nor frowning, but just wondering.

In her years of marriage, Sarah had learned the language of love to supplement her Okanogan. There were times she would secret away little bundles of pemmican to give to the boys in her retinue, more to establish a connection with them than to assuage hunger. They needed one another's courage. For the three, this journey would give them their first experience of the monstrous mountains legendary among their people—mountains to be breached only by the hardiest warriors.

At eight o'clock, the canoes beached for breakfast on a *batteur*, a river of water-laid sand that intertwined with the river of water. Horse meat, beans, and grease were the substance of every meal. Breakfast was a major stop which included a campfire and an opportunity to shave and scrub. After breakfast, they paddled another five hours before stopping for lunch at two, the only other meal of the day.

That night they camped early, at 7 p.m. The men were complaining of pain due to venereal disease—"Chinook love fever," Simpson called it, though it had been introduced by whites, not Chinooks. Already, seven men had been drummed out of the brigade because of it. Now it threatened to slow them down, being the chief complaint of five more men. Alex Ross applied what medication he could, while Simpson chafed against the low moral standards which were interfering with his travel speed.

On Thursday, the governor took time to line out the site of the new Kettle Falls Post. Named for the kettle-like holes the water had formed in the rocks, Kettle Falls was a major Spokane fishing hole and marketplace. The Spokane House business would be moved here, to the banks of the Columbia waterway. Trade would be more convenient here than at the old Sin-ho-man-naish village. (Convenient, that is, for the English.) Simpson surveyed the area, drew up the plans, laid the foundations, and had the place built in his head—all the work of an hour. A few Spokanes showed up and expressed hope that the removal of the post from their village would not affect their friendship with the white people. The days were vanishing when white traders located their posts adjacent to Native villages to build friendships with Native people, but Simpson couldn't appreciate the trend. He was more concerned about the economics of trade, the convenience of the traders, and the speed of travel. As the failed attempts of the Chinooks could attest, George Simpson was not one to build friendships.

They traveled on. As the days passed, the mornings became frostier and the panoramas more majestic. Scrub pine and juniper gave way to massive forests of virgin timber. The Shining Mountains emerged, snowy peaks glowing pink in the sunset.

After eight days of frosty mornings and glorious afternoons, they reached Boat Encampment[30] at the west end of the long portage across Athabasca Pass. From here, a single thread of commerce stretched to the breaking point across the Rocky Mountains. Messages tried to move back and forth along this thread in an oft-futile attempt to keep the Hudson's Bay empire together, but now the lines were buried in snow.

Boat Encampment was a majestic spot. Just north of a small island, the Columbia divided itself into tributaries. A broad alluvial plain provided ample space for camp—and for an arboretum of huge cedars, mammoths of the forest. Here was the terminus for the Hudson's Bay postal line. Letters were waiting for Governor Simpson, including one

---

30. Boat Encampment was located at the bend of the Columbia, about fifty miles southwest of Jasper, to the west of present-day Jasper Park.

from Chief Trader Laroque, stationed on the other side of the pass. He regretted to inform the governor that there was no food to be sent for their sustenance and no possibility of getting horses through. The letter brought news of one disaster after another throughout the HBC realm, and lacked even a single scrap of useful information or good cheer for a governor to hang a smile on. The letter put Simpson in a foul mood, and the men quickly learned to steer clear of him.

From here on, none of the tributaries could quite decide where their banks ought to be. The trail led east through ice water and mud full of last year's cattails. All voyageurs loaded themselves with two eighty-pound packs. One was worn on their backs, the other in front. These they would carry through a long, frozen swamp, up a precipitous mountain slope, across a pass of eternal snow, and on to the other terminus at the head-waters of the Athabasca River. For this trip there was to be neither fresh food nor horses.

"We shall have to make use of our legs; no joke," Simpson wrote in his diary.

At 2 p.m., after hiding their canoes on the island, they set out through swampland. Garry and Pelly carried parflêches strapped to their backs. Made by their mothers, these colorful rawhide boxes, filled with food and personal belongings, were their only reminder of the homes they had left behind.

There was no comforting love here. The boys sank up to their knees in mud, then waded to their thighs in freezing water to wash away the mud. The afternoon sun quickly receded behind the hemlocks to the southwest, and there was no escape from the nerve-numbing cold. Six miles they sloshed, never once stopping. There was no place to camp. At last they reached a second *batteur*, where they stopped for the night. Fires warmed their numb bodies into sensibility, and sleep allured them out of it again. Sarah could not minister comfort to Garry and Pelly because she had her own younger children to tend to, and they were crying much of the time.

On Saturday, the governor added a dram of whiskey to the normal starting routine. The *batteur* on which they had camped stretched eighteen miles to the east. The difficulty was that the stream shifted from side to side of the *batteur*, requiring them to ford it dozens of times. The early morning sun was too faint to thaw out clothing, which got wetter and icier with each crossing.

After four miles, Simpson was surprised by an outcry from behind: "*Monsieur le partisan*, it is the Iroquois. They are drunk and flat on their *derrières*. They not come with us." Here were those freemen again, mostly debauched Iroquois from the east who had taken from the white man everything bad and nothing good.

Fuming, Simpson ordered a breakfast stop, then stalked back to bring up the rear. Another of his crew met him with more information: "M'sieu Isaac, heem break into the keg of whiskey with his friends. Heem get mad about this march. Heem throw down his two packs into the *rivière*. They went downstream, *perdus*."

"What! He threw his provisions into the river?" Simpson was boiling under a frozen exterior. "That imbecile! As if our rations weren't scarce enough already!"

Realizing the potential for serious mutiny, Simpson marched the seven miles back to the beginning of the *batteur*, where Chief Trader McMillan was scolding the Iroquois—and they scolding him in return!

The governor picked up a hefty stick, strode up, and began to beat Isaac, lacerating his flesh and producing welts. "You will trap no more, you vomitous dog," he shouted. "I have threatened to confine you to the transport crews for life, and now it is done. I will teach you what price you pay for your imbecility. You have thrown your food away? I should let you starve, but I'd rather whip you. It gives me more pleasure."

Isaac cowered and dove into a snowbank to get away. Simpson stepped over to the keg, now half-empty, split it with a hatchet, and threw it into the river. So much for the curse of alcohol west of the mountains!

Shouts and moans filled the air, mingled with many oaths. Simpson ignored it all and stalked indignantly the seven miles back to a very late breakfast. Then he led the men another fifteen miles, crossing the icy water dozens of times. They camped at sunset. The tardy Iroquois freemen straggled in all night long after stumbling their way through the darkness.

. . .

By morning, ice was forming on the edges of the river. The men had to break through it a dozen times before breakfast. After nine more miles of sand, they reached the start of the Woods of the Big Hill, the seemingly endless slope that would take them to the pass.

Pelly, Garry, and several of the men were so numb from walking that they couldn't stand up. Being short, the boys had immersed more of their bodies in the ice water than anyone else. Alex Ross would have picked them up and carried them, but he had a heavy pack of his own, and he had to be concerned for Sarah, young Alex, and little Margaret. Simpson did not stop to build warming fires, because it wasn't breakfast time yet. Nothing, no, nothing could convince the governor to break his travel routine. Ross stayed back with Sarah to give his little family a chance to pick ice from their skin and rub their legs and feet to get their circulation flowing.

Kootenai Pelly was becoming more and more distressed at the punishment of the trail. His was a more sensitive nature than Spokan Garry's. He was close to tears; no words of comfort could help him. In all his imaginings at age fourteen, he had never dreamed of anything as hard as this. From his boyish point of view, the snowy hill before them was a challenge beyond endurance. It stretched up beyond the tops of the trees and into the clouds, an impossible pathway into the heavens. So this was the Backbone of the World.

All the others in the party seemed perfectly able to ascend it. The Canadians actually relished the walk, bragging of their abilities, competing for the heavy packs. At last, only the family of six remained at the *batteur*. Pelly wished he could go back, but that was out of the question. There was nothing for it but to plod on bravely. Alex Ross was not much at giving comfort. They forged on in silence, six together at the end of the line, each moving separately in his own private world of misery.

Things got worse. The Backbone of the World had to be climbed. This was not just a hill, but a true mountain, higher than any the boys had ever seen. Here, among thick trees at the foot of the mountain, the soft snow was a foot and a half deep. But each step upward plunged their moccasined feet a little deeper. There was only this consolation: others had packed the snow before them. Yet, even where the trail was packed, there were icicles that had fallen from the trees into the snow. These poked up into their feet like needles in a bed of cotton. The exertion of climbing caused them to perspire heavily. The perspiration froze, becoming a coat of ice over their skin and on their clothing. The ice would break around their knees and ankles as they walked, and the pieces fell down into their moccasins.

For a fourteen-year-old, this was too much. Kootenai Pelly began quietly to weep, his tears dripping out through eyes and nose. He clung to his medicine pouch, the only power that could help him survive this desperate crisis. Violent homesickness attacked him, along with the cold. He thought of the comforts of lodge and fire, of his father, Le Grand Queue. He dreamed of the warmth of the sweat bath; the hissing of the water as it hit the hot rocks; the closed-in protection of the igloo-like walls that held the hot steam so that your skin cried out for cool air.

But in this place there was only coldness, aloneness, violent struggle, a hill without an end. He wept more loudly, grieving the total loss of all things that had ever been dear to him, mourning a new life that seemed unbearably hard. His voice became a siren at the end of the marching line, announcing that something was wrong.

Yet the others were preoccupied with their own misery, and no one knew a word of Kutenai anyway. The straps of the boys' parflêches bit into their shoulders. Their feet were unbelievably cold. Yet the ice pinpricks reached past their benumbed nerve endings to find a place where pain might yet be inflicted, and the snow was approaching two feet deep.

The Forgotten Awakening

At 8 a.m., they reached a flat space well below the tree line. Here they stopped and ate breakfast. Kootenai Pelly and Spokan Garry brought up the rear. Pelly could not stop crying. The day before, he would have been completely chagrined to cry so openly in front of these men. But now his heart was so full of grief that there was no space left for pride.

The grownups turned a deaf ear to the sniveling boy. Such sounds had often been heard during brigades. Only Alex and Sarah Ross appreciated that Pelly had neither mother nor father to console him. The others saw his weeping as an irritation to be patiently ignored. No one considered it his duty to comfort him. Comforting was a lost art in this crowd.

Before the boys had had a chance to warm themselves by a fire or shave the ice off their legs, George Simpson was already off to conquer the Grand Côte, the Big Hill, to the pass. Simpson wore no pack, but had cedar shingles strapped to his moccasined feet. He was enjoying his role as forger of trails and was too busy to be concerned for the boys. The boys were Ross's concern. But Ross didn't know what to do for them. Spokan Garry kept his feelings to himself—though his courage was being tested to the limit. Pelly, a more sensitive lad, grieved every time he exhaled.

They reached the tree line, where the snow was seven feet deep. Here, Alex stopped his family to let the boys have a rest. They looked above them. The climb became much steeper here, then disappeared into clouds of blowing snow. A line of burden-bearing walkers stretched upward into the distant heights, switching back and forth up the hill. Each man appeared a little whiter than the one behind him, until the sight of them was no more. George Simpson had disappeared above them all.

The boys were at the edge of the forest. To the west, it stretched dark and unending, while the slope glared brilliantly white to the east, equally without end. It was painful to keep their eyes open in such a glare.

Just as the Rosses prepared to move on, a small bird, a phoebe, flew to a tree limb and began to sing its song—the first note high, the second a little lower, as if it were calling a name: "Phoe-bee, Phoe-bee." As it did, it jerked its tail down and down repeatedly as though trying to get the boys' attention.

The bird was unknown to either boy. Though its coat was an unpretentious gray, the piccolo-like call appealed to them as if it were addressing Pelly, wanting him to stop crying. The boys knew that animals do communicate to people, and they were attentive. Garry looked at the bird, then put his arm around Pelly and pointed to it.

"Look!" he said in Spokane. "She cries, 'Pell-ee, Pell-ee.'" His sing-song voice imitated the bird, and Pelly understood him immediately. His sadness melted. Was the bird a guardian spirit, sent to melt his grief?

"Pell-ee, Pell-ee," repeated the Kutenai, imitating the bird. He was smiling now, through his tears. In an instant, he had gained two friends: a bird and a boy. And the bird had given legitimacy to his new name.

His trials were bearable now, and he found new strength as he looked up into the brilliant snow. As for Garry, he determined to stay close to Pelly no matter what, for he needed a friend too. Love strengthened the receiver and the giver alike.

That bond of love was enjoyed by none of the other hikers, with the exception of the Ross family. The men were bound together by the rough rawhide straps of voyageur competition. Pelly and Garry were the only ones weak enough to admit that they needed love. Its cords bound them into a secret society whose mascot was a little gray bird. Hand in hand, the two boys continued on until the narrowness of the trail forced them back into single file.

After twelve straight hours of climbing, Simpson halted at the top of the slope. The men spread their tents on the snow and dropped on top of them, exhausted. That night, they didn't even bother crawling inside. There was neither wood for fires nor bare, soft ground in which to pound tent pegs.

The evening was clear and cold. Northern lights shimmered curtain-like in the darkness. Despite exhaustion, most of the men lay awake, too cold and miserable for sleep. The night was a battle against the cold trying to invade their pores to kill them. Pelly and Garry slept together under both their blankets, their bodies keeping each other warm. Sometimes human closeness is a matter of survival.

Two

The warm cocoon was shattered Monday at 3:30 a.m.: "*Levez, levez, levez!*" Every eye was grudgingly opened.

The sky was clear. The wind, deciding she could not turn these men away, had gone somewhere else. A full moon gave a ghostly pallor to the huge peaks and glaciers all around.

Packing up again, they trudged through deep snow, the leaders packing it down for the followers. Muscles already sore from the previous day rebelled against the high stepping required again. Garry and Pelly, still bringing up the rear, filed through drifts that were over their heads. At the first gleam of sun on the mountains, a roar of thunder was heard. But no, it was an avalanche that rushed down a mountain slope above them, but at a distance. Clouds of snow masked the dreadful force of crushing violence beneath.

This avalanche was a safe distance away, yet it created imaginings of disaster in everyone's mind. The men kept looking up the slopes, hoping to warn one another in time to escape death.

At 6 a.m., they arrived at the Committee's Punchbowl. Simpson allowed the men to drink a toast to the governor and committee in London, then he drove them onward.

At nine, they arrived at Camp Fusil, where they put up for breakfast. They were in scrawny forest now, most of the trees less than a foot thick at the base. Many had been chopped off six, ten, or twelve feet above snow level. Logs lay on the ground under the snow, the disintegrated platforms of bygone campfires. The men warmed themselves with a fire built on top of a new log platform laid over the snow. They had the best-tasting breakfast any of them could remember, though it consisted only of pemmican made months before from dried buffalo flesh and crushed rose hips.

The men swapped stories about giants that once came through the pass, chopping the trees high and using the trunks for kindling. It was just as well that neither Pelly nor Garry could understand English. Neither would have known that the trees had really been chopped down by other travelers when the snow level was even higher. Simpson sent two men ahead without packs, following the blazes on the trees, to get canoes patched and gummed at Rocky Mountain House.

At noon, the rest of the band continued on their way, having cut walking sticks to help support their lame and tired legs. Avalanches thundered all around them as the heat of the sun loosened the hold of snow on rock. It was an awesome scene, as though the mountains were grumbling at the intruders. But the men had already become less wary of these mountains that always cried wolf.

They followed the river flowing east from the Punchbowl until they arrived at the Grand Batteur, a huge stretch of river-laid sand. Here, at 6 p.m., they camped after wading waist-deep through ice water. Evening fires were used more for drying clothes than for roasting meat. Cold was a beast that confronted them in camp, whereas hunger was a wolf hovering at the edge of camp, more easily ignored.

. . .

At 3 a.m. Tuesday, the cry went up again: "*Levez, levez, levez.*" This time, eyes refused to open. Complaining muscles rebelled against the strain of more high stepping, more carrying. The packs had become somewhat lighter. Why, then, did they feel three times heavier? Feet were bruised and bloody, moccasins shredded and caked with ice, backs bruised from eighty-pound packs chafing against them. The men sounded and felt like mules. They groaned and complained and told each other of the avalanche that was sure to end their miserable existence in a moment, all of them together as one.

They stumbled in the dark, down a stream bed blocked with *bordineaux*, large ice jams standing vertically. At times, they traversed ice from which the river had receded underneath, leaving a fragile but heavy ice ceiling ready to cave in under their weight. These dangerous booby traps were indistinguishable from the more solid river ice. Everyone now carried a walking stick. With it they tapped their way, testing the sound of the stick on the ice.

At other places, they were forced to wade through water too rapid to form ice. They did so together, lining up and joining hands as they waded through so that none of them would be washed away.

Farther on, the streams were a tangled mass of ice tossed every which way. Soft snow made sculptures of the *bordineaux*, and the men often had the impression that white goblins were rising out of the earth to attack them.

At ten o'clock, the lead scout, attaining a crest on the path, spotted horses coming toward them from Chief Trader Laroque. The whole group joined him on the crest, raised a big cheer with what breath they could muster, let their packs drop to the ground, and sat down on them. A century before, horses had been introduced to North America. Every single member of the group thanked God, his lucky stars, fate, or whatever else he could think of to thank for the presence of horses. A trapper's best friend.

With the horses came a letter from the irrepressible Laroque. He reported that Norway House, a main Hudson's Bay depot, had burned completely to the ground. This crushing news gave Simpson an even greater sense of urgency to get back to Lake Winnipeg to direct Company affairs. Now, for certain, they could not afford to take an extended break.

• • •

By 6 a.m. Wednesday, all arrived at Rocky Mountain House, a cabin on a hillside surrounded at a distance by coniferous trees. All winter long, Rocky Mountain House had been accumulating letters. The postal funnel was plugged at the "impassable" pass—which Simpson had just somehow passed! From a large bundle of letters, the governor learned that the directors in London were pleased with his leadership. The news encouraged him in the exercise of his authority. In fact, he was so encouraged that he decided to use his authority to close Rocky Mountain House! He commented in his diary:

> One good consequence will arise from this change which is, that it will effectually put a stop to the practice of Gentlemen transporting their Families and heavy luggage across the Mountains. The Company require no transport. It is therefore quite unnecessary to keep a band of Horses, Horsekeeps and Hunters, as Single Gentlemen can or ought to be able to Walk. My wardrobe does not exceed 20 or 30 lbs., which my Servant can carry on his back and I do not see why theirs should be more weighty . . . Instead of Gentlemen consuming 10 Days or a Fortnight in the Mountains, studying their own comfort and that of their families, 5 Days are quite sufficient even on foot. I have done it in that time and at an earlier and more unfavorable Season than it was ever undertaken. Furthermore, I am ready to do it again. Our Chief Factors & Chief Traders ought to learn to do as I do, or, if incapable through Age or infirmity of doing their duty and meeting the

hardships & privations to which the Service exposes them, they ought in my opinion to withdraw and enjoy themselves on their retired Shares.[31]

Chief Trader Laroque soon learned the price of taking his ease. Because of his failure to get horses over the pass to the governor, the governor had learned that the trip could be made not only without horses, but without M'sieu Laroque! Perhaps M'sieu Laroque would learn in future to sweeten his letters with a little good news to assuage the hardships of others. Let M'sieu prepare himself to spend the rest of his days at the Red River Colony, built expressly to house HBC retirees.

Governor Simpson remained at Rocky Mountain House but six hours. By noon, he was ready for water travel again.

The boys had had time to thaw out and regain their circulation. Simpson, whose blood circulated more furiously than other men's, had never acknowledged any numbness in his limbs.

Another day's travel brought them to Jasper House, a lonely cabin and two outbuildings huddled together in a majestic river valley surrounded by tall peaks. A peak on the way to Jasper House was a majestic, pure white monolith that rose up out of the flat riverbed like some bleached bone jutting out from the skin of the earth—just like a vertebra. It really is the backbone of the world! Garry thought. Two days later, the party switched to horseback again and descended to the tiny outpost of Edmonton. The country was teeming with caribou, an animal new to the boys from west of the Great Divide.

At Edmonton, Simpson reminded himself how desperately he was needed to straighten the affairs of Norway House and of Red River Colony, which had suffered a crop failure. He decided not to delay here. And yet he could see that Garry and Pelly were exhausted from their travels. Whether from sympathy or to prevent them from slowing him down, he decided to leave the boys at Edmonton in the care of Alex Ross. They could join the flotilla of boats scheduled to depart ten days

---

31. Frederick Merk, *Fur Trade and Empire: George Simpson's Journal, 1824-25*, 147–148.

later while Simpson forged ahead. Pelly and Garry had time, at last, to catch their breath.

From their vantage point at Edmonton, the journey appeared as great a feat to the boys as any the bravest warriors of their people had ever accomplished. The trek had required of them every ounce of strength they possessed, had put iron in their souls, had forged a chain of trust between them.

It was well that they had learned these lessons now. These links of iron—the suffering, the challenge, the sense of accomplishment that had come to them through the *chipixa*—were the hardware with which the Master of Life was building a linkage with the white people. Life with the Long-hairs may have seemed foreboding, but there were brave deeds to be fought for and won. Crossing the backbone of the world was a great coup.

Some day we will tell The People of these things, they reminded themselves. They imagined themselves in the close protection of some sweat lodge, surrounded by friends and family, narrating their adventures. The greatest chiefs would listen to every word!

Here on the east side of the Backbone of the World, two young boys knew they had been appointed to a unique destiny in the history of their nations, a place of extraordinary challenge. And in the mild climate of Edmonton, they were beginning to warm up to it.

Three

At the Red River Colony, David Jones had emerged from a second abominably cold winter. Nothing could have prepared him for the extremes of temperature that blighted this lonely, hostile place.

The summer heat had seemed to fry his brain, destroying his power of thought. But now the temperatures were destroying, not the power to develop the sermon, but the voice to deliver it. Temperatures hovered as low as -40 degrees for days on end. He had to wear three greatcoats while preaching, yet his teeth still chattered. At church, there was a warm spot of twenty square feet around the woodstove. Here the schoolboys hovered—and became uncomfortably warm. Everyone else froze.

David's parsonage was so poorly constructed that wind came in through chinks between the logs and boards. His throat oozed phlegm. He was always spitting. Sometimes, after a coughing fit, he spat blood. Doctor Hamlyn diagnosed pleurisy and asthma.

Mosquitoes had been a plague early the previous summer. Now, as spring rolled out again, they were breeding in the melting snow. Nine months before, a kind woman had given David some netting for his bed. That was a mercy. But gray clouds of soprano buzzings would hover around him as he rode the ten miles north to his new church at Image Plain. At times, his face and hands were a mass of puffy welts.

The problem had been aggravated by the founding of the new church. The church at Image Plain was a landmark—to his ministry and to the landscape. He took pride in it. But with two congregations to serve, he was constantly traveling through mosquito-infested swamps, along wilderness paths and rutted cart-roads.

On this day, May 28, he was riding south from Image Plain to Fort Garry to dine with Governor Robert Pelly, his only friend, and with Donald MacKenzie, the factor, a man to avoid at all costs. The landscape was flat, the soil black, the air empty of wind and full of mosquitoes. As he rode along, he could not rid himself of dark thoughts. Rejection, despair, loneliness, a brooding sense of inferiority, the hopeless longing for simple love and goodness—all crowded into his mind at once, bringing with them cruel memories of frustrated hopes and homesickness.

During the previous year, David had asked a carpenter to make the doors for his church at Image Plain. But the craftsman, a Catholic, had never completed the work. Months later, David found out that Bishop Provencher had threatened to excommunicate the man if he helped the "infidel" build his "infidel church."

In January, the bishop had written to David to complain of a shortage of writing slates at his school. David had sent a package of six as a gesture of friendship. The bishop had sent a letter back in response—written in Latin! What a way of communicating: "We don't speak the same language, and that's just fine by me."

David continued to feel nothing but coldness coming from the east bank of the river where the Catholic church was located. Why, he asked himself, cannot the Catholics be receptive to a scrap of human fellowship, or to mere common respect and decency among pastors? This place needs a witness of Christian unity. We are not in the old country anymore. Out here in the wilderness, Christians must stick together. The Indians need to see our love for one another. What good is it if we just bring religious wars to the new country, to add to the wars that are already here?

David wrote in his journal of his loneliness: "I cannot be supported by any worldly hopes, prospects and acquisitions—Nothing but the experience of the freedom of body and mind indissolubly connected with the service of God can dispel the gloom which is so apt to collect around the insulated missionary."[32]

As for Donald MacKenzie and the upper crust of Fort Garry, their coldness had added a social dimension to the subzero winters of the colony. Already, the colony had developed a reputation as a closed society, very successful at making outsiders feel excluded. Fort Garry was the last place David Jones would choose to go for a good time, but Pelly had asked him to dinner, and he couldn't refuse his one friend.

David thought continually of his wife and parents in Wales—though such thoughts made him desperately homesick. He longed for a fellow missionary and had even requested one from the Church Missionary Society, but he had never heard back from them. They have no idea what it's like out here, he complained bitterly to God during his quiet times.

It wasn't just the cold and mosquitoes that tortured him. The ungodliness here was so thick you could cut it with a knife. He was standing against a tide, a Red River of sin. He felt like a lonely cattail trying to keep its roots in the teachings of Jesus while holding his place in the midst of a stream of violence and wickedness. He wondered about John West, his predecessor. Maybe he had discovered that the only way a Christian could survive out here was to rail against ungodliness. And yet—was that truly the best way? Carping and railing against sin did not seem to fit the spirit of Christ. And it hadn't born much fruit for West.

During the winter, starvation had struck the plains. The Assiniboins had decided to harass the colony by driving all the buffalo away. The Red River Colony, and Pembina to the south, were the pemmican capitals of

---

32. The Journal of David Jones, June 23, 1824.

the Hudson's Bay empire. But now, with the herds gone, the pemmican industry developed by the French Canadians and the Métis was in deep trouble. A band of French Canadian hunters had gone out searching for the herds—but hadn't found them. Instead, they had starved and nearly frozen to death in the snowy plains. Survivors had straggled in, full of whispered tales of cannibalism. The men, it was said, had eaten the dead in order to stay alive.

David believed the reports. He was not much impressed with the character of these French Canadians. Their rank ungodliness drew his spirit down into darkness. It was only with great effort that he could rise above their depressing influence into the light of hope and love.

He mused frequently about his hard lot. Things happen out here on the plains that can destroy the soul while the body yet lives, an outer shell containing nothing of importance. In this place, the most cheerful optimist must believe in the total depravity of man. Incest! Drunkenness! Horrible violence! Blatant marital unfaithfulness! Bondage to the sterling pound that destroys the character of men and women alike.

To live in the midst of such cruelty and lust was the severest of trials—harder to bear than mosquitoes, cold, and starvation.

David's one consolation was his work. A Sunday school had been started and already attracted one hundred and fifteen children. Church services were well attended, even in severe weather. Governor Robert Pelly was one of the regulars at the Upper Church each Sunday.

But what commanded David's attention, challenged his love, and excited his heart most was the school for Indian boys. He did not leave the affairs of this school entirely to its teacher, William Harbridge, but loved to spend time with the boys, being to them a real father. Had not the apostle Paul written, "I became your father in Christ Jesus"? David was learning the true meaning of those words. The boys were his greatest— his only—enduring comfort.

The school was located near the parsonage, with much garden space between the two buildings. David taught the boys how to plant, fertilize, weed, kill mice, chase crows away, and finally gather a harvest.

But even these pleasant thoughts led him to despair. For in the middle of them stood a giant tragedy from which the grief still filled his heart. Late that winter, his two most promising boys, who had taken the names William Sharpe and Joseph Harbridge, had taken sick. William Sharpe had died after a brief illness. It had been astonishing, the ease with which he had been struck down. Soon after, the equally vulnerable Joseph Harbridge had learned how easily Natives are struck down by the white man's sicknesses.

It had been the most shattering experience of David's life: the loss of two beloved boys in a single month. All his hopes for Joseph and William, to be ambassadors for Christ to the Assiniboin people, had turned to dust. Was God not shepherd and protector of his flock? Would it not have been a greater benefit if the boys had lived to spread the gospel of God's love to their people? The questions received no answer. God's ways, at times, were inscrutable.

Never before had David been reduced to such a walk of blind faith. "Faith is the substance of things hoped for, the evidence of things not seen," he reiterated to himself. But the words seemed now like a chattered nursery rhyme. For the moment, the "evidence" had been reduced to nothing, while the "not seen" was as big as all creation.

And what of the future? Where faith was tested, hope was tested too. If God had not protected the first two Indian boys to enroll in the school, what assurance did David have that other boys would not die at the school, discrediting his ministry and blighting the growing plant before it had a chance to bloom into a vibrant tribal church?

There was this one consolation: the boys had died as Christian believers. In that sense, they were the firstfruits of his ministry. The crushing disappointment of the deaths was forcing David to face up to his true motives for being in Assiniboia.

Am I, in fact, hoping to build a monument to myself? The school— what is it? An institution with a brief earthly life. Its only value is to produce eternal births, and that is all. The school itself is nothing. Jesus is everything.

The young parson entered the wooden gate of Fort Garry with fear and trembling. What new indignity might he be subjected to by the hostile gentlemen of the Company? As he entered the fort, David was conscious that his hands and face were blotched and swollen. His lungs wheezed to get rid of phlegm in his throat. Struggling against self-consciousness, he followed Robert Pelly into the sitting room, where Donald MacKenzie was speaking with Bishop Provencher.

MacKenzie was the law here, and he looked the part. He had an imperious gaze; with his light blue eyes he could freeze your heart solid. During his years in the West, it was said that he administered the law by wielding a tipi lodgepole. He was the only one big enough to even lift such an instrument, let alone swing it about and strike people with it. He was a godsend who had no use for God. Without him, the colony would have continued to be what George Simpson had once called it: a receptacle for freebooters and infamous characters of all descriptions. Simpson had added that there was no law, order, or regularity in the colony; every man was his own master, and the strongest and most desperate was he who succeeds best. For such as these there had come MacKenzie the Flattener with his Almighty Lodgepole.

Soon after coming to Red River to take over the place, MacKenzie had written back to the governor his feelings about his new assignment:

> …The Red River Settlers from the portrait I have of them are a distinct sort of beings somewhere between the half Indians and overgrown children. At times they need caressing and not unfrequently the discipline of the birch, in other words the iron rod of retribution. But in the present instance the latter not being within our reach, it behooves us to attempt by stratagem what we cannot compass by force. In the first place therefore all former scrapes and barefaced practices should be carefully avoided by every person holding a conspicuous station and the bottle and the girls so late

the bane must with monastic strictness be forborne. Order and religion likewise to be held in veneration; therefore with faces long and minds most pure and delicate shall you & I regularly attend the chapel in the coldest as well as the warmest weather, even should we slip a passage or two & ponder in mind the next resolves of Council at times....[33]

MacKenzie had been in his element discovering passes in Oregon and keeping order as leader of the Snake brigade. He was not a civilized man, and yet here he had to wear civilized clothes.

Led by Governor Pelly, the young, self-conscious David Jones entered into MacKenzie's vast presence. But the factor and the bishop scarcely acknowledged the Anglican parson. In their eyes, he was a nobody. The hour prior to dinner was filled with polite conversation, with David permanently on the fringes. Small talk hovered around their heads like a cloud of verbal mosquitoes.

Dinner came and went without incident. It was during the after-dinner conversation, attended by white clay pipes, that Robert Pelly made the announcement for which the guests had been invited.

"I think most of you know that my wife has been feeling poorly for many months. The winter climate has not been kind to her."

Everyone in the room sympathized. The woman had been through hell.

"Dr. Hamlyn has advised us to return to England. If we don't, I am afraid she won't last another year. We must leave next month. I have informed Governor Simpson of our intentions. There is every likelihood that he will appoint Mr. MacKenzie governor in my place. I just wanted to say: we hope to return one day. We have appreciated our friendship with all of you, and we wish you well."

So that was it. The colony was coming under control of the Company. A company town through and through. Donald MacKenzie was replacing Robert Pelly! David had prayed for a companion. Instead, God was tak-

---

33. Donald MacKenzie to Gov. Simpson, Ft. Garry, 27 July, 1823.

ing away the one companion he had, the one person to whom he could confide his struggles and share his Christian point of view.

David was speechless. His lungs were closing off. His breathing turned to wheezing. He did not even try to respond cheerily to this dismal announcement. Blackness threatened to close in on his spirit, a despair that expressed itself in the constriction of his throat. Aaagh! He was suffocating! He gasped noisily, so that the others looked at him, startled. In his heart, he cried out to God, though no one in the room heard his cries. David had no voice with which to cry.

Just at that moment, a servant admitted an Indian emissary into the room, who loudly delivered a message: "Sir, Governor Simpson's party come from Carlton. Him go to White Horse Plain. Him there now. Here!"—and he handed Pelly a note from Simpson.

The note described Simpson's desperate condition: he was horseless, foodless, and soaked to the skin, having crossed on foot the nine miles of swampland to the west of White Horse Plain. The Métis, who lived in those parts, were all gone hunting. Simpson needed help!

MacKenzie sprang up and ordered food, horses, and dry clothing sent to the governor. Then everyone went to bed.

• • •

Simpson arrived at midnight, riding his favorite horse, Jonathan. MacKenzie came out to the gate in his nightshirt and greeted the governor with a massive bear hug, all the more sincere because Simpson had so clearly proven himself a man's man whom MacKenzie could welcome into the fraternity of proven north-country leaders.

Simpson had not eaten (nor allowed anyone else to eat) the food sent with the horses. Eating would have slowed them down. So MacKenzie sat them all at table and fed them. At last, Simpson generously announced, "We rest here eight days."

During his stay, the governor did indeed appoint Donald MacKenzie to replace the departing Pelly. The government of Assiniboia was merging with the leadership of the Hudson's Bay Company. After the eight days had passed, Simpson left to inspect the gutted remains of Norway House near Lake Winnipeg. Then he was off to England, leaving MacKenzie to be king of Red River Colony.

A packet from Montreal brought David Jones news that his parents and wife were faring well back in Wales. He was consoled by this scrap of distant love, yet he felt more distant from God than ever, like a neglected piece of flotsam caught in a Red River backwater, rising and falling with the jetsam around him. Perhaps, he brooded, Jesus Christ is irrelevant here. Perhaps it is true: the only way to survive here is by brute force. Is the kindness of Christ a matter of insignificance in the real world?

Had he never committed his life to Christ, had he never stepped beyond the security of family and friends in Wales, had he never made a sacrifice of love for Jesus—then the coldness of his position here would not have dismayed him. Nothing ventured, nothing lost. But he had ventured everything for Jesus Christ, had cast all behind him, and the apparent distance that separated him from God cut him to the heart. David felt as though he had left God and his Christ back in Wales. When will this spiritual coldness end? God! Have mercy on me!

• • •

The situation of David Jones worsened on Wednesday, June 22, with the arrival of two Assiniboins from Beaver Creek—an old man and a woman who looked equally ancient. They led their horses to David's garden fence and stood there, singing a melancholy dirge. David soon discovered that they were the mother and grandfather of the deceased Joseph Harbridge.

What a sight they were! The grandfather, who wore only a loincloth, was nothing but folds of skin and protruding bones. And the mother! Years before, she had been scalped by a marauding war party. When the muscles of her head had healed, they had drawn her features, horribly contracted, into a twisted grimace. Inadequate wisps of hair hung about her protruding ears.

The two had heard of Joseph's death from his uncle and had ridden three hundred miles to mourn over the grave. David's servant, Donald Bannerman, translated their story: "We have not had food for six days. We are hungry. The boy's father was not well enough to come this trip. In his place, he sends four moose skins as a gift."

David smiled with true appreciation. He could not believe that the relatives had actually sent a gift. What an extraordinarily generous response, considering the circumstances. David could not comprehend it. His servant helped unload the skins and carry them to the parsonage. David fed the man and woman fish and potatoes, which they devoured voraciously.

"We will go to the grave tomorrow," they announced when they had finished—and refused David's invitation to sleep under his roof.

In the morning, the two appeared again, requesting that the servant conduct them to the grave. "We couldn't sleep at all last night," they complained. "Too near the grave of the boy."

David led them to the grave, where they howled and wailed for hours. They covered the grave with bark and sticks, and they mounted a board at the head, with a picture of a wolf painted on it. Then they took off their moccasins and lacerated the bottoms of their feet with knives. David tried to prevent them in this, but to no avail. After a quarter of an hour, they returned to the parsonage, leaving a trail of blood along the path from the cemetery.

Yet the two did not blame David for Joseph's death. For that, he was grateful. When it came time for them to depart, they expressed, through the servant, a genuine appreciation for the care David had given the boy. They promised to return in the fall with other relatives who wished to mourn.

Four

Kootenai Pelly and Spokan Garry made their way with the Rosses in a York boat from the burned-out ruins of Norway House, across the seas of Lake Winnipeg, then up the Red River at the south end of the lake. The York boat that carried them to their destination was a whitewashed craft curved into an arc, with high prow and high stern, shaped to resist heavy lake turbulence.

When they came to the big rapids on the Red River, everyone was ordered out of the boat, which was then dragged up onto logs that had been whittled into rollers. The boat was rolled south around the rapids, and the passengers were allowed to re-embark at the other end.

Finally, the colony made its first appearance as a series of cabins at the crest of the bank on the west side, then on the east. The Red River Colony consisted of a long, narrow series of plots with their ends abutting on the river. Cabins were arranged all up and down the river, especially on the west side, making it look as though a vast metropolis stretched on for miles. In reality, beyond a few hundred yards, there was nothing but a road connecting these ribbon-like plots together. Everyone loved a riverfront.

Like Jedediah Smith in the village of the Mountain Crows, Garry and Pelly sensed that their God-given destiny awaited them in this strange place, and they could only cling to the faith of their fathers—fingering their *sumesh* pouches as they did. The strangeness was accentuated as they passed a huge building with four wooden arms turning in a circle, around and around. The boys looked at Sarah to see if she might nod her head to reassure them about the object or explain it in some way. Sarah, however, had never seen such a thing, and could give no such reassurance. She'd had an argument with Alex that day and did not feel much like asking him what the contraption was, and so they all sat in ignorance about windmills.

Further on was another curiosity: the steeple of John West's Anglican church, known as the Upper Church, on the right, followed after ten minutes by the stunted twin steeples of Bishop Provencher's Catholic church on the left.

As the boat approached the main Red River dock, the Natives felt queasy, sensing the power of the white man's will, and sensing, too, their own vulnerability in the midst of it. They didn't understand half of what they were seeing, and they didn't know enough words to find out about it. Alex and Sarah knew Okanogan, which was a foreign language to both Pelly and Garry, and sign lingo was a poor substitute when there were so many things for which signs had not been invented. Besides, the Natives in the party were feeling insecure and out of sorts, and they drew an invisible cloak of protective silence around themselves and their ignorance. The only ones who talked were the French "tripmen." These transporters of goods had been known as "voyageurs." But the Red River colony was the avant-garde of English civilization, and brought new lingo with it to replace wilderness words. These tripmen were all business, and not the sort of people who would answer questions.

The Forgotten Awakening

Pelly and Garry sensed that they were not going to be highly regarded here, which was a new feeling for them, who were favorite sons in their own villages. Both remembered as if it were yesterday the grieving of the women as they had departed on this trip. Well, maybe they were going to die here. That was a real possibility.

Sarah did manage to reach out to them in her silence, to put her arms around their shoulders for reassurance. They snuggled up to her small body, receiving whatever she might give them by her touch.

The boat docked and was moored at the intersection of another river, which poured itself into the Red from the west. As the passengers stepped up on land, all three from the western tribes sensed that this step was the most important they would ever take. They were arriving into their destiny—Sarah's future with Ross, and the boys' with God. The boys' only reason for being here was that the Creator had required it of them and had also required them to suffer the loss of all things familiar. Their only assurance in this bereavement was that the Creator had sent them to this strange place by means of tribal prophecy, and it was that prophecy alone to which they could cling now, when the weight of its fulfillment bore down on them. They knew that greatness grew out of adversity, and they sensed that the Creator might allow some adversity even beyond the test of climbing the Backbone of the World. Without adversity and testing, how could anyone become a great warrior?—or a great spiritual leader, for that matter.

Kootenai Pelly did not warm up easily to the prospect of adversity. Back home, he had been an easygoing lad, laughing much, a budding artist who enjoyed fishing, singing, storytelling, and trapping. But his father, war chief of the Kutenais, had been quietly grieved at Pelly's inability to take an interest in the craft of battle. Sensing that he was now in the midst of a foreign—possibly hostile—people, Pelly shrank back for fear of what might come.

Spokan Garry, a more outgoing boy, forged out ahead into the new world, leaving his friend behind, drawn by curiosity about this new and wondrous place. One astonishment after another greeted him. First, the place was unremittingly flat. Not a lump of a hill was to be seen in any direction once they had gotten up out of the river channel. Second, the soil here was not red or brown like normal earth, but as black as the raven's wings. Third, the lanes were full of carts such as he had never seen before, with wheels shaped like saucers. These wheels squeaked so loudly that the city was one horrible symphony of piercing shrieks.

Why don't they put bear grease there? he thought. Do they like this sound?

The place was humming with people. Twelve hundred of them lived here, not counting a village of Métis to the west and another of Salteaux to the north.

They entered the wooden gates of Fort Garry, where Alex Ross looked for someone to report to. Sarah and the children tagged along—and walked into a horror.

For there, coming out of post headquarters, was the huge and menacing bulk of Donald MacKenzie. Sarah recoiled: What? Him? Here? MacKenzie had been a brigade leader when her husband had been factor at Fort Nez Percé on the Columbia River. It was where they had been married. MacKenzie had appeared as a crass, imperious, threatening portent, a man of violence. Alex had never mentioned that the giant was stationed here. Pelly and Garry sensed Sarah's fear and took up positions behind her as she tried to hide behind her husband. MacKenzie had grown, if it were possible, even bigger than in Oregon, where the constant stress and challenge of exploration had kept him almost trim at three hundred pounds. Now he had become obese, his Oregonian brawn covered by a layer of Red River fat.

Alex Ross had never liked the man. MacKenzie had completely outclassed him as an explorer and brigade leader. His thoughts were acid: Why, the man has become positively gross. He must weigh four hundred pounds! Or more!

But he said only, "Mr. MacKenzie, we ha' arrived from the Columbia District with the two boys requested by the governor. What'll be done with 'em?"

MacKenzie looked contemptuously at the two boys, as if he wanted to pound them into the ground with his bare fist. The boys had never seen anyone so massive.

Ross, oblivious to their fear, moved along to discharge his duty: turning over the boys to whoever was going to take charge of them.

"You'd best take 'em to the schoolhouse yonder," MacKenzie barked, waving his hairy paw in the northerly direction they should go. Clearly, he had no patience with a Christian pastor, with Indian boys, or with an unimpressive squaw. Wanting to deliver himself from their useless presence, he walked on. Before he left, though, he shoved a letter into Ross's hand and added, "It's fer the parson, when you see him."

Disregarding MacKenzie's direction to the schoolhouse, the six found their way straight to the Anglican parsonage, knocked on the door, and were greeted there by David Jones. Garry and Pelly couldn't help but notice the nearby tall white clapboard building with the pointed tower on top, and they were curious about it. This was surely the same building they had seen from the river, but they were more curious about the man who was going to welcome them here and hopefully care for them—and they were hoping that he would not be like Alex Ross, George Simpson, or Donald MacKenzie.

David Jones, when he appeared at last, was a pleasant surprise and a vast relief. Still feeling like a stranger in a foreign land, David could immediately sense the insecurities of these boys from the west. All the loneliness of his own heart reached out to them in an unrestrained joy, almost a repressed sob. He could not help himself. He scooped them up in an un-English hug, then recovered himself and greeted Sarah and Alex Ross as a gentleman should have done.

Silently, unconsciously, Garry and Pelly sidled over to the man who had so warmly greeted them. They sensed that there were no barriers with him, and no need for barriers. His heart had touched theirs, and in their boyish innocence, they saw no reason to hold back. They needed love. He needed to give love. The deal was struck almost before it had begun to be bargained. From now on, they would trust David Jones to be their father, to show them what this place was all about.

From David's point of view, the Red River Colony was a bridge, a place where people could meet from all sides of a vast chasm. It was a place as foreign to him as it was to the Spokane and the Kutenai—a middling place Christ had appointed for his own purposes. Each of them had traveled vast distances, invited by God to have interactions here. None of them knew what would come of the meeting. David had wondered why God had appointed such a bleak, flat, black, cold, uninviting place to be his bridge among the nations, but he saw now that ease and comfort do not link people together. Adversity was more likely to unite hearts. People who had to rely on each other in hard times could learn from each other what God wanted them to learn. In foreign lands, people saw their need more clearly than at home, in comfort and security. David saw this more clearly than the boys, but even the boys instinctively sensed their need for David.

Ross gave the letter to David and took his family off to find lodgings without so much as a good-bye. Sarah said good-bye and threw in a parting hug to everyone. David opened the letter hurriedly during this moment, and discovered—oh, what joy!—an answer to his request for help from the Church Missionary Society. One William Cochran would be arriving on the next boat from England!

The goodness of God has broken through this darkness at last—twice in a moment, he breathed in a paroxysm of thanks.

David spent the next day, July 2, getting the boys settled in at the school's bunkhouse, then readying his sermon for the Lord's Day. He decided to preach on his favorite text, "These things have I written unto you that believe on the name of the Son of God, that ye may know that ye have eternal life."

The following day, everyone showed up for church. William Garrioch, the new teacher at the school, brought the twelve boys and two girls to join the congregation, which was made up mostly of lower-class retirees of the Company. Alex and Sarah Ross were there with little Alexander and Margaret. Ross sat in the back row with his family, whereas the boys sat up front, eager to know what this was all about.

The Forgotten Awakening

Sarah discovered within the first five minutes that something was wrong: she sensed an uneasiness in Alex, and it put her ill at ease too. He kept fuming under his breath, but she did not know what his trouble was, only that her husband was wrapping his habitual disrespect around the new pastor, David Jones. She decided to keep quiet and let him keep the matter to himself. She had learned that Alex Ross had a great deal of dust in his soul, and it was best to let it settle so that she didn't have to breathe it into her own soul too. Perhaps Alex was just jealous that he was not the one preaching, as he had sometimes done at HBC posts out west.

As for Pelly and Garry, they could understand nothing of the service, because they knew almost no English. Yet they received the smile and the warmth of David's heart through his message.

William Garrioch, a man of humble heart, rosy cheeks, and encouraging word, had recently replaced the previous teacher, William Harbridge, who had been a chronic complainer and a man of narrow spirit. The two boys immediately warmed up to Garrioch, and he to them. He quietly showed them with smiles and gentle correction how to behave in an Anglican church.

After church, Ross went to Fort Garry to find out when his position as schoolteacher was to begin. George Simpson had promised him the job, but Simpson was off setting straight the situation at Norway House at the north end of the lake, so the best Ross could do was to check with Donald MacKenzie to see if Simpson had left word about his new duties. He found MacKenzie pressing furs by the post's warehouse.

"Governor Simpson promised me a teaching post at the school here. I don't suppose you'd know anything about it?"

MacKenzie looked up from his work, a vague aura of pity covering his face. Teaching boys in a school was, in his mind, a long step down from fur brigade leader, but MacKenzie knew that Alex Ross had been demoted so far down that even that lowly position was not going to be offered him. In fact, it looked like Ross had been sent here to get him out of the way entirely.

"Governor didn't say a thing about it."

That was all. MacKenzie had no more words to dispense. He didn't like words; he was a man of action. He had his own feelings about being cooped up here in Fort Garry, and he experienced a sense of inner glee at seeing Alex demoted to an utterly irrelevant status in the Company. He and Ross had fought over every decision for years, and MacKenzie had never met a man he disliked more.

But then MacKenzie thought better of his silence, deciding to jab the truth farther into Ross's thick hide. "The school's taught by William Garrioch, and the governor has no authority over it. David Jones and the Church Missionary Society put whoever they want in the school. I can't see what governor was thinking to promise you such a position."

He watched Ross squirm with intense disappointment, then turned the dagger in Ross's soul: "But you did such a good job of delivering that letter I gave you yesterday, may I offer you the position of postman?"

Ross was shocked: What? Delivering other people's mail? Is he joking? I, who have been factor of Fort Nez Percé? He stomped out of the fort, stabbed to the bones.

Yet, when Alex Ross had gotten over the shock and humiliation of realizing that he had been brought to Red River to be cast aside, he had to face facts. He came crawling back to Donald MacKenzie and took the job of postman. A pittance of a salary came with the job, and, Ross realized, out here mere survival required just such a pittance.

• • •

At the school, William Garrioch's first job was to teach the boys English, a task he set about with relish. The boys were eager to learn the language, for it was their only hope of communicating well with everyone else, or even with each other. It would take weeks to learn even how to handle the equipment of learning: pens and pen holders, alphabet cards, slates and slate pencils, and copybooks for learning to form letters on paper. They fell quickly to their slates and were soon learning to form the letters of the English alphabet.

The Forgotten Awakening

On September 30, David Jones heard a knock on his door. He opened it to find a half-dozen Assiniboins, come from Brandon House to mourn over the grave of Joseph Harbridge. They were a different group from the first. The leader, a youngster with a violent temper, got his face next to the face of David's servant Donald.

"*Scoutaywaubo! Scoutaywaubo!*" he shouted, demanding firewater. His leggings were fringed with scalp hair. He wore the wizened skin of a raven as a headpiece, its beak covering his forehead, its tail covering his neck.

David stood up to the bully and told him firmly that he had no firewater. Sensing that he meant it, the whole group turned and departed. The last man in the party turned back to David and requested help in finding the boy's grave. David sent Donald to lead the way to the graveyard nearby.

That evening, the Assiniboins shrieked so loudly that their voices could be heard half a mile up and down the river. Garry and Pelly, practicing their lessons in the bunkhouse, heard the familiar sound of Indian mourning and came out to learn where it was coming from. They saw the family; they saw the grave—and they knew that a Native boy had died at the school.

David had wished to spare them that.

While the Assiniboins were yet grieving, the boys noticed an eerie glow in the clouds to the west. The sun was going down in a blaze of brilliant color. Someone shouted: "Grass fire!"

Soon everyone was frantically running to and fro, trying to organize firefighting parties. Within an hour, the whole flat horizon was ablaze, lighting up the clouds in the gathering darkness. Someone grabbed Pelly and Garry and gave them each a skin with which to flog the ground. They joined the people who were beating the black earth and the crackling grass.

Smoke blew over the town, reaching its fingers into lungs. It stung the eyes and clouded vision. The smell of it was unbearable.

The charred air carried evil noises too. The Assiniboins continued to shriek, their voices clearly audible from the graveyard. "My child, why did you leave me! Why go out of my sight so early? Who will feed you in the long journey you have undertaken?"

The boys understood none of the words the Assiniboins chanted. But they knew their meaning nonetheless. The devilish sights and sounds filled the westerners with dread. As they pounded the ground with pieces of buffalo hide, Garry and Pelly could only wonder in private what distress might await them in this strange new place. Here at the place of the Red River, with pastor and teacher gone elsewhere, their vision was clouded, and strangers mourned the death of their sons. Suddenly it dawned on them that their own imperiled future remained as obscure as ever.

Five

When the Reverend William Cochran arrived at the Red River Colony, he brought with him a surprise: his wife and infant son.

The arrival of three, not one, drastically changed David Jones's plans. He moved out of the parsonage to give the new couple the advantage of its privacy and four-room spaciousness. He moved into the schoolmaster's quarters at one end of the church, a cramped space partitioned off from the sanctuary. William Garrioch had built his own house, leaving this inadequate little apartment vacant.

Yet the move to such quarters was but small sacrifice, from David's point of view, compared to the hope of Christian fellowship, of hot meals cooked by Mrs. Cochran, and of companionship in the work. How often he had learned that a short-term sacrifice produces long-term gains!

William Cochran turned out to be a twenty-nine-year-old, muscular farm boy turned evangelist. He had a massive chin and a massive forehead, between which beamed a kindly, shrewd face. He wore wire-rimmed glasses with lenses shaped like two hoes—round at the nose, boxy at the hinges. These gave him an intelligent appearance, yet in manners he remained forever a guileless country boy.

It was well that the Cochrans had come, for David desperately needed their moral support. Sickness and disappointments multiplied during the winter of 1825–1826. The weather was as cold as the winter before it, the temperatures frequently reaching -40 degrees.

Now another Native boy, James Hope, became feverish, then bedridden. David visited him daily. As he looked into the boy's face, he seemed to see Joseph Harbridge and William Sharpe, who had sickened and died just one year before. David fretted: Is this loss of boys to become an annual occurrence? The cold is killing them with its icicle daggers. How can I ask tribal chiefs to give their sons into my care when I cannot guarantee their survival?

David prayed about the situation through January and February. He spent much time by the bedside of James Hope, praying for him and seeking God's mercy. In a very real sense, if James Hope were to die, hope itself would die with him. For David, this was a crisis, despite the companionship of the Cochrans. The entire mission was fueled by hope. Without it they might as well pack up and go home.

On February 28, both pastors decided to spend an extended time of prayer over James's bed. As they prayed together, David whispered to William his doubts.

"William, we lost two this time last year. It's this cursed cold and snow, I feel sure. The boys do all right through three seasons. But the winters kill them—and we don't have the means to save them. And where is God in all this? Why does God allow them to come here, if only to die?"

Cochran replied, "Aye, it's a mystery and a consternation, all right. But one thing I've learned. Even if God keeps his own counsel, he knows what he's doing." They returned to prayer.

Just then, an astonishing thing happened. James Hope, feverish, suffering, delirious and gasping for air, began to form a word between his gasps and coughs: "Jesus!" He gasped, then said it again: "Jesus!" Each breath came in with a gasp and exhaled with the name of Jesus. James was praying in his delirium.

From that moment, his condition improved. By March 2, David was able to write in his journal that James Hope was entirely well. An overwhelming sense of relief washed over him. It seemed to him that hope itself had been healed of disease.

But on the very day of James's healing, disturbing news came from other quarters. The French Canadians had been out hunting for buffalo, as in other winters. Again, they had found no herds, and they had been reduced to abject starvation as they wandered out on the prairies. Again, they were straggling back to Red River with horrible tales of murder and cannibalism.

One of these Frenchmen burst into Fort Garry when David was there. In David's presence, he described to Donald MacKenzie the desperate need for food among the Canadians who were making their way back to the colony. The missionary's sensibilities were assaulted, not only by the story of men eating men, but by the cursing and profanity mingled in with it. The name of Jesus had been a staff of life for James Hope. But from the mouth of this Frenchman, it was a knife jabbed into David's heart. That night, David wrote in his journal:

> He who feels at liberty to curse his God—his soul—his
> seven sacraments and all that his ritual teaches him to rever-
> ence will not stand in need of much temptation to commit an
> outrage upon his fellow creature in order to relieve himself.[34]

During those evil March days, one intrigue followed another. The desperate freemen tried to save themselves and their families by violence. First, they turned their hopes to Fort Garry, where there were stores of grain purchased from the Scottish settlers. Three or four ringleaders

---

34. *Journal of David Jones*, March 2, 1827.

ALEXANDER ROSS

The first white man to live among the Okanogans, he was also among the first to write of the Plateau tribes and of the early fur trade.

From *Fur Hunters of the Far West*

DR. JOHN McLOUGHLIN

Chief Factor of Fort Vancouver, King of Old Oregon, The White-headed Eagle.

JEDEDIAN SMITH

The only known sketch. Mercifully, the artist filled in the gaps in his face.

SPOKAN GARRY

Garry, during the years he was most sought out as an ambassadorial representative of the Plateau tribes.

SPOKAN GARRY

Garry at the end of his life. His biographer said he was a man who
lived too long.

GEORGE SIMPSON

The most powerful man in Rupert's Land

WILLIAM COCHRAN

With David Jones, William Cochran was the greatest influence on Spokan Garry and Kootenai Pelly. As far as we know, neither man had any idea that they were the fullfilment of tribal prophecy. They attributed the great spiritual hunger of the tribes to simple good-heartedness.

"The Protestant Church, And Mission School, at the Red River Colony" by C Heath Sculp.

Taken from *The Rainbow in the North*

PETER SKENE
OGDEN

Two of the
greatest explorers
of the American
West.

DONALD MacKENZIE

Taken from *History of Chautauqua County* by Andrew W. Young

plotted a raid on the fort to plunder the storehouses and steal the grain, but an informant tipped off Donald MacKenzie, who personally led an armed force to arrest the plotters. He rattled their heads together and placed them in jail at the fort.

This action did not feed families or solve the crisis. Other ringleaders soon emerged, more resentful and cantankerous than ever. These turned their attention to the Scottish settlers, who had raised corn and barley the previous fall and who now enjoyed the fruits of their labors. The Canadians told one another that this grain would be more easily taken than that in the fort. There was no Donald MacKenzie here to rattle their heads together.

When David Jones heard of the plot, he organized his congregation into a charitable militia who went from door to door collecting food and grain donations. Hard-bitten Scottish residents reminded the missionaries that these same Canadians had turned a deaf ear toward their hunger two winters before, selling meat to them at exorbitant prices.

In reply, David and William gave them a gentle sermon about the higher road of Christian love. "We must do it as to the Lord," they repeated from one home to the next. Few could refuse them or their cadre of gleaners, who included the boys in the school. At the end of several days of intense effort, many sacks of grain had been collected and turned over to Donald MacKenzie. MacKenzie, in turn, gave the grain to Bishop Provencher to distribute to the French.

The plotting ceased. The sense of desperation was drained away. Several days later, David received a letter from MacKenzie.

> Dear Sir.
>
> I am requested by the Gentlemen directing the Catholic Mission to present their thanks and the thanks of their congregation to you and Mr. Cochran for your zeal and beneficence; as also to the many charitable individuals who joined in your contribution towards relieving the Freemen during their present distress.[35]

---

35. Journal of David Jones, March 2, 1826.

Well, even MacKenzie could act the gentleman and appreciate nobility when he saw it. But as to the relative effectiveness of brute force and Christian love, there were few hearts converted. Donald MacKenzie continued to believe in the motto of the Hudson's Bay Company: the words of Satan from the book of Job, "Skin for Skin." David Jones and William Cochran continued to believe in the motto of Jesus: "Love one another as I have loved you."

The latter motto, made credible by those who were living it out, was beginning to have its effect on Spokan Garry and Kootenai Pelly. "Skin for Skin" was nothing new. But the other motto opened up new possibilities, and they were trying to evaluate how the spirit of it would be received back home. Was it possible that the tribes west of the mountains could learn to treat each other by the laws of love?

From time to time Donald MacKenzie would come to church, bringing with him the "gentlemen" from Fort Garry—the lordly English who felt an obligation to occasionally bestow their presence on the parson from Wales. It was the most disagreeable of all duties for MacKenzie, who didn't believe in sitting still for an hour, didn't believe in churches, in God, in worshiping anything, in teaching Indians Christianity or agriculture—in short, who opposed everything that David stood for. Above all, Donald MacKenzie didn't believe in pretense. Yet he was obliged to follow orders, though he complained bitterly to Simpson.

David followed the tradition of shaking hands with all who left the church after the service. When MacKenzie showed up one day, David winced inside, sensing that Donald was about to lodgepole him with words.

"So how are the wee brown boys doing with their slates and their schoolbooks? Have we turned them yet into proper Englishmen with a garden in every home?"

David ignored the sarcastic reference to the garden plots he had arranged for the boys in front of the bunkhouse and kept smiling as best he could. But then MacKenzie turned to Alex Ross, who stood in line behind him, and said, "Mark my words, Mr. Ross. All your ideas about getting the Natives to trap will fly out the window once the brown-skins learn the hoe and the plow. These parsons here are cutting the livelihood of the Company right out from under us. Pretty soon, you and I shall have to set trap for ourselves. But then, if it be fer God, well, we'll have to bear our cross, won't we?"

David cringed at such gross sentiments so rudely spoken, and wondered why God had allowed Robert Pelly to be replaced by such a one.

Six

For years afterward, everyone agreed that the winter of 1825–1826 was the longest, the coldest, and the snowiest of any in memory. When spring arrived, the snow refused to melt on schedule. Cold hovered over the mountains and clung to the prairies below. The north country was still breathing her crystal breath from the frozen tundra, where arctic wolf and polar bear had adapted themselves to her harsh ways. David Jones and William Cochran were imitating the wolf and the bear, for they had learned that three greatcoats are better than one on days when the north wind insists on her own way.

Even by late April, the snows had not begun to melt in earnest; the rivers were still low. Few suspected that the worst of the winter's wrath was yet to come. For the time being, David remarked to William that the planting of barley and wheat was delayed by weeks because of the lingering blasts of winter.

Suddenly, during the last week of April, the seasons changed. There were four days of spring. Then, before the week was out, hot summer arrived. The snows melted with a vengeance, all at once, from Red River to Athabasca Pass. By Saturday the river courses were full, and early on Sunday, April 30, they overflowed their banks. For the first time since the new church at Image Plain had been organized, no pastor was able to get to it to lead services. Melted snow was moving, swift and muddy, toward Lake Winnipeg, spreading out over the land and carrying away everything that tried to stand before it. Every drop of water was fleeing the mountains like people trying to escape a house on fire.

The Upper Church, the school, and the parsonage had been built on a small knoll, thanks to John West, who believed that a church steeple should rise above all other man-made structures. Several dozen people now flocked to the church, hovering around it and bemoaning their losses, real or imagined. Property was being deposited in the mission compound, dragged and carted there from homes even now filling with water.

The ice that had ceilinged Red River all winter—a solid sheet four feet thick—separated from its banks without breaking. It rose up entire, like a hammered thumbnail rising above swollen flesh, soon to fall away.

At 8 p.m., the ice began to move down its channel. With deafening cracking noises, it knocked over trees and wiped out cabins. Then it slammed into some hillocks, where it remained wedged.

At nightfall, the weather turned wintry again, five degrees below freezing. Clouds overtook the colony, and a freezing rain, mixed with snow, drove the homeless into the church. They crowded together there, trying to keep each other warm.

Spokan Garry and Kootenai Pelly were with their schoolmates in the bunkhouse, where they could hear the cattle moaning as if the world were at an end. They, like the cattle, wondered if *they* were at an end. But the English words they had learned enabled them to communicate with each other, and they encouraged one another, trying to keep their heads above the surface of their fears.

"If we were home, we would move to higher ground. But there is no higher ground here," observed Garry.

"If worst comes to worst, we can climb the tree in front of the parsonage," replied Pelly, who had a habit of waiting for the other to initiate conversation. Both fingered their *sumesh* pouches constantly.

David Jones looked in on the boys from time to time, but he and the Cochrans were overwhelmed with the task of housing, feeding, and comforting all the homeless families that were flocking to their hill. "He that feedeth the ravens when they are hungry can and will provide for us," he would say wherever he went. "In every disaster there are the seeds of blessing. Trust God's infinite wisdom." David recognized that fear was as much a danger as flood, and faith would be needed to survive both. Sixty-three refugees had arrived already, housed now in the sanctuary of the Upper Church.

By the evening of May 4, the water had risen until it covered the church graveyard and swept within four feet of church and parsonage. In the black of night, everyone in the church, the parsonage, and the bunkhouse was alarmed to hear the ice moving away. With a bone-jarring crunch, followed by a twisting, creaking, and loud crackling, it irritably announced that it was going somewhere else to find better company up north.

When the people ventured out the next morning, they discovered that the ice had demolished four more homes as a last gesture of ill will. Many cattle had been swept away, as had all the maples and oaks in the front yard of the parsonage. The patriarchal elm that had been growing there for centuries was chopped off clean.

Garry and Pelly looked at the clean stump, looked at each other, and thought: So much for the safety of the big tree.

"We await the issue of his gracious hand," David wrote in his journal.

David visited the boys in the school, encouraging them to trust in a sovereign God and to see this trial as "ordained of God for our good, for in the end he is gracious toward those who humble themselves before his almighty hand. What good is it to trust him only when all is going well?

We must learn to trust him in trials too. Then we will see how he uses trials to teach and purify us."

That Sunday, William Cochran preached on the trials of Job. "God is doing an unsearchable thing, beyond understanding. We must learn to trust him in the midst of trouble. He alone can exalt us to safety. It is his right to take away all other supports, until only he remains. He is faithful. Cling to him."

The water level had risen to the ceilings of many homes. When that happened, the wooden structures were lifted off their foundations and carried away. Alarmed and helpless retirees stared thoughtfully as various homes moved past their windows toward Lake Winnipeg. "Look, there goes the old Harbridge cottage. Och, an' Governor Pelly's house follows right behind, an' the stockade gate o' Fort Douglas is floating yonder, ye see?"

In late afternoon, the wooden bastions of Fort Garry swept past the parsonage windows, together with the carcasses of dead cattle and the ruins of innumerable possessions—chairs, tables, boxes, carts, and carioles. It occurred to all of them: How many of our possessions are made of wood! Everything wooden is floating away, while only we ourselves remain above destruction.

The Bible provided the only comfort. The "leaves bound together" birthed the miracle of thankfulness. The inhabitants of Red River Colony were moving to higher ground, Native lads and bearded Scots together, moving to a higher point of view. "Everything that my Father hath not planted shall be rooted up," as the missionaries kept saying.

The snow kept melting; the waters kept rising for days. As far as the eye could see, there was nothing but water. The little group on the church eminence had the impression of being Noah's family.

From time to time, they would carefully wade out to retrieve some valuable object and drag it to dry ground. Yet by May 13, even the grounds of the church were inundated. At 10 p.m., the water entered the church itself.

William Cochran organized the schoolboys into a work party, using leftover timbers to build a stage above the roof of the parsonage. By Sunday the stage, thirty feet square, was completed.

William placed his wife, the Indian boys and girls, and a dozen other settlers on the stage, while David organized a work party to place the heaviest possessions in the loft of the church. David's purpose was not so much to spare the possessions as to weigh down the church building in case the water rose up to the ceiling. Those who did not stay on Mr. Cochran's stage huddled together with the cows on a small hillock near the school. A foot and a half of water surged through the parsonage, three and a half feet through the church.

Pelly and Garry, inseparable friends, spent the night of May 14 on the stage. It was impossible to sleep, though they were dead tired from the work of building the stage and of lifting possessions to the sanctuary loft. The sound of running water haunted them in the darkness. Yet, they were learning to put their trust in a caring God. Their medicine pouches, filled with what Garrioch called "oddments," seemed less and less powerful. Where did the power come from to master the trials of life? From the spirits, or from Creator?

It was an experiment, whether to believe the two missionaries or not. Their trust in Jesus, whom they thought of as the Master of Life, was contagious. They seemed so very confident of God's care, even though they faced the same losses everyone else had to face. The boys would not have paid much attention to the missionaries but for the inner resilience that shone in them now through severe adversity. Perhaps the Master of Life is closer than The People have believed? Perhaps the comforts of the *sumesh* pouch are not needed?

That night, the weather turned foul. A terrific lightning storm swept toward the boys on the wings of the north wind. As Pelly and Garry looked out from their stage toward the watery western horizon, flashes of lightning were mirrored in the black water. As the storm advanced, thunder sounded like cannon firing invisible shot that never landed anywhere. The mirrored lightning drew near, seeming to come from below and above all at once. Pelly and Garry were surrounded by it, completely engulfed in the flashes that appeared to rise up out of the water.

Then the winds came across the face of the deep, blowing with such force that they shook the stage alarmingly. Everything solid, stable, and secure was being shaken. Annie Cochran came to the boys, put her gentle arms around them, and prayed with them amidst the sound and fury. Her presence took the edge off their fear. She stayed with them through the night, as David and William comforted the others elsewhere. They sensed: Love is a secure foundation in the midst of trouble.

• • •

By the next day, the water level had risen several more feet—as far as the eye could see. The sheer volume of it staggered the imagination. The church had six and a half feet of water now, an increase of three feet in a day. That meant that the total volume of water for miles and miles in all directions had increased by three feet, all of it lumbering northward, trying to get back to the place of its spawning.

At 1 p.m., a Hudson's Bay man arrived in a York boat to take some of the people off the stage and place them on a high bank several miles up the Assiniboin River. The man explained to David and the Cochrans, "The bairnies on the brae need a minister. Ye'd better come, fer the need be greater there."

David was hard put whether to stay or go with the boat. The boys of the school, trained from childhood to demonstrate courage at such times, stood glued to their places on the platform. The whites, who remembered no such training, rushed pell-mell into the boat. David and the Cochrans were pushed along with them. In seconds, they had embarked, leaving the schoolboys on the stage.

Garry and Pelly, standing among the others, outdid each other in acting brave. But David, from his perch on the York boat, sensed their anxiety. Immediately, his misgivings for having left them came out to haunt him. Why didn't I resist the tide of people leaving the stage? Will we ever see the boys again? If a calamity should destroy the parsonage, how will I ever forgive myself?

When the boat arrived at the "brae" of the Assiniboin, the missionaries found one hundred and thirty Hudson's Bay tents pitched along a narrow mound. They lodged a makeshift village of Scots, French Canadians, and Métis. Nearby were tipis full of Salteaux families. Boatloads of Scottish settlers were arriving daily. Some six hundred and fifty people, with their cattle, sled dogs, and horses, were all milling around together in a hodgepodge impossible to comprehend. The boatman had been right after all: the need was greater here. The pastors were overwhelmed with injured, frightened, homeless people seeking help and prayer.

On the following day, Donald MacKenzie arrived at 3 a.m. in a York boat. He advised the missionaries to bring everything they could carry from the mission compound. "It'll all go. There's no hope fer it. This right here is the only safe ground for tens of miles around. Your churches'll be washed away by tomorrow." MacKenzie considered himself a realist. It was against his nature to give false hope—or true hope either.

His words, spoken in the dark with no sympathy, depressed David and doubled his anxiety for the boys. Despite that, David allowed Mr. Cochran to be the one to pick up the Native children from the platform, while he stayed behind ministering to the crowds and waiting for the boys' return.

After an eternity of waiting, Cochran and MacKenzie showed up with the children just before midnight. The boys were hugged, fed, and brought under blankets. With a quiet voice, in private, William reported to David what he had found. His face reflected anxiety, disappointment, even terror: "The current around the church has increased. It has swept away all our fences, swept the graveyard clean, and it looks like it will take all the buildings away, too. It is just as Mr. MacKenzie said. But thank God, the boys are safe and sound. They have stood the test of bravery far better than others twice their age."

"They are all that matters. As to the rest, God's will be done," replied David. "And may he support us and give us faith in his promises. This is our only ground for rejoicing."

In his journal he wrote: "The Lord can make his gospel a fountain of living water even in the midst of deserts and under the most discouraging circumstances."[36]

During the following two days, David rowed twice over the slow-moving waters to the Upper Church. On the second day, he looked for a water-level mark he had etched on a window frame during the first trip. The mark was only an inch under water! The flood was peaking!

That night, another boat floated by the encampment. A Frenchman shouted out in the darkness, "It is one sea, a sheet of water from this *rivière* clear to the Missouri. Indian villages have been wiped out *entière*. We have the flood of Noah, yes?"

On Friday, the two missionaries held a thanksgiving service, attended by hordes of people of all ages. But later that night, a violent wind rose up, blowing from out of the blackness. It seemed to resent the thankfulness of the people. For people dwelling in a tent village, it was the worst possible turn of events. Wasn't the flood enough, they asked one another, that a gale must now be added to it?

The wind scoured everything, forcing its way into every nook and cranny of tent, wagon, and boat. It discovered every loose object and whipped it away. It lashed the waters until the air was full of spray. It blew away the entire fleet of Hudson's Bay boats. It blew the sides of the tents horizontal; they snapped and flapped like flags.

David rushed to the mainstay of their tent and held it erect. But all loose belongings under its shelter were blown away. Anne Cochran, Spokan Garry, and Kootenai Pelly tried desperately to hold on to their few belongings.

Then the lightning visited the camp, to renew its terrible mischief. On this night, the lightning leapt in great horizontal streaks across the sky, almost without intermission. The whole camp was lit up, as if a limpid, flickering sun were trying to shed light through cracks in the sky.

A quarter of a mile upwind, somebody's lantern blew into the grass. Immediately, despite the wetness all around, the grass caught fire. Within minutes, a blaze was reaching into the sky, fanned by the wind. David

---

36. *Journal of David Jones*, Sunday, May 21, 1826.

called to Garry and Pelly to take his place at the tent pole while he ran up to the blaze. He cried out an alarm and organized a firefighting brigade.

The fire was the last straw. David cried out to God in despair. "Dear God, not a fire. Have mercy. Have mercy!" he shouted angrily at the top of his lungs. Within minutes, a heavy new downpour began, making firefighting efforts superfluous. David stood wordlessly in the rain and soaked up the answer to prayer. An hour more, and the winds and lightning gave way to a steady pounding of rain.

• • •

By morning, it appeared that there was not a tipi or tent left standing. All had blown flat. A pale sun was trying to announce its presence behind leftover clouds.

Amidst the confusing melee of people trying to regain shelter under shredded tents, David seized a spyglass and searched for evidence of the mission buildings far to the east. It was as though he were on a mountain peak, looking for another distant peak across an ocean of water. He aimed his glass toward where the Upper Church should be. Did it stand? Yes! He could make out each of the buildings of the compound in the distance. All of them were still standing except a few cattle sheds, the Indian bunkhouse, and the servants' quarters.

On Saturday, May 20, another boat arrived with news from Pembina to the south: the water level had fallen! Immediately, people examined the water's edge at their feet. Yes! It had fallen too. The crisis had passed in the midst of the storm, hidden imperceptibly under the wind. Boats were retrieved from hither and yon, from where they were caught on fallen trees and snagged in the midst of the flotsam. On the next day, Sunday, a third of the camp turned out for thanksgiving services.

Later that week, amid an increasing plague of mosquitoes, David boated to the new church, the one he himself had built at Image Plain. It, like the other, was still standing, though the settlers' homes were under twelve feet of water. Yet it was not entirely a happy discovery. With tears streaming down his mosquito-bitten face, he inspected the precious glass windows he had installed with his own hands. Shattered! He sloshed into the sanctuary to find the benches he had built. Broken! The pulpit he had ordered built by a professional carpenter—thrown into a corner! The plaster lovingly troweled onto the walls, cracked and falling off!

"Child of my own rearing," he wept. "Have I taken too much pride in the work of my hands? Have I become too much distracted with pulpits and glass windows?"

Fighting back tears, he stood motionless for half an hour, absorbing the destruction around him, adapting his thoughts to the changed scene, probing for the meaning, for God's purpose in all this disrepair. Then, straightening himself, taking a deep breath, looking upward again, he continued with his thoughts. Will not the gospel sound just as good from behind a table? Surely, my idol is thrown down. Yet God has kept for himself a place for worship.

With tears still in his eyes, David Jones knelt on the dry surface of the upended pulpit and thanked God for using a flood as a surgeon's knife to carefully cut away everything unnecessary, while leaving the one thing of importance.

The praise of God.

He moved on. Finding some of his Image Plain congregation, he held a thanksgiving service among them. He was astonished at how happy they were—truly thankful for the mercies of God in the midst of disaster. David had gone there to minister to them. Yet now they ministered their joy to him at his hour of loss.

He felt closer to his people than ever before. They were closer to each other too, for God had taken away all their fences and washed away all their walls. A new spirit of faith and love searched for expression in song. The congregation sang with great gusto:

God is the treasure of my soul
A source of lasting joy.
A joy which want shall not impale
Nor Death itself destroy.[37]

---

37. Scottish hymn quoted in the *Journal of David Jones*, Sunday, May 28.

The Forgotten Awakening

During the week that followed, the waters began to recede.

One day, when David rowed to the Upper Church, he found several French Canadians looting the gutted building. Thoroughly disgusted, he chased them away and gathered up the loot they had dropped in their retreat.

"Looting churches!" he complained to his servant Donald. "Some people have no shame!" He and Donald decided to spend the nights there to deter pilfering. They slept in the attic of the parsonage, one of the few dry and undisturbed corners in the whole colony.

Seven

By Monday, June 12, Spokan Garry and Kootenai Pelly were back at the Indian school, sleeping in the schoolhouse itself until another bunkhouse could be built. On that day, the plowing began in preparation for the planting of wheat and barley. The two boys, with the others, took their turns at the tree-root plow.

For Garry and Pelly, the planting allowed them time to think, to question. What of the Master of Life? What of the white-skinned ones? What are they teaching us? Is their teaching good?

Spokan Garry could see through the severe test of the flood: Among the *chipixa* are those who observe the Creator's laws, and others who do not—who, in the midst of affliction, choose to live like the animals. Affliction is like the Backbone of the World, Garry thought. From it, all people flow either in one direction or the other, toward God or away from him. Garry's original belief that white people would be a race of holy *sama* had long since been revised in the face of reality. Among the whites there were scoundrels, just as there were among his own people. Each person must be judged on his own merits.

As for David Jones and the Cochrans, the flood had purged them of impurities in their character. "God is forging a people of iron," they said to their people. "God is building a church strong enough to blaze a wilderness trail. Wooden wheels are not good enough here. God is adding to the church iron rims, so that his people can get to their destination without further calamity." The flood had tested the iron in their souls, had drained away doubt, arrogance, jealousy, and small-mindedness. The missionaries and their two churches had come through the test strengthened.

If, as some said, this flood was Satan's attempt to destroy the church, David and William had a ready reply: "God knows what he is doing, and Satan cannot hold a candle to God's power. Jesus is the Author of Life. 'In him and for him and through him are all things made that are made.' 'God hath put all things under his feet, and gave him to be the head over all things to the church, which is his body.' If he, from time to time, lets bad things happen to us, it is for his own hidden purposes. We cannot always see those purposes when we are under the test. But one day, we will look back and understand his wisdom."

Kootenai Pelly and Spokan Garry didn't see it clearly yet, but the great flood would be their Great Divide, their entry into a new watershed. They were ready to cling, not to the spirits of the animal world, nor to the medicine bags they had brought from home, but to the God who stood above all these things and gave assurance of his love—the assurance they had clearly seen in David Jones and William and Ann Cochran.

Spokan Garry never thought of himself as "converting to the white man's religion," though that was what the missionaries hoped for. To him, the Bible held the secrets foretold by ancient prophecy—prophecy that had spread out along the tributaries of the Great River decades before. Both boys saw biblical faith as truth revealed by the Creator for all nations. The People already believed in Quilent-satmen, He-made-us. He was well remembered by every tribe on the Columbia Plateau. Now he had sent Pelly and Garry here to learn of Jesus. Jesus had joined Native and white man together for a transaction of his own making, with its fullest repercussions yet to be revealed.

Spokan Garry asked new questions never before asked by The People: How real, how present is the Master of Life to us in the concerns of daily life? Does he work through angelic or earthly spirits, or does he prefer to work directly? Should we put our confidence in animal spirits, or in the Master of Life himself? Did some great thing happen many years ago as David Jones said—something that broke down a wall of separation between all people and Quilent-satmen? Is the name of Jesus a stronger talisman than all the others, a *sumesh* pouch that has made all others obsolete? Does God give, through Jesus, an invisible "white stone with a new name written on it, known only to him who receives it"?

The pastors seemed to have a *sumesh* pouch planted deep in their lives. And now, perhaps, the Master of Life was ready to give each of the boys a white stone to put in just such a *sumesh* pouch in their own hearts.

• • •

To Spokan Garry, as to all the boys in the school, the scythe was an unfamiliar contraption. To cut hay required strenuous exercise in the hot September sun, far more strenuous than the work of dipping a net for salmon in refreshing Spokane streams. Cutting hay strained muscles— the same muscles over and over again until the shoulders ached and you couldn't sleep at night. Blisters formed at the base of every finger, and the flies bit you on your dripping back. This labor brought no glory.

But the hay must be taken in, or the cattle will get nothing to eat this winter. At least so says Reverend Cochran, and didn't Father, Old Chief, and Chongulloosoon tell us to listen to the *chipixa*?

And yet, by midafternoon, rebellion rose up hot in Garry, as in all the others. He angrily dropped his scythe on the ground and stalked off, leaving Mr. Cochran to do for himself.

And this the parson did, providing an example, that they might see that he was not above hard labor, that he was not merely using the boys as his personal slaves. Gradually, he coaxed them back and assured them that—come February—they would appreciate the wisdom of this way.

Eventually, Garry began to adapt his ideas to a new teaching: feed the hay to the cattle, and you will have meat during the winter. You will not have to find buffalo herds east of the mountains, nor fight the Piegans for the right to hunt them.

After the hay came the wheat and the barley, which had to be cut and threshed. Reverend Cochran explained, "Because we planted the barley late, it must now be cut unripe, ye see, or it'll be destroyed prematurely by fall winds and rain."

Then the corn came into ripeness, provided it was not first devoured by Sir Crow and Master Grub. Mr. Cochran stationed the boys in the fields during the last week before the harvest to preserve the corn from marauders. Garry and Pelly thought alike: Fighting birds is less glorious than fighting Piegans; do we really have to do this? But Mr. Cochran was the teacher now. The People's teachers were too far away to be consulted.

Finally, the land had to be plowed so that the dead plants would enrich the soil for next year's crops. This, too, was hard and inglorious work—standing atop a tree root tipped with iron as two oxen dragged it across the ground.

The boys were too light to make the plow dig much of a furrow. But some things could not be learned in Mr. Garrioch's classroom—they could only be learned by doing them. When the boys threw down the plow and stalked off angrily because it hit a rock and jumped up at them, William personally comforted them, took the plow himself, placed their hands next to his, and completed the job with them. It was slow work—a labor of love: the plowing up of the old ways, and the sowing of the new.

In the midst of all this labor, the weather turned cold and rainy, and Ann Cochran became ill. By the end of September, she was bedridden.

William was beside himself. Yet he prayed, "Lord, it is good for us to be sifted like wheat in order that we may know what spirit we are of. If it were not so, I fear that we would glory in our strength, and imagine that we could run in the path of duty without your aid. You leave us alone that we may learn from experience: without you we can do nothing."

For the boys, the idea that affliction was God's threshing fork took a little getting used to, though William Cochran modeled it well. But it proved to be, for both Garry and Pelly, a profound seed of thought that sprouted into all sorts of new ideas about Creator and his ways.

Mr. Garrioch, the teacher at the school, was a good model too, a kind and humble man. At first, the boys mistook his gentleness for weakness, but it did not take them long to learn the difference between the two.

One day, Mr. Garrioch caught Spokan Garry fighting with another boy, Harry Spencer. After determining that Garry had provoked the fight, he pulled his belt from around his waist and commanded Garry to come to him. He took up the boy in his arms so that Garry's hands were confined in his embrace. Then he thrashed Garry's bottom. The boy was so fearful of the pain—to him thrashing was a new form of punishment—that, as he grimaced, he accidentally bit his teacher's ear during the whipping.

Garrioch set the boy down and felt his ear. It was bleeding! Spokan Garry looked horrified. "Me—I did not mean . . ." he stumbled. But Garrioch didn't need the words, for he was a man of intuitive understanding, and he bore Garry no ill will for taking a piece out of his ear. He smiled kindly with a "That's all right now," then let the boy return to his desk and placed a handkerchief over the ear to stop the bleeding.

Kootenai Pelly thought nothing of the thrashing, for it was a commonplace for Kutenai parents to spank their children. His parents had frequently ridiculed the Blackfeet people across the mountains for their lack of child discipline: "And now see what sort they have turned out to be," his father would add with finality, as though no further explanation were needed. But Spokan Garry didn't think much of the practice. And he vowed that he never would.

Despite occasional whippings, Garry never considered running away from the school—partly because of the plainspoken love of his teachers, and partly because he knew his father was expecting him to learn great new mysteries to teach The People someday. He refused to disappoint his father. And beyond that, the Creator himself had him on a great adventure. To say no to that adventure was to reject life itself.

Several of David's sermons had spoken about how God disciplines those he loves. Even Jesus, at the center of these sermons, had received discipline and submitted to it. Jesus was becoming a familiar person, the one who portrayed the Creator in human flesh. It was as though God had become a man, to show humans what God is really like. And in their turn the two parsons were portraying Jesus in human flesh, to show as best they could what Jesus was like. It was these portrayals that made all the difference in the world for Garry and Pelly. Clearly, the new faith was a good deal more than just words on a page from leaves bound together. The leaves described a reality that could truly change a person's life.

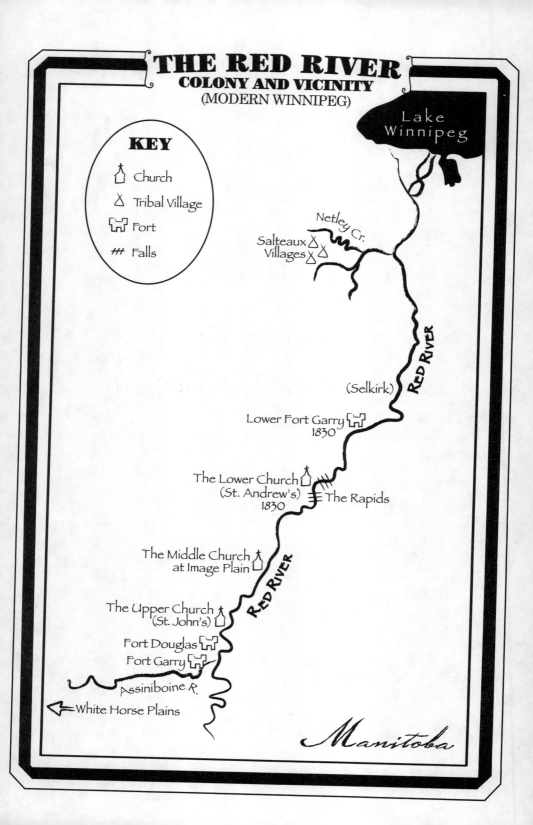

THE RED RIVER
COLONY AND VICINITY
(MODERN WINNIPEG)

KEY

⛪ Church

△ Tribal Village

🏰 Fort

〰 Falls

Lake Winnipeg

Netley Cr.

Salteaux Villages

RED RIVER

(Selkirk)

Lower Fort Garry 1830

The Lower Church (St. Andrew's) 1830

The Rapids

The Middle Church at Image Plain

The Upper Church (St. John's)

RED RIVER

Fort Douglas

Fort Garry

Assiniboine R.

← White Horse Plains

Manitoba

Part V:
Plowing of the Ground
1827-1828

Before you whites came to trouble the ground, our rivers were full of fish and our woods of deer; our creeks abounded in beavers, and our plains were covered with buffaloes. But now we are brought to poverty. Our beavers are gone for ever, our buffaloes are fled to the lands of our enemies, the number of our fish is diminished, our cats and our rats are few in number, the geese are afraid to pass over the smoke of your chimneys, and we are left to starve. While you whites are growing rich upon the very dust of our fathers, troubling the plains with the plough, covering them with cows in the summer, and in winter feeding your cattle with hay from the very swamps whence our beavers have been driven![38]

—Pigwys, Chief of the Salteaux, 1826

I am obliged to be minister, clerk, schoolmaster, arbitrator, agricultural director, and many other things, to this mixed and barbarous people; and it is no sinecure. They are scattered over twelve miles of country, without roads, full of swamps and miry creeks, where in wet weather I have the utmost difficulty in reaching them. I have everything to teach them, to enter into all their personal concerns, to be a peacemaker, and to teach them to manage their temporal affairs. Wearying as all this is to the flesh, it is very beneficial to the people: it leads them to look on me as one of themselves; they feel they can depend on my friendship, they know that I shall advise them only for their own good; and this leads them to listen with a willing ear when I tell them of spiritual things.[39]

—Journal of William Cochran

38. Quoted from the Journal of William Cochran. Tucker, *The Rainbow of the North,* 87-88
39. Tucker, *The Rainbow in the North,* 54.

One

The dawning of 1827 proved to William Cochran that the appalling coldness of the previous winter had not been a fluke. Despite the big man's warm personality and padded physique, he was cold all the time. The agricultural parson was only now getting used to wearing two greatcoats under his black robe while he conducted services. He looked like a black pumpkin reading Scripture from atop the pulpit. William preferred wrapping his feet in blankets, rather than David Jones's recommended wool stockings underneath buffalo-hide shoes. Both men were growing adept at turning the pages of the Book of Common Prayer, hymnal, and Bible while wearing wool mittens.

The Lower Church, at Image Plain, was the coldest of the two they served, for there was only one woodstove there, and that church could only be reached by a bitterly cold horseback ride of several miles through snow and wind. The wind had absolutely nothing to stop it, and the drifting quickly covered all trace of rut and roadbed. Even in the twin-stoved Upper Church, invisible draughts blew from unseen chink to unseen chink, as though the walls themselves had lungs full of frozen air. Besides, the stoves did not warm the air at the front of the sanctuary. It was a measure of these pastors' love that they had provided for the warmth of their people before they had provided for their own.

Spokan Garry and Kootenai Pelly learned to get to church early and reserve for themselves a place near a stove. Here, much conversation occurred with youngsters from other tribes. When Garry discovered that none of them had heard of the Master of Life before coming here, he eagerly filled them in with stories of Circling Raven, of the plague, the fall of ashes, the emergence of the Master of Life tradition, and the Dream Dance of the western tribes to help them remember the prophecies.

At another time, David said to Garry and Pelly around the stove, "Has anyone explained to the two of you how you got your names—the meaning of them?"

Garry and Pelly looked quizzically at each other. No, no one had explained that.

"Nicholas Garry was the founder of this mission, a great man who is as responsible as anyone for this school being here at all. And Robert Pelly was the one who helped build the school, while he was in charge of Assiniboia. Without them, there'd be no school, and I'd be still in far-off Wales." The thought was illuminating to both boys. Neither of their tribes had the habit of naming people after other people. They would look into the nature of the person to be named, a peculiar characteristic, or a particular event that had marked them for life. Naming someone after someone else was a new idea that took some getting used to, because they knew that each person was unique in God's sight, and no one should try to be someone else.

Amazingly, despite the bitter cold, the work prospered. The people came to church in ever-increasing throngs, the congregation doubling, doubling again, and doubling again. The floods had not only torn down their fences but drawn them closer to God. The people had pitched right into the rebuilding of both churches, as though the demolishing had been a challenge to their Scottish spunk and their Christian faith. Churches that had been built in the beginning by a few hands were restored by many. Affliction tentatively united the colonists, even bridging the respectful but artificial gap that separated laity from clergy.

William Cochran aided in this. He had a way of making Christian truth practical, of presenting it in homey ways that farmers, trappers, and boatmen could understand—just as Jesus had done for Galilean fishermen and Judaean shepherds.

William's knowledge of agriculture, too, was helping to bridge the gaps that yawned everywhere in the colony. One thing the colonists had in common: they all had to eat. In the fall of 1826, William had shown the people how to harvest the late-planted barley while it was still green. Despite his warnings about it, many of the inexperienced farmers had failed to take in their harvest in time. Grubs had eaten much of the corn, and wandering war parties continued to drive the buffalo away. As a result, many farmers, as well as hunters, had to face the winter with short provisions.

William Cochran, however, had made sure that the missionaries themselves—and the boys at the school—were well stocked for the winter. His expertise in agriculture was immediately vindicated in the eyes of all. Those who had listened to the parson were eating well. Those who hadn't weren't, but were forced to come to the ones who had learned from the agriculturalist. The abundance of food even in midwinter was not lost on Garry, who saw the relevance of agriculture for his people in spite of the humbling work and the difficulties with grubs, locusts, drought, crows, and endless labor.

Yet it was not expertise alone that earned respect for the two rectors. It was their love.

Late in January, David Jones received a visit from one George Robertson, a settler with an empty larder and a reputation for ungraciousness. Just one year before, David had called at Robertson's home to collect a food offering for the starving French. Robertson had cursed him to his face and refused to donate any food at all.

Now the dinner tables were turned. Robertson's crop had failed. In the humiliation of hunger, the ungracious wretch had remembered that David Jones cared about the hungry. Dirty and bewhiskered, he showed up at David's door wearing a grimy brown coat and a sheepish smile.

"Revr'n, sir, we be stairvin' over 't the cottage, 'n' we've na had a grain o' bairley to chew on these last day or twa. Do ye ha' some bairley bread?"

For David, the request was especially galling. He remembered the unwelcome soup of obscenities this man had fed him the previous winter. There was nothing that rankled him more than the name of Jesus being dragged through the teeth of unbelievers. He had told himself: these cloddish heathen know not what they do. They haven't the slightest idea of how their swearing offends Christians. If I were to speak that way about this man's father or beloved Scottish ancestor, he would strike me in the face. Yet he thinks nothing of dragging my king down into his dirt.

David swallowed his indignation and replied quietly, "Come in, and close the door quickly behind you." He was looking at Robertson's mouth and not his eyes. His own face, he knew, betrayed the contempt he felt, yet his conscience told him that Christ commanded love, not contempt.

He fished among hot words for a few cool ones that would speak truth in love. "Mr. Robertson, we have a Teacher who uses the circumstances of life as a mirror to show us our true selves. God has brought you to your knees so that next time you might have pity on others who come to you on theirs."

"Aye," was the only response. Robertson spoke the word with true, if temporary, humility.

David continued, "Be sure of this: We reap what we sow; God will not be mocked. Yet God is merciful, and he wishes mercy on you, I'll be bound. Mercy triumphs over judgment."

"Aye," said George Robertson, more hopefully this time. Like most of the Scots, he was a man of few words, and Gaelic ones at that, under most circumstances.

David Jones sighed within himself. "Here, now. God has been good to us by supplying Mr. Cochran, who knows how to plow up fallow ground and sow a seed in it. Here are some potatoes that he gave me but yesterday, and some barley soup his Annie made the day before. Now come with me out to the shed, and I'll give you a sack of barley seed, so you'll have something to plant in the spring. Mind, keep the rats out of it."

"Obliged, I be obliged, aye," said the Scot as David led him through the cold to an outbuilding. Robertson was not smiling. The whole experience was painfully humiliating. It was a nuisance that, in order to keep body and soul together, a man must endure such humiliation. But he took the food and the seed with a smile of relief nonetheless.

The parsons' plainspoken, homespun love, like their agriculture, was not lost on Spokan Garry and Kootenai Pelly. During these days, they were sizing up the missionaries and the other *chipixa* of Red River. Just as the Scottish settlers had refused to give over their lands to violent floods, they saw too that the missionaries refused to allow hatred to master them, though a flood of it pushed against them from every corner. If there was stubborn pride in the Scottish settlers, there was equally stubborn love in the missionaries. The same love that won the hearts of Scottish fathers and their children, bringing them to church, also won over the two boys from the Columbia District. David Jones possessed the basic integrity they had come to expect from their own fathers and spiritual leaders, and the gospel of Jesus shone well from such a setting.

Another event made a deep impact on the boys. In March, an epidemic of influenza struck the colony. The "general sickness" afflicted people in different ways. David Jones developed a sore throat that kept him from talking for two weeks. William Cochran coughed even louder than he spoke. These aggravations afflicted many of the white people. Despite them, church and Sunday school were well attended, even when half-sick people were obliged to wade through melting snow to get there.

It was the Indians and mixed-bloods who suffered the most from the epidemic. They were seized with the most wretched vomiting. Confined to bed day after day, many became increasingly dehydrated, as the missionaries and Dr. Hamlyn tried to nurse them to health. Especially hard-hit by the sickness was a mixed-blood Cree teenager named Harry Spencer.

In the midst of the epidemic, the river began to rise under the ice, as mountain snows far to the west began once again to melt. Fear spread with the influenza throughout the lonely colony: What if the floods come again? Now, with so many sick! We shall perish in this cursed place! God have mercy on us!

Dozens of settlers began moving their cattle onto high hills miles away from their homes.

On Easter Sunday, David was preaching from John 10:10, "I know my sheep and my sheep know me." In the middle of his sermon, a loud crack from the direction of the river startled everyone. The ice was heard to move. By the end of the service, the sound of its crashing was dying away. Before the last word of benediction had been spoken, the people rushed out and down to the waterside.

The water level was nowhere near flood stage. A sigh of relief gave way to general rejoicing, and to the beginning of planting season. A spirit of thankfulness filled the colony—filled, too, the sermons of the pastors for weeks to come. "You see how God has cared for us," William told the boys. "Though our churches were filled with water and our houses floated away, has not God preserved us and given us what we need?"

It was true. Who could deny it? All their needs had been cared for, all winter long.

Pelly and Garry reflected on this teaching. The whites reverenced, not the creation, but the Creator. The creation was to be used, harnessed, plowed—but not treated with reverence. The whites used the earth, planted it as a garden, made it do what they wanted. They bent it to help them; they said that the Creator had given it as a gift—in the same way that the white man gave gifts to The People, gifts of iron from the earth's belly. If The People did not believe that it was right to mine the iron from her depths, was it not hypocritical to delight in the weapons made from the iron?

And what was the result of this teaching about the earth? They, Garry and Pelly, did not starve during the winters. But the buffalo hunters did. It was a lesson. Let The People learn to plant, and no longer only to hunt and trap.

Though hunger had been beaten, influenza had not. So many people were afflicted that the number available to sow seed was cut in half. Up and down the west side of the Red River, the land had been divided into agricultural lots a half mile or more in length and only a few hundred feet or yards in width. This arrangement allowed each colonist a snippet of river access at the east end of his long, narrow field. One could look north and south across these flat, coal-black parcels and observe a dozen neighbors sowing their wheat and planting their potatoes, one after another into the distance.

William sowed wheat, while David harrowed it. Spokan Garry and Kootenai Pelly joined the group that plucked out roots and stones.

During the following week, the boys went to the parsonage to learn how to cut seed potatoes. Ann Cochran, wearing scarf and apron, was the teacher. She had a singsong voice full of bubbly energy.

"Leave an eye on each one, you see," she said, demonstrating with a paring knife. "Each eye'll produce a half-dozen more potatoes in the fall. Do it right, and I'll bake a cake that'll taste jolly good tonight after the work's done."

That evening, after the planting, William took the boys back to the parsonage for the promised reward. The aroma infused the whole atmosphere with goodness.

"And now, what heavenly, angelic delight has my Betsy prepared for us?" William sang. He alone called her Betsy. Still wearing her full-length white apron, she brought the masterpiece—a cake with real frosting—into the sitting room.

"Ah!" exclaimed her husband, donning his wire-rimmed spectacles to see the masterpiece better. "A king's reward—and complete with sugar icing! Now these boys'll see if I haven't married the finest baker in Assiniboia!"

It was not the cake alone that delighted Spokan Garry. It was the warmth of the Cochran household, their good-hearted jokes, the sense that they believed in him, that they were on his side. The Cochrans were much younger than his own parents, yet they seemed to have the same care for him that his own parents had.

But the upper crust of Hudson's Bay society were beginning to suspect that William Cochran was nothing but a plowboy, and his wife a common countryside busybody. They kept their distance from the Cochrans and their love-warmed home. George Simpson, on occasional visits to the Upper Church, did not find William Cochran as stimulating in conversation as he had found David Jones. Cochran was too common.

David was still ministering to the sick—especially to Harry Spencer, who was sinking fast during the week after Easter. On April 25, David called on him at the makeshift hospital Dr. Hamlyn had set up in a vacant cabin during the epidemic. Harry, his lips cracked, his face white, seemed scarcely conscious.

David asked with quiet anxiety, "Do you want me to bring you anything?" He abhorred his feeling of helplessness at times like this.

The boy opened his black eyes wide. He looked piercingly at David, not replying to the question. A mysterious peace shone from his face, though he had been through a most violent sickness. Harry was looking at David as though about to speak solemn words, words that he did not want the minister to take lightly.

"The boys at the school," he gasped between breaths. "Tell them, tell them . . . Jesus Christ has saved poor Harry's soul!"

Something at once joyous and tragic shone into the room through the windows of Harry's eyes—like a sunset made partly of sunlight, partly of clouds. Assurance of salvation was mingled with the premonition of death. David was lifted and crushed all at once. He felt like a seed potato in Anne Cochran's hand, being sliced up so that more plants could grow from him. Every Indian death pierced him to the core. What good could come from these tragedies?

Harry sank into unconsciousness. David ran his fingers through the boy's black hair, cut into bangs over his eyebrows. He wept quietly for an hour. He later confessed these tears in his diary—bitter tears that flowed from love chopped off. They were the same tears that the prophet Circling Raven had once shed in the midst of another sickness, tears of frustration and pain, of helplessness in death and the disappointments of life.

Before the night was out, Harry Spencer was gone. David was with him when he passed away.

In the morning light, with eyes emptied of all tears, David looked out the window and across the flat, black plain. He saw William Cochran and the Indian boys just starting their planting of the potatoes. A verse of Scripture came to mind: "They that sow in tears shall reap in joy. He that goeth forth and weepeth, bearing precious seed, shall doubtless come again with rejoicing, bringing his sheaves with him."

David ran out and told the boys Harry's last words: "Jesus Christ has saved poor Harry's soul." They were dark-hulled seeds, those words— planted in the lives of the two boys from across the Great Divide, fertil- ized by the death of their speaker, and watered with the tears of a grieving pastor. Yet the pastor was not wailing, weeping, or singing a dirge. His eyes grieved, yes, but his mouth smiled. Garry and Pelly saw his grief, and they noticed his joy too.

The Kutenai and the Spokane would have sung a dirge for Harry— but the boys sensed that dirges were not appropriate here. They were to learn new ways, to think new thoughts. There would be no cutting of hair, no painting of faces, no slaughtering of horses, no shouting the words of mourning—"Why have you gone far from me?" David Jones was showing them a different way. Whether it was a better way or not, they could not tell.

Harry Spencer was dead, but his words lived. They were not the words of a white man, but of a Native like themselves, spoken with in- ner certainty, almost prophetically—"Jesus Christ has saved poor Harry's soul."

Two

William Cochran was plowing and harrowing a field he had cleared the previous fall. He was showing Kootenai Pelly and Spokan Garry how to work the soil into hills with a hoe. As he put four kernels of last year's corn into the hand of each boy, he taught a rhyme that his father had taught him: "One for the blackbird, one for the crow; one for the grub, and one to grow. Aye, that's right! Four kernels to the hill, and ye'll find a good crop come September. One out of four is about what you can expect in this fallen world of ours."

Garry and Pelly were understanding English now. They spoke it, too—with a Scottish burr. Long ago the two boys had set aside their alphabet cards. They were reading from books now, although *Alison's Abridged History of England* held but little interest for them.

Garry had taken to wearing the white man's clothes. A Scottish tam became his head wear, and a white shirt and gray wool trousers replaced deerskin. In this, he became the Indian counterpart to American trappers like Jed Smith, who had taken on Indian clothing and customs. One thing he absolutely refused to do like the white men, however, was to tuck in his shirt. He hated the feel of being tucked in and buttoned down. He also refused to wear the white man's shoes.

June was the month for catching sturgeon in Lake Winnipeg, the great lake to the north beyond Netley Creek. The monsters of the deep were harvested for lamp oil. A hundred pounds of oil could be extracted from each of the gigantic carcasses. For Pelly, the catching of the sturgeon brought back memories of great canoe trips on the Kutenai River, of listening to the orders of the Fish Chief, of torches shining across the water all night long. They had been exciting, the sturgeon hunts. But when he said to Garry, "You catch sturgeon?" Garry replied, "What is sturgeon?" Garry had to admit that the biggest fish he had ever caught was a mere salmon.

During this month, many of the boys at the school took employment as tripmen, manning the York boats that took brigades hither and yon. The school and the churches thinned out considerably, to the consternation of David and William, who chafed to each other about it.

The Métis—offspring of French-Canadian and Native people—went off on their separate journey in June, a traditional buffalo hunt. Garry and Pelly observed another curiosity: amphibious transportation. The Métis brought their screeching Red River carts south to the Assiniboin River near Fort Garry. Then they took the dish-shaped wheels off, tied them to the bottoms of the carts, and pushed the carts into the river. The buoyant crafts floated easily to the south side of the river, where the men untied the wheels to begin the journey beyond Turtle Mountain to the plains of the Souris and the Coteau of the Missouri.

The Métis were hoping for a good hunt this year. A band of Assiniboins had reported that the Sioux were giving up their harassment of the colony—they would no longer chase the buffalo away. The Métis were jubilant: the Company paid well for pemmican, which was the main product of the early hunt.

At the end of July, the Métis returned. Their returning carts were loaded with bags of pemmican. The Métis had carved the meat into thin strips and prepared the pemmican at Pembina to the south.

Pembina, a mere collection of shacks on the prairie, was a great pemmican town. There, the dried strips were pounded to a pulp over pieces of rawhide spread out on the prairie. Then the Métis would pour the meat into bags made of buffalo hide. Melted buffalo fat would be poured into each bag until it was full.

The Métis did not trouble themselves about finesse in this process. No one ever doted over pemmican the way the American trapper Bill Sublette doted over Crow buffalo jerky in Saint Louis. No, pemmican was full of long hairs, pebbles, and grit, and it would never be mistaken for gourmet food. Its advantage was that it could conveniently be carried on trips, and it would last forever without spoiling. People would rot before pemmican would. And anyway, the rough customers who rode the York boats and canoes to the Athabasca River and Great Slave Lake scarcely noticed hairs, pebbles, or grit. They were a boorish lot who had pebbles for teeth and hair on their stomach linings. What were a few extra pebbles and hairs to them? The *haut cuisinerie* of a Paris chef would have been wasted on them. Let them eat pemmican.

· · ·

On a Sunday late in May, David Jones preached on Luke 18:18: "Master, what shall I do to inherit eternal life?"

At the end of the service, David challenged the boys in the school to make Jesus the Master of *their* lives; then, he said, they would receive the promise of eternal life. But they would receive this only if they made Jesus their lord and master and agreed to do as he said.

The sermon struck a chord in Garry, but not the one David intended. Garry approached his mentor with a question later that day, trying to put together what his people believed with what David taught. He was always trying to go from what he knew to what he did not know. It was like crossing a river. He did not move to a new stone until he was sure it was anchored well in the bottom of the creek.

Accosting David Jones outside the parsonage, Garry asked: "Is Jesus the sun? You spoke of the Master of Life today. Is he the sun?"

"Yes, Jesus is the Son of God," came the reply.

Garry could see that the parson was not tracking. He already knew that Jesus was the Son of God, that He-made-us had a Son named He-saves-us.

"No, is he *the sun?*" Garry pointed to the sun. Many of the tribes in the West had become convinced that the being revealed in the white men's book was the sun. They called the sun "Master of Life," believing that the great being to be revealed by the white men would be the sun. "You spoke about the Master of Life today. Is he the sun? I have not heard you say so, but . . ."

David, horrified, replied, "He most certainly is not the sun! You must not think any such thing. You must not worship the sun."

"No, no! That's not what I meant. We worship Amotkan, He-who-dwells-on-high. We call him also Quilent-satmen, He-who-made-us. My people do not worship the sun. But my people have taught that the one to be revealed by the white teachers will be the sun."

"Sun? The sun?" David was trying to leap over barriers of thought, to understand how Garry's people thought, to anchor the gospel in a mind that revered nature. It was not easy, but words came to him little by little, and he looked earnestly into Garry's eyes.

"Well, you must not worship the sun. But when it comes to that, Jesus is the Sun of Righteousness. Perhaps the thought is not so far off track after all. Jesus is light, and there is no darkness in him at all. And if we want to follow him, we must walk in the light. It is like walking in sunlight. Following Jesus is like walking in sunlight."

Garry thought: David Jones always has a good way of explaining things. A friendly way. He anchors the next stone in the bottom of the stream, so you can take your other foot off the last one without losing your balance. Garry began to think about what it means to walk in the light without worshiping the sun.

As a result of his thinking, he accepted David Jones's invitation to follow Jesus.

• • •

On June 24, a solemn occasion arrived. As a result of their receptiveness to Christian teaching, the two from the Columbia District were baptized, along with eight other boys in the school. Pelly and Garry had decided to cut their hair short, so when the water was sprinkled on their foreheads, it dribbled off their noses and onto their shoulders. A smiling David Jones repeated the words:

"I baptize thee in the name of the Father and of the Son and of the Holy Ghost."

For David, it was an occasion of great joy, the birthing of two souls into the care of Jesus. He loved Pelly and Garry as though they were his own sons. "I became your father in Christ Jesus," he would quote to them frequently, and they knew he meant it.

This baptism was entirely different from the premature and ridiculous ritual performed so casually by George Simpson. Because they had received the love of God through his representatives, the baptism this time held meaning. It was a mystery, a spiritual threshold, to both boys. They were used to spiritual mysteries. Their people had always been deeply in touch with the spirit world, whereas many English had lost touch with the mystery of creation and had grown obtuse toward spiritual things. David and William's journals were full of exasperation about the spiritual thickness of the English, who had grown hardened in material preoccupations and Enlightenment skepticism. To many English, baptism was nothing more than a religious ritual performed by the officials of the established church, a meaningless mass of religious gobbledygook. Once the ritual was over, it could be easily forgotten. Yet, even though they didn't believe in it, they still thought Christianity was better than any other religion because, in their minds, it was English.

But baptism meant much more than that to Spokan Garry and Kootenai Pelly. In the back of their minds sounded the words of their friend, the Cree lad Harry Spencer, who had passed away the previous winter. His words still echoed in their hearts: "Jesus Christ has saved poor Harry's soul. Tell the others! Jesus Christ has saved poor Harry's soul!" The whole event had made a deep impression, and the retelling of it had not died down even now. The mystery of the spirit world had invaded Harry's life at death, and whatever had happened to him, they—Pelly and Garry—wanted in on it. They wanted to walk in the sunlight. That is why they agreed to be baptized, though the ritual itself left them feeling little different than they had felt before.

• • •

Locusts descended on the harvest that fall. William Cochran railed against them, describing them as a species of animal that devours plants not because it is hungry, but for the sheer love of destruction. Then, typical of his approach in preaching, he compared locusts to the power of sin that will eat a man's soul until there is nothing left. After church, the people would go out to see the destruction of the cornfields—nothing left but stumps—and they would see also the destructiveness of sin.

Nonetheless, there was a good harvest of barley, wheat, potatoes, and corn that fall. Despite a cloud of locusts and a plague of worms, the harvest was again proving to be a fitting reward for all the labors of clearing, plowing, harrowing, and planting. Food bins were actually overfull for the first time in Red River memory.

That fall, William Cochran told David Jones that he had his eye on some more land near the Rapids, some six miles north of David's church at Image Plain—the place where they had rolled the York boats on logs. The Rapids, he said, would be a good place for a third church. He was thinking of building a home there too.

He said to David, "I'd like to sow where another man has not yet planted. John West started the church at the Forks; you built the church at Image Plain. Now I believe God would have me create a farm and a church, and maybe, if all goes well, an agricultural community of Natives somewhere between the Rapids and Netley Creek."

David was excited for his friend, and yet he felt a distancing between himself and William. The old loneliness, which had first engulfed him upon his arrival at the colony, was reaching back to claim him. But he said nothing of that.

Then came the annual November cold, sickness, and bad news. David began to suffer severe headaches. Then an outbreak of whooping cough struck the boys at the school, carrying two of them to their graves. A few girls had been added to the school, and David worried about their constitutions, so lacking in resistance to disease.

But thoroughly unexpected was the news William brought back to David from a trip to Pembina. Cochran had hoped to purchase some sheep, brought up the Mississippi from Saint Louis, but the sheep had not arrived. William explained to his chagrined yokefellow:

"Winnebagoes just the other side of the Mississippi are on the warpath. They are turning back all shipments coming upriver, and the agent in Saint Louis is unwilling to risk the loss of his stock. There'll be no sheep this year, I'm afraid. Our Indian girls will just have to keep spinning buffalo wool. It's a poor substitute for the real thing, I know."

William filled David in with as much as he knew about the Winnebagoes, a tribe neither of them had heard of before. That night, November 21, David wrote in his journal his deeply troubling thoughts:

> The Winnebagoes, a tribe roaming from Lake Michigan to the waters of the Mississippi, are said to have committed various aggressions and outrages on the Americans in the neighborhood of Prairie du Chien, a settlement about four miles below the falls of S. Anthony; in consequence of this the Americans sent their *gens d'armée* into the woods and took about sixty prisoners, out of which the Governor selected eighteen and ordered them to be executed! What a lesson does this teach us of the state of things in the interior of North America! Under a government professedly Christian—where liberty and equality are the boasted principles of their constitution; eighteen of the aboriginal possessors of the soil are hung at the caprice of an individual; a death in the estimation of the Indian the most degrading in nature, and from which his mind would revolt a thousand times more than from the idea of a month's torture inflicted in the usual

way! Poor, degraded and persecuted Indian! Where is now thy title of "Lord of the land?" Unhappy representative of a once fearless and independent race! . . . Every man possessing the least spark of feeling—of humanity—of generosity, of any principle which can be credit to his nature must burn with indignation at the very idea of such conduct; and I trust that this transaction will cause a voice to be heard in the Congress. . . .[40]

David knew nothing of the explorer-turned-politician William Clark's difficulty in finding a sense of outrage in the U. S. Congress. Clark believed that once a victorious people had conquered their enemies, they should reach out to strengthen and restore the defeated people. But Clark's voice was becoming fainter and fainter.

As for David, he knew only his own outrage and shame. He was embarrassed by his race—by the ease with which white people destroyed all who came before them. To William he said, "It is as though we have become locusts, and as we sweep down upon the land, we are devouring everything in our path."

• • •

Mercifully, Spokan Garry and Kootenai Pelly did not hear of these outrages. Their minds were focused on the west. They dreamed of returning home to tell their families and friends all they had learned at Red River. They longed to sit naked in the sweat lodge, then plunge into the river as in the old days. They longed to speak with their parents, to see them smile and wonder at all they would tell.

That winter, William Cochran took the students ice fishing. Certain places on the Assiniboin River were known for good fishing. The big parson took the fifteen boys and four girls from the school out on the ice, where they sawed a hole and built a rough shack over it. Fish

---

40. *Journal of David Jones*, November 21, 1827.

were becoming a more and more important staple of the colony, partly
through the suggestion of Kootenai Pelly, who had fished more than any
of them and whose people had been ice-fishing for centuries.

For a week, they took turns dangling a line into the hole. William
Cochran let them leave school for this work. In his mind, the real school
was out there on the ice. He saw little use for traditional classical education. He wanted Native children to learn how to survive winters, for he
saw the suffering of the local tribes. He was intensely aware, from his
conversations with the local chief, Pigwys, that it was the white peoples'
encroachment that was creating this suffering, but bemoaning that fact
didn't help anyone deal with their hunger.

Excited children from eight to eighteen pulled up fish one after another through four holes in the ice. Most, including Spokan Garry, had
never fished through ice before. The school was not only a place for Natives to learn from white people, but also to give to each other from their
own distinct lifeways. Kootenai Pelly was in his element as teacher of this
winter skill that others knew nothing about.

Then came Sunday—the "Sabbath," as it was known to the Anglicans.
"There'll be no work on the Sabbath, even fishing," insisted Cochran. So,
as usual, the nineteen children attended Sunday school and worship, and
played at draughts or the Indian game of hand in the evening.

The next day, Garry and Pelly and a friend, Henry Budd, went out to
the ice shack. From the bank they could see that strangers were occupy-
ing it. The boys approached warily. A French Canadian was there in the
doorway, smoking a pipe and whittling a gewgaw. Garry spoke to him in
a brogue like that of his teacher, Mr. Garrioch: "This be our shack."

Two fat, whiskered, sneering Frenchmen came out and joined the
other. "Yesterday, you have left this place. Now we are here. *Au revoir, mes
petits garçons*."

The three boys ran back to the school and reported the affair to Mr.
Garrioch and Reverend Cochran. Cochran stormed down to the river,
beating fist into palm. He charged out on the ice with a determined tread,
opened the door, and said to the men huddled inside: "You have taken

our fishing hole while my boys were observing the Sabbath. Kindly give it back." His words were measured, but his voice was threatening, and he was bigger than any of the Frenchmen. Unfortunately, the Frenchies were too many for him to dislodge, and they knew it. They stood their ground.

Never again did William Cochran collect food offerings for the French. He was not as forgiving as David Jones.

• • •

As for David Jones, he was more and more encouraged by the growth of his ministry. The two churches were filled to overflowing with Scots, Orkney Islanders, English, Indians, and mixed-bloods. What a joy it was to see the uniting together of people of such diverse tribes and tongues! "Does this not speak well for the future of the continent?" he observed to William Garrioch one day.

Only the English failed to attend church in increasing numbers. When a new boy, just arrived, referred to Christianity as "the white man's re-ligion," David corrected him with much warmth in his speech. "White men! They are the last to come to church." It was true: the darker the skin color, the more enthusiasm for Jesus Christ. Added to the general lack of interest of the Hudson's Bay aristocracy in serving Christ, the English considered the mixed-bloods and the Indians to be beneath their rank, and they all knew that they would have to mingle with them if they came to church. There was, after all, something decidedly un-British in the way people of diverse backgrounds were coming together during wor-ship services. They believed that in heaven there would be special loges reserved just for them. They would have started their own upper-crust church, but Jones and Cochran were the only Anglican pastors for hun-dreds of miles in all directions. On most Sundays, the English protested against their lowly style by staying away.

The winters were unkind to David. He became severely stricken with pleurisy and asthma. While riding horse cariole between churches, the cold air seemed to destroy the very fabric of his lungs. Many times, he was so weakened by the task of preaching that he had to be helped down from the pulpit afterward. Dr. Hamlyn was recommending a sabbatical holiday in Wales.

It did not help his condition when, on May 5, he was nearly drowned in freezing water. He had just launched his canoe in the rain-swollen creek that ran between the church and the parsonage. A sudden gust of wind caught hold of the raised bow of the craft, swung it around, and banged it into a tree at the water's edge. David tried to prevent the disaster, but he only succeeded in breaking his paddle and launching himself into the water. The creek was still full of ice; David was paralyzed with cold, and his body went into shock. He managed to stagger to the bunkhouse where Kootenai Pelly helped him to the stove and covered him with blankets until he was restored. "It was only by the mercy of God that I managed to crawl out of the water," he chattered.

William Cochran showed up that afternoon and learned of David's brush with death. Always on the lookout for lessons to teach the boys, he went out and brought in a chunk of ice. "You see this ice?" He held it up before them as though they had never seen ice before. "It nearly killed Reverend Jones, it did. But we can make a friend of it. Now, come with me, and you'll see."

He led them back out to the creek. "Pick up, each of you, as much ice as you can hold."

Accordingly they picked up armloads, which they carried in their shirts, held out in front of them like aprons. "Now, bring it to the north side o' the schoolhouse." They followed him through the fenced garden plots to the back of the building.

"Now we dig a hole in the shade, and bury the ice here."

The boys glanced at each other in quiet amusement. The ritual seemed to signify that they had killed an enemy—not that they had made a friend of the ice.

But in time, the buried ice proved to be friendly enough, especially with the arrival of summer. With it, they cooled all manner of drinks and foods in the hot summer sun. The cold cache lasted well into July! This idea will be useful to the people, thought the Spokane and the Kutenai.

It was a significant lesson: the winter can be tamed. The white people have learned to extract comfort from curse, to make even the winter serve them. It has been well worthwhile to live with them. The People had wisdom when they sent us to this place. We feel like storehouses filled to overflowing with knowledge until we can hold no more. Surely it is time for us to go back and teach what we have learned?

Three

The first occasion for breaking open the ice cache occurred when Governor Simpson showed up on one of his whirlwind trips to set everything straight throughout the continent. The last week of May, he entered the new Fort Garry, which was being built out of limestone so that it would not float away if there were any more floods.[41] He slapped Donald MacKenzie on the back and proposed a second trek out to the Columbia District.

Later that week, on May 31, Simpson and MacKenzie were riding to the parsonage north of Fort Garry. With them rode MacKenzie's German-born wife, Adelgonde. The two had been married by David Jones two years before in the parsonage. Addie had brought a slight civilizing influence to her gigantic husband and she even helped out with the school from time to time.

Whenever Simpson was around, the MacKenzies had to learn how to listen quietly while their superior bestowed his orders and opinions. Today, the governor was full of words.

---

41. It is the rear gate of that stone fort that remains preserved at the heart of Winnipeg today.

"By God, this Cochran is a disappointment!" he was saying. "Donald, he's a regular country bumpkin! And his wife: a low-class dollymop! Oh, she tries to cover it up—likes to appear as a great woman of prayer. But underneath! Well, a low-level vixen she will always be. Don't you agree? Entirely unsuitable as a teacher for the daughters of the Company." During the last year, Ann Cochran had started a school for Company officers' children. George Simpson did not approve. Yet he was not over the school and had no authority to change it.

The rotund MacKenzie kept Simpson's ball rolling as both engaged in their favorite pastime of railing against the Christian missionaries. "And I think ye should ken it, sir: Cochran has talked your David Jones into startin' an Indian farmin' village—and gettin' the Salteaux to come live in it."

The news brought visible consternation to Simpson's face. "What? Teach them farming? The Indians? He'll do nothing of the sort! What is he about, this Mr. Cochran? Why can't he take a lesson from Bishop Provencher? Do the Catholics teach their people to farm? Soon this country parson will have our 'breeds so they won't man our York boats or set their traps! I shall have to straighten out this Northumberland nincompoop."

Donald and Adelgonde smiled at the thought.

The three soon arrived at the parsonage where they were to dine. All three were dressed in their finest dinner wear. Donald had slimmed down to about three hundred pounds to please his wife—and for another reason too. While on the Columbia, his weight had given him an advantage over other men; but here, it merely invited ridicule. The men had started calling him "Fat MacKenzie." Back in the Oregon country they had named a pass after him. But here, heroic deeds were forgotten in the highly competitive atmosphere of Fort Garry, which filled itself to overflowing with slander. It was a unique feature of the civilized that they forgot how to honor people even when they deserved it.

Spokan Garry, Kootenai Pelly, and Henry Budd had been chosen to serve table for the visit of the Company dignitaries. The three boys had become especially close friends since their baptism that summer. They were also the missionaries' pride and joy.

Spokan Garry let the dignitaries into the house. The lower level had two rooms, with sleeping quarters upstairs. Garry took the greatcoats, hung them on pegs beside the stairs, and ushered the guests into the combined kitchen, dining room, and sitting room on the left. Ann Cochran and David Jones were there to welcome them. William had not yet arrived.

It was a cozy room, made of horizontal beams placed *pièce-sur-pièce* into grooves in the corner posts. It also boasted real glass windows with curtains. Trunks adorned the corners of the room, for the missionaries kept all their clothes in trunks, not in wardrobes or closets. (A "closet" was a place for people to close themselves off for prayer, not a place for hanging clothes.)

A bright fire graced the large limestone fireplace, which poured its unwanted heat into the room. The wealthy could afford a separate, free-standing kitchen, but neither the Cochrans nor the Joneses were wealthy. Two spider pans were straddling coals, raked to one side of the hearth, to keep food warm without burning it. The delicious smell of potatoes and venison invited everyone to dinner.

Ann Cochran was in the awkward position of serving people who, she knew, looked down their noses at her because of her low-class origins. She was largely silent throughout the evening, cooking and serving from a sense of duty and putting on a brave face in the presence of her detractors.

"And where's Reverend Cochran?" Donald MacKenzie inquired pleasantly.

"He be a-plowin' the cornfield. Did you see him not?" said Ann, trying to be affable.

In the last three years, Cochran had increased the acreage from three to twenty-four. But this was the last clearing he would create here. Not a minute later, they heard a large cowbell clanging outside, an undignified *mooo*, and the voice of the missing Cochran, preaching to someone:

"Now, now Bessie! Remember Jesus wants us all to learn servant-hood. Be a good gairl now, and bear up under your suffering without complaint, and you shall have your reward."

Simpson and MacKenzie looked out the window—and saw William Cochran riding to dinner on a cow! They glanced surreptitiously at each other. What is the Church of England coming to, that it ordains such as these for men of the cloth? said Simpson to himself. The Cochrans' status fell yet another notch in his eyes.

But the warmhearted parson burst into the room with a broad smile and words of genuine humility. "Och, the time got away from me. Please accept my apology for my tardiness. And me, tryin' to teach the boys to be on time. Now you boys may learn a lesson about the embarrassment o' bein' late."

"Quite all right, I'm sure," said the guests.

David Jones, always eager to say the good word, smoothed over the awkwardness. "We shall have plenty of wheat and corn to sell the Company this year, thanks to Mr. Cochran."

"Yes, corn is all well and good," MacKenzie said. Inside, he chafed. Corn, corn. We didn't come here to talk of corn!

"Look here," piped Simpson. "It's good that you have invited the two boys from the Columbia tonight. Fact is, I'm on my way to the Columbia soon, and I thought the lads might want to write to their families to reassure them, you know. I'd be happy to read their letters to their parents, if they would like to write home. I trust they have learned how to write!"

"To be sure," Cochran beamed proudly.

Garry and Pelly pricked up their ears. Their minds raced with excitement, and with words for their parents. They began to imagine not only writing home, but going home.

Garry thought: Oh, for the quiet waters that sweep past the village, the breeze in the pines at twilight, the fresh grandeur of the Great Mountain, the gentle jokes of uncle Chunguloosoon.

By the time they snapped out of their daydreaming, the company was seated at dinner. Simpson was talking again, quite animatedly, his forehead shining in the firelight. "Now, Reverend Cochran, what's this I hear of a harebrained scheme to start an agricultural village among the Salteaux? This is merely rumor, is it not?"

"Rumor?" The saintly smile vanished from the face of the big parson. Having taken the seat nearest the fire, he was nothing but a black silhouette. The visitors could not make out his expression.

"Far from rumor, sir. Far from rumor! Apart from such a plan, it is impossible to teach the Native men. We have but women and children here. That is well, as far as it goes, of course. The school proceeds well, but we cannot reach the men until we shall manage to get them settled in a community. As long as they are wandering about, they are lost to any improvement in their condition, material or spiritual. They like to hunt buffalo and forage for food, but the buffalo and the food are disappearing with the wilderness. They must learn new ways. Mr. MacKenzie is well aware of the starvation that threatens them every winter. In winter, the families are dependent upon the children we have taught here. More and more we see desperate families coming here to beg from our boys! Their wandering habits are a thing of the past. These people must be weaned from wildness."

David was tensing up. He felt an asthma attack coming on. He excused himself from the table. Donald MacKenzie refused to confirm or deny the story of starvation. Starving Salteaux were simply not his concern. Neither was starvation a concern to George Simpson, who had seen plenty of Natives starving throughout the West, and had grown accustomed to the sight.

Governor Simpson felt suddenly warm. His words were hot too. "It is not in the best interests of the Company that you start a farming town for Indians. We rely on these Natives to perform various duties as Company servants. What is good for the Company is good for all. Remember: you are here by invitation of the Company. Take care to remember that."

Cochran paused, swallowing hard. There was an even hotter fire growing within him, and his words exploded like a log popping sparks from the fireplace: "The Company is not Lord! Jesus Christ is Lord! We must all give account to him, and what is the Company doing for these poor Indians, but to bring starvation upon them? These boys who sit by our fire here have learned that they need not starve in winter. But what of the countless host of their kinsmen who will die this winter because they are too feeble to walk and too poor to ride—and their tribes wish to move with the buffalo across the snow? Does the Company not care about them?"

His voice was rising out of control, his smile barely concealing his passion. Ann surreptitiously patted him on the lap in an effort to calm him down.

As for George Simpson, he was disliking the parson still more with each passing moment. What! Is all the world's righteousness concentrated in this country bumpkin?

Donald MacKenzie belched loudly, trying to communicate what he thought of Cochran. "Chasin' the buffalo. Snarin' deer. Starvin' in winter. 'Tis their way. If you try to change 'em, you do 'em muckle wrong. This I ken, Mr. Cochran: the Indians willna change. Och, they be a wild people, like moose and beaver, and tied to their ways. When the wilderness goes, they go with it. The Company is not here to settle the land, only to take its pelts. The Indians understand that. They accept us, and we accept them. Dinna teach 'em the white man's ways. Dinna settle 'em in your towns. And dinna teach 'em agriculture." MacKenzie finished, belching a second time, to the chagrin of Adelgonde, who moved away from him slightly.

Garry and Pelly heard this speech, but it came from one who had not shown them a moment's kindness, and they did not give it weight.

Cochran, incensed by the arrogance of both men, decided to take Simpson down a peg. "The Company uses the Indian women for relationships of convenience! Is it not true that the gentlemen never really intend to marry the Native women?"

Simpson winced. Cochran's words were a dagger to his heart, an invasion of his private morals, a shattering of his boundary markers. He could not believe the sheer cheek of the man. Cochran was turning out to be another John West, that infernal meddler who had founded the mission here.

Yet the parson continued to press in. "Why are these gentlemen of yours so reluctant to have their marriages blessed by the church? Why do we see so few Company officers in church on the Sabbath?"

Simpson entered a stony silence. Cochran was not a Company employee, so the governor had no leverage over the man apart from threatening words. Such words had always worked on everyone else. He couldn't tolerate his powerlessness in the face of an antagonist who had found his voice.

David Jones reentered the room from outside, where he had been wheezing. Observing the hard silence in the room, he thought it best to break it. "I regret my poor health. I am afraid these climates are getting the better of me. Perhaps now is a good time to inform you all. Mr. Cochran and I have decided: I will have to be making a trip back to Wales. Support for our work has been flagging, and we must build it up if we can. Perhaps the Welsh weather will do me some good as well."

David, like Garry and Pelly, longed for home. This meeting place in the wilderness was a gift of God, to be sure. But he was visualizing the gentle streams and thatched roofs, the country gardens and stuccoed cottages of his boyhood. In this he differed from William and Ann Cochran, who no longer saw England as their home. The plans William was making that spring, to build a house at the Rapids, certified that they were ready to make this place a permanent home. William was no longer thinking of himself as a missionary to Red River Colony, but rather as resident pastor.

Everyone left the parsonage disgruntled that night—everyone, that is, except the two from the Columbia, whose thoughts of home had kindled a longing to go home. Each knew that his destiny was not here. Red River was only a way station in a pilgrimage the Creator had appointed for them. In the meantime, they had decided to write letters to inform their people that all was well, and that the white man's book had not disappointed them.

Part VI:
The Calamity
1828

Kitzunginun's father was chief when the Smith party came. A relation of ours from the Umpqua was visiting at our village. No Coos enters a stranger's camp until he is invited but this relation went right in and opened up a carcass of an elk hanging on a tree in the camp. The cook threatened him and drove him out of camp. This made him mad. He wanted our people to attack the brigade but the war chief and the peace chief said "No." So he went to the Hanis band near Empire and they refused also so he went ahead to the Umpqua and told them to attack the hunters when they came. His father was from our people but his mother was Umpqua so he belonged to them. The Umpquas made trouble for Smith.

—Testimony of George Wasson Bundy to J. M. Maloney, July 1931.
from *Campsites of Jedediah Smith on the Oregon Coast*

At the moment of attack Mr. Smith was off with two men in a Canoe to ascend and examine Bridge River, a stream that flows into the Umpqua, to see if he could find a road to take his Horses . . . a short time after Mr. Smith's departure, there being about a hundred Indians in the Camp and the Americans busy arranging their arms which got wet the day previous, the Indians suddenly rushed on them . . . .

—John McLoughlin to Governor, Assistant Gov'r & Committee,
Hudson's Bay Co., August 10, 1828

One

The Snake Brigade had been going out each year under the guidance of Peter Skene Ogden. He kept pushing the brigade outward in ever-widening forays, down to Grand Lake.[42] What George Simpson had called the most dangerous and disagreeable assignment in the realm, Ogden was turning into an opportunity for discovery. He knew how to use the alluring powers of the wilderness to his advantage.

The Snake country was a deceptive serpent. Smiling wantonly, she beckoned to those *pauvres* with her twittering aspen trees, her rich buffalo meat, her broad freedoms, and her soft, brown women. But when they got to know her more intimately, she revealed to them her true face: the nightmarish, black-painted visage of a Blood warrior. Her true voice proved to be the gargling caw of a raven. Her pleasant limbs terminated in the claws of a grizzly, and her heart was as cold as the winter of 1827–1828.

---

42. Great Salt Lake.

Yet they loved her, and every Christmas, they longed for the next brigade to take them back to her. After they had been with her for ten months, a dwindling number of men took pride that they had survived her embrace another year. The Native women of the brigade took pride, too, in their arts, vying with each other to produce the best-dressed plews in the realm.

Ogden wrote of the '27 brigade on March 13:

All obliged to sleep out in pouring rain and without blankets. Not one complaint. This life makes a young man sixty in a few years. Wading in cold water all day, they earn 10 shillings per beaver. A convict at Botany Bay is a gentleman at ease compared to my trappers. Still they are happy. A roving life suits them. They would regard it as a punishment to be sent to Canada.[43]

Within two years of that journal entry, the veteran guide they called Grand Paul would lose his life—scarred, weary, his face lined—at the ripe age of twenty-nine. He would be one of the last survivors of those early days with Donald MacKenzie, Finan McDonald, and Alex Ross, most of his trap mates already killed by violence, snows, or accidents. The Snake country was unmerciful.

But the trappers were rough too. Ogden knew how to play the roughness of country against men so as to milk the best out of both. In that skill, he surpassed even David Thompson.

But head and shoulders above both Thompson and Ogden stood a giant who was milking the best out of the entire Columbia District, from the Rogue River to Puget Sound, from Rocky Mountain House to Grand Lake.

By 1828, John McLoughlin had been chief factor at Fort Vancouver for four years. In the days of David Thompson, the transvestite Kutenai prophetess Kokomenepeca had prophesied that giants were coming to unsettle the earth. McLoughlin was a giant, but his destiny was not to

---

43. E.E. Rich, *The Letters of John McLoughlin*, lxvii.

unsettle the earth, but to settle it. Not that the chief factor ever tried to form settlements on the Columbia. Just the reverse. His orders were to prevent the settlement of the District so that it would be more permanently lucrative for British trappers. He was a settler of the earth in another way. He was one who stilled earthquakes—who settled the dust that other men kicked into the air. To him was given the rare power to bring peace, stability, unity, and respect wherever his authority reached—wherever, that is, the Columbia River reached.

That power had been tested immediately after George Simpson had smashed his whiskey into the flagpole of Fort Vancouver and shoved off up the Columbia to pick up his two Native lads at the mouth of the Spokane. Concomly had sent a diplomatic party to the new fort to trade furs. His rival, Casseno, had waited for him in ambush, ready to do to him what Concomly had done to others when the British post had been in Concomly's bailiwick. But McLoughlin had sent an armed force to protect the Chinooks, and Chief Concomly had been vindicated in his faith. McLoughlin was a man after his own heart, a man who knew how to wield authority.

Casseno, afraid of alienating the British, had remained friendly too. John McLoughlin was using British influence to bring peace among the tribes. If Alex Ross had seen it, he would not have believed it. Likewise, every American who had offended Piegans by trading with Crows would have been astonished.

All tribes must be permitted to trade with the King George men! It was a new idea, and McLoughlin alone made it work. "We will play no favorites," he said. "We will be enemies with no one but those who declare war on us. We will not permit access to the fort to be blocked by Casseno or by anyone else."

To bolster his strategy, McLoughlin invited the chiefs from all around to visit the fort. He greeted them with his most impressive diplomatic array, showed them his cannons, gave them a tour of his fortifications, and extended a hand of warm welcome to them all. He was the picture of benevolent power.

Concomly respected McLoughlin absolutely. Not only had the new factor protected Chinook trading rights, he also refused his men the right to use liquor as a tool of the trade. Concomly appreciated that impressive bit of leadership twice over. Not only did it show McLoughlin to be a man of authority, but it protected Concomly's son, Cassacas, from the drunken rages that had embarrassed his father in the days of old Fort George. Concomly made a pact with McLoughlin to keep the firewater out of the area for good. Their common dislike for alcohol made them partners in diplomacy. McLoughlin purchased an entire shipload of rum from the Russians, just to keep it away from the tribes. The rum stayed untouched in his storehouse as long as he remained Chief Factor at Fort Vancouver.

As if all that were not enough to vindicate the judgment of Concomly, old One-eye also managed to secure a marital alliance between McLoughlin's stepson, Thomas McKay, and his own daughter, *Timmee*, The Maiden. Concomly was smacking his lips, thinking of himself once again as the big sturgeon in a great river of minnows.

Concomly was not alone in his respect for the chief factor. Virtually all the people—Kanaka, Canadian, Kelawatset, Clallum, and Clatsop—recognized McLoughlin as *hyas tyee*, Chief of Chiefs, and paid him respect accordingly. They called him *Pee-kin*, the White-headed Eagle, not only because he possessed, at forty-three, a mane of white hair that fell to his shoulders; nor because he was so large at six foot four that he looked down on everyone from above; nor because he always wore black formal wear like the eagle; nor yet because his pale gray-blue eyes could pierce you at a hundred yards. They called him Pee-kin for his character, his very nature—for by his character he soared above other persons and the trifles that preoccupied them.

Alex Ross had never awakened such respect, nor had the red-bearded giant Finan McDonald, nor Duncan McDougal, nor Donald MacKenzie, nor Archibald MacDonald.

When the wilderness beckoned to men to free themselves from conscience and live like animals, John McLoughlin held up his hand against her. If a man could keep his standards in the midst of the erosive power of the Columbia Gorge, he could keep his standards anywhere. Such a man was worthy to be listened to, all agreed.

McLoughlin, despite his roughness, his violent demeanor, and his autocratic ways, was a man of conscience, and the people believed in him. They loved to follow him. They hoped in what he hoped for and listened to his voice. The spiritual hopes awakened by tribal prophets like Yuree-rachen and by David Thompson seemed to find embodiment in Pee-kin. He provided a space for order that pushed back the encroaching chaos of the great shaking of nations that was destroying whole peoples throughout the continent. And so the nations up and down *Tacoussah-tesseh* had, by 1828, learned to trust him implicitly.

Two

The sun was down. Oil lamps dimly lit the interior of the factor's house, a large log structure of two stories. Two men, Alexander McLeod and Thomas McKay, had just departed. John McLoughlin's wife, Margaret, her wide cheekbones reflecting her Cree blood, came into the bedroom where her husband was sitting. The bed was too short for McLoughlin's frame, but the factor had ordered it that size on purpose, because he believed it was healthier to sleep sitting up. At present, his feet were resting on a metal box filled with hot coals. He was trying to get them warmed up before getting into bed. An unusually large, oval beaver pelt, punctured by two eyeholes, did double-duty as a throw rug nearby. On the wall hung a buffalo robe, faced with black lining—more of a wall decoration than an article of clothing. Eloisa and David, their children, were sound asleep in the next room.

Margaret approached her husband silently. At fifty-four, she was nine years older than McLoughlin. Yet her hair was jet black, while his was as white as milk. She was only slightly on the heavy side, with a quiet spirit. Reflecting another side of her ancestry, she wore the softly rustling dress of a Frenchwoman, with a fringe of white lace at her neck. Standing, Margaret was no taller than her husband sitting on the bed.

Using the French language they shared, the factor spoke: "These Clallums. They'll be giving us trouble no more."

The woman said nothing in reply, but understood.

McLoughlin sat pensive as his feet warmed to the heater and his speech warmed to his subject. "The Clallums will learn to respect white men, to obey the laws of decency. Those murderers! Five of our best men, brutally hacked to pieces! And their wives—slaves! The butchers do not yet know with whom they have to deal!"

He reflected on the events of the last few days. He had sent Chief Trader Alexander McLeod to teach them a lesson. McLeod, taking a party to Puget Sound, had found the Indians devious and unrepentant. McLeod had given them every chance to surrender the murderers and restore the women—but the Clallums had toyed with him. So McLeod had fired upon their village from the ship *Cadboro* and then landed a party of men to burn their village and their fleet of forty-six canoes. They had torched the main Clallum village at Port Townsend—and all without the loss of a single Englishman. It was a lesson taught.

And yet . . .

Something about McLeod was unsettling the factor's heart this night.

McLeod is a little man. His post is already too big for him, and he cannot grow up fast enough to fill the niche. Always arguing, defending himself, overreacting, losing perspective. The torching of Port Townsend was one torching too many. He shouldn't have gone that far. Justice against murderers is one thing. Taking vengeance against innocent villagers is quite another. How many times have I said it: in teaching the Indians our justice, there must be reminders of our goodwill; in the midst of retribution, there must be mercy.

The Eagle spoke again. "*Vraiment!* But McLeod is going to make us some enemies we don't need, if we're not careful."

241

"*Oui*," the woman replied, and added in French, "He's a brash man, too much like Thomas, but lacking Thomas's strength." Thomas McKay was her son by Alexander McKay, the late Northwester and Astorian who had lost his life years before.

Her husband continued. "But the deed's already done. There're times when I think: to get things done right, you have to do them yourself. McLeod is too intent on proving himself to know what's good for the District. And the more he proves himself, the more he proves himself poor."

He took a draw on his pipe. Margaret sat down next to him and fondled his chin. After sixteen years, they were still in love with each other. His love for her had been a model of faithfulness. He wanted no more Duncan McDougals, marrying for sexual convenience and business partnership, then abandoning their *femmes du pays* when transferred to other districts. McLoughlin expected Company servants and gentlemen to be as faithful to their Native wives as he was to Margaret. If they weren't, he gave them the cold of his eye and the back of his hand. There had been a sharp decline in marriages of convenience, despite the bad example of George Simpson at York Fort—and *his* Margaret. The factor required Company servants to take off their hats in the presence of his wife. Native women were to be treated with respect like any white woman, and there was an end to it!

The stillness of the fireside was shattered by a racket from outside the gate. It was 10 p.m. The gate was closed for the night. Yet someone was shouting, "*Wawa nowitka klatawa inside!*"

The factor put down his pipe and ran out the door. He seized the bolt in the man-sized postern of the great gate, opened the door, and confronted the commotion.

Several Tillamooks were demanding entry. In their midst was a wretched-looking white man. His linsey-woolsey trousers were in rags. He had no other clothes and was suffering from exposure. His back was a festering wound; his black beard was full of dirt. His skin was sunburned and bitten, his hands scabby on the palms. He was at least as tall as McLoughlin, but seemed struck dumb by some unknown terror. He was almost too weak to stand.

McLoughlin, who had learned medicine as a young man, brought the stranger up the steps of his house and into the visitor's hall, a large room with several comfortable chairs. Two elk heads flanking an Indian cedar-bark blanket stared down on the scene as if they knew the stranger's secrets. The wounded man plopped into a chair as though it were heaven. Margaret brought whiskey while McLoughlin washed the wounds. It was well past eleven before the stranger found his tongue.

"Who are you?" McLoughlin asked for the sixth time.

Some scarcely perceptible change occurred in the stranger, as though the sight of Margaret, the taste of the whiskey, and the sounds of human kindness opened a postern inside him. "I am Arthur Black. I belong to the party of Jedediah Smith—of Smith, Jackson, and Sublette."

McLoughlin winced at the name. Smith! He's the one who created that stink with Ogden and the loss of our freemen three years ago. This man, Arthur Black, was with Smith at Flathead Post. I am sure of it.

The black-bearded American continued: "Eighteen men! And I'm the only survivor!" He broke down and wept for sheer grief and frustration. Everyone was silent for several minutes. There was nothing to be said until Arthur continued his pathetic story.

"Jedediah Smith was leadin' us north from San Jose, nineteen of us and near three hundred head o' horses. Come up the Buenaventura, then over to the coast till we come amongst the Umpquas. By July, we had two hundred and twenty-five horses and mules left, and was campin' July 14 with a hundred Injuns next door. All of a sudden, they rose up and hacked our whole group to pieces. I was standing at the edge, got stabbed in the hands and a tomahawk in the back, but made my escape. Before I got free, I saw my friend Virgin hacked to pieces. Tom Dawes was swimming away, but not fast enough . . . all our men bein' hacked apart . . . blood all over the ground." His words trailed off into weeping.

The Eagle's face fell. First the Clallums. Now this. It was as though an earthquake were shattering the peace everywhere at once from some seismic point deep underground.

Black kept talking. "For four days I wandered in the woods, half-dazed. Then I come out to the ocean. An Injun come out of nowhere . . . tried to take my knife. I pounded his skull, he ran away . . . Three days later seven of 'em come at me, took everything I had. After that, I lived on nothin' but frogs, snails, roots 'n' berries. Finally made it to these people, who befriended me an' brought me here. They saved my life." He gestured to the Tillamooks.

McLoughlin turned to one of his freemen who had helped them find the way to the fort. He gave one simple order: "Get LaFramboise."

The man went off and returned with a second man in tow. Michel LaFramboise was a short, broad Frenchman with a big head, dark hair, and a whaler's beard—a fringe lining the jaw and no mustache. Black had been explaining the apparent cause of the massacre—a stolen axe—but now McLoughlin turned to the Frenchman.

"Michel, you ken the Umpquas," he said. "It seems a party o' Yankees has been wiped out. Go to your people there. See if you can get any word from old Centernose about survivors. Scare up some runners to help you. I'll expect word in a fortnight."

The stumpy Michel LaFramboise was as great a contrast to the towering McLoughlin as could be imagined. About all these two men had in common was their employment by the Company. If McLoughlin believed in sobriety, marital faithfulness, and virtue, LaFramboise was accomplished in wine, women, and song. The Company, he insisted, had no right to interfere with a man's pleasures. It was said of LaFramboise that he had a woman in every tribe and a cache of wine on every river. He was also the best scout in McLoughlin's employ. He knew the Willamette Valley, the coast, and the Natives better than any other man alive. And because he had submitted to tribal marriage rites in village after village, he was regarded as "brother" in village after village.

"*Oui, Monsieur le docteur, toute suite!*" Michel replied. "I go first t'ing in the morning." His breath was alcoholic. He had been fetched without warning.

McLoughlin grimaced, but he concluded: This assignment will dry him out soon enough!

Three

Two days later, John McLoughlin was in front of the fort superintending the plowing of a field of "pease." Lightning-lit grass fires had been burning for weeks throughout the Willamette Valley. The smoke, trapped between two mountain ranges, was producing a choking haze throughout the valley. The sun appeared as a red-orange disk directly overhead.

Ah, noon. They'll be serving dinner soon, he observed. Perhaps the governor'll arrive today. He'll be surprised when he gets here. Much has changed in four years. Simpson will be pleased by the self-sufficiency of the fort. We have drastically reduced imports from England.

From the river a mile away, a commotion was growing. A dozen men started up the cart path toward the fort. They were shouting, gesturing. When one of them saw the factor, he shouted, "*Bostons chako. Bostons olo, kokshut.*"

What? Bostons! There are other American survivors?

Within minutes, McLoughlin was face-to-face with John Turner, Richard Leland, and that most disagreeable gadfly, Jedediah Smith! The three were in rags, destitute, and suffering from exposure.

He led them into the fort, the Tillamook guides following. At that moment the cook was in front of the dinner hall, ringing the dinner bell. An imposing monument, the bell hung from a tripod covered with a thin pyramid of cedar shakes.

McLoughlin led the Americans between the two bastions and past the bell to his house. On the way, Jedediah came face-to-face with Peter Skene Ogden. Ogden did not recognize him at first. Jed was heavily bearded and bedraggled. But when Arthur Black shouted a loud "halloo," ran to his friends, and bear-hugged them, recognition dawned on Ogden too.

That torn ear! That scarred forehead! Jedediah Smith, the scum!

A flood of bad memories swept to mind from the most painful event of Ogden's career. Trapping the region east of Grand Lake—Great Salt Lake—he had lost his freemen to the Americans, who promised better prices and great freedoms. Ogden had suffered personal indignities and even threats to his life—and had been summarily ejected from the area, to report to his superiors a financial loss. If he had not been tarred and feathered, it was only because of the want of tar and feathers.

True, Jedediah Smith had not been present, but he had caused the whole situation by his infernal meddling, his snooping, and above all, his mapmaking. Everything Governor Simpson had warned about had taken place. The British and the Americans were deep into a fierce competition, and alcohol was becoming the lure that each side used to get the Natives to trap for them. Jedediah Smith, being the first name in Smith, Jackson, and Sublette, was widely blamed for this deteriorating situation.

Ogden exchanged knowing looks with McLoughlin. The Americans stank with a most un-British odor. Both Ogden and McLoughlin were struggling with a moral obligation to shelter, feed, and bind up the wounds of their enemies. Arthur Black had been disagreeable enough. But Jedediah Smith?

Speak a rough word! Laugh in their faces! Lock them outside the gate! It would be a mercy for everyone! That was what they wanted to do. Instead, they brought the sly, cunning Yankees into the main house and treated their wounds.

McLoughlin sat Jedediah at table and produced venison, ham, and beef. As Jedediah talked, the factor quickly discerned that his story matched Black's. The Tillamooks, too, confirmed that the massacre had resulted from a dispute over an axe—at least, such was the intertribal gossip.

"I have already sent one o' my best guides with Indian runners to fetch word o' your belongings and any survivors," McLoughlin said.

Jed replied, "Sir, these Indians are the worst butchers I've met within all my travels. If you would consider a punitive expedition against them, it'd be a great favor to me if you would let me ride along."

McLoughlin cleared his throat. "I ken well enough how you must feel, Mr. Smith. We have just lost five of our best men among the Clallums o' Puget Sound. It so happens that I do plan an expedition to the south, but what sort of expedition it'll be remains to be seen." The factor turned to a servant. "Send fer Mr. McLeod." The servant scurried off.

McLoughlin carried on. "We canna have the Indians murderin' people with impunity. We have found from the beginnin': the only way to keep order among the tribes is by bringin' home to 'em the certainty o' retribution when they violate the laws o' conscience. Still, I must wait for my man LaFramboise to return before we can be sure what is the correct course."

Jedediah, still seething from the worst disaster of his life, found McLoughlin's evenhandedness a trial, yet he squelched his own retort, sensing the wisdom of the factor of Fort Vancouver. Years of enmity against British fur interests competed with the new respect he was feeling for a man who invited respect by his mere presence in a room. Jedediah adopted a "wait and see" attitude. At the same time, he knew that he himself was being evaluated, and it was an uncomfortable position.

For his part, McLoughlin well knew that fur brigades accumulate all sorts of riffraff, and who was to say that the Umpquas were not justified in their brutality? Americans were well-known for stupidity, brutality, and immorality, and it seemed likely that the wrong was not all on the side of the Umpquas. He would let LaFramboise smell the matter out.

Jedediah ate well, but he refused even the single glass of port offered him at dinner. Jedediah's family, like most Methodists, had never imbibed. In a few minutes, a servant ushered in a short man in his thirties, dressed in a waistcoat and black trousers under his greatcoat. His skin was pale, his beard brown. He looked as though he had spent too much time under Oregon clouds. His manner was dark, stiff, and formal, rather like a smouldering campfire under Oregon drizzle.

"Ah!" the factor shouted as he took up his after-dinner pipe. "Mr. Smith, I would have you meet Mr. Alexander McLeod. Mr. McLeod, meet Mr. Jedediah Smith, one o' our competitors."

McLeod did not move, but nodded nervously, looking at Jedediah, then the floor. The factor continued: "Mr. McLeod, we shall have to divert the Southern Brigade for an errand o' mercy. On your way south, I want you to see what o' Mr. Smith's peltries an' horses you can recover from the tribes around Bridge River. Then you can move on to explore the beaver waters to the south, beyond Fort Umpqua."

McLeod was speechless. His eyes said, Errand of mercy? For these vermin? Look at them. Dirty. Ragged. Common riffraff! And plotting against us these many years. Convince me they deserve mercy!

He looked at the floor and said, stiffly, "Aye, sir. Did you have in mind to punish the Indians?"

"That we have not decided. We shall await LaFramboise before makin' the decision. In the meantime, get your brigade together with speed. You dinna ken what snowy passes you may have to cross south o' the old post. Maybe Mr. Smith can tell us what he kens o' that country."

McLeod looked as though information from Smith & Co. would be as welcome as a live skunk in a beaver trap. With the arrival of Jedediah Smith, the Southern Brigade itself was beginning to stink. Every new edict from the chief factor was less tolerable than the last.

McLeod fumed: Love thy enemies! Puke! How can you run a brigade on advice like that? The whole idea makes me sick!

And the Indians were distasteful medicine, too. Because of them, now he was going to have to do a kind deed for the survivors of a massacre.

Avenging our losses at the Clallums was a kick. But avenging the Yankees is a sick joke!

. . .

During the weeks of preparation for the trip south, Jedediah reviewed his years in the wilderness and all his dealing with the Indians, trying to comprehend what good his wanderings had done. On balance, his contacts with Native people had been favorable, and he couldn't believe that it had all been for nothing—though at present, bitterness was an overwhelming enemy that triumphed for a season. *At times like this, things seem worse than they really are*, he reminded himself. Yet on balance, his relations with the people of the land had been quite positive.

There had been the impoverished little villages of "Diggers," as his men called them, desperately poor people west of South Pass who dug their food out of the ground. All their villages, one after another, had been empty by the time Jedediah arrived, with columns of smoke their only greeting. He soon learned that they kept brush piles always at the ready, waiting to be torched at the first sign of slave-raiding parties from the Plains tribes to the east. As soon as danger came, these horseless people would light the fires as a warning to the next village, and run off to hide in the hills. For all they had known, the white men were just another raiding party looking for slaves.

The degree to which slavery was practiced there had surprised Jedediah. But it shouldn't have. Had not Lewis and Clark found slaves among the tribes of the upper Missouri and freed one of them, Sacajawea, to return her to her people among the Shoshones?

Then, in the mountain camp of Conmarrowap, the Ute chief, he had experienced firsthand the indignities forced on slaves. The hugely corpulent chief had just taken two slaves. Jedediah tried to finagle a treaty between Conmarrowap and the Shoshone chief Cotillon, and he had purchased the two slaves out of their misery.

Moving south, he had come upon the "San-pitches," another desperately poor tribe, to whom he gave some of his precious buffalo jerky. Not a popular decision with his trappers.

Further along, there had been the desert, a place of starvation for man and beast, where they met the Mojaves, tall men and short women clothed with blue tattoos and little else. He had circled north, crossed the mountains, and traipsed across the desert back to rendezvous, nearly dying of thirst. Then he had made the whole trip to the Mojaves a second time.

And then came the Mojave massacre. Several men killed. A desperate search with the survivors through the desert, trying to find water. And then he had learned the reason for his troubles: the Spanish had warned the Mojaves to be on the lookout for Americans. The Spanish were the real culprits. Or so he reasoned at the time.

After months of detention by Governor Echeandia in a Spanish jail, he had finally sailed to San Francisco, hoteled it with Father Duran at San Jose, purchased three hundred horses, and begun his journey north to Fort Vancouver. The year before, he had concluded that the mountains and the desert east of them offered no passage for a herd of horses, so now he was searching out a route north.

All along the way, there were Native tribes, and the farther he went, the more he realized that none of them had ever seen a white man before. The Miwoks were idle little people with villages ensconced among the waterways of the Buenaventura, eating acorns, acorns, and more acorns. This was the one food they didn't have to chase down.

North of that tribe were the Maidu. He would never forget chasing a young girl in good fun, only to see her fall down dead before he could give her the gift he had intended for her. Died of fright! The words he had written in his journal came back to him now: "Could it be that we who call ourselves Christians present such a fearsome picture to a little girl of the wild that she would die merely by looking at us?"[44] His appearance

---

44. Journal of Jedediah Smith, March 1, 1828. Sullivan, *Travels of Jedediah Smith*. 65.

had caused some family a deep tragedy not unlike what he was coping with now. He had tried to leave presents—but they had been so very inadequate to make up for the loss.

During the last several years, Jedediah had become aware through such events that the first meeting of very diverse cultures was bound to be frought with misunderstanding and tragedy, two invisible enemies working against everyone—both white and native. Now that he was on the other side of the table, coping with the consequences of this enmity, he was trying to grasp after God's higher point of view, trying to discern how God would have him overcome the deep bitterness that was eating him alive.

North of the Maidu were the Wintuns, a totally innocent people who rarely wore clothes. He remembered a field of clover with young girls sprawled out completely naked. And a group of Wintun men who, upon seeing the white trappers, began a violent dance as though to ward off these evil spirits with white skin.

Soon Jedediah was moving their horses down into dark ravines. As the land became morose and unfriendly, so did the people of the land. From now on, he would find arrows in the flanks of the horses, shot by invisible warriors at the tops of the ravines. The clouds rained danger and destruction.

These were the Hupas, the "short-haired" tribes, and the Karoks. And finally he had met the Yuroks, the Tolowas, the Chetcos, the Calapooya, and the Coos peoples, encountered while riding up by way of the ocean beach into Oregon. Here he began to encounter the Chinook jargon, trade language of the coast.

Every tribe had been unique. The very idea that there were people called *Indians*, as though they were a monolithic group to be treated all together as one, was completely useless. There were hundreds of distinct tribes and families of tribes, each with its own way of thinking, living, speaking; their lifeways shaped distinctly from all the others. The land shaped these people. Different types of land had produced wildly differ-ent types of people. And almost all had been friendly, once they got over the shock of seeing men with white skin. The Mojaves would have been congenial—and had been congenial—but for the Spanish egging them on prior to Jedediah's second visit.

As the trauma of the most recent massacre began to recede, his past experiences came forward to give perspective. A wealth of memories, most of them positive, began to play their own more favorable and melodious tune in Jedediah's soul. Pain was, after all, only one of the instruments in the orchestra contributing to the symphony of his life.

Four

By Sunday, September 6, though LaFramboise had not yet showed up, the factor gave orders to delay no longer. The Southern Brigade was off, and the Americans with it, to see what could be gained of the stolen belongings and horses. McLoughlin sent sealed instructions, to be opened only upon arrival at the Umpqua.

Alex McLeod was the most undisciplined, lackadaisical, lazy brigade leader Jed had ever met. The tardy caravan consisted of a batteau thirty-two feet long and a small canoe. The two crafts made such slow progress that, by evening, they had barely gained the mouth of the Willamette—a distance of only four miles—downstream, and in good weather.

Well, they had discovered a leak in the batteau.

Jedediah fumed: What do they pay this McLeod to do, if not to make sure the boats are caulked? What incompetence! How does McLoughlin stand for it?

On Sunday, with one man bailing constantly, they managed to traverse the twenty-five miles up the Willamette to the falls, and even to portage their baggage the three hundred yards around the chutes. There, a boat more water-worthy awaited them.

On Monday, about a mile below Champoeg, they met Michel LaFramboise *en canoe* with Thomas McKay and several Natives. Michel shouted across the water, "We are come from the Umpqua. I have just send Nasti to Chief Centernose. He say the ones that do this trouble ware Kelawatset. All property ees scattered all ovair the countryside."

LaFramboise and McKay joined the group. They all camped at Champoeg, the Hudson's Bay horse camp. Thomas McKay (Dr. McLoughlin's stepson) was a tall, muscular, dark-faced man of thirty, who showed none of his stepfather's polish. He walked with a limp and swore frequently. His eyes, peering out from under heavy brown eyebrows, seemed always to sparkle with extreme emotion—pleasure, disgust, friendship, or enmity, depending upon the mood of the moment.

Champoeg, a point of land in a bend of the Willamette River, had been a place of trade among the tribes for centuries. Every spring, the Klamaths brought slaves to sell to the tribes of the north. The Hudson's Bay Company had taken over the place as a kind of depot and abolished the slave trade, but now Champoeg was a mess. Grass fires had turned everything black. The horses had scattered.

In the midst of the desolation, McLeod decided neither to press on, nor to look for the horses. LaFramboise was certain that the men needed a regale, and he prevailed upon the Scot, in the name of tradition, to have one—now that they were no longer under the eyes of Dr. McLoughlin. So they broke out a keg and, for three days, drained it empty.

Jedediah's opinion of McLeod sank still lower during the regale. The whole camp was either drunk or sick. Little work was done but for the completion of a few packsaddles, made from branches hewed and lashed to form an X.

During this time, LaFramboise went back to Fort Vancouver, then arrived back with two notes from McLoughlin—one for Jedediah, the other for McLeod. Jedediah received his note with little enthusiasm, for it placed him completely at the mercy of Alex McLeod. McLeod was pleased to read that Dr. McLoughlin was giving him discretion in the matter of retaliation against the Kelawatsets.

The camp ran out of food. No hunters were appointed to supply the larders. Jedediah didn't want to go hungry, so he went out and brought back a deer to feed the besotted crew. Several men ran out into the meadow to chase down some horses. It did not occur to them that horses run faster than men; they caught none. All complained at night of headaches.

On Saturday the 13th, the men, working in concert, surrounded some horses and transferred the packs to horseback. But just at that moment, the skies clouded over and rain pelted the blackened earth. McLeod considered such weather a complete hindrance to further travel, and kept his men in tents. Many of them, after all, claimed to be sick.

For the next two weeks, the weather changed from "rain" to "flying showers" to "less rain" to "clouds"—as McLeod duly recorded in his journal. But even Alexander McLeod could not keep his men from wanting to make some progress, so they made their wet way to the mouth of the Santiam.

McLeod kept complaining about the wild mustangs or marrons that kept running off. Every morning, valuable time was required to chase them down. Jedediah pointed out to some of the men that horses could be hobbled by tying together the right front and the left rear legs. His suggestions were ignored. Jedediah exercised his frustrations by going hunting. By the 30th, so many horses had run off that McLeod was forced to purchase new animals at an exorbitant price from the local Natives.

In October, Indian summer set in. The caravan entered the mountains to the south of the Willamette Valley. Rumors passed like wildfire among the French Canadians that the Indians from here on had all turned hostile and were waiting to ambush them.

Michel squashed the rumors: "I have been to Old Fort Umpqua. Centernose was there. He say the Umpqua have many of Monsieur Smith's stolen goods. The word has gone out among all the tribes that we come with a large force. Tribes fear us still; they run from us; they wonder what we will do to them."

LaFramboise gestured with his hands when he spoke, frequently clapping and waving. His beard looked like a dark shadow under his chin. The men respected him. Who else had the courage to ride through these forests alone? True, Jedediah did the same during his hunting trips, but they could not bring themselves to respect an American, especially one who had come to them on his knees and in rags.

On October 9, they reached the Umpqua River and camped on the north side, across from the "Old Establishment." Old Fort McKay, founded a few years earlier by McLeod and LaFramboise, was nothing but a collection of ramshackle log huts, but it made a good meeting place, and the group stayed put, awaiting the arrival of the Umpqua chief, Centernose, sometimes called "St. Arnoose" by the British.

In the meantime, several Umpquas wandered into camp, bringing reports that four Americans had made their way to the Coos villages and were staying there. The rumor was plausible. While Jed was among the Tillamooks, they had received coastal gossip that only eleven bodies remained after the massacre, out of the total of eighteen. Perhaps three or four others had survived.

It was time to open John McLoughlin's sealed instructions. Alex McLeod tore open the seals and perused the letter. It said that he should not pay for Smith's furs or merchandise. He should invite the Indians to trade as usual, but when the Indians tried to sell American goods to them, McLeod should say, "These goods were stolen from the Americans. You must request payment from the thieves who murdered their rightful owners. We will take them and give them back to Mr. Smith."

So the Company would neither punish the Indians nor reward them by buying stolen goods. Jedediah marveled at the diplomacy! The factor had kept the orders sealed to prevent his men from telling their Indian wives, who would warn their relatives—and the Americans would have recovered nothing. As Jedediah's respect for McLeod plummeted, McLoughlin kept gaining stature in his eyes.

On the 11th, Centernose and a dozen warriors arrived for the annual trade fair, just walking into camp without fanfare. Centernose was a straightforward, self-confident man, but somewhat shriveled—well past his prime. He explained through the interpreter, Nasti, "I visited the Kelawatsets and bought many of Mr. Smith's horses. The massacre happened because of a stolen axe. The brave who stole it resented being tied up by Mr. Smith, and he tried to get the whole tribe to retaliate. He was overruled. His pride was hurt. He changed his mind and convinced the other tribes to attack. He claimed these white men were of a different nation from the King George men and were there to make war on the Company."

Jedediah confirmed the incident with the axe, then asked Centernose, "Do you know of any survivors? We hear that four men may have made their way to the Coos."

The wizened chief shook his head. "I know nothing of this."

McLeod added, "Be so good as to send a runner to the Coos. We shall appreciate getting word back."

The chief did not respond to the request, but asked, "Is it your plan to make war on the Kelawatsets? The Umpquas will gladly take up arms against them. We are friends of the King George men."

McLeod replied, "No. We only wish to restore Mr. Smith's property to him. It may be that the Kelawatsets thought they were doing us a favor by killing the Boston men. But we all want to be friends and to have peace. Mr. Smith's goods must be returned."

The following day, Michel LaFramboise came to Alex McLeod over breakfast and reported a private conversation. "The chief confide to me. He do not understand why we are helping the Americains. The Americains ware bragging to the Kelawatsets how they would come in, slam-bang, an' force the English out of here. Now the English help Americains. They have nevair heard of such a t'ing before."

McLeod grew livid. "Damn their hides, these Yankee bastards! And damn McLoughlin for bringing us here. So we are reduced to chasing down these pompous Yankees' horses and giving them back to the kindhearted

Mr. Smith? 'Thank you very kindly,' says Mr. Smith! 'You are entirely welcome,' says the good doctor." McLeod cursed for three minutes.

"Eh well," concluded the Frenchman at last. "It ees our lot. T' rains begin. Let us do t'is disagreeable job an' make ze Americains pay for everyt'ing. T'is man Smith t'inks he is a good Christian and a great huntair. As for me, I would like to be quit of him as soon as possible."

. . .

On Friday, October 17, Jedediah Smith and Arthur Black joined McLeod's party to descend the Umpqua River. Centernose provided six canoes. McLeod ordered a band of horses to accompany them, to bring them back upriver when they were finished. The horses betrayed McLeod's skepticism: he doubted that they would find Jedediah's horses alive. Leland and Turner were left at Old Fort McKay with Tom McKay. The others boarded the canoes.

As if to confirm McLeod's pessimism, the party came upon a slaughtering ground two days later. Half a dozen horses had been killed and carved up by the Umpquas. They were buzzard food now.

"Makes you sick," Arthur said to Jedediah as they tried to get upwind from the stench. "These people don't appreciate a good horse, even when it's dropped in their lap. First they think it's a toy, to ride up 'n' down the beach on. Then they kill it fer meat, 'cause they ain't got the gumption to go after bear."

Jed was thoughtful. "It was unwise—thinkin' we could drive a herd all the way to rendezvous. But the treatment the horses got from the Mexicans was worse even than this—lettin' 'em starve to death slowly in pens." The two men stared at the dismal scene of rotting flesh, inwardly mourning the futility of nine months' hard labor driving horses up mountains and through quagmires from San Gabriel.

By the 21st, Indian summer had ended for good. The flotilla of canoes arrived at a large Umpqua village amid pattering rain.

Centernose brought out armloads of Jedediah's property: three fire-arms, boxes of medicine, pencils, two shirts, forty-two otter pelts, one hundred and sixty-three beaver, and several books—including his Bible!

Picking up his Bible, Jedediah felt as though he were being united with his best friend. He checked it over—it had not been harmed. No prophet had stirred up interest in it among the Umpquas—they saw no use for books of any kind.

As Jedediah continued on his way, he picked up more and more belongings, including his journals and maps. He sent Arthur Black back to Fort McKay with them.

• • •

On November 12, after a heavy storm, they finally arrived at the infamous Bridge River—the site of the massacre.

For Jedediah, there came an overpowering queasiness as the canoe neared the point of land beneath the cliff. His stomach churned. The canoes made for the island, but he could not take his eyes off the point. He didn't want to visit this place—and yet he knew that he must. He felt that he could not bear the sight of the place of the massacre, yet some mysterious force drew him to it. He wished Arthur had remained with him to help him face this moment, but at least he had his Bible now.

Yet his Bible was a silent friend. Darkness was enveloping Jedediah, as though he had been plunged into a sea of despair, bitterness and defeat. He did not open his Bible because he knew that it would challenge his bitterness, and he was not ready to let it be challenged.

After setting up camp, he sneaked off in a canoe and paddled the waters to the old campsite. He went alone. He didn't trust himself in front of men who had no care for him.

The scene was just as he had seen it from the hillside. No one had come back here—the bodies had decomposed where they lay, slowly turning into rag-covered skeletons. The rags identified the bones.

There, over by the fire, was Ransa. There, near the horse pen under the cliff, LaPlant had fallen. Over there, James Reed, who'd been talking to Tom Virgin near the water's edge. And there—oh God!—was Harrison. Poor Harrison! His clerk, Harrison Rogers, had been a constant source of Christian fellowship all along the way.

Jed cried out loud, so loud that the men heard him all the way back at camp. His cries echoed off the cliff, frightened the seagulls from the snags, and drove the woodpeckers away. This torrent of grief was what he had feared—it seized him and carried him away he knew not where. When he had visited this place and given himself over to his grief, would he end up embittered, cynical, a furnace of revenge? Is this where the wilderness pathway led you?—inevitably cursing everything good while plotting the destruction of "savages"? What good is the sextant in your soul when that sextant leads you here, to this place of carnage and calamity?

The other massacres had been different. After each, the challenge of survival had distracted him from dealing with his pain. The other two massacres—Arikara and Mojave—had cut him only skin deep. But this one had cut his heart out. He felt as though he had died. He wished his own bones were here among the rest. He visualized that wretch who had organized this murder. He wanted his bones here too.

Darkness overwhelmed him as the sun went down. He was drowning in a sea of grief and anger, bleak pain mocking all his hopes. Curse God and die, it said. Where is your God now? Violence always prevails in the end. Your ideas? They are civilized ideas. But this is the real world, unvarnished by your civility. Where is your love now? You are surrounded by men who hold you in contempt. They spit on your Puritan ancestors and your Methodist fervor alike. The friends you invested your life in—they lie in pieces at your feet! The treasures you worked so hard for—they pass through the hands of ignorant savages who would rather cut them to pieces than appreciate their worth.

Jedediah wept in an agony of grief. He was being sifted like wheat. Would anything of him remain after the sifting was done? It seemed that darkness had come to take a permanent foothold in his life. Would he ever have faith again? Was this where youth ended, innocence was lost, and cynicism set in for the rest of your days? An arrow had pierced his heart. The shaft had broken off, but the head was still buried in him. And Jedediah had not the power to heal himself.

They are coming over . . . McLeod and the men in a canoe. They have shovels . . . they are going to bury the men . . . I can't face them. Ah, the woods, the ferns.

Jedediah ran into the forest to grieve, following the invisible track of Arthur Black. He cried inside, but only scraping sounds came from his throat. He grieved for three massacres all at once—Arikara, Mohave, Umpqua. He grieved for the shattering of his dreams, the burial of his hope that faith and love would triumph over evil. He wept into a fallen log covered with soft moss. His mind was a whirring confusion of memories all mixed together. The Arikara chief Gray Eyes. The incompetent brigade leader McLeod. The officious Echeandia at San Gabriel. The cold and suspicious Father Duran at San Jose. The barbaric savage Mike Fink. The cynical Alex Ross. What a sea of imperfection!

The wilderness woman wins. She violates all standards, demolishes goodness, ignores morality, wrecks all beauty. She slashes bodies. Hacks off heads. Grasps the hair and tears it off, leaving a bloody gash in God's handiwork. She demands her way, and who can stop her? Jedediah had tried to sneak past her in the Oregon fog. But no. She had found him out. She had awakened from her slumber and demanded her toll of human lives.

And where is your Jesus now?

• • •

Sometime in the night, Jedediah stumbled back to the point of slaughter. The skeletons had been buried. His canoe was still at the water's edge, left for him by those who had seen him go into the woods. He paddled back to camp and plopped down on his epishamore. He was exhausted, as though he had been fighting the most difficult battle of his life. The buried arrowhead in his soul troubled his dreams.

Five

That fall, Governor Simpson arrived at Fort Vancouver and began to change everything, as was his custom. In fact, he was supervising the erection of a new Fort Vancouver.

He said to the factor, "Why on earth did I put the fort so far from the river? I must have been daft. Let the fort be torn down and moved. Then old La Pierre won't have to keep fetching water from so far away every day. Besides, the stockade pickets are rotting away."

"Indeed," replied McLoughlin, deciding to keep further commentary to himself.

Once the decision was made, neither factor nor governor was inclined to let it rest very long. By mid-December, a new fifteen-foot-high stockade was raised a mile to the southwest.[45] Each vertical was placed in a three-foot-deep trench, the first pointing up, the second down, and so

---

45. This is the present location of Fort Vancouver National Monument.

on, so that no gaps appeared between the pickets. The stockade was built in the shape of a parallelogram of Douglas fir, the tree they had just named for David Douglas, the botanist who had recently visited the fort.

Timber for the factor's house was piled inside, the pile growing daily as construction progressed. The lumber was floated down from the saw-mill, located five miles upriver on one of the few rapid streams in the vicinity. The new house was to be made of sawn timber. Indians were impressed by the mystery of the straight-edged lumber. It took hours of patient carving for them to produce the single circle of flat planking they used for their doors, yet here were thousands of canoe lengths of deftly carved boards, produced in the same amount of time.

The governor was a believer in gardens, so he personally supervised the new one, lining it out beyond the north gate close to the factor's house. By placing the fort here, they were able to keep the same fourteen acres of corn, eight of oats, five of barley, and fourteen of peas. It was all very satisfying: visualizing, dreaming, then carving out a place in the wilderness. Putting your stamp on the world. Civilization. Commerce. Prosperity. Making the land produce.

Here is a challenge you can sink your teeth into, George Simpson exulted. Then he walked back along the new path that had been worn between the two sites. It was 4:30; surely supper would be ready soon.

The air was drizzly as usual. He entered the old factor's house as if it were his own. He removed his high hat, covered with oilskin to protect it from the rain; then his greatcoat, covered with a sheen of wetness. He hung both on a peg in the hallway, then mounted the steps to his room to get dressed for dinner.

Emerging shortly in dinner attire, he moved through the hallway to the dining hall. People were in the dining room, even before the ringing of the five o'clock bell. That was unusual.

Is there a meeting? he queried.

Dr. McLoughlin was shouting—violently—so that his voice resounded into the hallway:

"What do you mean, sir, showing up here at this time o' year? I gave you explicit instructions to move south to the headwaters o' the Buenaventura!"

A timid Scottish reply was barely audible. "B-but the men was ailing, sir. An' it was raining. Nothin' but rain morning, noon, and night. The lowlands're completely inundated."

"Then travel the ridges, you imbecile!"

"But the horses kept wanderin' off. Really, sir, they are the most unruly horses in all creation!"

Simpson entered the room and saw that the person with the factor was Alex McLeod. McLoughlin didn't pause his unmerciful lashing to acknowledge the governor. "Horses have nothing to do with it! You came back here so you and your men could warm your buttocks by your firesides! Your men ware ailing, ware they? So you think, do you, that this is a wee hospital? 'Send your men hame, and call good Dr. John, an' he'll apply a salve'?"

The Eagle, speaking the last words in falsetto, strode three paces to the mouse as if to devour him. He transfixed him with his pale eyes. The mouse was cornered. Its brown fur quivered. Its eyes looked into the eyes of the Eagle as if to say, "It is your lot to devour such vermin as me. I give myself up."

"Such a poor excuse for a trader I ha' never seen in all my life! Mr. McLeod, you will get your men togither and lead them out o' here within the week. You will lead them beyond the Umpqua to the headwaters o' the Buenaventura. There you will send 'em out to trap. If it rains, put on your capotes. If the men get sick, apply medicines. If the boats leak, caulk them. If the horses wander, hobble them. But I'll be damned if you will not trap the headwaters o' the Buenaventura and bring us back some peltries!"

The mouse scampered away to lick its wounds, swallow its anger, and obey—grateful that it had been allowed to live another day, but it made one more mistake—it cursed Jesus Christ as it went out the door. This was an intolerable offense to the Eagle. He reached out for the scruff of

McLeod's neck, grasped it firmly, and shouted, "Take the Lord's name in vain again, an' I'll tie you to the cannon and have you whipped!"

The mouse scampered off.

At that moment the dinner bell rang. Simpson waited until the bell stopped tolling, then chimed in. "My dear man, could that poor devil really have deserved such a tongue-lashing?"

McLoughlin, without reply, moved his eyes toward a third party, who had been standing silently in the corner. Suddenly aware of the third person, Simpson kept mum. Disputes among English gentlemen should not be aired in front of strangers.

"Governor Simpson, may I introduce you to Mr. Jedediah Smith?" the factor said.

Jed came forward and shook hands. Simpson looked awkward and tried to smile.

Jedediah, just the reverse, was trying to conceal a smile. McLoughlin's rebuke of McLeod had given him one of the most pleasant moments of his life, for the arrogant McLeod had done nothing but torment him the entire journey south and north again. Besides, McLeod had proven to be the most inept, careless brigade leader he had ever seen, so there was healing in McLoughlin's reaction. A judgment had been rendered, and the justice of it healed that part of his grief caused by McLeod's stupidity, laziness, slovenliness, gross incompetence, and ungraciousness to a desperate man.

Jedediah Smith needed protection. He needed a hospital for his wounded spirit. McLoughlin's hospitality was both bastion and hospital to him, a true sanctuary. Jedediah looked to John McLoughlin with tears in his eyes, tears of gratitude and respect, as of a wounded child to the white-haired father who draws boundaries of protection. Righteousness, to a fur man, had to do with the proper treatment of horses, medicines, alcohol, clothing, furs, traps, and fur men. Jedediah, seeing a man of righteousness, instantly respected him.

On the other hand, Governor Simpson felt that the factor had been a little hard on McLeod, and he was not at all sure that the American Smith deserved the sanctuary of a Hudson's Bay post. He withdrew his hand as quickly as possible from an unwelcome handshake, not wanting to appear either charitable or vulnerable. Simpson spoke to Jedediah:

"The factor has already filled me in as to your unfortunate encounter with the Indians. It was the fault of those wretched savages, I am sure." Simpson said the last words in a way to imply that he was not sure about it at all. If Jedediah had run afoul of the Indians, it was surely because neither the Indians nor the American trappers could learn to be civilized.

Jedediah felt the sting of his skepticism. This Simpson was ready to believe the worst of him while pretending not to. The English! Always masters of pretense!

Several men now entered the room through the so-called "witches' door," built so its top resembled a cross and its bottom a Bible—traditionally meant to protect against witches' curses.

As a matter of fact, the dinner hall admitted no women at all—witches or not—except during worship services. Peter Skene Ogden came first, immaculately dressed, like the others, with velvet stock and collar to his ears. The clerk, Frank Ermatinger, followed Ogden, a finely dressed, pleasant elf with a bulbous nose. The spry Tom McKay came limping in, smirking and dressed in a Scottish kilt and sporran—in every way Ermatinger's opposite. Mr. Manson, overseer of the building construction, entered next, followed by Robert Bruce, the horticulturist, huffing and puffing after the exertion of ringing the dinner bell. Alex McLeod was conspicuous by his absence.

The factor sat at the head of the mahogany table (recently imported from London) with Governor Simpson on his right, Chief Trader Ogden next, and so on by rank, with the four Americans seated at the far end. None of the Americans enjoyed a gentlemanly pedigree.

Two candlesticks with beeswax tapers decorated the table, providing a cheery and smokeless light which exposed the faces of everyone to everyone. The light sparkled off the Messina-pattern Spodeware platters and tureens, but left the corners of the room in murky darkness. The effect was to draw everyone close together around the table, as though the rays of candlelight were strings that tied the company to each other. No light from the setting sun made its way through the Oregon clouds and tiny windowpanes, or "window lights," as they were called. The fire had been lit in the two fireplaces, one at either end of the room, but these glowed rather than blazed. All in all, there was little to distract the men from their conversation.

Servants entered from the kitchen, a separate building, bringing mostly leftovers from the heavy noon meal. It was quite a repast for the middle of the wilderness: a course of soup followed by trays of vegetables, cold duck, and hot venison.

There was music, too. A gigantic highlander dressed in kilts of Royal Stuart plaid played a loud *pibroch* as he walked around the table. The music raised goosebumps on Jedediah's skin. The Pibroch of Donald Dhu, played with ear-shattering power in that enclosed room, required an end to conversation.

When the piper finished, he sat down in an armchair near the door. The factor prayed, and the conversation flowed after the prayer as the servants served the soup from the tureen.

"Mr. Smith has braved the perils o' the south, leading a herd o' horses from California," McLoughlin said to the governor. "Quite an accomplishment, I should say—uncharted wilderness all the way. And he has made maps as well, maps he doesna mind sharin' wi' us."

"Splendid!" said the ferret in black, and then fell silent, not wanting to praise the Americans overmuch.

McLoughlin forged on. "The maps'll be useful to Mr. McLeod, provided we ever get our Southern Brigade underway. It seems to have gotten stuck here at the fort! A pity our Mr. McLeod does not have Mr. Smith's way with horses!"

"A pity," inserted Simpson, "that Mr. Smith should have lost his horses to the Indians." Simpson's voice had a well-used cutting edge, which seemed to grow sharper the more the knife was used. "I fear the carelessness of the Americans will encourage the Indians to be more aggressive."

"Nah!" said the wild man Tom McKay, as though the governor's words had caused offense. "We took care o' that. We got 'em in the palm o' our hand now. Nothin' to fear. Michel an' me, we can see how things are. Dr. John, he had the Umpquas go to the Kellywatsets fer payment fer the horses they stole. Wouldn't let McLeod pay fer 'em. Umpquas give us all the horses, hoo, hoo." McKay's chin was dripping soup.

Jedediah spoke up, apparently close to tears. "That was a fine piece of diplomacy, Dr. McLoughlin. My men were careless, I'll admit. I gave orders to my clerk not to let any of the Indians into camp, but they were camped nearby, and he probably didn't have the heart, or perhaps the means, to keep 'em out. He paid dearly for his mistake." A few throats cleared uncomfortably. Everyone around the table sensed the terrible emotion behind Jedediah's words.

The kindly Frank Ermatinger spoke, finishing his soup and reaching for a platter of venison. "You'll find the Indians respond to strength, not to a soft heart, Mr. Smith. If you show 'em you're master of the situation, they'll respect you. Don't take their lands, but show 'em how they can profit from the trade. All the while, let 'em see your eight-pounders and your muskets, and they'll soon know what's what."

"Well put, man," Simpson chimed in. "You Americans have an unfortunate way of botching relations with the Natives. Positively indiscreet. It is little wonder you lose so many men to their depredations. Mind you, I say this in Christian charity. I hear the Americans have lost some five hundred men to Indian attacks. We have lost barely a dozen to the Indians, most of them from the Snake Brigade. Your downfall is the lack of discipline in your ranks. 'Every man for himself,' you keep nattering. Ha! The Indians know how incapable you are of organized action. The right hand promises one thing, while the left takes it away and offers something else. Soon the Natives don't know whom to believe. You fight with each other and you encourage drinking, and you practically invite them to steal your horses."

Big Arthur Black spoke up, his beard quivering with emotion as he glowered at the little governor. "Hold up there! If your freemen or your

Mr. McLeod are any clue about British horse-handling, I'd say you could learn some lessons from us."

"Granted," McLoughlin interrupted, holding up his hands as if to close the subject. He thought it inhospitable to feed his guests such bitter accusations along with their soup.

But Simpson was intent on pressing home his point. "Well, I don't see how you Americans can keep order in your ranks when your leaders are mere trappers who have risen up from the rank and file. We all know what happens when the father tells his son to take charge of the household. The other brothers immediately resent the new master and make plans to undermine his authority. A father who does that invites rebellion and anarchy. You can't have real freedom in anarchy. 'Liberty, equality, fraternity!' Pah! Look what happened to Robespierre."

Simpson was just warming up to the conversation, but Arthur Black was warming up too. "So then you put gentlemen and lords over your brigades, do you?—men like Mr. McLeod? Eh?"

Peter Skene Ogden coughed loudly. He had not been well since the last Snake Brigade, and he seemed to be avoiding conversation now.

McLoughlin leapt in again. "Come now, gentlemen. We can all make ourselves look good by comparing our own cream to the other man's sour milk."

McLoughlin gave Simpson a glare, warning him off. Jedediah, who felt the odds against him—Turner and Black were outclassed, and Richard Leland was an Englishman with divided loyalties—felt gratitude for John McLoughlin's defense.

"I can say positively," McLoughlin continued, "that Mr. Smith and his partners have portrayed none o' the qualities o' which you speak. And as for liquor, I wager Mr. Smith'll not even partake o' the wine at this table, let alone sell whiskey to Indians. Yet I will say to you, Mr. Smith, in all candor: we fear what the encroachment o' the Americans'll mean to the stability o' the region. Not everyone in the American camp is so right-minded as you. Mr. Ogden tells me o' one Johnson Gardner, a case in point."

Jedediah laid down his fork. The whole history of British-American competition was suddenly on the table, and he was losing his appetite. "I must apologize for Mr. Gardner. I was away exploring while he was inciting your freemen at rendezvous three years ago, but I learned of it afterward. I admit that our men had an unruly way, but we are able to keep reins on them most of the time, especially where liquor is concerned. I permit no liquor to be traded to the Indians, and my partners are in complete agreement."

"Well, there is good news." Peter Ogden spoke, his forced enthusiasm barely hiding an air of skepticism. Ogden had been avoiding conversation like a poker player guarding his cards. But by now he sensed Jedediah's sincerity and vulnerability, and he laid his cards down.

"Liquor will destroy the country for everyone, British and Americans alike, if we are not careful. It would be well if we could come to some gentlemen's agreement about how far the competition'll go between us. Both the land and its people will fare better if we can keep out of each other's hair."

Jedediah sensed in the request the same spirit of fairness that prevailed in the thoughts of William Clark. Clark utterly distrusted the British, but Jedediah could not help but think, If only he could be here and sense the spirit of John McLoughlin! If only he could hear the words of Peter Ogden and sense his real concern. What a little face-to-face conversation among Christian gentlemen wouldn't accomplish!

Jedediah had hardly thought the words when McLoughlin made that very point. "Here, now," he said, "we're all Christians around the table. Surely we can come to terms with our differences, so that everyone may come out the winner."

Despite Simpson's inflammatory opening words, the candlelight was pulling all the men into harmony. Or maybe it was the factor's way of managing the conversation. There was emerging at the table a desire to play the fur trade not as bitter enemies, but as friendly combatants abiding by gentlemen's rules. Simpson began to see what was happening and decided to shut his mouth.

Peter Ogden jumped to take advantage of the emerging spirit of co-operation—it seemed to be just what he had been waiting for. He had harbored resentment against Jedediah Smith since 1825, but recently, admiration had been growing to replace it. Jedediah's disaster and humiliation had worked in him an unexpected sympathy. While the other men had treated Jedediah's struggles with contempt, in Ogden those struggles had engendered respect for a fellow explorer who had experienced the worst the wilderness could throw at a man. "You have explored the headwaters of the Buenaventura, we hear. Could you tell us what you have found?"

Jedediah smiled weakly. He suddenly had no compunctions about steering the British to the south—and Ogden's newfound admiration was mutual. He had already returned the favor of McLoughlin's hospitality by giving his host valuable knowledge of the Buenaventura—the river Escalante claimed to have located northeast of Presidio San Francisco.[46]

"The Mexicans are poor explorers and even worse trappers," he said. "The word *beaver* doesn't even appear in their vocabulary! They think it some sort of fish."

Tittering filled the room.

Jedediah added, "Beaver abound in the tributaries of the Buenaventura as far as we explored, but they avoid the higher elevations. I have given Dr. McLoughlin maps to copy. By now, we both know that the Buenaventura does not move east, but north from San Francisco Bay. I find no hint of a river to connect the Great Salt Lake with the Pacific Ocean. There is only a vast expanse of desert, thinly populated by the most miserably poor people I ever saw. West of the desert is a wall of mountains, completely impenetrable and covered by eternal snows."

"Will we be able to trap below the forty-second parallel into California without incurring hostilities from Mexico?" McLoughlin inquired.

Jedediah snorted. "The Mexicans hardly know what's happening fifty miles from San Francisco. Your men would have no difficulty, provided they make it past the mountains at the forty-second parallel."

---

46. That is, the Sacramento River.

McLoughlin nodded, smiling in his appreciation. "This is most use-ful, and I thank you kindly. But we are more concerned to come to some agreement over the Snake Country."

Governor Simpson put in, "The Snake is all more or less trapped out at any rate. Your men will find little to reward you in that region."

McLoughlin added, "We dinna presume to claim the Bear Lake for ourselves, which we well ken to be the favorite place for your trade fairs. But north o' Lewis's River we'd all benefit from an agreement. You stay east o' the Height o' Land, an' we'll stay west. What d' you say?"

Silence followed. All eyes were on Jedediah. McLoughlin took a pinch of after-dinner snuff from a horn container. A log popped in the fireplace, while another snapped in reply from its opponent. The magnates of the Honorable Company became silent, hoping that Jedediah would agree to a bargain which the two governments had been unable to reach after years of negotiating.

"Yes, I think it would be for the best," Jedediah said at last. "Leave the Blackfoot and Crow lands for us to trap. We'll leave you the Flatheads. Sublette told me the Blackfoot territories are full of beaver, very little disturbed by the trap. We can direct our men toward the upper Missouri. I promise you this: I will do everything I can to persuade my partners of it." Jedediah, who had met with William Clark on a trip back to Saint Louis in the fall of 1825, felt that Clark would surely approve.

The conversation continued on lighter themes after that. As the men retired to the sitting room, Jedediah struck up a conversation with Mr. Bruce, who described his experiments in growing apple trees and in coaxing the wild strawberry to yield large, edible berries.

Six

On Christmas Day, there was no work, only festivity. Music filled the air, the music of fiddle and Jew's harp, of recorder and bagpipe. Indians who hovered around the fort gambled all day long, playing the game of hand. No snow had fallen west of the mountains yet this year, so there were footraces among people of a dozen nationalities—Owyhees (Hawaiians) against Canadians, Scotsmen against Americans, Iroquois against Chinooks.

Alcohol was kept to a minimum. The only time the Hudson's Bay Company permitted the free flow of Scotch was for regales at the outset of a brigade—and even then, the leadership allowed it reluctantly.

McLoughlin read the Anglican services for Christmas Day. Then he added a Catholic service in a style suitable to his French Canadians. The factor's spiritual leadership meant more to Jedediah Smith than all the paid clergymen lumped together back east. That McLoughlin led services in French for the Catholics deeply affected him. Here was a man whose Christianity rose above mere English tradition. McLoughlin's God was higher than the kings of England, and higher than the Hudson's Bay Company too. Here was the Eagle, a creature who flew large circles above all other creatures and saw further than they did. His love, faith, and righteousness reached out and embraced people different from himself, yet without violating his own integrity.

Worship services were the only occasions when the lowborn were allowed into the gentlemen's dining room. Worship at Fort Vancouver broke down barriers that English gentry insisted on at all other times. Company servants, gentlemen, women, and Natives all met together, believing for the moment in a God who makes no distinctions. It seemed the English under McLoughlin were willing to be a little less English for the sake of God. David Jones, at Red River Colony, would have been astonished at McLoughlin's success in drawing even the English to church.

The Scripture reading for that day, intoned from the massive six-inch-thick Bible McLoughlin used, seemed a prophecy of the people gathered in the dining hall:

> He that is mighty hath done to me great things; and holy
> is his name. And his mercy is on them that fear him from gen-
> eration to generation. He hath showed strength with his arm;
> he hath scattered the proud in the imagination of their hearts.
> He hath put down the mighty from their seats, and exalted
> them of low degree.

As for Jedediah, John McLoughlin had exalted the low degree of his estimation of the British people in the few weeks he had known him. Yes, the White-headed Eagle was at times harsh, but his harshness was reserved for the shifty and the shiftless. To the weak and the destitute, he was gentle and caring. The factor personified God's Word appropriately to this rough country. Jedediah's faith in God's power to triumph over evil was somehow restored during that Christmas Day service. Righteousness heals.

Even Governor Simpson felt a deeper kindness that day. Not that Simpson ever took ownership of the Christmas spirit. In fact, he disliked festivities, grousing to anyone who would listen, "Why do these infernal games go on and on? Christmas is a waste of time! And doesn't the factor look ridiculous dancing with that Indian woman he calls his wife? And those two brats are insufferable—David and Eloisa! Ugh!" Eloisa was McLoughlin's blonde eleven-year-old. David, the factor's son, had an unfortunate reputation for haughtiness and naughtiness.

Yet despite all his complaints, something lifted Simpson up that Christmas. A contagious infection of goodwill required the governor to broaden his loves. By the next day, inexplicably, he had softened toward Jedediah and the Americans. In that charitable mood, he decided to offer a fair price for the peltries and the horses recovered from the Umpqua massacre.

The felt urgency of Jedediah's removal from the British post was itself removed from the American explorer's heart. Suddenly content to stay at Fort Vancouver for the winter, he accepted the governor's offer of $3 per skin ("Though they are the worst I ever saw!" Simpson complained loudly) and the forty shillings per horse ("Sight unseen, mind you") and thanked his host for allowing him to stay.

As spring approached, Jedediah packed up and prepared to head east to rendezvous with his partners, David Jackson and Bill Sublette. For five years, he had explored the walled garden and had met its people. But he sensed that his time here was finished. Fort Vancouver had been a city of refuge for him, a hospital for his wounded soul, but he still wanted to go home. He missed his family terribly, and in his morning prayer times, he sensed that God was closing a door. These mountains would see him no more.

On March 12, he headed east, passing through Kettle Falls and stopping a day at Flathead Post, where he had, four years before, spread the

The Forgotten Awakening

extraordinary news that Quilent-satmen had a son. This time there was no sign of any tribes at the post—the place was vacant, a hotel only for foxes and ground squirrels. He had not the least idea of how deeply his presence there four years before had affected key tribal leaders, and he knew nothing of what was about to happen in the lives of those key players in a new drama about to take place throughout the secret garden of his childhood dreams.

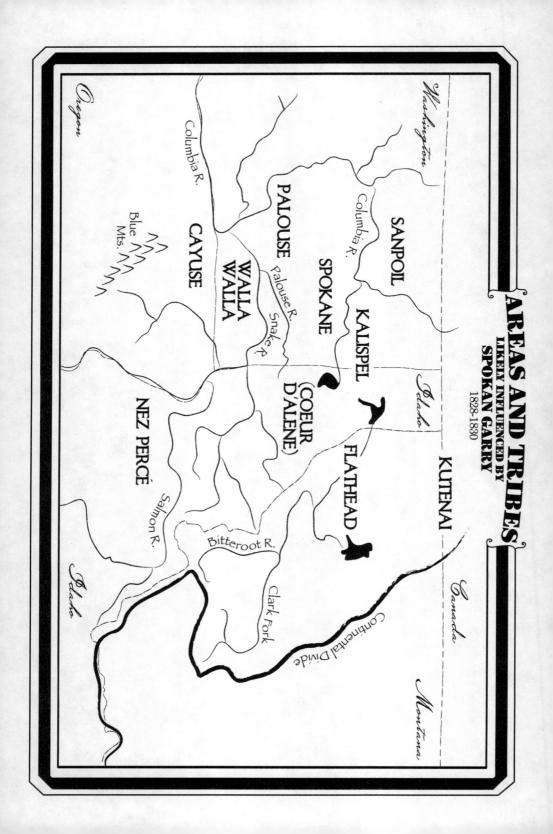

AREAS AND TRIBES
LIKELY INFLUENCED BY SPOKAN GARRY
1828-1830

Oregon

Washington

Columbia R.

Columbia R.

SANPOIL

PALOUSE

Blue Mts.

CAYUSE

WALLA WALLA

PALOUSE

Palouse R.

Snake R.

SPOKANE

KALISPEL

(COEUR D'ALENE)

FLATHEAD

Idaho

KUTENAI

Canada

Montana

NEZ PERCÉ

Salmon R.

Bitteroot R.

Clark Fork

Continental Divide

Idaho

Part VII:
The Sowing of the Seed
1829 — 1831

By coincidence, the beginning of the close association between the Sahaptin-Salish peoples and large numbers of American trappers which became significant about 1830, occurred simultaneously with a dramatic and remarkably influential introduction of Christian ideas among the home villages of those Indians. The Americans in the mountains had nothing to do with it and were unaware of what was taking place. But . . . it worked abrupt and profound changes in the behavior of many of the plateau tribes beginning in the winter of 1829–30, and accounted in large measure for some of the Americans' attitudes about them that differed sharply from earlier British estimates of their conduct.[47]

—Alvin M. Josephy, *The Nez Percé Indians and the Opening of the West*

. . . .(I)t was the prior existence of the Prophet Dance which explains both the ready acceptance of Christianity at its point of introduction and its rapid spread.[48]

—Leslie Spier, *The Prophet Dance of the Northwest*

Garry and Pelly appear to have made a tremendous impression upon their own and neighboring tribes with their recitation of what they knew about the white man's religion. No record exists of what they taught but the evidence would suggest their main outline was somewhat as follows. God, spoken of as the Great Spirit, created the world, sustained it, and cared for his people. Jesus Christ, the Son of God lived, died and rose again for the salvation of mankind. He was referred to as the "Master of Life." Sunday was God's Sabbath and no work should be done on that day. The Ten Commandments and their elaboration and explanation in the catechism of the Book of Common Prayer was the basis for a Christan life. Those who obeyed these injunctions went to heaven, those who disobeyed them, to hell. Prayers were to be said morning and night, as well as grace before meals. They showed their Bibles and Prayer Books

---

47. Alvin Josephy, *The Nez Percé Indians*, 73-74.
48. Leslie Spier, *The Prophet Dance*, 30.

which were regarded as the "white man's book of heaven." They urged peace among the tribes and with the whites. They told the tribes that their Christian teachers were known as "Black Robes."[49]

—Thomas Jessett, *Chief Spokan Garry*

I am concerned to say that the Coutanais Boy Pelly died last Spring [1831] at Red River; his complaint was an affection of the Liver. Every care & attention were paid to the poor Lad during his illness both by the Revd. Mr. Jones, under whose charge he was, and by the medical Gentlemen at the Settlement. To guard against any misrepresentations on this subject I send the Spokan Lad Garry across, whose Statements I hope will satisfy the natives that no blame in reference to the Fate of the Lad can by possibility attach to those under whose care he was.

—George Simpson to C. T. Francis Heron, York Fact., 27th June, 1831

---

49. Thomas Jessett, *Chief Spokan Garry*, 34

One

The Columbia River was now a familiar antagonist to George Simpson. He set out on March 25, 1829, to ascend the river toward the village of Spokan Garry. Simpson carried the letter Garry had written to his father on the night of the governor's visit to the Cochrans. Word had reached him that Garry's father, Illim-spokanee, had died before his son could return, and he was unsure of the reception that awaited him in the village.

Privacy was not guaranteed by the Hudson's Bay mail service. The governor read the letter to tribal villages hither and yon throughout the Columbia District. It was a useful letter. It seemed to bring peace and happiness wherever it was read. He sensed that the information contained in it would be of genuine interest to all the tribes of the area. As a result, all the tribes to whom he read the letter learned that the return of Spokan Garry and Kootenai Pelly was imminent.

Leaving the brigade at Kettle Falls, Simpson rode south through late-melting snow to his destination, arriving at the Spokane village by late afternoon. The village appeared unchanged from the days of the prophet Circling Raven, who had first foretold the coming of the white-skinned ones. The reed-mat lodges were more serene now than at any time in memory. Nothing remained of the adjacent Spokane House, which had at one time been a bustling meeting place and market for trade goods, but for now, the *chipixa* had gone elsewhere.

Within minutes, the whole village was assembled to hear news of Slough-keetcha. Simpson mounted a fallen log at the southwest edge of the village of gray reed-mat lodges. The people, covered with skin ponchos, looked up at him with expectancy, much as they had done when Circling Raven had delivered his prophecy. The old ones remembered how the ground had been covered with white ash. Those who now looked up at Simpson were curious to know what might issue now from the prophecies of the prophet.

"I bring good tidings from Spokan Garry," the governor said loudly. He cleared his throat, savoring the drama of the moment. "The boy has learned much. Now he has written a letter. The letter is addressed to his father and mother, but I will read it to everyone, because everyone seems interested." He cleared his throat again, eyeing the family of the boy, who looked up with patient eagerness. A translator was ready to convey it to the throng. Simpson read:

Church Mission House, Red River. June 6th, 1828.

My dear father and mother: I am very glad that I can write to you, and that I can tell you that I am well. I have never been sick since I came to this place and have always had food to eat and clothes to put on. I can now read much of that book that the Great Spirit has given to the white people to tell them what they must do so that when they die they may go to the good country. This book tells us that there is a time coming when Indians as well as white men shall know what the Great Spirit has said in this book, and what they ought to do to please him. I wish, my dear father and mother, that you, my sisters and brothers, and all my country people knew these things. Give my love to my uncle Chongulloosoon. And to all my aunts; and I would thank you to send me a deer skin. The great Illemechum who you saw before takes this letter; be good to the white people for they are good to us. This from your son, Slough-keetcha.[50]

Chongulloosoon, brother of Illim-spokanee, stepped forward, encouraged by the reference to his name. He spoke with a tight, thin voice which barely reached as far as Simpson.

"I am Chongulloosoon. Many moons have passed since the nephew of Chongulloosoon went away. Is it not time for Slough-keetcha to return here to his people? Let him know again the warmth of the sweat lodge, the cool of the river, the spearing of the salmon, and the laughter of his people. Let Slough-keetcha return this summer, when the sun melts the snows on the Backbone of the World. Or has Slough-keetcha forgotten how to snare the rabbit, to hunt the deer, to retrieve the salmon, and to speak the tongue of The People? Let the Chief of the Long-hairs make reply."

"I assure you," replied the governor, "the boy will return forthwith. I am only sorry to hear of the passing of his father, who will not have the pleasure of hearing of the boy's adventures from his own lips."

"We are old," Chongulloosoon continued. "The winter before last was a hard one. Even your man, Jaco Finlay, did not survive it. He remained at the site of your old post after it was torn down. He refused to go to Kettle Falls. He lived on camas root. He loved our people. Now he is dead. As with Jaco Finlay, so with our people. We starved that winter. Who is to say that Chongulloosoon will survive another winter? Let me look into the eyes of Slough-keetcha again before the bitter snows come. And let him teach The People what he has learned among the Long-hairs."

---

50. *Journal of David Jones*, June 6, 1828.

Simpson replied, his voice fluttering, "He has learned much, I assure you, much to help your people eat well all winter long. He has learned to plant, to grow food, as we do at all our posts."

"It is good," replied Chongulloosoon, but then he thought, Why does the white chief speak merely of food? The prophecy, the things of the spirit world—these are what we want to hear of.

Simpson continued, "I will send him to you this summer. I will send him across the Height of Land with the brigade. Expect him not six months hence."

There was much excitement when this news was translated. The old ones remembered the night the skies had burned to ashes and fallen to the ground. It seemed that the old prophecies, at long last, were about to shed their light for The People.

Two

George Simpson arrived back at Red River on June 1 and told David Jones how eager the western tribes were for a visit from Pelly and Garry. The boys packed their belongings late that summer and joined the fall brigade.

But in the middle of the bustle of preparation, Simpson himself showed up outside the bunkhouse to deliver bad news to Garry: "Er, I regret to be the bearer of evil tidings, but your father passed away this year. Regretfully, you will not see him when you return." The governor was doing his best to be sympathetic, but he was not a sympathetic sort of man, especially toward Native people. Garry felt no connection with him. He left the governor standing at the door and sat down on his bunk by himself. He needed to be by himself now, and he retreated into his own little world of memories, while Simpson shrugged his shoulders and walked off. Sadness overwhelmed him, and he was close to tears. A few minutes later, Kootenai Pelly came in the door, and the two had a long and tearful conversation that made both of them even more eager to go home. "We can't assume that our villages will be as we left them," Pelly concluded. "We don't know what has happened since we left. We must prepare ourselves for surprises."

. . .

A week later, the boys had rejoined the fall brigade and were retracing the route to the Columbia and to Fort Colvile at Kettle Falls. They arrived in October.

Nothing could have prepared them for what greeted them at Kettle Falls. Beneath the single log tower of the fort, a huge throng of people had gathered, not just Spokanes and Kutenais, but crowds from every tribal group for a hundred miles in all directions. After George Simpson's visit, word had passed from mouth to mouth at fishing holes and trade fairs: "The two boys, sent to learn the book of the *sama*, are returning. They will tell what they have learned!"

The throngs were not lowbrow rabble, but chiefs and their families. Garry was himself descended from the greatest chief ever produced on the Columbia Plateau, the great Say-ump-kin, who was his great-grandfather and who was also the great-grandfather of many other chiefs of the Plateau. He had blood ties with chiefs of the Nez Percés and the Coeur d'Alenes as well as the Spokanes, but the gathering together of such diverse peoples in one place spoke volumes of the great peace that was imminent, binding together people who had been bitter rivals for centuries.

Garry and Pelly were young—not even twenty—but the appearance of such crowds, who had showed up just to see them, made them realize that their boyhood was finished. They recognized few familiar faces in the crowds. And since they were dressed in English and Scottish clothes (including Garry's tam-o'-shanter and billowing white shirt), few even of their friends recognized them. Even Pelly's father, Le Grand Queue, and Garry's brother and sister, Sultz-lee and Quint-qua-a'pee, wondered whether the two boys hadn't gotten lost somewhere along the way, to be replaced by these strangers. But Pelly and Garry recognized their families, ran up to them with delight, and threw their arms around them. Family members seemed at once nervous and gleeful: excited for the reunion but unsure what to expect.

Garry recognized immediately that he had become a prophetic fulfillment, a multi-tribal phenomenon. He pulled himself away from his family, for the entire crowd had come to see him and Pelly, and they were all wondering what was to happen next. He had to address the crowd. Standing under the peak-roofed blockhouse of the fort, he raised his hands in greeting: palms up, palms down, palms to the crowd. Every voice was stilled.

But Slough-keetcha had forgotten much of his Salish! He could only speak in Scottish-flavored English learned from his teacher, Mr. Garrioch. He cleared his throat and spoke slowly, awkwardly.

"I am Slough-keetcha. The white men call me Spokan Garry. I come from over the Backbone of the World, where I ha' been with the white teachers o' the book, at a place called Red River."

He could see that most of the people did not understand him. Though their hearts were eager, their eyes were dull. No one had arranged for a translator. Even if they had, so many linguistic groups were present that a single translator would have done little good for the majority.

He changed course, speaking still in English: "Those o' you who ken my speech, tell your people that we ha' much to tell. We'll come to you, to your villages. We will tell what we ha' learned. Speak with us today. We'll make arrangements to visit you from our villages."

The rest of the day was taken up in scheduling meetings between the boys and the villages of various tribal chiefs near and far. Their two families would have to wait their turn. But the appointment-making was completed at last, the people started to pack up, and Garry and Pelly turned to those who had waited patiently for them. Neither boy could speak more than broken words of his own language, yet both families were expert with hugs, smiles, and gestures, and in the end, all the discomfort of the language barrier disappeared into a heap of hugs and joking.

Garry rode with several dozen Spokanes to his village. All the while, he was trying desperately to remember the words of his own language and the names of his people. How much he had forgotten! Yet the people were proud of him and respected him as a spiritual leader—before he had even opened his mouth.

In light of the death of his father, Chongulloosoon quickly became a second father to him, and he stayed in his uncle's lodge.

First thing next day, he entered the sweat lodge with his brothers and uncles. He had not so completely forgotten the ways of The People as it had seemed at first. Just the opposite: he had borne in mind the pleasure of the sweat lodge since the cold hell of Athabasca Pass had frozen it permanently into his imagination. In the sweat lodge, his brothers told all that had happened since he left, including the death of their father and the dismantling of Spokane House. He, in turn, talked endlessly of church steeples, York boats, squeaking carts, windmills grinding grain, raven-black soil, and ice fishing. And as he talked, the language returned, enabling him to become an ambassador between peoples. This, he soon learned, was his destiny, and he learned to fit—uncomfortably at first—into an ambassador's clothes.

As for Kootenai Pelly, his father had brought him, as a gift, a beautiful white stallion. This was no ordinary horse, but a buffalo horse, a five-mile horse, the rarest of all steeds. It could keep pace with a buffalo cow for five miles. The spirited animal pranced proudly and pawed the ground. It seemed to be aware of its prowess, but horseback riding had not been a frequent pastime at Red River. The people of the colony rode more often on carioles and Red River carts than on horses. Pelly had grown rusty in his riding skills.

On the long journey north back to his village, the stallion reared up at the edge of a riverbank. Pelly careened, falling heavily on a rock, then rolling over a precipice, screaming. The screams echoed from the hills.

Le Grand Queue leapt to the ground and sped to where his son was lying on his back.

"My back, Father, my back," was all Pelly could say. He was in agony.

They made a travois for him, according to Plains Indian practice, and they placed him gently on it. In this way, the renowned son of Le Grand Queue was brought home to his people on a stretcher.

Three

Pelly's injury put him out of commission as an emissary for the new teaching. News of his fall raced through the forest. It soon reached the village of Spokan Garry. Its implication was this: Garry would have to visit all the tribal villages by himself. Except for the Kutenais, the whole weight of prophetic fulfillment was falling on him.

He began with his own village. Assembling all the people, he smoked the pipe with them, then spoke to attentive crowds. The old ones remembered Circling Raven, who had stood where Garry now stood thirty-seven years before. They marveled to hear his prophecy fulfilled in their eyes.

"The book of the *chipixa* is a message from the Great Spirit about the Master of Life. It is for all the tribes and nations. It says: Quilent-satmen has sent his only Son to lead us closer to him."

Chongulloosoon spoke up. "Your father spoke of these things. We already know these things from the men at the fort. You, Slough-keetcha, you know our ways. Tell us so we will understand."

Garry continued, "The Son came from above to clear the air of mist and ashes. He spoke of righteousness. He told us to please God by doing right. This is what is right: we must love our Creator and worship him, following his laws revealed in his book. Those who live like the animals—they are wrong."

So far, Garry knew he was just covering old ground—things The People already knew and practiced. But suddenly, his mind filled with images of William Cochran and David Jones. Some of what they had said and lived was truly new for The People. William Cochran had taught the principles of agriculture—and those principles had spread mercies to all people, both white and Native, during the starving times. Garry would teach those principles one day. There would be time for that. But it was David Jones who had lived out the deeper things: the principles of forgiveness, loving your enemy, living at peace with all people insofar as it falls to you—being like Jesus, who forgave His enemies. And this was what Garry focused on now.

"Quilent-satmen sent the Master of Life: his name is Jesus, Sun of Righteousness. God's Son became a human, with flesh and blood like us. He showed us what Quilent-satmen is like, a perfect image of his own heart. But when he came, his own tribe rejected him, spat on him, dishonored him, and finally condemned him to death, though he had done only good for them. They stretched him out on a tree and pounded iron spikes through his hands and feet. They killed him, and it was a long, painful death. This is what happened to the Son of Creator. And as he was dying, He said, 'Father, forgive them, for they don't know what they are doing.'"

This word nailed the listeners to Garry's words. Or rather, the words were like nails in their hearts. "Oy, oy," they cried, horrified. The whole idea of God being a man was difficult enough. Now they saw a misty picture of a death on a tree. And a word of forgiveness in the midst of that death. This, surely, was something Quilent-satmen would do. It had the ring of truth.

"This showed the forgiving heart of Creator, a heart to forgive enemies. This is how God is toward us: forgiving us. His heart is to forgive. Then when Jesus died, God raised him from the dead, to show that his way, the way of love and forgiveness, will win in the end. Quilent-satmen wants us to learn this way, the way of peace. Even toward our traditional enemies. Even them. I saw this practiced at Red River by the Black Robes. God can give this power to us. He gave this power to the men who taught me."

Garry was thinking of David Jones, his heart of love toward people who had tormented him, even toward Bishop Provencher, who had not shown love toward David. It was a love that came from God and strengthened you from within. By God's power, you could overcome evil with good.

This word about loving enemies was like a bomb exploding in the middle of the village. It was new, yet The People sensed the wisdom of it, even though no one had heard such a thing before, except from Koo-koo-sint, David Thompson. This was revelation from the spirit realm. And as outlandish as it was, few questioned it. The new idea was accepted almost immediately. It seemed to them that this was what they had been looking for all along. Imagine if all the tribes could hear this word, what peace there would be all around. Surely this was the secret that had been trying to break forth: peace among the tribes, brought by the Master of Life, Jesus.

During the coming weeks, they gave gifts to Slough-keetcha, the traditional way of honoring a prophet. With those gifts, which included several horses, Garry began his teaching tour among the other tribes who had opened the door for him.

• • •

Before the first snows came, Garry traveled from village to village, preaching the new message. He was drawn into the work by the intense curiosity of the people. He rode south to the Nez Percés. There he spoke to the shrewd Hallalhotsoot, and to the old man, Bloody Chief. Both men liked the teaching, thought it credible, and proclaimed Garry a great teacher. Before he left, they expressed the desire to send at least two Nez Percé boys with him to attend the Red River school.

"Perhaps there will be some from other tribes who will wish to send their sons," Garry said to the Nez Percés. "I will send word when the spring fur brigade returns east across the Backbone of the World. We plan to go back with them."

He preached among the Cayuses and the Walla Wallas before returning back home. In his own village, he spoke of Jesus to the respected Spokane headman, Old Chief. Old Chief gave his eleven-year-old son to go with Garry to Red River. Garry toured the other Spokane villages, preaching the message of forgiveness and love, using stories from Red River as illustrations.

As Garry taught the new teaching, whole villages were affected. Routines were changed to include regular morning and evening prayer to honor the Master of Life—whose name, they now knew, was Jesus. Sundays were set aside for observance of the Lord's Day—no work was permitted. Garry taught the people a few of the white man's songs and the people continued with the simple dance dating from the time of the old prophets—the prophet dance, still used to commemorate the old prophecies—which included a time of confession of sin, and the consecration of the heart to God the Creator.

The message first introduced by David Thompson, that the tribes should live in peace and protect the weak, became generally accepted doctrine. Intertribal squabbling was reduced to an occasional ill remark. Tribes that had fought each other for centuries learned to forgive and forget. Peace prevailed.

The Ten Commandments became generally known and accepted, reinforcing ancient tribal ethics. Only in the area of monogamy was there serious quibbling with the new teaching. The abundance of women in comparison to men made the teaching impractical, or so thought the majority.

Acts of thievery became downright rare throughout much of the Columbia Plateau, as the already principled leaders enforced their will on the scurrilous. Sexual codes were tightened even tighter than before. Lying had always been rare—but now it became virtually nonexistent.

Garry allowed the people to give him a new name: *Ilimhu-spokanee*—Chief Sun. In part this was because they couldn't pronounce his new name. The word "Garry" came out sounding like "Jerry."

Only among the Coeur d'Alenes to the east did he receive a cool reception. Their prophets—another Circling Raven and his son, Twisted Earth, had told them to look for "Black Robes," and Garry did not wear the proper clothing to be the fulfillment they sought.[51] But elsewhere, his fame spread like wildfire.

The people were dry tinder. Slough-keetcha was appointed as a whirling fire-drill to set the twigs afire.

---

51. A different man from the Spokane prophet, this Circling Raven was of an older generation. His son, Twisted Earth, was a contemporary of the Spokane prophet toward the end of the eighteenth century.

Four

In the spring, Slough-keetcha, accompanied by his brother and his uncle Chongulloosoon, took his message to the Flatheads. Word of his preaching had piqued the curiosity of Chief Insula. The Flatheads had picked up rumors of it at Kettle Falls and at Horse Prairie during trade fairs.

The three Spokanes rode east past the falls and along the well-worn trail to Flathead Post, finally arriving at the village of Insula on Flathead Lake. The trail was new to Spokan Garry, but his uncle had traversed it many times.

The Flathead village consisted of a circle of three dozen buffalo-skin tipis on the shore of the broad, scenic lake. The lodges had a unique appearance: the Flatheads left the buffalo tails on their lodge hides, incorporating them into the design of every tipi.

Fresh-cut lodgepoles were everywhere, ready to replace the old ones for the new year. Between the tipis were a dozen or more horse corrals made of green poles lashed together. The village was as prosperous as it was beautiful, facing a range of snow-capped mountains across the expanse of water.

Insula was inspecting and grooming his favorite warhorse when the three Spokanes arrived. After introductions, he invited them into his lodge. The interior was bright with the afternoon sun, all the more so because the tipi, by Flathead custom, was furnished with no interior lining.

Insula seated himself at the tripod backrest opposite the door. From it hung his *sumesh* bundle and his weapons. He invited his guests to be seated on the cattail-mat floor and ordered food to be brought.

"My elder brothers, you have journeyed far. You have spent two days in the journey?"

Chongulloosoon presented a protocol gift of sweet grass and tobacco, then replied, "We stopped overnight at Flathead Post. We used the shelters there, for they are seldom used by the white people anymore—only by foxes and mice."

"Uhnh, we go there less and less. We prefer the trade of the Long-knives these days. They love to trade with us at the Hoary-headed Fathers."

Slough-keetcha did not know the place, which the white men called "The Grand Tetons."

Turning to Garry, Insula said, "But this year the Long-knives did not come. We traded with Chief McGillivray at Fort Colvile. At Kettle Falls, we learned that you have been three winters among the white teachers, learning from them of Amotkan. Is this true?"

Slough-keetcha replied, "Yes, it is true."

Insula paused. A long, pensive moment passed, in which only their breathing was heard. Then he said:

"Long ago, the prophet Shining Shirt foretold these days. He said that the white people would give us the laws of the Creator. He even counseled us to have but one wife. This, he said, was what Amotkan preferred us to do. Shining Shirt himself divorced the younger sister of his sister-wives, so certain was he of this teaching. But this counsel was hard for us to follow, as you can see"—and, smiling, he pointed to his two wives, who were serving soup in dishes.

Soon the men were eating the soup with horn spoons. Garry replied, "This is just what the white men teach, that every man should have but one wife! It is the counsel of the Master of Life in the leaves bound together."

Insula bantered back, "But how is this possible? There are many more women than men in our villages! We would have many frustrated women if we followed this advice!" Insula's broad face beamed. He and Chongulloosoon shared knowing looks.

Slough-keetcha, on the other hand, was baffled by the question. He thought, there are many implications to what I have learned. Many things I have not yet thought through. I wish Pelly were here. He is a thinker. He would have thought of these things already.

Insula continued. "Still, it is evident that the prophecies of Shining Shirt are accurate. And do the teachers wear black robes, as he foresaw?"

"Yes. They wear black robes when they lead worship."

Garry marveled within himself as he spoke. The Spokanes had been unaware of the ancient prophet Shining Shirt. The more widely Garry traveled, the more he realized that the Great Spirit had prepared all the surrounding tribes for just the teachings he was now giving them.

Insula was still talking. "And what of the talisman Shining Shirt gave to the Salish warriors, which he told them to bite before they went off into battle with the Piegans?" He drew in the dirt floor, between two mats, the sign of the cross. Then he went on.

"A village of the Kalispels to the west was besieged by Piegans who greatly outnumbered them. The warriors went out to fight them. Shining Shirt instructed them to bite the cross. Two refused to bite it, and they were the only two injured in the battle! This talisman has much power! What do you know of it?"

"The cross is the sign of the Son of the Creator. The Son came to earth and died on a cross, a piece of wood shaped like you have drawn. Then he was brought back to life, to show that death had no power over him. The empty cross has been his sign ever since."

Insula replied, "I saw the same sign on the book carried by the man called Smith, the Man of the Book. I have seen it, too, at Flathead Post, and on the book of the trader, Ogden."

"Shining Shirt had much else to say," Insula continued after a pause. "He said that the white man will cause all wars to cease throughout the land. He said that the power with which the white man brings peace will also reduce our people to poverty. He said that it would be useless to resist; that we must, at all costs, make peace with the whites. What have you found out about this?"

"Elder brother," replied Slough-keetcha, "I know nothing of these prophecies. This is true—about the white man's power. They have large guns and great houses such as you have never seen. They sail on great boats, far bigger than any canoe, and they have much knowledge, beyond what we have."

"Shining Shirt said it would be so." The chief's voice was low, guttural. The atmosphere inside the sun-drenched tipi seemed darker than it had been.

"But the white people also have good hearts. They wish to share their knowledge with us. They are kind," Garry added, and he told stories, drawing on his years with David Jones, William Garrioch, and the Cochrans.

Insula listened, but he grimaced as he replied. "And yet, I have seen much of them I do not like. Some of them are as you say, but others are skunks and weasels. They seduce our girls; they sell their firewater to our young men to corrupt them; they lie; they cheat; they cannot be trusted. How do you account for this?"

"Not all white people serve the Master of Life. Some choose to live like the animals."

"Ah! They are of *Emtep?*"

"Just as our own people are—some good, some bad—so are they."

The conversation stretched on into the night, as Slough-keetcha attempted to satisfy the curiosity of the Flathead chief. They finished the evening by singing a prayer to Amotkan, He-who-dwells-on-high, thanking him for the words of guidance he had given them before any of them had received their names.

• • •

Two weeks later, Slough-keetcha, alias Ilimhu-spokanee, was once again Spokan Garry, translating a speech for Factor Simon McGillivray at Fort Colvile. With him was Kootenai Pelly, still ailing from a damaged liver. Garry was surrounded by the fruits of his successful preaching. Five other boys ranging from twelve to seventeen years old had been given over by their fathers for education at the Red River school: a Cayuse, a second Kutenai, two Nez Percés, and the son of Old Chief, who had been renamed Spokan Berens.

Dr. Hamlyn, the Company physician, was there to travel back to Red River with the caravan. He had been to the Columbia District to add his medical expertise to the knowledge of Dr. McLoughlin, but when he examined Kootenai Pelly, his face fell. He did what he could.

On April 20, the brigade departed, taking not two, but seven chiefs' sons to the school at Red River. All seven were given new names by the white people—for this, too, had been prophesied by that great *sgumoiga*, Shining Shirt. Now it was their turn to face the extraordinary odyssey of crossing the Backbone of the World, but they had Garry and Pelly to help them.

Five

Having crossed the Backbone of the World a third time, Spokan Garry and Kootenai Pelly excitedly brought their friends to the mission school at Red River. It was with a sense of privilege and pride that Garry showed his five new friends the wonders of the Red River Colony. Garry borrowed a cart from the mission compound, hitched up an old gray mare, and piled the five others into the cart. The five had readily adopted their new names: Kootenai Collins, Cayuse Halket, the Nez Percés Ellis and Pitt, and Spokan Berens. Pelly was in no condition to rattle around in a springless cart over the foot-deep ruts of springtime, now hardened by the summer sun. He stayed in the bunkhouse.

The cart squeaked its ungreased wooden wheels down winding lanes behind the old nag that obediently pulled it. The boys stood inside the cart, their nostrils full of the stench of horse manure, their hands clinging to the poles lashed together that formed the sides of the cart. The wheels screeched unmercifully, but the boys thought it all great fun, and, imitating the screeching by voice, doubled the sheer volume of the racket halfway to Fort Garry. It was an easy way to relax in the midst of the language barriers that still separated them. Laughter, like gift giving, was a universal language.

At the fort, some men were building a powder magazine out of limestone quarried from the riverbank. Garry commented in sign lingo and English, "Remember what I said about the flood? The wood houses floated right away! See there! They are building this house out of stone so it won't float on water."

The others, who had not believed Garry's story about the flood, now didn't know what to believe. Their lives were so full of things they had once thought impossible, they were having to trust Garry to tell the truth despite all the improbable claims he made. When he would make another one of his incredible statements, they would just fall silent and listen, not letting on whether they believed him or not. All their foundations for judging truth from falsehood had been jerked out from under them, and only Garry was yet trusted enough to help them discern hard fact from gross exaggeration.

Alex Ross happened to be passing by delivering mail. He greeted Garry in his stiff, dour manner and explained like a museum tour guide that the whole fort was to be rebuilt of stone, and that there were plans to build another fort like it near Grand Rapids, fifteen miles north.[52]

Next, Garry took them to the great windmill. They all stood gaping up at it as its four tattered arms turned slowly in the wind like an ancient scarecrow who couldn't decide which way was up.

"It is for grinding the grain into flour, for bread," Garry explained.

As the cart groaned on, he showed them the church at Image Plain, five miles to the north, and then went on to the Rapids, another ten. There he looked for Parson Cochran and Ann, for the words of David Jones still rung in his ears with the startling news: "William is starting a new church there among the Salteaux. And he has already cleared seven acres for planting."

---

52. Lower Fort Garry has been restored as a provincial park north of Winnipeg, Manitoba.

Garry was eager to introduce his five friends to the Cochrans and to tell them proudly of the success of his preaching. The flat, black-mud road had changed considerably since Garry had first arrived, for there were no longer any trees left standing anywhere near it. The place looked like a huge, barren slab of black slate, stretching on and on to infinity, covered by crops just ripening—and by nothing else.

William and Anne spotted the cart well before it reached their rustic hut, and they came running out to meet it. If the truth were told, they had never expected to see Spokan Garry again—had even told each other that he would remain with his people and forget everything they had taught him. But no! Here he was, and five others with him! They were so surprised to see Garry that Reverend Cochran accidentally dropped his wire-rimmed glasses off his nose, and they went flying to the ground. Both the Cochrans believed in hugs, so uncharacteristic of the British spirit, and with their arms around Garry, they approached the door of their hut.

The Cochrans' new home was a thatch-roofed log shack, the most primitive affair imaginable, especially in comparison to the parsonage at the Upper Church. Garry noticed that, except for a couple of rude benches, the place was bare. There was literally nothing here—except the warmth of the Cochrans themselves. And that, he reflected, was a great deal.

Garry let the news burst from him: "Pelly fell from a horse and has been almost bedridden all these months. But my people wanted nothing so much as to hear what I learned from you and Parson Jones. I spent the whole time preaching to them and to all the villages for miles around!"

"Thank the Lord!" William replied. "He gives us more than we can ask or think." Smiling at their conversation, Ann took up the work she had been doing before the boys arrived—grinding last year's wheat into flour. William had dug up two smooth stones from the riverbank, and she was grinding the one on the other, with the grain in between. Then she strained the rock chips from the flour with a piece of muslin. It was the crudest method imaginable—but there was no windmill at the Rapids.

She spoke as she ground the flour: "We'll be buildin' a chairch soon, just over there." Her voice lilted upward at the end of each phrase as though it were a question. "But wood be scarce these days, as you can no doubt see. Mr. Cochran pairchased a wee plot o' woods there on the east bank, some o' the last trees left standin' within ten mile."

"You wouldn't like to help us put up the new sanctuary, would you now?" William asked. "We'll be needin' some strong arms like yours."

"Aye, we'd like tha'." said Garry in his best Scotch brogue.

But it was not to be. On August 14, David Jones returned from Wales with his wife, and the two of them made an immediate hit with the upper crust of Red River. After considerable fixing up and preparation, the two of them moved into the parsonage in October and made themselves thoroughly comfortable. Garry was involved in all these preparations, so David asked Garry and the others to become involved in the construction of a new Indian bunkhouse. Garry, out of commitment to his spiritual mentor, felt obliged to help with that project, whereas he scarcely ever saw the Cochrans anymore.

During David's visit to Wales the previous year, William had written for support from the Church Missionary Society, hoping that David would put in a good word for him in building his new church. When the support had not come through, some hard words had passed from William toward his yokefellow in Wales.

Now that the two of them had taken over the parsonage, William and Ann began to tell each other, "David made room for us in his heart at fairst because he was lonely. Now that his wife is with him, he's not so keen to help us. He don't need us anymore." The more they spoke these thoughts to each other, the more they appeared as truth. David no longer seemed like a yokefellow of Christ. He seemed increasingly like an Englishman sucking up to the upper crust at Fort Garry—and to that English hypocrite, George Simpson.

Garry sensed that a good deal more had changed hereabouts than just the removal of the trees. There was a barrenness that he could not quite put his finger on, but he sensed it in his spirit. He also sensed that he would see very little of the Cochrans from now on. William had his eyes on other Natives and other projects that did not include the Red River Colony and the school. Much of the warmth that had exuded from the pastors of this little colony seemed to have dissipated. A somberness surrounded the colony now, deepening with the passing of months.

• • •

On August 20, Governor Simpson arrived on a York boat, bringing a teenaged English girl with him. Donald and Adelgonde MacKenzie came out of the fort to greet the governor at the riverside.

"And who be this charming filly?" MacKenzie inquired of the little girl, who could not have been more than eighteen. He eyed her as a bull buffalo would eye a new cow in his harem.

Simpson replied, before Donald could say anything foolish, "Meet my new bride, Frances. Frances: this is our chief factor, Donald MacKenzie, and his wife, Adelgonde."

The MacKenzies flinched as though doused by a bucket of freezing water. Adelgonde thought, but didn't say, Why, the girl is less than half the governor's age. He surely does know how to rob the cradle!

Everyone knew that the governor had gone off to England to get married. He had, in fact, "pensioned off" his "old concern," Margaret, who in his mind had too much Indian blood to qualify for a real marriage. Generously, Simpson had coupled her to someone else and provided a monthly stipend for her and for his children by her. This was, in the minds of English gentlemen, a thoroughly acceptable—even generous—solution to the problem of finding sexual satisfaction in the wilderness. No one was shocked about it, but to bring such an innocent babe to this wild place! High society banter was full of *this* shocking development for weeks.

Another change had taken place, too: the school had a new teacher by the name of John Bunn. He was a stricter man than William Garrioch, but his love for the boys shone through his strictness. He taught well and quickly earned the boys' respect.

Shortly after the fall term began, a shipment of logs arrived from up the Assiniboine River. The logs were destined to become the new bunkhouse.

At about that time, William Cochran received a severe wound in the knee. A house he was building fell on him, the result of a lack of assistance in raising it. As a result, David was preoccupied with the pastoral work of two parishes, and it was John Bunn who supervised the building of the new bunkhouse. The accident threw into sharp relief the isolation of the Cochrans, in contrast to the abundant help that David Jones was getting for his work at Red River.

The five new boys and Spokan Garry worked together on the bunkhouse even before they could speak easily to each other. They dragged the logs to the school by horse and chain. They axed and adzed the logs to shape, including the four corner posts, grooved to receive the ends of the horizontal logs. They raised the timbers, chinked them with clay, made the rafters and the shingles, and installed windows, all with the help and supervision of John Bunn. English was taught in the process, as John carefully labeled everything by its English name. Two kinds of teaching—language and carpentry—were fused together in one outdoor classroom.

Bunn was a good teacher in all these skills, and the end product was more expertly crafted than the parsonage had been. Last to be installed was the door, which had an iron handle but no lock. None of the houses in the colony had locks.

• • •

One day during Sunday worship, several of the Scots got up during the middle of the service—and noisily walked right out of the church! Garry spoke to David about the act of rudeness, sensing that something was wrong. David tried to explain the situation so Garry could explain to his friends from the western tribes.

"Alex Ross happened to read some remarks I put in the missionary register about how the Indians are making more spiritual progress than the Scottish. I am afraid he's taken offense, and many of the Scots are up in arms. You see, they have their own way of worshiping God. They call themselves 'Presbyterians.' Their way is as different from ours as we are from the Catholics. We have tried to bring them along, to do it their way as best we could, but they are never satisfied!"

Garry could not grasp this divisiveness. Did not these people believe in loving your enemy?

During the next week, Alex Ross himself showed up at David's door, spokesman for a dozen Scots that crowded around behind him. He explained his mission: "Long these many years, we ha' adapted oursel's to your Anglican ways. But none o' us is well content to keep it up. You have obliged us to be Anglicans long enough!"

David replied, "You speak as though we were trying to force our ways on everyone."

"Aye. By keepin' out all choices but yours."

"What? Do you think we have plotted to keep out Presbyterians from the colony?"

"'Tis what we suspect. We shall go direct to the governor and request a Presbyterian clergyman."

David was flabbergasted. Yet he said to himself, the Presbyterians have been persecuted for centuries. They always think they're being persecuted—it's in their blood.

The truth was that Alex Ross, whom Simpson had promised a teaching position at the colony, had been stewing about the loss of position ever since. Not only that, but as leader of the Snake Brigade, Ross had been privileged to lead worship in Scottish Presbyterian fashion. Here at Red River all the churches were Anglican, and no one was asking him to lead a worship service. All his ideas about what he would do with himself here had come to nothing. The Red River Colony was a retirement colony, mostly for people who were done with life and had nothing more to do than fish. Alex Ross had to find something to do, and being an agitator for Presbyterian colonists was what came to hand.

Spokan Garry was not present at this confrontation, but the dour-looking Scots made it known that they were disgruntled with Anglicanism, and Garry could sense the bad feeling at every worship service. The air was thick with it. The protesters would cluck their tongues, whisper loudly during prayers, and stonily refuse to sing Anglican hymns. They interpreted the simplest liturgical decisions as being "against" them, signs of a return to the days of the Stuart kings, forcing Anglicanism on the Scottish Kirk. Forgiveness, for them, was the least attainable of all virtues.

David wrote in his journal:

> The most interesting feature in our church here has hitherto been its unity—the total amalgamation within its walls of petty names and distinctions, the identification of all classes who hold the faith as it is in Jesus within the only, one, and common bond of the Gospel. Through the malignity of a few individuals who care for none of these things, this interesting feature will be lost the moment lines of distinction begin to be drawn. And I am very doubtful what effect may be produced on the minds of our Indian(s) . . .[53]

What effect indeed. The bad feeling was an embarrassment to Spokan Garry in front of his friends—who also sensed the rift. It was another change since he had been away, and it seemed that all the changes were negative ones.

The passage into the winter of 1831 was marked by huge clouds of birds flying overhead—first pigeons, then blackbirds. The boys had to stand in the fields for hours on end and chase them away from the corn and the barley. Garry told them that their efforts would be well rewarded the following winter. He stood with them in the fields and tried to make the tedium easier to bear with conversations about home.

After harvest, the weather began to turn cold as the legendary Red River winter made its ugly appearance. In an effort to conserve wood, stoves were not stoked up in advance of worship: the pastors lit them only a few minutes prior to services. Often, when Pelly and Garry arrived at church, the entire building, inside and out, would be covered with

---

53. *Journal of David Jones*, August 5, 1830.

frost and ice—an ice palace. Frost covered even the Bible, the pulpit, the prayerbook, and the ceilings. As the room warmed up, the water would drip down on the people, spattering the pages of their Bibles. It was as though the wood of the sanctuary was mourning the loss of the trees.

One evening in December, Garry rode home from Image Plain with David Jones after the Tuesday prayer meeting. Their horse cariole sped along on the surface of the hard-packed snow in the dusk. The harnesses, studded with bells, brightened the atmosphere of the lonely road with their jingling. All else was silence, until Garry put his thoughts into words.

"Governor Simpson—he got rid o' Margaret, his Indian wife. Now he has an English wife. What do you think o' that?"

David spoke through the wool scarf that was wrapped around his face. "He was not strictly married to Margaret, not by English law." David had not yet discerned the thrust or the import of the question.

"No. But he had her. He had children from her. Is this the way of God?"

Garry's conversation with the Flathead Insula and his remembrance of Shining Shirt were still fresh in his mind. He was trying to decide what he would teach when he went back home—trying to determine what God really wanted, and what was merely the white man's way. "Is it God's will for a man to have but one wife, or is it no'? The governor does no' think much o' Indian people. I ken that Factor MacKenzie doesn't either. But what does God think?"

Beginning to comprehend, David replied, "The governor has made the Company his God. We must let these men live as they choose. But God has commanded us to live with one woman until death separates us—so that children can grow up learning faithfulness. God is faithful in his love for us, and he wants us to be faithful until death, just as Jesus was faithful in his love for us. So it is God's will that we have but one wife."

"Yes, but what of our tribes in the west, where we have many more women than men? The men die in battle and on buffalo hunts. Most of the men who remain have at least two wives. Often they are sisters."

David paused, wrestling with the question, then spoke what came to mind. "When the people learn to farm and live at peace with each other, there will be more men. You see, the many parts of God's plan fit together."

"But in the meantime? Before that day, may we not bend to the old ways?"

David felt that he should stick to what he knew. "God has made it clear: when we follow Jesus, we must follow the teaching of the apostles. Each man is to have but one wife."

Garry saw the theory, as Insula had. But the theory seemed to fit other people better than his own. Besides, the governor in his own insolent way showed that biblical ideas could be bent to fit with practical realities.

Sensing Garry's doubt, David spoke more firmly. "You see, do you not, that I am faithful to my wife? I do not expect of you anything that I do not practice myself." It was not an unexpected position. David's own life had always been his final argument. He left William Cochran to rail against the practices of the gentlemen of the Honourable Company. It was not David's way to rail against anyone. He considered it his duty to live by the standards he taught and let his life be his best sermon. He was more likely to make friends of his enemies that way.

Garry, still struggling with the whole question of monogamy, spoke of it with Kootenai Pelly and was astonished to find out that no Kutenai ever took more than one wife. Quoting a Kutenai proverb, Pelly said, "No one can make use of more than one wife. One is enough for any man."

Nonetheless, Spokan Garry was not convinced.

• • •

On New Year's Day, David invited William and Ann Cochran to the Upper Church for dinner with the youngsters from the two schools— Pelly and Garry's school and the Cochrans' new school at the Rapids.

New Year's Day brought a great celebration in the best English tradition. The women had prepared roast beef, corn, raisins, bread, and plum pudding. Benches in the schoolhouse were rearranged around makeshift tables. The dinner was a banquet of laughter, which the few glasses of spilled milk could not quench. Afterward, the tables were removed and the floor opened for dancing—English style—while John Bunn played his fiddle.

After the affair was finished, the Cochrans loaded up several carioles with children and formed a caravan back to the Rapids. William struggled the whole way with his resentment against the Joneses, which he had successfully hidden under wraps during the festivities.

"The Joneses have developed quite a prosperous life for themselves," he said to his wife. His thoughts continued internally. *Now we must go back to our hovel where every grain must be crushed between two rocks, and we must hold church in a hut.* His mind would not let him alone, and he sat next to Ann thoroughly preoccupied with thoughts he dared not admit to his wife. And his knee still ached.

But after they had passed Image Plain, a sight emerged in the gathering darkness that jerked the parson out of his thoughts. A small poplar tree stood by the side of the road, a lonely and forlorn orphan that had somehow escaped the axe. An Indian woman hovered around it. She was carving it with a knife. William recognized her: she was a Salteaux from the village of Pigwys at Netley Creek. He didn't know her name, but he knew what she was doing.

"Betsy, that woman is taking the inner rind of that tree for food."

"Dear God," Ann gasped, groping for words to express her shock.

The caravan came to a halt. William got out of the cariole. The woman glanced at him dolefully, her eyes dull with patient resignation. She said nothing. She expected nothing. For her, this was life, the inevitable. Poplar rinds had always been her food when all else failed. But now, trees had vanished for miles around, and even the small sustenance they provided had been taken from her people.

On the ground were scattered scraps of the whitish outer bark, and in her hand, strands of red. She would take these strands home, boil them, and feed them to her family.

"No trees now," she said in Salteaux.

"This is the last straw," William mumbled to his wife—and bundled the woman into the cariole between them. "This spring, I will go to Pigwys and see if I can persuade him to let us build a permanent agricultural community for the Salteaux. These people cannot survive by foraging. The herds are vanishing, and even the trees have disappeared. They must be taught how to plant crops and raise livestock."

"You know he won't listen. He believes his people know more than we do."

"There must be a way. I have to try."

The sight of the starving woman crashed into William's life without gentleness, crushing his resentment against the Joneses almost by accident. He forgot the vision of a warm house, raisin cakes, and roast beef banquets behind him, and he set his eyes on a new dream—a farming village among the people of Pigwys. His mind raced along new lines now: What is my poverty, when placed against the life-threatening deprivation of the Natives? At least we have enough to eat. To Ann he said, almost joyously, "This is my destiny. It is what God has given to me, what he has prepared even from the time I learned to farm in Northumberland, and if I must die to my own comfort for the sake of the comfort of this woman who is shivering next to me, so be it."

Six

Kootenai Pelly had never ceased to have pain since his fall from the stallion. He had been under Doctor Hamlyn's constant care, but the pain had only increased.

Finally, on Palm Sunday, a grim David Jones and John Bunn carried him on a stretcher from the new bunkhouse into the parlor of the parsonage, where a cot was set up for him. Here the Joneses could nurse him hour by hour.

Pelly had always been a quiet one. He disliked being the center of attention. If the truth were told, he hadn't minded being confined to quarters this past year and letting Garry do all the traveling. He thought deeply during his times of solitude; he disliked small talk and large convocations. His parents had taught him well the Kutenai philosophy, "Do not shout, do not laugh loudly. Do not let anyone hear you beyond the lodge where you are staying, or the old women will ridicule you. Don't be a mischief boy."

Pain was forcing him to be more dependent on other people now, and he could no longer remain so aloof. His close friends, Spokan Garry and David Jones, were a comfort to his pain. Conversation helped to distract him from it, and their faith helped him when he could not find distraction.

Mrs. Jones (for that is what they all called David's wife, a more formal woman than Ann Cochran), treated Pelly as one of her own children, washing his clothes and feeding him soup from her table. She did this for seven days, but on Easter, the family was consumed with church activities, and they had to leave Pelly quite alone the whole day. At the end of the day, they returned home exhausted and went to bed, but Pelly, who had slept all day, was wide awake.

Was it a mistake coming back here? he asked himself as he lay awake through the long night. Would the village shamans have had more success in healing my liver? Yet they had many months to try, and could do nothing. He recalled how the Shaman Society had discussed his case. They had gathered around him to sing the sickness out of his body—had tried to draw the malady out of his mouth, but had admitted in the end, "it takes strong power to pull sickness out of the mouth."

Pelly thought, Dr. Hamlyn is not a shaman. He is more like the wise women. He knows herbs and preparations.

The Kutenai boy wondered about the sayings he had heard as a child. Were there omens that predicted my death? Did a bird fly into the lodge? He tried to remember. I remember one day a tear falling unexpectedly from the eye of He-who-walks-into-the-forest. Perhaps that was an omen. Did Mother touch a part of a deer kill that she was forbidden to touch? He didn't know, and he wasn't sure if it mattered.

Those were the old ways of explaining tragedies, but now he was not sure that they were right. He sensed that his time was near, and he was trying to understand why he should die so young.

His childhood came back to him in poignant vignettes. He remembered the first time, at age six, that he shot a crane feeding in the swamps near the village. How proud he was to have supplied food for his family. He remembered, too, his first deer hunt, when, after the first fall of snow, he and his father had gone into the eastern forests with the Deer Chief. Le Grand Queue had spoken of him with pride after he shot his first deer. "The boy is quiet, but he shoots straight and true; mark it well." His father had been a good teacher.

How I miss you, Father! Tears welled up in his eyes.

The next year, he had sought his guardian spirit. But David Jones had told him that Jesus was all the guardian spirit he needed. David had not required him to throw away his medicine bundle, but the bundle had become less and less important to him over the years.

Pelly opened his eyes wide and looked about him in the darkness of the parsonage. A woodstove was the main feature of the room. It had a long stovepipe that stretched the length of the room, to throw out as much heat as possible as the heat meandered through it. "Woodstoves are better than fireplaces," Reverend Cochran had said. Reverend Cochran had been right.

Bouquets of dried herbs graced the walls, interspersed with a few augurs and bellows. A canoe paddle, a jingle-bell harness, a straw broom, David's walking stick, and snowshoes occupied the corner near the door. A writing desk recently brought from Wales stood in the near corner, with a cane-seat chair in front of it. The desk, its front side folded down, was littered with the papers of David's journal, with quill pens and ink powder.

This was David's room. It reflected his personality, his interests. It was a cozy, simple room, like David himself.

The wood in the stove, brought by raft from across Lake Winnipeg, snapped and popped comfortably. The brass warming pan, filled with coals, had not been needed to warm the beds tonight. The Joneses were lavishing love on him, using the precious wood to keep him snug.

The sturgeon-oil lamps had been extinguished. All the room was bathed in cold moonlight from the window. The light accentuated the pitcher and basin on the side table.

The teaching of the white men is a comfort.

Christian moral teaching had differed little from the traditions of the fathers, serving to confirm his own people's lifeways. "You are good at wrestling in a woman's arms, but you are a coward in wrestling warriors," they used to tell him, thinking to shame him out of sexual wantonness—and he had blushed every time. He had never had any leanings toward sexual wantonness, but they had just wanted to make sure.

Even the habit of worship on the first day of every week was not new, for the Old Ones had instructed the same, from some ancient tradition of the *San-ka*, the old name for his people.

Reverend Jones's teaching had been easy to accept, a welcome progression, the next logical step. In accepting Christian teaching, Pelly, more than Garry, had not felt himself to be stepping beyond the bounds of what was safe, familiar, and secure. Even now, on his deathbed, he felt secure. He saw that Jesus was a San-ka.

On Monday, David received a visitor—Mr. W.K. Smith, a teacher who had just been hired for the school at the Rapids. He was a stiff, formal man, cold and dour, with a domineering nose to match his personality. A carbon copy of Alexander Ross. Yet he had come to the parsonage out of concern for the sick boy, something Ross never would have done.

"You have, I am told, the boy Pelly convalescing here?" he inquired of David.

"Yes, he is in the parlor. Come in."

W.K. Smith asked the questions expected of an evangelical Christian schoolmaster.

"Pelly, do you pray?"

"Yes, sir."

"And what do you pray for?"

"I pray to God to pardon my sins and wash my soul."

"Good lad." W.K. Smith smiled. The boy had given the right answers. The new teacher had no idea of the depth of Pelly's faith, for Pelly had not shared it freely, even with his own father. W.K. Smith prayed briefly and then left, quite satisfied. The school had done its job well.

David remained with the boy all afternoon. Pelly could converse more freely with him, for David was a trusted mentor.

"Sir, do you remember the great flood?" he asked.

"I remember it well," replied the Anglican.

"You said then that troubles are not a sign that God hates you, but that God loves you."

"Yes. God disciplines those he loves. He removes our comfort and ease when they no longer suit what he is teaching us."

"This is a good idea. God taught you . . . you taught me . . . a good idea."

Pelly was not thinking as clearly as he had the previous night. His mind was spinning; he was moving in and out of consciousness. He was looking at David, and suddenly his father was there, in David's place. Yes. His father was there in the room with him—Le Grand Queue, his face streaked with red. He felt compelled to say the words to his father that he had never had the courage to say when he was with them.

"Father! The Great Spirit has sent me to teach you."

"I am here!" Le Grand Queue replied.

"The Great Spirit wants you to keep following the ways of righteousness, even though I must die. He says to keep on confessing our sins. I am sorry I did not say it when I was with you. But since you have come here now, it is not too late. Follow Jesus. He is San-ka. He is one of us!"

David was kneeling at the cot, holding Pelly's hand, listening to the delirious boy instruct his father. Sorrow threatened to overwhelm him.

It was the same heart-wrenching poignancy that had torn him at the death of Joseph Sharpe, William Harbridge, and the other boys who had died at the school. David wept, the tears rolling silently down mosquito-bitten cheeks.

David thought, I trained Pelly to teach his people of Christ. But this is the only teaching he will ever accomplish—a dream produced by fever delirium! Yet I thank you, Father, that he has come to know you. Now let me learn from him the lessons he learned from me.

Kootenai Pelly did not last out the day. By suppertime, he was gone.

They let people come to the parsonage on Tuesday to pay their last respects. Garry came and wept his heart out—mourning the loss of a friend who was closer than a brother. He could not forget a certain bird that had cried "Pellee, Pellee" during their journey over the Backbone of the World. Their friendship had been birthed that day, and now it had to be buried in the ground.

On Wednesday, they buried Pelly near the graveyard by the church. Pelly's garden was nearby, where William and David had labored to teach him about "pease, carrots, and potatoes." David preached a homily on "Except a corn of wheat fall into the ground and die, it abideth alone; but if it die, it bringeth forth much fruit."

On the other side were the graves of Joseph Sharpe and William Harbridge, who had died just before Pelly arrived. Their deaths had been a premonition of harm after all.

David was the last to leave the graveyard that somber afternoon. He stayed there long because he was full of grief—heavy, heart-wrenching grief. After twenty minutes of bitter weeping, he sighed, stretched out his arms toward the open grave, and said, "Adieu, my friend."

He went to the parsonage within view of the grave. Avoiding conversation with his wife, he went alone to his desk. Pelly's cot had not yet been removed. He took up his pen and wrote:

> I once thought it probable I might be placed among his Tribe, and often pictured to myself years of youthful intercourse with him in our Maker's service; but the Society determined otherwise, and he is gone! Moral and Political changes may pass over this country and render it either more populous or more deserted, but whether a desolate wilderness or a crowded city, here is one spot which will ever stand linked in my memory with the most treasured recollections as the place from whence some Indian pilgrims stepped into the chariot of separation which rolled them from earth to

heaven. We may again meet there with joy, where no difference of language will frustrate our communion, and where our views and motives shall be far better appreciated than they are here.[54]

George Simpson did not attend the funeral, but the news of the Kutenai's death greatly upset him. "Damn! This is a serious turn—and a bleeding nuisance. We'll have to send an envoy to explain things—tell the father it wasn't our fault."

The culmination of all his fussing was that Spokan Garry was chosen as envoy to Le Grand Queue to "tell the father it wasn't their fault." Hadn't his letter of last year brought peace and comfort wherever it was read? Imagine what the boy himself could do for a grieving father!

Garry departed with the next Company brigade a month later to bear the grim message to the people of the Kutenai River that the son of their greatest chief was dead.

---

54. *Journal of David Jones,* Easter Monday, 1831.

Seven

Le Grand Queue of the San-ka—the Kutenai—stood next to the Fish Chief, He-who-walks-into-the-forest. Their faces were painted red; their hair braided into three braids, with a fourth braidlet on top. Le Grand Queue was adorned with weasel tails at the end of each braid. His deer-hide shirt was adorned with elaborate cutout patterns flowing from the neck and down the sleeves. A choker of pipe beads circled his neck, and several long necklaces testified to his preference for the color blue.

The two men were preparing their people for an evening of fishing on the Kutenai River, that watery stream of life that poured itself past their village, linking it to several other Kutenai villages upriver. A great number of canoes lined the water's edge, each made of whole bark carefully peeled from mountain trees and stretched around a rib cage of cedar. The canoes had a unique shape, long at the bottom and short on top, like the old Roman warships designed to ram other ships beneath the water's surface.

Well before sundown, He-who-walks-into-the-forest led a flotilla of twenty canoes out onto the water. All through the night they stood athwart their canoes, holding their torches with one hand, thrusting their spears into the salmon with the other. By morning, every canoe had returned laden with such weight that the vessels seemed to be floating underwater.

Le Grand Queue, named by the French for the braid that had at one time stretched down his back, returned to his lodge and was greeted by his wife, who handed him his pipe. His fishing had been enjoyable, and he was exultant. He filled the pipe with a mixture of tobacco and *kinnikinic*. Then he sat down in front of his lodge, lit the pipe, and pointed the stem toward the setting sun to ward off bad luck. After this ritual, he began to chant his evening devotions, alternately singing and smoking. He was at peace with himself.

The Great Spirit had blessed him, for he had over thirty broken horses and a large herd of unbroken ones. Under his guidance the village was as prosperous as it had ever been, and so he held firm to his chieftainship. It had been many years—was it twenty-three or twenty-four?—since he had gone in quest of the powers of the chief. Then he had received a new song. He had sung the song to The People, had been elected to the post, and had proven himself capable, for it was art, not war, that proved one eligible for chieftainship among the Kutenai. Not a single year had passed but what the village had increased in horses, had prospered in the fall salmon and late-fall deer hunts, and had enjoyed protection from those noisy and obnoxious neighbors, the People-who-dwell-by-the-lake, the ones the whites called Flathead. Under his leadership, the Kutenai had formed a buffalo-hunting pact with the Flatheads—the first one in history—and a few of his people had even ventured east to take the buffalo of the plains across the mountains.

He thought much of his son in the east, at far-off Red River. Perhaps if I smoke and pray faithfully, he will prosper and return to us to become Band Chief. This was his fondest hope.

Sending his invalid son back to Red River had set him on edge. It was the last thing he would have done if the decision had rested with him, but he remembered still his son's words: "Father, the wise women have not brought healing. The pain is still there. But there is a man at Red River who knows much. He is not a shaman, but he knows much of herbs and preparations. Perhaps he will bring healing. I will go back. Besides, there was a boy who prayed to Jesus, and he was healed. It was great medicine. Jesus has great spirit powers."

The southern Kutenai rarely crossed the mountains into the eastern plains. Le Grand Queue knew well the danger of the northern trail, and of the Blackfeet who lived to the east of the pass.

"Are you sure you are strong enough to make this journey?" he had cautioned. "Yes," his son had said. But the word had come from his faith and courage, not from inner certainty.

Le Grand Queue was interrupted in his musing by an argument outside his lodge. The lodge itself was a tipi made of dogbane, sewn together and arranged like thatch in four circular bands around the cone of lodge-poles. The door was a mat of horizontal dogbane that hung over a square opening. Emerging through this opening, the chief confronted two men, Looks-at-the-ground and The Bent One, who were arguing violently, even coming to blows. This behavior was unusual among the Kutenais, and Le Grand Queue moved quickly to break up the fight.

Looks-at-the-ground defended himself: "He stole from me the dried sturgeon we caught last week. It was gone. I searched his lodge. It was there."

"Has it come to this?" Le Grand Queue remonstrated. "Is there not much food? Have we San-ka stopped looking out for each other?" His gaze accosted Looks-at-the-ground.

"Stealing cannot be tolerated among us," Looks-at-the-ground reminded the Band Chief. "It is contrary to the ways of the San-ka."

The Bent One cringed and said nothing. He was appropriately named, for he had a curved spine, almost a hunched back. It limited him severely in the hunt. He was an old man who seemed burdened at the prospect of living another year.

"What you say is true," replied Le Grand Queue, "but there is a higher righteousness. It is not our way to steal, we all agree. Such is the way of the Piegans across the mountains. But there is a higher law yet. You should have noticed that The Bent One was desperate. You should have given him the sturgeon so that he would not be reduced to stealing it! Give him double what he took!"

The chief, miffed that there should be even the semblance of poverty under his benign leadership, stared daggers at the others. If there is anything worse than stealing, he said to himself, it is stinginess. Wrong never grows in one man's lodge alone.

"Wait here," he added irritably—and he went into his lodge and brought out three trout. He gave two to The Bent One and one to Looks-at-the-ground. Like David Jones, he recognized the power of his own example in preserving righteousness among his people. Moreover, he didn't want Looks-at-the-ground to resent his judgment. Judgment must be tempered with love, he concluded to himself. So will we preserve harmony in the village. When we lose harmony, life is not worth living.

The hard resentment vanished from the face of Looks-at-the-ground as he received the trout. It made the chastisement against his stinginess easier to swallow. He went off mollified, willing to obey the chief's command.

The Bent One, likewise, straightened a little as he walked away. He had said nothing the whole time. Now he was glad he had thrown himself on the mercy of the chief.

. . .

At the close of the day, as the sun was setting, another commotion was heard to the south of the village. The chief donned his hat made of a horse's mane, sown in a circle with the hair flattened to form a brim all round.

Walking to the commotion, Le Grand Queue recognized that two strangers had entered the camp. But no, they were not strangers. One was the Salish lad, Spokan Garry; the other his uncle, Chongulloosoon. He remembered them from the meeting at Fort Colvile.

"You have come far," he said amid the general uproar. But the foreigners did not speak his language. So with gestures, he drew them to his lodge and sent for The Bent One. The old hunchback had Salish relatives and knew the Salish tongue.

"Let me see if I can get you something to eat. Please, sit down," the chief said to his guests. It was dark inside his lodge, but his wife was just kindling a fire. Her mother was also present, and the chief said to his wife, "Tell your mother to prepare fish for our guests."

Spokan Garry noticed that whenever the chief addressed his mother-in-law, he did so through his wife, never once speaking directly to her nor she to him. This practice he thought strange, but he was learning to adjust to many strange customs as he traveled far and wide among non-Salish nations.

The Bent One arrived and quickly learned that he was to be an interpreter. His face reflected his pride at being so privileged—until he had to translate the first words of Spokan Garry.

"My uncle and I have come bearing news. We are sorry to say it: six moons ago, your son died. It was the damaged liver. He never recovered after his fall from the horse."

Le Grand Queue betrayed no emotion. He sat paralyzed, as though pierced with a poisoned arrow. A cloud of darkness filled the lodge. Death itself seemed to have come in through the dogbane thatch. He said nothing, but uttered muffled cries. The two women began to ululate at the top of their voices, their cries piercing the lodge-cover. Every villager knew why the two Spokanes had come: the son of the War Chief was dead.

It was the darkest night of Le Grand Queue's life. He wanted to go off and mourn, yet etiquette required him to play the host to his guests.

His best friend and confidant, He-who-walks-into-the-forest, was away on another all-night fishing trip. The sun had set, shrouding the camp with darkness.

Will the sun ever shine again?

Spokan Garry said awkwardly, "He was my best friend. We were brothers. I grieve as you do."

But Le Grand Queue didn't seem to hear him. He was in a world of his own. He had apparently cut off communication with the outside world to spare himself its pain. Or perhaps he was treasuring the memory of his only son in a way that allowed no others to participate.

Spokan Garry and Chongulloosoon looked at each other unhappily. It was a poor place to be—guests in the lodge of the very man to whom they had given such devastating news. The Bent One, seeing the awkwardness of the situation, invited the two messengers to stay in his lodge overnight. Conversing freely with them on the way, he assured them that the chief would soon recover from the shock.

The whole village retired early. The usual gambling games and entertainments were canceled. The people, if they spoke at all, spoke in whispers and gestures.

On the following day, Garry asked The Bent One to go with him to the lodge of Le Grand Queue. "We must try to help him in his grief," he explained, and The Bent One agreed. They made their way to the lodge, past women who were building and repairing four-legged pyramidal drying racks.

The three comforters were met at the door by the women of the lodge, whose faces reflected concern, grief, and lack of sleep.

"He is as he was when you left," a woman replied to their inquiries.

They soon saw that it was so. Le Grand Queue was seated by the fire exactly where they had left him, grief etched on his lordly face. Behind him, a cuirass attested to his prowess in battle, a breastplate made entirely of dogbane, but its owner had been wounded with an unseen spear to the heart, and he seemed to be dying.

Garry spoke: "Will the War Chief listen to us? We, too, have been pierced by your loss."

No reply. Garry pressed ahead anyway, with The Bent One interpreting.

"Your son was best friend to me. We spent many hours together. No doubt, he told you of the great flood. It happened during the Moon-of-snow-melting, five years ago. Water rose up all around the school where we lived. Pelly and I saw it together. We lived through it our first year at the school. Everything was uprooted by it—entirely swept away! Many trees, lodges, animals, even the wood headboards from the graves of the dead. We saw them float past, washed away by the water. Only we ourselves were saved, by standing on a platform above our schoolhouse."

The chief's eyes were riveted to Garry's mouth, but his face showed no comprehension.

Garry continued. "The Master of Life used the flood to speak to us. He said that everything is changing. Much that we have known must be swept away. We must suffer the loss of all things. But the Master of Life loves us, and he came to us many years ago to assure us that nothing else matters—only his love for us, for all of us must one day endure the loss of all things. He alone remains. Your son knew these words; he died in peace. He would want you to be at peace, though your grief is great. My grief, too, was great when I saw that he had died. But I know this: your son heard the words of the Master of Life. His spirit lives with Creator. To know this took the bitterness out of my grief."

There was no visible response to these words, though the women of the lodge seemed grateful that Garry had come, and they seemed more at peace than before. Presently, they ushered the visitors out into the light. Within the hour, Garry and Chongulloosoon prepared to depart. Nothing more could be said.

A little later, in the midst of their preparations, the canoes returned from the fishing expedition. Unexpectedly, Le Grand Queue emerged from his lodge to greet them. He had unbraided his hair, and his face was unpainted now. But he seemed to have emerged from his silence and spiritual isolation. Garry, relieved, breathed a sigh of relief.

The Fish Chief began to divide the salmon into equal lots, destined for each of the lodges. Though gathering other food was left to the initiative of the provident, the salmon hunt was divided equally among all. The poorest Kutenai would receive the same allotment as the Fish Chief, who did the allotting.

Garry had planned to leave quietly during these activities, but when they began actually to go, Le Grand Queue heard of it, and he had the presence of mind to give a command to his herald. Something in Garry's words, apparently, had soothed Le Grand Queue after all. He was functioning again.

The young town crier went about immediately, informing everyone that the two Salish guests were about to depart. At that, someone from every lodge found a scrap of food and brought it to the visitors. "You must have food for your journey," they said as they gave fish, dried venison, camas root, pemmican, and crane tidbits. Now, well stocked with food for their journey, they were bid farewell in proper Kutenai style.

• • •

Spokan Garry, accompanied by his uncle, returned to their home, to that corner of land at the mouth of the Little Spokan, that quiet place below the falls that stop the salmon. He was not sure whether he had helped soothe the grief of Le Grand Queue or not, but he had his own people to think about now.

A week after his arrival home, on the very spot where Finan McDonald had once built a fur post, Garry set up a tule-mat building next to the river. It had a bell, which he used to call his people together on Sundays so that he could teach them of the Master of Life from the leaves bound together. Teach them, too, the wisdom of the planting of seeds.

Epilogue

Jedediah Smith had become by 1831 the most important explorer of the American West. His biographer, Dale Morgan, summarized, "Everywhere he touched his pencil, west of the continental divide, Jedediah made cartographic news."[55] On top of this, his fascination with the indigenous peoples yet unknown to white society made him in many cases the first white person those tribes had ever laid eyes on. Everywhere he went, he got to know them, honored them with protocol gifts, and protected them as best he could from the occasional violence of his own men. He gave us the first ethnographic notes ever jotted down about many of these tribes. Morgan and Wheat summarize: "his is close to a comprehensive catalogue of the Indian peoples of the American West."[56]

The most famous and useful of all his discoveries was South Pass. Unlike the northern route through the Rockies opened up by Lewis and Clark, South Pass provided a potential wagon road up the Platte River and across the mountains into Idaho. This pass was the hidden passage that opened up the Oregon Trail. The first wagon to cross South Pass and continue on into Idaho was that which carried the first missionaries, the Whitmans and the Spaldings, in 1836, to settle among the Plateau tribes.[57] Narcissa Whitman and Eliza Spalding were the first two women to cross the Rockies and settle in the West.

---

55. Morgan and Wheat, *Jedediah Smith and His Maps of the West*, 40.
56. Morgan and Wheat, 83.
57. Of course, other wagons had already crossed the pass, bringing supplies to trapper rendezvouses.

The Forgotten Awakening

Jedediah did not live long enough to see the pass he discovered used by thousands of emigrants on the Oregon Trail. In 1831, he organized a trade expedition with his brothers, Austin and Peter, and his longtime partners, Dave Jackson, Bill Sublette, and Tom "Broken Hand" Fitzpatrick. Along the Santa Fe Trail, he was ambushed by a roving band of Comanches while looking for water in the infamous Journada of southwest Kansas. He died at age thirty-three, a shining candle snuffed out too soon.

Spokan Garry lived out the Christian lifestyle he learned at Red River—yet not as a "white man's Indian," but as one who stood between cultures to bring reconciliation in the name of Jesus. As the first Christian evangelist in the American West, he offered the tribes neither the sophisticated theology of eastern denominations nor their religious paraphernalia, yet all the evidence shows that his spiritual influence throughout the region was profound. He had not the authority under the Anglican Church to baptize anyone, but clad in a broad-brimmed hat and a red bandana, with his shirt never tucked in, he taught from the Minor Catechism David Jones had given him and stressed the Ten Commandments as God's immutable law. (Under this influence, the most well-known of all Nez Percé Christians of that period, Hallalhotsoot, became known as "Lawyer.") Garry also taught daily morning and evening prayer and the observance of Sunday as the Sabbath—the Lord's Day. Within a year or two, these patterns began to be observed everywhere on the Columbia Plateau.

More difficult to describe is the heart change that the teachings brought. These are the things that indicate spiritual awakening—a sense of deep repentance, a hunger for purity of life, an eagerness to please God in an ethic defined by the Ten Commandments. Literature of the period points to a widespread, deep spiritual awakening on the Columbia Plateau, the sort of thing that only God can produce. All the writers were at a loss to explain how the movement they observed among the tribes could have originated. It was the last thing any of them expected.

The first and most astonishing event was the 1831 Nez Percé delegation to Saint Louis. This consisted of four and possibly seven men who
traveled with Fontanelle's fur brigade from their village in present Idaho. Tipyahlanah (Eagle), Hi-yuts-to-henin (Rabbit-skin Leggings), Tawis
Geejumnin (No Horns On His Head) and Ka-ou-pu (Man of the Morning) visited William Clark in Saint Louis, the first Native people from
west of the mountains Clark had seen since the Voyage of Discovery.

We can only imagine what a reunion that must have been. William
Clark had turned much of his home into a celebratory museum of Native American lifeways. Alvin Josephy summarizes what happened at the
meeting: "During the course of the interview he was told of their people's growing interest in the white man's religion, and was led to understand that the Indians would welcome receiving a missionary who could
instruct them in the Bible."[58]

When word of this got around back east, it caused an immediate stir
and provoked a response, but there was no comprehension of what had
prompted the invitation. During the following years, many others saw
this Native thirst for the knowledge of Jesus Christ—and likewise did
not comprehend the story behind what they saw.

In 1832, Captain Benjamin Louis Eulalie de Bonneville lived among
the Nez Percés for a season, attempting to develop a trade in furs. His
biography, written by Washington Irving, reveals his impressions of the
new faith of the Plateau tribes just three years after Garry's ministry
had begun:

> "They are certainly more like a nation of saints than a
> horde of savages. In fact, the antibelligerent policy of this
> tribe may have sprung from the doctrines of Christian char-
> ity" . . . [Irving continues]: The worthy captain . . . exerted
> himself, during his sojourn among this simple and well-dis-
> posed people, to inculcate as far as he was able, the gentle
> and humanizing precepts of the Christian faith . . . "Many a
> time," says he, "was my little lodge thronged, or rather piled

---

58. Alvin Josephy, *The Nez Percé Indians & the Opening of the Northwest*, 97.

with hearers, for they lay on the ground, one leaning over
the other, until there was no further room, all listening with
greedy ears to the wonders which the Great Spirit had revealed to the white man.[59]

Elsewhere, Bonneville describes a typical religious observance from
other tribes in 1832–1833:

Sunday is invariably kept sacred among these tribes. They
will not raise their camp on that day, unless in extreme cases of danger or hunger; neither will they hunt, nor fish, nor
trade, nor perform any kind of labor on that day. A part of it
is passed in prayer and religious ceremonies. Some chief, who
is generally at the same time what is called a "medicine man"
assembles the community. After invoking blessings from the
Deity, he addresses the assemblage, exhorting them to good
conduct; to be diligent in providing for their families; to ab-
stain from lying and stealing; to avoid quarreling or cheating
in their play, to be just and hospitable to all strangers who
may be among them. Prayers and exhortations are also made,
early in the morning on week days. Sometimes, all this is done
by the chief from horseback; moving slowly about the camp,
with his hat on, and uttering his exhortations with a loud
voice. On all occasions, the bystanders listen with profound
attention; and at the end of every sentence respond one word
in unison, apparently equivalent to an amen.[60]

Perhaps the most extraordinary evidence of deep cultural change
brought on by the teachings of Jesus had to do with attitudes about war.
Captain Bonneville was living among the Nez Percés when they were
raided by Blackfeet from the east and many horses were stolen. When

---

59. Washington Irving, *Bonneville's Adventures*, 101–102.
60. Thomas Jessett, *Chief Spokan Garry*, 49.

the Nez Percés did nothing about it, Bonneville exhorted them to be more manly—whereupon one of them replied, "It is bad to go to war for revenge. The Great Spirit has given us a heart for peace, not war."[61]

It was these Christian seeds of peace, planted early among the Plateau tribes, that so confused these tribes later when white people provoked them to war. (See Dee Brown's *Bury My Heart At Wounded Knee*.) Even after the Nez Percé chief Joseph decided to abandon these Christian convictions, the Flatheads to the north still refused to join in Chief Joseph's war. Their opposition to war with white people was rooted in the prophecies of Shining Shirt.

In April of 1833, the American trapper Nathaniel Wyeth reported the following observations among the Flatheads:

> . . . every morning some important Indian addresses either heaven or his countrymen or both, I believe exhorting the one to good conduct to each other and to the strangers among them and to the other to bestow his blessings   he finishes with "I am done" and the whole set up an exclamation in concord   during the whole time Sunday there is more parade or prayer as above   nothing is done Sunday in the way of trade with these Indians nor in playing games and they seldom fish or kill game or raise camp   while prayers are being said on week days everyone ceases whatever vocation he is about   if on horseback he dismounts and holds his horse on the spot until all is done. Theft is a thing almost unknown among them and is punished by flogging . . . the women are closely covered and chaste.[62]

Warren Ferris, another American trapper, records the following about the Pend d'Oreilles, Flatheads, and Nez Percés: "Their ancient superstitions have given place to the more enlightened views of the christian faith,

---

61. Josephy, *The Nez Percé Indians & the Opening of the Northwest*, 93.
62. Jessett, *Chief Spokan Garry*, 52.

and they seem to have become deeply and profitably impressed with the great truth of the gospel. They appear to be very devout and orderly, and never eat, drink, or sleep without giving thanks to God." [63]

From the journals of William Marshall Anderson, a trapper who got to know the Nez Percé chief, Kentuck, and the Flathead chief, Insula, at the 1834 trapper rendezvous:

> June 16, 1834: Three of the Nezpercés came to us from the other camp. The elder of the Indians is called Kentuck. This is a nickname given to him in consequence of his continual endeavours to sing "the hunters of Kentucky.["] He is called "the bulls-head" in his own language. This tribe like the flatheads is remarkable for their more than Christian *[in margin*: I mean as practiced in what are called Christian countries] practice of honesty, veracity and every moral virtue which every philosopher & professor so much laud, and practice so little. There are now four missionaries on their route to the nation of flat-heads. If they can only succeed in making them such as the white-men are, & not such as they should be, it would be charity for the messengers of civilization, to desist. I believe these are the only people on the globe with whom the aforesaid virtues are generally practiced realities not admired Utopian dreams. They "bona fide" despise and discountenance lying, stealing and begging . . . [64]

John K. Townsend, an ornithologist, observed a group of Cayuses, Chinooks and Nez Percés in 1834:

> The whole thirteen were soon collected at the call of one whom they had chosen for their chief, and seated with sober, sedate countenance around a large fire. After remaining in perfect silence for perhaps fifteen minutes, the chief commenced an harangue in a solemn and impressive tone,

---

63. Josephy, *The Nez Percé Indians*, 90.
64. Dale Morgan, ed.: *The Journals of William Marshall Anderson*, 132.

reminding them of the object for which they were thus assembled, that of worshipping the "Great Spirit who made the light and the darkness the fire and the water," and assured them that if they offered up their prayers to him with but "one tongue," they would certainly be accepted. He then rose from his squatting position to his knees, and his example was followed by all the others. In this situation he commenced a prayer, consisting of short sentences uttered rapidly but with great apparent fervor, his hands clasped upon his breast, and his eyes cast upwards with a beseeching look towards heaven. At the conclusion of each sentence, a choral response of a few words was made, accompanied by a low moaning. The prayer lasted about twenty minutes. After its conclusion the chief, still maintaining the same position of his body and hands, but with his head bent to his breast, commenced a kind of psalm or sacred song, in which the whole company presently joined. The song was a simple expression of a few sounds, no intelligible words being uttered. It resembled the words, Ho-ha-ho-ha-ho-ha-ha-a, commencing in a low tone, and gradually swelling to a full, round, and beautifully modulated chorus. During the song, the clasped hands of the worshippers were moved rapidly across the breast, and their bodies swung with great energy to the time of the music. The chief ended the song he had commenced, by a kind of swelling groan, which was echoed in chorus . . . The whole ceremony occupied perhaps one and a half hours; a short silence then succeeded, after which each Indian rose from the ground, and diappeared in the darkness.[65]

The following year, Dr. Gairdner, surgeon at Fort Vancouver, observed religious services of the Walla Wallas. These may have been the result of Cayuse Halket's influence, one of the boys taken to the school

---

65. Jessett, *Chief Spokan Garry*, 54–55.

by Garry, who had returned from Red River by then. The chief of the Walla Walla band was Peopeo Moxmox, Yellow Bird, who eventually sent his son to the first mission school in Oregon in the Willamette Valley and became a great proponent of Christian missions among his people. His people worshiped like this:

> The whole tribe, who are here at present, men, women and children, to the number of about 200, were assembled in their craal, squatted on their hams; the chief and the chief men at the head arranged in a circle; these last officiated; towards this circle the rest of the assembly were turned, arranged in regular ranks, very similar to a European congregation. The service began by the chief's making a short address, in a low tone, which was repeated by a man at his left hand, in short sentences, as they were uttered by the chief. This was followed by a prayer pronounced by the chief standing, the rest kneeling. At certain intervals there was a pause, when all present gave a simultaneous groan. After the prayer there were fifteen hymns, in which the whole congregation joined: these hymns were sung by five or six of the men in the circle, who acted as leaders of the choir; during this hymn, all were kneeling, and kept moving their arms up and down, as if to aid in keeping time. The airs were simple, resembling the monotonous Indian song which I have heard them sing while paddling their canoes. Each was somewhat different from the other. All kept good time, and there were no discordant voices. The hymns were succeeded by a prayer, as at first, and then the service ended . . . It is about five years since these things found their way among the Indians of the Upper Columbia.[66]

How we evaluate these religious expressions will depend in large part on our worldview. As Brad Long and I wrote in *The Collapse of the Brass Heaven*, our worldview is an inner model of how the world operates.

---

66. Jessett, *Chief Spokan Garry*, 58.

The paradigms (or ingredients) of our worldview open our eyes to some things, while blinding us to others.

Don Richardson gives us the best paradigm to bring to these events in the Columbia Plateau in the 18th and 19th centuries, to help us interpret them meaningfully. In *Eternity in their Hearts*, he shows that God reaches out to cultures to begin to draw them to Jesus, by providing glimpses and revelations about Jesus before the gospel is introduced to them by the Christian Church. In that way, the people within the receiving culture are less likely to see the Christian gospel as an unfriendly intrusion.

For generations, Native people from the Columbia Plateau have been trying to tell us that their greatest cultural heroes received prophetic revelations from the Creator during the 18th century.[67] Many of these revelations specifically prepared their cultures to receive the gospel when it came. Neither today's secularists, nor 19th century missionaries, have been able to appreciate these revelations, and so they have discounted them, but why don't we take these people at their word? Don Richardson's paradigm will help us see that God may well have been reaching out in his gentle way to woo the First Nations to himself, but our worldview must contain a paradigm for the power of God to appreciate this part of our history. The briefest review of Leslie Spier's *The Prophet Dance* would indicate that there were a great many prophecies throughout the Columbia Plateau; we probably don't know more than a fraction of them.

If the gospel writer Matthew had been as skeptical today as we are of the testimonies of Native people, he never would have included the story about the Magi in his gospel (Matthew 2). Of course, there was syncretism in these early religious expressions. And yet, because of God's gentleness, whole nations were trying to find their way across uncharted ground to discover who Jesus is. We cannot expect them to have had perfect doctrine instantly.

The overwhelming impression that we gather from these early accounts is that Spokan Garry had contextualized the Christian gospel to

---

67. See my website, TheForgottenAwakening.com, for examples.

the cultures of the tribes so that whole villages were able to embrace it and move toward Jesus together.[68] Virtually everyone who met the Plateau tribes during the 1830s spoke well of them and described what looked like earnest Christian prayer and worship emerging from lives of impeccable moral standards. Captain Bonneville concluded, "A Christian missionary or two, and some trifling assistance from government, to protect them from the predatory and warlike tribes, might lay the foundation of a Christian people in the midst of the great western wilderness, who would 'wear the Americans near their hearts.'"[69]

Who could have imagined that those missionaries would arrive right on schedule and establish themselves among the tribes, only to be bitterly resented by the very tribes that had requested them! With the Whitman massacre on November 29, 1847—by the once-peaceful Cayuses—all hope of attaining Bonneville's vision was shattered.

There was, after all, one exception to the long list of those who appreciated the Plateau tribes: the missionaries themselves. Their theology often prevented them from seeing what God was already doing among the tribes, except in the most negative terms. Here, for example, is an excerpt from the journal of missionary Asa B. Smith, reflecting on the Nez Percé delegation that went to Saint Louis in 1831:

> With what motives these individuals [the delegation] went it is difficult to determine. To suppose that it was any thing but selfish motives, is to suppose that good can come out of the natural heart. Were I to judge of their motives by what I see now among the people I should say it was nothing but selfishness. Doubtless there was curiosity to find out something about the christian religion. There has been much said about the desire of this people for instruction but it is quite evident what it is for. It is not usually the common people that express much desire only the chiefs & principal men. These manifest a

---

68. It is extremely important to differentiate between contextualization and syncretism. I recommend two books, both available at Wiconi.com: Adrian Jacobs' *Aboriginal Christianity the way it was meant to be*, and Richard Twiss's *Culture, Christ and Kingdom Study Guide*.
69. Josephy, *The Nez Percé Indians*, 116.

great fondness for hearing something new & telling of it & by so doing they gather many about them & increase their influence & sustain their dignity among the people.[70]

Often, the early missionaries brought with them theological assumptions that God could not possibly have done anything among the tribes apart from themselves and their missions efforts. These were judged to be "spiritual." Everything before them was to be attributed to "the natural man." After all, these people were "heathen" and "savages."

Spokan Garry's biographer, Thomas Jessett, briefly traced the journey of Samuel Parker, the first missionary who responded to the request of the Nez Percé delegation. Parker lived among the Nez Percés for a short time, and the man known as Kentuck took a particular interest in him. The aging Parker witnessed the profound faith of these people, admiringly and appreciatively. But Jessett comments: "Parker's revivalistic and Calvinistic[71] background made him unwilling to recognize the religious practices of this group as possessing any value whatsoever."[72]

Another writer, commenting on the missionaries who moved in among the Spokanes, wrote, "There does not appear to have been much co-operation between the Rev. [Cushing] Eels and [Elkanah] Walker and Spokane Garry, and it is the personal impression of the writer that these self-sacrificing and devout missionaries were temperamentally incapable of a sympathetic understanding of the Indian character, or of fully availing themselves of Spokane Garry's services and previous efforts, or of successfully cultivating what has been stated to have been 'as fertile soil as could be found in the Northwest for the planting of Christian teachings.'"[73]

70. Clifford Drury, ed. *The Diaries and Letters of Henry H. Spalding and Asa Bowen Smith Relating to the Nez Perce Mission, 1838–1842*, 106-7. Quoted in Alvin Josephy, *The Nez Percé Indians*, 668.
71. Calvinism does not create spiritual awakening. Prayer does. By the 1820s, many Calvinists had become utterly prayerless. Charles Finney had to cut through the shackles of hyper-Calvinism before he saw any spiritual awakening in his ministry during the 1820s. By the midthirties, he too bemoaned the trailing off of God's power. The power of God was not renewed in the land until the great prayer revival of 1857.
72. Jessett, *Chief Spokan Garry*, 62
73. William S. Lewis, *The Case for Spokane Garry*, 43.

The Native response to the missionaries was summed up in the following statement about Marcus Whitman:

> Had he come into our country determined to heal our sick and respect our church, we would have welcomed Dr. Whitman. But he was so negative towards the Indians in his looks, his actions, his medicines, and his beliefs, that he would never have believed the Predictions of Circling Raven, called "The Raven Cycle." Our beliefs were not as simple as Dr. Whitman and others claimed them to be, in the substitute faith they brought. Unfamiliar with Indian customs, they imagined that the Indians' religion was merely animism, but it was not. We all looked up to the sun a hundred years ago, as we did to the rivers and the trees. But we did not worship them.[74]

The appreciation of motive and temperament is in the eye of the beholder. Why were David Jones and William Cochran so successful in their efforts at Red River, whereas the later efforts—those of A.B. Smith, the Cushing Eels, and the Elkanah Walkers, for example—were not? David Jones at Red River had an entirely different view of these tribes. Commenting on Garry and Pelly's return to Red River with five other chiefs' sons, he wrote:

> This shews very evidently the confidence placed by the natives there on the good faith of the White people, and also the value which they attach to Christian instruction, indeed every person conversant with them represent their desires on this head as being extremely ardent. And I think it a feature peculiarly new and interesting as connected with these Indians that their desire for teachers is not associated with any ideas of temporal benefit and aggrandizement.[75]

---

74. Chief Joseph Seltice, *Saga of the Coeur d'Alene Indians*, 43-44. As stated elsewhere, the Circling Raven mentioned here was a prophet who lived a generation earlier than the Circling Raven portrayed in this story.

75. *Journal of David Jones*, July 25, 1831. What this quote also shows is that, by the time Spokan Garry had returned to Red River, Jones was much more assured of his Christian devotion than when Garry had left Red River. At that time, David Jones had expressed some private reservations about the sincerity of Garry's conversion.

Much has been written about what went wrong in western missions so that a situation of so much promise turned poisonous so quickly, (That question is beyond the scope of this book. I recommend Alvin Josephy, *The Nez Percé Indians*, for a fair and balanced description of those disastrous years.) but the success of the Red River school, of Pastors Jones and Cochran, seems to be rooted in the fact that they were able to convince the boys in their care that they were loved by God and by themselves. With that kind of foundation, those boys' Christian faith lasted their whole lives, in spite of severe provocations later on—sometimes from missionaries.

One of the great ironies that emerges from this story is that the narrow doctrines of denomination, so important to the missionaries themselves, destroyed in the minds of the tribes the integrity of the very faith the missionaries preached. Here again, David Jones was unique: he sought fellowship with Catholics, Presbyterians, and other Christians. His was the spirit expressed in 1 John 4:7: "Everyone who loves has been born of God and knows God." Native people knew this truth even when it eluded many missionaries.

In the 1840s, thousands of settlers moved across South Pass and began to build towns, threatening to displace the tribes. On top of that, an epidemic of measles broke out in 1847, carrying off the Red River–trained Nez Percé Chief Ellis and hundreds of other Natives. By then, the tribes had become so resentful and distrustful of the missionaries in their midst that they blamed them unfairly for these disasters. Of course, they were deeply frightened that their whole way of life, their very existence, was threatened. As it surely was.

Those who remained from the earlier days—John McLoughlin and Peter Skene Ogden—did what they could to keep the peace. They were still trusted. But the new generation of American immigrants did not respect these men as Jedediah had learned to do, and as the tribes still did. Their sage advice, which could have helped avoid many disasters, was ignored. After all, they were British.

The Forgotten Awakening

As for Spokan Garry, he became a true ambassador during the 50's and 60's, speaking out courageously for interracial love and reconciliation, but the white immigrants who had taken over the land would have none of it.

In 1887, a group of white people led by one Schyler Doak took over Garry's house and land by force. Garry was made to understand that he was a foreigner and that if he wanted to own land, he should become a U.S. citizen and apply at the land office. Garry's last years were years of profound poverty and dishonor. He, with his blind wife, Nina, and his daughter, Nellie, lived penniless in a tipi at Hangman's Creek on land that no white man cared to own—and site of the military defeat and humiliation of the Spokane people. During his last days, he was a squatter on land his people had called home for centuries.

A friend of mine, Brian Huseland of Spokane, recently held Spokan Garry's Bible in his hands. It opened to Psalm 69, as though its owner had frequently turned there to his favorite passage of Scripture. This psalm gives us a picture of Garry's faith in the later years of his life:

Save me, O God; for the waters are come in unto my soul . . .
They that hate me without a cause are more than the hairs of mine head; they that would destroy me, being my enemies wrongfully, are mighty: then I restored that which I took not away . . .

Draw nigh unto my soul, and redeem it; deliver me because of mine enemies.
Thou hast known my reproach, and my shame, and my dishonor; mine adversaries are all before thee . . .
Reproach hath broken my heart, and I am full of heaviness . . .
Let thy salvation, O God, set me up on high.
I will praise the name of God with a song, and will magnify him with thanksgiving.

(Psalm 69:1, 4, 18–20, 30)

We revere heroes of nonviolence only when they succeed in winning political victories and turning the tides of injustice, yet history is full of men and women who maintained a walk of Christian love, achieving great integrity even when political victories eluded them. Shall we not honor such as these also?

The history of white America demonstrates that we white Americans could never quite figure out whether we were supposed to love Native people with the love of Jesus or wipe them off the face of the earth. At heart, the doctrine of Manifest Destiny, which dominated western expansion beginning in the 1840s, was the harmless belief that America was to stretch "from sea to shining sea," but as this doctrine evolved, it was twisted to mean, "We're here now; you Indians should disappear from sea to shining sea." That Christian people went along with this twist is the greatest of all tragedies. It destroyed the potential of the Christian gospel to become the basic uniting impulse of America. How can we recover what we have lost?

Postscript

This manuscript was a labor of love for over twenty years. As I worked on this story, I was continually filled with an inner certainty that the White-Native narrative on this continent is not finished. Jesus the Great Redeemer has a redemptive ending to this story which is yet to emerge.

As I finished the manuscript, I was astonished to see events unfold that confirmed this sense of hope. To begin with, on June 11, 2008, Canadian Prime Minister Stephen Harper officially asked forgiveness of all the First Nations of Canada for the abuses committed under the Indian Residential School Program. As Chief Kenny Blacksmith of the James Bay Cree said, "Our Canadian Prime Minister is the first to explicitly ask forgiveness. This leaves our people in a position to respond. We can either choose to hold on to the past, or embrace freedom, which is available through an act of forgiveness."

Chief Blacksmith organized a "Journey of Freedom" through twenty First Nations, Inuit, Métis, and regional centers, culminating in the Forgiveness Summit in Ottawa, June 11–13, 2010. He continued: "Forgiveness is not political. It is not legislative. Forgiveness is spiritual. Therefore, we need to respond spiritually. This six-month spiritual journey will make ready the hearts of our people to formally respond to the apology and to the specific request for forgiveness of Prime Minister Harper this June." This event happened just as I wrote this postscript. I believe it was the start of something deeply transformational in Canada. (A description of the summit, including Chief Blacksmith's speech, is available at www.canadianchristianity.com/nationalupdates/100630forgiven.html. I also highly recommend a visit to Chief Blacksmith's website, www.GatheringNations.ca.)

Simultaneously, in the U.S., thanks to the leadership of then-Senator Sam Brownback, a joint resolution was passed by the U.S. Congress, apologizing for the injustices perpetrated against First Americans (see www.nativeres.org).

It seems to me that movements and events like the Forgiveness Summit are just exactly what has been needed, not only in Canada, but in the United States. Repentance and forgiveness open the way for new possibilities of mutual respect so that our two peoples can walk in the light again. I trust that www.i4give.ca, which contains messages and videos from the Journey of Freedom and the Forgiveness Summit, will remain on the web for many years to come to shine light for the rest of us.

A second hopeful sign just now is the number of places around the world where God is moving powerfully among indigenous people. The *Transformations* videos of George Otis (www.SentinelGroup.com) are documenting these moves of God and the healing of the land that results. I particularly recommend the story of Almolonga, Guatemala, in *Transformations*; the awakening of the Inuits of Hudson's Bay in *Transformations II*; and the story of the Fiji awakening in *Let the Sea Resound* as stories well worth seeing. If a picture is worth a thousand words, videos like these are worth a million. What all these stories affirm for us is the need for extraordinary prayer, without which there can be no fresh start.

A third hopeful sign is the emergence of a whole new kind of indigenous Christian ministry in America and throughout the world, one that more or less picks up where Spokan Garry left off. One of the pictures of Spokan Garry I have included in these pages shows Garry in the prime of life as a Christian leader. Garry is not dressed as a white man, but as a Spokane Native. He made no assumption that Christians should wear western clothing or practice western culture in order to be Christian. This refusal to adopt white culture was surely a central reason why later missionaries devalued and overlooked his contribution as a Christian evangelist. They assumed, because he chose to retain his Native identity, that his ministry wasn't really Christian. It didn't have a "Christian" appearance to them. But he had entered into a relationship with Christ partly through his own culture, as a result of tribal prophecy. He understood, better than the missionaries did, that God is above cultures. Jesus straddles all the cultures, and he does not play favorites. While God used some white people to inform the faith of the Plateau tribes, Garry's

Christian leadership emerged from within Native culture and he never abandoned it. His model of leadership was fully Christian and fully Native at the same time.

Dozens of indigenous Christian ministries are growing up today in the U.S. and Canada which express Christian faith within the context of Nativeness. The gist of their message? You can be fully Native and fully Christian at the same time. This is a new idea (at least, within the last century).

Richard Twiss (Lakotah) has demonstrated that God has a high calling waiting for indigenous people in this country. God can use Native people to proclaim Jesus throughout the world in a powerful way, but let them take with them their regalia, their music, and their dance. Richard is a public spokesman for this movement, and his website, www.Wiconi. com, is an excellent place to obtain resources from many of the leaders of the movement.

Perhaps the three best vision statements for this movement come from Richard Twiss and Adrian Jacobs (Cayuga, a member of the Six Nations Iroquois Confederacy), available at Wiconi.com. They are *One Church Many Tribes: Following Jesus the Way God Made You* by Richard Twiss, along with the excellent resource *Culture, Christ and Kingdom Study Guide*; and *Aboriginal Christianity the Way It Was Meant To Be* by Adrian Jacobs.

Jonathan Maracle (Mohawk) is living out all these principles in music with his team of musicians, Broken Walls (www.BrokenWalls.com). As the name implies, Broken Walls is heavily committed to the reconciliation message mentioned above, but from a solid base of approaching Jesus from within Native culture.

Terry LeBlanc (Mi'kmaq/Acadian) heads up My People International in Canada, a training-focused ministry program for Native North Americans. See his excellent ministry website, www.MyPeopleInternational.com.

Dr. Suuqiina's teaching on "what defiles the land," coming from an Inuit perspective, caused me to understand biblical teaching about land in a way my own white culture could not do. Through Dr. Suuqiina and his wife, Qaumaniq (Cherokee), I began to see how heavily my view of the Bible is shaped by my European perspective, which has almost nothing to say about a biblical view of land.

Randy Woodley (Cherokee) has helped me realize, again, how much of my own Christian faith has been imprisoned by my white-European-modern-secular-materialist skepticism. God is not necessarily wedded to pulpits and pews, even when we are. (Go to www.EaglesWingsMinistry.com.)

These ministries are proliferating just now, and I feel sure that they will multiply exponentially in the future. See the links at www.Wiconi.com for more examples.

Ministries like these, which pursue Jesus from within Native culture, are sparking much debate within indigenous Christian circles. This debate is inevitable and necessary—and long overdue. The process of Christ's permeating a culture is a messy one, as every ambassador for Christ across cultural boundaries must know, regardless of the culture.

Some of us palefaces may wonder about all this. It may be well for us to do a little historical review, to gain perspective about contextualized ministry. Let's go back to the days when we of English background were ourselves the indigenous people.

It is the fifth century. We are pagan Celts. We live in Ireland, Wales, Scotland, and England, before any of those lands possessed those names. Rome is once again trying to take over our island peoples. They consider us to be barbarians, probably because we are. They speak Latin; we speak Gaelic. They are cultured; we are not.

Now here comes the Christian church, relying heavily on the Roman government as a tool to spread Christianity. We Celtic tribes do not like this. We prefer our ways, and we don't feel like becoming Latinized and Romanized. The church keeps trying to do this anyway, and they succeed only minimally in their project of Christianizing the British Isles. Finally, they give up and withdraw, leaving the few churches they planted to fend for themselves.

One day, God gets hold of Patrick, a teenage boy from one of those few Christian families in Britain. According to his autobiography,[76] he is captured by an Irish raiding party and sold into slavery in Ireland. Working as a slave, he is mysteriously overwhelmed by a spirit of prayer day and night. He simply cannot stop praying. Then he is miraculously set free, prepared for ministry (in Celtic Gaul, not at Rome), and finally anointed by the Holy Spirit to return to the land of his captivity to acquaint the Irish with Jesus. Often, he continues to be overwhelmed by a spirit of prayer, and he wonders where these prayers are coming from— "sighs too deep for words" (Romans 8:26, RSV). By the power of God flowing through Patrick, with no Roman system to offer, thousands of Celts embrace Christ.

The process God used in Patrick's life was so transformational that, by the end of one generation, Ireland had become a Christian nation. Contextualization (letting the gospel become Celtic) was so complete that to this day Patrick is regarded as an Irishman. The Irish Celts then turned their attention to bring this very friendly gospel to Scotland, Wales, Cornwall, Anglo-Saxon England, and the tribes of Europe, not by imposing a foreign system and converting people to it one by one, but by letting the power of God flow through them so that their cultures themselves were transformed by Jesus.

God's way works. In his book *How the Irish Saved Civilization*, Thomas Cahill summarizes: "[The] thirty-year span of Patrick's mission in the middle of the fifth century encompasses a period of change so rapid and extreme that Europe will never see its like again . . . [A]s the Roman lands went from peace to chaos, the land of Ireland was rushing even more rapidly from chaos to peace."

That's transformation, but that is not what happened in America among indigenous peoples.

For a picture of the opposite way—man's way, not God's—we turn to the Stuart kings of England: James I, Charles I, and Charles II. These

---

76. *Classics of Western Spirituality: Celtic Spirituality*, 67-83.

are the kings who colonized America beginning at Jamestown. Because of the King James Bible, which was being translated just as Jamestown was being settled, most people today think of James as a wonderful Christian king. Those people likely have never examined James's life. (I recommend David Stewart's book, *The Cradle King*, for anyone who wants to look beneath the surface.)

James grew up in a Scotland full of prayer and God's power to awaken hearts. Real Christianity was being reborn there by the power of God in the sixteenth century. So many people were coming to Christ that John Knox wrote, "It was as if men had rained from the clouds."

All this spiritual awakening was profoundly distasteful to James, who had grown up in the midst of it. When he became not only king of Scotland, but also king of England, he used the English church system to clamp down on the Scottish Kirk, which was still in a state of spiritual awakening. He immediately imprisoned John Welch (son-in-law of John Knox) and other Christian leaders. This began a "sad time" for Scotland, of which God had spoken to John Welch before it happened.[77]

James believed that God had ordained a system of perfect order, a spiritual chain of command system with himself at the top. Spiritual awakenings, in his mind, were too messy to be endured. He never thought, "Not by might, nor by power, but by my Spirit" (Zechariah 4:6, KJV). Using Scottish prisons and English swords, he set out to impose his will on the unruly Scottish Kirk and on all other Christians who opposed him. The Scots, in their turn, dared to rebuke him, saying that only Jesus had a right to control the church and that Jesus had his own way of appointing church leaders. The Scots had experienced God's way, and they agreed together that God's way was worth dying for, compared to the empty religious system of domination and control coming from James.

James also set out to impose his will on Native tribes in the Virginia Colony at Jamestown. His personal representative, Thomas West, Lord de la Warre, committed the first recorded massacre of Native men, women,

---

77. John Howie, *Scots Worthies* (NY: Robert Carter, 1854), 295–8.

and children on this continent, the massacre of the Paspahegh people in 1610. (The Paspaheghs had the misfortune to be the tribe on whose land Jamestown was built. Never heard of them? That's because they ceased to exist in 1610.)

Not long after that came the kidnap-conversion of Pocahontas, who was taken from her father Powhatan by force, dressed in English clothes, and removed to England. This highhanded way of treating Native people came to be seen as normal Christian behavior under James. That Chief Powhatan and the Virginia tribes might not have enjoyed this kind of treatment seems to have been overlooked until recently. I recommend two books for further reading: Helen Rountree's *Pocahontas, Powhatan and Opechancanough* and Linwood Custalow's *The True Story of Pocahontas*. Linwood Custalow is Mattaponi, the tribe of Pocahontas.

Patterns that started with James grew like a virus in a petri dish under his son and grandson. If you had the misfortune to be either a Native American or a Scottish Christian in these years, you discovered that Christian kings who abandon the power of God to create their own governmental alternatives can become truly monstrous. Thousands of Scottish Christians covenanted together to resist the religious imperialism of Charles I, and tens of thousands lost their lives resisting Charles II. These Stuart kings were also responsible for imprisoning some of the most famous Christians of their day: John Bunyan (author of *Pilgrim's Progress*), George Fox (founder of the Society of Friends), and William Penn (founder of Pennsylvania), all men of Christian vulnerability, deep prayer, and love, who were trying to live out the true way of Jesus. (William Penn's relationship to Native people is clearly and beautifully portrayed by Darrell and Lorrie Fields in *The Seed of a Nation*.)

Unfortunately, it was these kings who became the first taste of Christianity among the Virginia tribes. Their pattern of domination and control set a precedent for this continent, and that is what prevailed here, rather than the type of Christianity modeled out by Patrick among the Celts. Once a precedent has been established, it is free to grow until it fills a place.

Scotland and the American tribes mirror each other in this. By the end of the eighteenth century, both cultures were under full assault. In Scotland, it became illegal to play a bagpipe, speak Gaelic, or wear a kilt. Under King George, all forms of Scottishness were considered an act of rebellion against the king. Likewise here: by the twentieth century, all forms of Native culture were to be rooted out by a system of government-controlled, church-run schools. "Kill the Indian and save the person" became the philosophy of this system, and all this was happening under the banner of "Christianity."

As a person of Scottish ancestry, I would like to point out that this season of cultural genocide has ended for my people, and I believe the way it ended could be instructive for us today in the U.S. and Canada as we seek healing from similar mistakes we have made among First Americans.

Queen Victoria was a ruler who actually put her Christianity into practice as queen, but she had the misfortune to lose her husband in the prime of life: Prince Albert, whom she loved with all her heart. After his death, she went into a profound grief that lasted for years. It was as though she too had died. Just when it seemed she would never snap out of this, she hired a Scot named John Brown as her bodyguard. This man somehow reached into that deep well of grief, and Queen Victoria began to feel cared for in some mysterious way. (I have found no evidence that John Brown was a Christian, nor that he had a physical relationship with the queen.)

What *did* happen is this: Queen Victoria ended up spending a long time in Scotland, getting to know the Scottish people, whom she came to love. Her family and the politicians of the day could not account for her long sojourn there. But in Scotland, not only was she healed of her deep grief, she also led the way in healing centuries of prejudice and bitterness between the English and the Scottish people. She wrote a book about the Scots, *Queen Victoria's Scottish Diaries*, which changed hearts and melted centuries of hurt.

That melting is what we need here on the American continent between white Europeans and First Americans, and it is happening today by people who are willing to just listen to God and surrender their lives to him. We need more of God's way and less of man's, and that is going to require us white people to give up our highhandedness, this spirit of domination and control, and practice real Christianity. "Not by power . . ."

There is no substitute for genuine love—for people quite simply getting to know each other, spending time together, and building trust while engaged in mutual discovery. There are plenty of examples of such people in our history, but, unfortunately, they have been a minority.

Darrell and Lorrie Fields's book, *The Seed of a Nation*, is an excellent visionary statement based on the wisdom of William Penn, a man who practiced his Christianity. I highly recommend it. So are the writings of John Dawson, especially *Healing the Wounds of America* and his little booklet *What Christians Should Know About Reconciliation*, published for the International Reconciliation Coalition.

It is time for *indigenous cultures* to come to Christ and experience kingdom transformation. This sort of spiritual awakening, like that which transformed Ireland years ago, would go well beyond setting up foreign churches and "converting" a few people to attend them. What seems about to happen now is the belated redemption of entire Native cultures because God values the people of those cultures for who they are. "Just as I am, without one plea." This is not a song we Christians have sung among indigenous communities—yet its message is true, and it is time that its truth be heard.

What St. Patrick showed us years ago is that, *in the end*, the weakness of Christ is stronger than the power of human control. Men like Spokan Garry and Jedediah Smith lived this out in their own ways, seeking to break down dividing walls that separate peoples behind massive barriers of misunderstanding. I believe that, in the end, their way will prevail. The story of White-Native relations in this country does not have a good ending yet. But Jesus the Great Redeemer specializes in giving redemptive endings to our stories, and he is the One we can trust to redeem this story.

Acknowledgments

I have badgered a great many people in the process of writing this book, and even though it was their job to let me badger them, I still appreciate their help with my research before it ever got to the publisher—a process that took over twenty years. In fact, the research and writing of this book has taken so long that the people who helped me may have forgotten all about their assistance. Nonetheless:

First, let me thank the librarians at the Library of Congress, the libraries of Virginia Commonwealth University and the University of Richmond, the Virginia State Library, and above all, the Henrico County Library Adult Services desk. Let me thank the staff at the Manitoba Historical Society, especially Carol Barbee. I wish to thank the staff of the Manitoba Provincial Archives in Winnipeg, especially Judith Hudson Beattie; the staff of the Fort Garry Historical Society, especially Geraldine Hamilton; and the kind people who guided me around St. Andrews Church, which was founded by William Cochran in Lockport, Manitoba. I am indebted for the help of the people at the Hudson's Bay Company Archives and the Church Missionary Society Archives. I wish to thank the staff of Fort Vancouver National Park in Vancouver, Washington, where Dr. McLoughlin held forth for many years. The tour guides at John McLoughlin's house, too, were full of information and perspective. And I wish to thank the kind people of the Missouri Historical Society for letting me handle the journals of Jedediah Smith and William Ashley.

Most of the sites I portray, both in the Pacific Northwest (where I lived for many years) and in the Winnipeg area, I visited firsthand so that I could imagine the stories that played out in those locales. Thank you, Carla, my wife, for accompanying me in bumping down some of the poorest excuses for roads ever imagined as we retraced the steps of Jedediah Smith and Spokan Garry.

The Forgotten Awakening

A number of Native people gave me help in evaluating and critiquing my manuscript as it grew, including my friends Richard Twiss (Lakotah), Randy Woodley (Cherokee), Troy Adkins (Chickahominy) and his wife Kelly (Cherokee), and Tim Lucas (Tuscarora). I wish to also thank Pastor John Knight and Mr. Brian Huseland, both of Spokane, who encouraged me at two critically important times. God used you for me, brothers. Above all, I wish to express appreciation for Mildred Iyall, the late great granddaughter of Spokan Garry, and her husband, Daniel, who encouraged me when I most needed encouragement.

Finally, I would like to thank the late Christian musician Tom Howard, who produced an album entitled *The Hidden Passage* just as I was researching Jedediah Smith's discovery of South Pass and the tribes west of the Rockies. The music of this album mysteriously and profoundly expressed the spirit of the forgotten awakening as I wrote this material. It kept me going through all my research and writing; to this day it never grows old. (The album has recently been reissued under the title *Sanctuary Shelter*.) God uses the arts to reach hearts in ways that the head cannot comprehend.

Bibliography

- "A Brief Sketch of the Life and Labours of Archdeacon Cockran." Religious Tract Society, 1872.
- Billon, Frederick. *Annals of St. Louis*. St. Louis: G.I. Jones & Co., 1886.
- Cartwright, Peter. *Autobiography of Peter Cartwright*. Nashville: Abingdon Press, 1956.
- Catlin, George. *Letters & Notes on the Manners, Customs & Conditions of North American Indians*. New York: Dover Publications, 1973.
- Chittenden, Hiram Martin. *The American Fur Trade of the Far West*. New York: Barnes and Noble, 1935.
- Clark, W. P. *The Indian Sign Language*. Philadelphia: L. R. Hamersly & Co., 1885.
- Cline, Gloria Griffen. *Peter Skene Ogden & the Hudson's Bay Co*. Norman, OK: University of Oklahoma Press, 1974.
- Clyman, James. *Journal of a Mountain Man*. Missoula, MT: Mountain Press, 1984. Linda Hasselstrom, ed.
- Corney, Peter. *Early Northern Pacific Voyages*. Honolulu: Thomas G. Thrum, 1896.
- Coutts, Robert. "St. Andrew's Parish 1829–1929, and the Church Missionary Society in Red River." Unpublished.
- Dale, Harrison Clifford. *The Ashley-Smith Explorations and the Discovery of a Central Route to the Pacific 1822–1829 (with the Original Journals)*. Glendale, CA: Arthur H. Clark, 1941.
- Drury, Clifford M. "Oregon Indians in the Red River School." *The Pacific Historical Review*, Vol. VII #1, March 1938.

• Elliott, T.C., ed. "Journal of Alexander Ross; Snake Country Expedition, 1824." *Oregon Historical Society Quarterly,* Vol. XIV, #4, December 1913.

—"The Peter Skene Ogden Journals." *Oregon Historical Society Quarterly,* Vol. XI, #2, 4, June, December 1910.

—"Peter Skene Ogden, Fur Trader." *Oregon Historical Society Quarterly,* Vol. XI #3, September 1910.

• Fogdall, Alberta Brooks. *Royal Family of the Columbia.* Fairfield, WA: Ye Galleon Press, 1978.

• Fuller, Myron L. *The New Madrid Earthquake.* Washington, DC: U.S. Geological Survey Bulletin 494, 1912.

• Hussey, John A. *The History of Fort Vancouver and Its Physical Structure.* Portland, OR: Abbot, Kerns & Bell, 1959.

• "Interpretive Manual for St. Andrew's National Historic Park." Unpublished.

• Irving, Washington. *Astoria.* Portland, OR: Binfords & Mort, 1967.

—*The Adventures of Captain Bonneville, U.S.A., in the Rocky Mountain and the Far West.* New York: G. P. Putnam, 1855.

• Jessett, Thomas Edwin. *Chief Spokan Garry, 1811–1892: Christian, Statesman, and Friend of the White Man.* Minneapolis: T. S. Denison, 1960.

• Jones, David. *The Journals and Letters of David Jones, 1825–1832.* Unpublished.

• Johnson, Olga W. *Flathead & Kootenay.* Glendale, CA: A. H. Clark, 1969.

• Josephy, Alvin M., Jr. *The Nez Percé Indians & the Opening of the Northwest.* New Haven, CT: Yale University Press, 1965.

• Lavender, David. *The Fist in the Wilderness.* Garden City, NY: Doubleday, 1964.

—*Land of Giants: The Drive to the Pacific Northwest 1750–1950.* Garden City, NY: Doubleday, 1956.

• Lewis, William S. "The Case of Spokane Garry." *Bulletin of the Spokane Historical Society* Vol. I, #1, January 1917.

• Lionberger, I. H. *The Annals of St. Louis and A Brief Account of Its Foundation and Progress 1764–1928.* St. Louis: Missouri Historical Society, 1930.

• MacKenzie, Cecil. *Donald MacKenzie, King of the Northwest*. Los Angeles: I. Deach, Jr, 1937.

• Merk, Frederick. *Fur Trade and Empire: George Simpson's Journal 1824–5*. Cambridge, MA: Harvard Univ. Press, 1931.

—"Snake Country Expedition, 1824–25: An Episode of Fur Trade and Empire." *Oregon Historical Quarterly*, Vol. XXXV, #2, June 1934.

• Miller, Christopher. *Prophetic Worlds: Indians & Whites on the Columbia Plateau*. New Brunswick, NY: Rutgers University Press, 1985.

• Miller, David E., ed. "Peter Skene Ogden's Journal of His Expedition to Utah, 1825." *Utah Historical Quarterly*, Vol. XX, #2, April 1952.

—"William Kittson's Journal Covering Peter Skene Ogden's 1824–1825 Snake Country Expedition." *Utah Historical Quarterly*, Vol. XXII, #2, April 1954.

• Morgan, Dale L., and Carl I. Wheat. *Jedediah Smith and His Maps of the American West*. San Francisco: California Historical Society, 1954.

—*Jedediah Smith & the Opening of the West*. Indianapolis: Bobbs-Merrill, 1953.

• Morgan, Dale L. *The West of William Ashley*. Denver: Old West Publishing Co., 1964.

• Morton, Arthur S. *Sir George Simpson: Overseas Governor of the Hudson's Bay Company*. Portland, OR: Binfords-Mort, 1944.

• Morton, W. L. *Manitoba: A History*. Toronto: University of Toronto Press, 1957.

• Ogden, Peter Skene. *Traits of American Indian Life & Character*. San Francisco: The Grabhorn Press, 1933.

• Oliphant, J. Orin. "George Simpson and Oregon Missions." *Pacific Historical Review*, Vol. VI, #3, September 1937.

• Porter, Kenneth Wiggins. *John Jacob Astor, Business Man*. Cambridge, MA: Harvard University Press, 1931.

• Ray, Verne F. *Lower Chinook Ethnographic Notes*. Seattle: University of Washington Press, 1938.

• Rich, E.E., ed. *Part of a Dispatch From George Simpson Esq., Governor of Rupert's Land To the Governor & Committee of the Hudson's Bay Company, London*. London: The Hudson's Bay Record Society, 1947.

—*Peter Skene Ogden's Snake Country Journals, 1824–25 and 1825–26*. London, The Hudson's Bay Record Society, 1950.

—*The Letters of John McLoughlin From Fort Vancouver to the Governor and Committee, 1825–38*. London: The Hudson's Bay Record Society, 1941.

• Ross, Alexander. *Adventures of the First Settlers On the Oregon or Columbia River*. Ann Arbor, MI: Ann Arbor University Microfilms, Inc., 1966.

—*Fur Hunters of the Far West*. Norman, OK: University of Oklahoma Press, 1956.

—*The Red River Settlement*. Smith, Elder & Co., 1856.

• Ruby, Robert H., and John A. Brown. *Indians of the Pacific Northwest: A History*. Norman, OK: University of Oklahoma Press, 1981.

—*The Spokane Indians: Children of the Sun*. Norman, OK: University of Oklahoma Press, 1970.

• Santee, J. F. "Concomly and the Chinooks." *The Oregon Historical Quarterly*, Vol. XXXIII, #3, September 1932.

• Scharf, J. T. *History of St. Louis City and County*. Philadelphia: Louis H. Everts & Co., 1883.

• Spencer, Omar C. "Chief Cassino." *The Oregon Historical Quarterly*, Vol. XXXIV, #1, March 1933.

• Spier, Leslie. *The Prophet Dance of the Northwest and Its Derivatives; The Source of the Ghost Dance*. Menasha, WI: General Series in Anthropology, I. 1935.

• Stewart, Alan. *The Cradle King: The Life of James VI and I, the First Monarch of a United Great Britain*. New York: St. Martins, 2003.

• Sullivan, Maurice S. *Jedediah Smith, Trader & Trailbreaker*. New York, Press of the Pioneers, 1937.

—*The Travels of Jedediah Smith*. Santa Ana, CA: Fine Arts Press, 1934.

• Sunder, John E. *Bill Sublette, Mountain Man*. Norman, OK: University of Oklahoma Press, 1959.

• Thomas, Edward Harper. *Chinook: A History and Dictionary of the Northwest Trade Jargon*. Portland, OR: The Metropolitan Press, 1935.

• Thompson, David. *Travels In Western N. America*. Toronto: MacMillan of Canada, 1971.

• Tucker, Sarah. *The Rainbow in the North: A Short Account of the First Establishment of Christianity in Rupert's Land by the Church Missionary Society.* London: James Nisbet & Co., 1853.

• Turney-High, Harry Holbert. *Ethnography of the Kutenai.* Menasha, WI: American Anthropological Association, 1941.

——*The Flathead Indians of Montana.* Menasha, WI: American Anthropological Association, 1937. Memoirs of the American Anthropological Association, #48.

• Victor, Mrs. Frances. *River of the West.* Oakland, CA: Brooks-Sterling Co., 1974.

• West, John. *The Substance of a Journal During a Residence at the Red River Colony.* London: L. B. Seeley & Son, 1827.

• Wynecoop, David C. *Children of the Sun.* Wellpinit, WA: 1969.

About the Author

Doug McMurry lives in Virginia with his wife, Carla, to whom he is very happily married. The two of them have founded a prayer center, The Clearing Where Eagles Fly, adjacent to the Chickahominy River where, in 1610, the first peace treaty was signed between whites and Natives on this continent. Their main prayer burden is that the indigenous tribes from sea to shining sea will rise up and achieve their God-given destiny as the host peoples of this continent.

Descended from John Alden, Myles Standish, and several other Plymouth Rock Pilgrims, Doug believes that the United States will not achieve its true destiny until the indigenous tribes are honored as our host peoples and treated accordingly.

Those who are interested in The Clearing are invited to check out its website at www.TheClearing.us. Doug has also created a website, www.TheForgottenAwakening.com, which conveys the complete prophecies described in this book, along with their sources and the context in which each was given.

As of 2011, Doug reports that two other books are in the offing. *How Friendship Came to Barrows Creek* is a story for children about reconciliation. *Glory Through Time* traces the role of prayer in the great transformational movements of Western history.